MIDNIGHT THIRSTS

Books by Greg Herren

BOURBON STREET BLUES

JACKSON SQUARE JAZZ

Books by Michael Thomas Ford

LAST SUMMER

LOOKING FOR IT

MASTERS OF MIDNIGHT
(with William J. Mann, Jeff Mann, and Sean Wolfe)

Books by Sean Wolfe

MASTERS OF MIDNIGHT
(with William J. Mann, Michael Thomas Ford, and Jeff Mann)

MAN OF MY DREAMS
(with Dave Benbow, Jon Jeffrey, and Ben Tyler)

Published by Kensington Publishing Corporation

MIDNIGHT THIRSTS

GREG HERREN

MICHAEL THOMAS FORD

TIMOTHY RIDGE

SEAN WOLFE

KENSINGTON BOOKS
http://www.kensingtonbooks.com

KENSINGTON BOOKS are published by

Kensington Publishing Corp.
850 Third Avenue
New York, NY 10022

All Kensington titles, imprints and distributed lines are available at special quantity discounts for bulk purchases for sales promotion, premiums, fund raising, educational or institutional use.

Special book excerpts or customized printings can also be created to fit specific needs. For details, write or phone the office of the Kensington Special Sales Manager: Kensington Publishing Corp., 850 Third Avenue, New York, NY, 10022. Attn. Special Sales Department. Phone: 1-800-221-2647.

ISBN 0-7582-0663-1

First Kensington Trade Paperback Printing: September 2004
10 9 8 7 6 5 4 3 2

Printed in the United States of America

Contents

The Nightwatchers

Greg Herren

Chapter One

Go home, old man, Rachel thought, tapping her black fingernails on the counter.

It was a quarter till nine, fifteen minutes before she could lock the doors. Everything was clean, and the cash register was already counted down. All she really had left to do was dump the remains of the day's coffee down the sink, lock the cash drawer in the safe, and turn everything off. She'd be gone by ten minutes after at the latest.

She glanced out the big windows fronting the coffee shop. The streetlight just outside cast a yellowish glow in the thick mist pressing against the glass. She shivered and looked back at the old man. He was sitting at one of the tables in the far corner, with the same cup of coffee he'd ordered when he came in around seven thirty. He hadn't touched it. It was still as full as when she'd filled the cup, only no steam was coming off the black surface now. He didn't seem to be watching for anyone, or waiting. He never glanced at his watch, which she'd spotted as a platinum Tag Heuer, nor did he ever look out the window. Every once in a while he would look up from his newspaper and catch her staring. He'd smile and nod, then go back to his reading.

Apparently, he was determined to read every word.

She stood up, bending backward so her back cracked. The night had been really slow. The Jazz Café, even on weeknights, usually was good for at least thirty to forty dollars in tips. Tonight, when she'd counted out the tip jar, it yielded less than seven dollars. Just enough to get her a pack of cigarettes and a twenty-ounce Diet Coke at Quartermaster Deli on her way back to her apartment. *It wasn't,* she thought, wiping down the counter yet again, *even worth coming in for.*

Usually on this kind of night, cold and damp and wet, Rachel was kept hopping with orders for triple lattes. The tables would be full of people who would come in shivering, bundled up against the cold wetness in the air, which seemed to penetrate even the thickest coat. They'd hold their steaming cups of coffee with both reddened hands, talking and laughing. Some would be doing their homework on laptops.

She liked busy nights, when the orders kept coming and the tip jar filled. Then, the time seemed to fly by, her closing shift passing in the blink of an eye. She hated the slow nights, when every passing minute seemed to take an eternity. She glanced back at the clock on the wall, then back at the old man. *If you would just leave,* she thought, *I could go ahead and close early.*

He's kind of good-looking, she thought as she sipped her tepid cup of green tea, *for an older guy.*

At that moment he looked up, and their eyes met. His were blue, a deep blue with some green in it. Once again, he nodded his head to her and smiled, but this time he didn't go back to his newspaper. He held her eyes.

Not to worry, my child. I'll be gone soon enough.

She turned away, shaking her head, the hair on the back of her head standing up. She felt a little nauseated. All she'd eaten was a bagel with cream cheese. The damned tips, she thought. She'd hoped to get enough money tonight to get something to eat after work. That wasn't an option now.

That's it, she decided. Her blood sugar was low.

He couldn't have read her mind; he couldn't have talked to her without speaking. That was crazy; that kind of thing didn't happen in real life. No, her imagination was working overtime because she was bored and her blood sugar was low.

She turned back to the counter. He was standing there. He was smiling at her. He was handsome—she amended her earlier thought. There was something kind in his smile, and his pinkish-white face was free of lines. He might not be as old as she'd thought, despite his thick white hair, which hung past his ears. His clothes were immaculately pressed and looked expensive. There was a big sapphire ring on his right hand.

"I didn't mean to startle you." He inclined his head slightly to her. "My apologies."

British, she thought, *or maybe Australian.*

"It's all right." She forced an awkward smile, the kind she usually used on difficult customers who didn't seem to know what they wanted or changed their mind when she was halfway through making their drink.

"Trust your instincts." He bowed his head, then turned and walked out the front door.

She watched him for a moment, hugging herself tightly, until he disappeared into the fog outside.

"Get a grip, girl," she said aloud, walking faster than necessary to the door to turn the lock and drop the blinds. She stopped at his table to pick up his coffee cup.

Beside it sat a hundred-dollar bill and a small cream-colored business card.

She stared at the money, then reached for the card.

"Nigel Witherspoon, Nightwatcher." She turned it over. Written on the back, in a spidery hand in red ink, were the words "Your friend is in danger. Trust your instincts."

She slipped the card into her pocket. *Crazy old man*, she thought, picking up the hundred-dollar bill and smiling at it.

Looked like she could have that cheeseburger after all.

For a moment she thought she smelled roses, then shook her head and went back to closing up the shop.

Philip Rutledge turned up the collar of his black leather jacket as he stepped outside his apartment building on Ursulines Street.

It's like stepping back in time, he thought as he stood looking up and down the street. The mist hid the telephone lines hanging overhead. The lanterns on the fronts of houses, glowing through the whiteness, could have been gaslit. A horse-drawn carriage rode by, empty except for the driver, and in the silence all he could hear was the clomping of horseshoes against the pavement. To his right, he could hear the clicking of boot heels against the sidewalk, but even squinting he couldn't see who was making the sound, until he suddenly appeared, the mist seeming to part. The man was in full nineteenth-century attire, from the top hat to the cane, to the boots, to the cloak flying behind him. The man nodded at Philip as he went past, a slight smile on his face. Philip stood there and watched the man continue on his way up the street.

The man disappeared into the mist at the corner. Philip grinned to himself. *Maybe he's a ghost*, he thought, reaching for a cigarette as he carefully made his way down the five concrete steps from his building's front door. He stood there for just a moment, staring into the mist where the man had disappeared, lighting the cigarette and walking down to the corner at Burgundy. The man was gone, vanished as if he'd never been there at all. *Definitely a ghost*, he thought. Everyone knew the French Quarter was full of ghosts, and on a night like this it was even easier to believe. He ran a hand through his thick, dark blond hair, which was cut short on the sides and long on the top. His hair was already damp from the mist. Condensation was forming on his jacket. The night air was still; there was no breeze; there was no sound anywhere.

I love New Orleans in the mist, he reflected as he started walking up Burgundy Street. He loved the timelessness, this feeling that he was walking in a different era. The spell of the mist could last for a while. The streets were deserted—no tourists anywhere, no one out walking their dogs. It was easy to imagine the women in their hoopskirts just inside the walls of the old houses lining the sidewalks, sipping wine out of crystal and laughing at the jokes of the men as they ate by candlelight. Every house's shutters were closed and latched against the night.

As he approached the corner of Burgundy and St. Ann, he heard footsteps echoing behind him.

A chill went up his body. He stopped walking, standing there, his head cocked to one side, listening.

Nothing. There was nothing to hear except the distant sound of cars driving down Rampart Street, a block away.

Stop scaring yourself, he thought, dropping his cigarette and grinding it out beneath his boot. *It's just a weird night, that's all; stop letting your imagination run away with you. You'll never be able to get hard if you keep this up.*

He lit another cigarette, turning and looking behind. He couldn't see more than a few feet; it was pointless. But again, his senses seemed to trigger something, a feeling that something was back there, watching, waiting . . . He peered through the mist, squinting, straining his eyes. Nothing.

He took a drag on his cigarette and started walking again. Just nerves, that's all it was, the mist so thick and damp and, well, cloying. He inhaled and blew the smoke out through his nose. He passed under a streetlamp and stopped there for a moment. He cocked his head, straining to hear. He could have sworn . . .

There! A cautious footstep, then silence.

His heart began to beat faster.

Maybe it's just someone walking their dog, he thought, looking back down Burgundy Street. *But then, why don't I hear the dog?*

He started walking again, trying to keep the sound of his own steps as silent as possible. Surely, he reasoned, no one was going to be out trying to mug people tonight.

The French Quarter wasn't completely safe. Once away from the neon and crowds of Bourbon Street, in the silent darkness of the lower Quarter, muggers plied their trade, pulling knives or guns or simply jumping the unsuspecting solo pedestrian after night fell. Attention must be paid to surroundings, awareness at its peak for safety. Philip had never been mugged, but he rarely came staggering home drunk in the wee hours of the morning alone.

There. Another step, then another stealthy one followed.

He fought to keep his breathing under control. Just because there was someone back there didn't mean he was going to be mugged.

St. Ann was only a half block away. There would be people around; the Rawhide Bar was there on the corner. Safety.

He started walking just a little faster, trying not to break into a run.

The steps behind kept pace.

His breathing started coming quicker, beads of sweat forming at his brow line. There was dampness under his arms. He tossed the cigarette away into the street.

A car went by, its headlights glowing against the white blanket, illuminating shapes and forms. He stopped and looked back as the lights swept along the sidewalk, until the glowing red taillights vanished.

There was no one there.

He took several deep breaths and started laughing as his heart rate slowed.

Idiot. He grinned, heading for the corner. *You just heard your own footsteps echo; that's all it was.*

He flagged down a United cab at the corner, which was a lucky break. He was running a little late. On his way out, his phone had rung. Once he heard his mother's voice on the other end, he regretted not letting his machine answer. It was the same conversation it always was: "When are you going to get a real job? . . . You can't work at a coffee shop forever . . . We didn't spend all that money on college for you to spend the rest of your life making lattes."

"How are you ever going to buy a house?" she would ask. "A car? What about retirement? You're young now; you think you don't have to worry about these things, but you have to start planning, Philip. You have to think about your future."

His future. He'd applied for plenty of jobs since graduating last summer. Nothing.

His mother, of course, didn't know he made plenty of extra money. The ad in the local gay paper, with his bare torso and a beeper number, was quite successful. It had been running now for several years, and his mother would be quite shocked if she knew how much money was sitting in his savings account at the Whitney Bank.

He ground his cigarette out on the sidewalk. Arthur, the man in Uptown he was going to see, would give him several crisp brand-new hundred-dollar bills.

What would his dear Southern Baptist mother say if he told her that he could make three hundred dollars, cash, for doing nothing more than standing in front of an old, lonely man while wearing nothing but a jockstrap?

He climbed into the cab. The driver was a black woman with feather earrings dangling down to her shoulders. Thick dreadlocks hung down her back. "Where to, darlin'?"

"Fifteen twenty-three Octavia."

She nodded and turned the meter on.

Other than the employees, Rachel was the only person in the Quartermaster Deli.

Sitting at the long table, waiting for her mushroom bacon cheeseburger to cool off enough to eat, she kept watch out the plate glass window. Her cigarette burned in the metal ashtray coated with the resin of thousands of previous cigarettes. She took another drink of her Diet Pepsi. The half joint she'd smoked on her way through the Quarter had mellowed her out . . . although she had this eerie feeling, as she'd walked through the thick mist, that someone was following her.

Paranoia will destroy ya, she thought, her eyes still fixated on the swirling mist outside the glass. She shook her head. Stop looking for something that's not there.

"Looking for ghosts?" the woman behind the cash register called over to her. A Marlboro dangled from her lips. Her curly black hair stood out at all crazy angles from her scalp, and she was wearing too much pancake makeup and too much black eyeliner. Her body seemed shapeless in the battered old LSU sweatshirt hanging almost down to her knees.

Rachel turned and smiled at her. "It's a haunted night."

The woman shrugged. "If you believe in that stuff."

Rachel turned back to her window. She believed. The big old house on State Street that she'd grown up in was haunted. Her parents and older siblings didn't believe her, and she eventually gave up trying to make them understand. She saw them everywhere: the old woman in black who paced the halls upstairs, the lovers who met in the gazebo in the backyard around midnight, and the young boy playing in the garden just outside the dining room windows with a ball just after sunset every day, who sometimes would smile at her and beckon to her to come and play just for a little while. They'd even sent her to a psychiatrist once, thinking she was emotionally needy, a little too desperate for attention—perhaps that was why she made up the ridiculous stories.

She'd hated her family then, for not believing her, for finding it easier to believe she was unbalanced or insane than to accept that their house was haunted.

Philip was the only one who believed her, and sometimes she wondered if he did or was just humoring her out of friendship.

At least if he doesn't, he has the decency to pretend, she thought, picking up her burger and taking a bite.

Trust your instincts.

She spun her head, looking out the window again. The old man was standing on the opposite corner, staring at her through the glass. She forced herself to swallow, even though her stomach was turning. He nodded to her, then turned and walked up Bourbon Street, vanishing into the mist.

Trembling slightly, she stared down at the burger, appetite gone.

The radio in the cab was tuned to an R & B oldies station. Gladys Knight and the Pips. He remembered the song vaguely but couldn't recall the name.

He looked out the window as the cab drove out of the Quarter and headed Uptown. The black jock he had on underneath his baggy jeans was pinching him slightly below the right cheek. He shifted in the seat, trying to get the strap to move down.

"You okay back there?"

He looked up. Her dark chocolate eyes were watching him in the rearview mirror. Her voice was a deep alto, without inflection or tone. Each syllable was the same note.

He shrugged. "Yeah, I'm fine."

"On your way home?"

"Work."

"What do you do?"

How do I answer that? he wondered. Hell, she was a New Orleans cab driver. She'd seen and heard it all before. "I'm an escort."

She nodded. "Are you careful?"

"Yeah." He resisted the urge to say, *I'm not stupid.* He knew other escorts didn't care about condoms. He saw them online all the time, peddling their bareback wares. He sometimes wondered why they didn't care. Sure, there were drugs and stuff now, so it wasn't a death sentence like it used to be, but you needed insurance to get the drugs, right? It wasn't like they were passing them out for free. Why take such a risk? His friend Rory, the one who'd gotten him to place his ad in the first place, was willing to go condom-free.

"If they pay extra." Rory shrugged, uncaring. Rory never bothered to get tested, either. He could be passing it along to his foolish customers.

Philip shuddered. The cab was rolling along St. Charles Avenue now. The streetcar clanged past them, glowing eerily in the mist. Huge oaks lined the Avenue, their thick branches arching over it like a tunnel. They stopped at the light at Napoleon, the redness glowing through the mist. He glanced out the window.

A blond man was standing on the corner, looking right at him.

He was good-looking, tall, with long white-blond hair hanging to his shoulders. He was wearing a black overcoat over tight black jeans. His eyes were an intense blue, as though shot through with lights.

The man smiled at him and waved.

Philip stared at him.

They were in bed together, the blond man's hard body pressed against his as they kissed. It was a tender kiss, the kind that lovers share, rather than the frantic face-eating kind driven by lust for a stranger. His lips were strong, firm, yet gentle and almost sweet. Philip leaned his head back, and the blond man started kissing his chin, his outstretched neck, sending tremors through Philip's body. The scent of lilacs and roses was heavy in the air, and Philip luxuriated in the smell as his body enjoyed the feel of the silk sheets against his back, his butt, his legs. Philip put his hands on the blond's back, feeling the strength of the rippling muscles there, trailing them down as the back narrowed and then began to curve outward into the hard, round muscles of his ass. The blond man was now kissing the cleft in the center of Philip's chest, while the fingers of one hand were stroking a nipple . . .

The light changed, and the cab started moving again.

Philip's eyes opened. He stared at the dreadlocks hanging down over the headrest.

He turned and looked out the back window.

The man was gone, like he'd never been there in the first place.

Philip shook his head. *What the fuck?* He reached into his jacket pocket and pulled out his crumpled pack of cigarettes. “Do you mind if I smoke?” he asked as he shook one out.

“Just open the window.” She smiled at him in the rearview mirror, showing gold caps on her front teeth. “Don’t bother me none, but you’d be amazed at the way some people bitch.”

He cracked the window, and the cold, damp air slapped him in the face. His hand was shaking as he shook out a cigarette and lit it.

What the hell was that? he wondered, inhaling the smoke and blowing it out the window. He turned and looked back, but he couldn’t see anything through the mist other than the headlights of the car behind him, the low hanging branches of the massive oaks, and the occasional streetlamp.

New Orleans is a haunted city. Maybe it was just a ghost.

He smiled to himself. Rachel Spielman, his best friend, whose apartment was just across the hall from his, claimed to see ghosts all the time.

“So many people have died violently here,” she would say, rolling a joint. “Is it any wonder the city is full of ghosts?”

He didn’t believe in the supernatural, ghosts, werewolves, witches—any of that. Bogeymen to scare children into behaving was all it was, old stories coming down from the less-educated times, when an eclipse was a sign of God’s anger. Rachel did, so he always humored her and listened to her wild stories of the ghosts in her parents’ house. It was part of her charm, part of the reason he liked her so much. A vivid imagination.

He tossed the cigarette out the window as the cab turned onto Octavia Street. She pulled up in front of Arthur’s house. “Nine seventy-five,” she said without looking back, expertly flipping the meter off.

He pulled a ten and a five out of his wallet and handed them over the seat to her. “Keep it,” he said.

“Thanks, man.” She flashed her gold teeth at him. “You be careful, okay?”

“I’m always careful.”

Her smile faded as he opened the door. “There’s some weird energy in the city tonight,” she warned, “so be on your guard.”

He looked at her for a moment, trying to decide if she was serious, and then climbed out of the cab. "You don't have to wait till I'm inside."

She shrugged. "Suit yourself, man." He shut the door, and she pulled away from the curb. He stood there, watching the red taillights disappear into the mist.

The street was deserted. He looked around and exhaled in relief.

Did you think you'd see him again? he asked himself as he went up the walk to the front door. *You're getting as crazy as Rachel.* He climbed the steps to the verandah. A porch swing swayed gently, as if someone had just gotten out of it. Wrought-iron chairs beaded with condensation were scattered around, empty and forlorn. Green-painted shutters stood sentry beside darkened windows. A fountain in the side yard bubbled, water flowing through a marble urn held aloft by a bare-breasted woman. The front door was oak, half of it stained glass in the pattern of a Madonna and child, the Madonna smiling down at her giggling infant. The house, a huge old Victorian, seemed cold and uninviting. He pushed the buzzer, hearing the bell clang inside. Footsteps approached the door. He looked back to the street. It was still empty. The door swung open.

Arthur was in his early seventies, a retired professor of English from Tulane University. His head was completely bald, white, crisscrossed with bluish veins. Long gray hairs hung from his nostrils. He was wearing a long red velvet robe that brushed the floor. His bare feet protruded from beneath its hem. His toenails were long and yellowed. His watery blue eyes were bloodshot. He smelled of sour Scotch. He always drank several Scotches before Philip arrived.

"Philip." His voice was slightly slurred from the liquor. "Do come in, my dear boy." He smiled, yellowed teeth over bluish gums. He didn't look well, not that he ever did.

Philip stepped past him into the house. It was always spotlessly clean, everything in its appointed place, yet it always smelled musty, the air stale. Philip removed his coat and hung it on the coat tree just inside the front door. He walked down the hallway to the living room. The curtains were closed, as they always were. It was as though light and fresh air had abandoned the house many years before.

If ever a house was meant to be haunted, he thought as he untied his shoes and removed them, *it was this one.*

Arthur stood in the doorway. His glass of Scotch sat on an end table, next to the reclining chair where Arthur always sat. The ice was melted. The half-empty bottle stood, uncapped, next to it. Philip knew Arthur would not come into the room until he was undressed. He never did. Arthur didn't want to touch him, as though somehow he were unclean. Philip placed his shoes on the hearth, then removed his socks. He stood back up and pulled his sweatshirt over his head. It was cold in the house, and goose bumps rose on his bare skin. He folded the sweatshirt and placed it next to his shoes. Arthur liked everything to be neat. Philip undid his belt, unbuttoned the fly of his jeans, and slid them down. He stepped out of them and folded them, placing them on top of the sweatshirt.

With only the black jockstrap on, he turned and faced Arthur, his legs apart, his pelvis thrust forward a little.

Arthur smiled, pale lips parting to show his almost predatory teeth. "Beautiful, yes, simply beautiful." He stepped into the room and removed his robe. His skin was pale white, pale enough to see the blue veins, and hung in folds from his arms. A patch of gray hair stood in the center of his flabby, sagging chest. His belly was round and hung over the gray pubic hair, the small pink cock, the even smaller balls beneath. He sat down in the chair and reached for his Scotch, taking a drink and smacking his lips. Philip turned so his back was to him, then bent over forward, bending his knees slightly, so the muscled orbs of his ass were rounded and uplifted, framed by the straps of the black jock. He glanced up at the antique clock on the mantel.

Arthur was breathing heavier. Philip knew without looking that the little red cock was now hard, being stroked. Arthur never wanted to touch him, which was fine with Philip. He didn't want to be close to Arthur, to feel that old, papery skin, to smell the stale Scotch on his breath or the slightly sour odor of his body. He shifted his weight from one foot to the other, flexing each cheek in order. This was so much easier than the others, the closeted overweight married guys from out of town, who wanted to fuck him or be fucked, to have their moist, sour-smelling cocks sucked, their balls touched.

"So pretty," Arthur breathed.

Philip straightened back up, bringing his arms up over his head, making the muscles of his back stand out, standing like that for a few minutes, watching the second hand on the clock moving ever so slowly around the Roman numbers on its face. He turned sideways, posing, his right arm dropping and flexing so the muscles of his pecs and shoulders jumped out, while looking at a point slightly above Arthur's head. His own cock was still soft. That was fine as long as the jock was still on, but when it was time for the jock to come off, his cock had to be erect, ready to be stroked.

He climbed up on the coffee table, flexing his arms again. He avoided looking at Arthur, and started thinking about something erotic, something to get his cock to start stirring.

The man in the mist.

That handsome face.

The blond hair, the blue eyes.

The blue eyes with the hint of unforeseen pleasures in them.

He smelled lilac and rose again, felt the silk sheets against his skin.

His dick began to stiffen.

He saw the blond man unbuttoning his own shirt, revealing marble-like skin, muscles finely etched in relief like a sculpture, the round, pink nipples on his large chest erect and hard. The tufts of blond hair running from the navel downward, hinting of what was below.

He imagined what the man smelled like, how his lips would taste, how his skin would feel against his own.

He was hard now, the head of his cock sticking out above the waist-band of the jock.

He slid the jock down, spitting into his other hand, which he used to start stroking his dick.

"So pretty," Arthur said again.

And Philip lost himself in the reverie of the fantasy from the cab, the blond man's mouth and tongue working on his neck, his chest, then his stomach. Philip closed his eyes, imagining himself back in the room that smelled of lilac and rose, his skin lying on sheets of silk as candles flickered in a warm, soft breeze. "I love you so," the blond man whispered, his fingers probing the cleft between Philip's cheeks, looking for the entryway into his body.

Philip brought up his free hand to pinch his own nipple.

Arthur was breathing faster; he could hear him. "So pretty, so pretty," he repeated over and over again, like always, and Philip began rubbing his thumb over the head of his own cock, the precum starting to leak out a bit, using the sticky drops of fluid to further lubricate his cock as he rubbed; and in his mind he was far away, far from this spooky, stale old house with an old man sitting on the couch in front of him, in a bed with the blond man, who was sucking Philip's cock while probing Philip's asshole with his fingers. Philip imagined looking down on that white-blond head as it moved up and down, worshipping Philip's cock as though it were a totem.

Philip heard the gasps as Arthur's little cock ejected its few drops of semen.

His own was ready, the cum rising in him, his balls tightening, and even though Arthur liked him to be silent, he cried out as he reached the point, his juices spilling out of him.

He opened his eyes.

"So pretty," Arthur said again, his own eyes closed.

So pretty.

Chapter Two

"Keep the change," Philip said as he slid out of the cab in front of his building on Ursulines.

"Thanks." The cabbie, an older white man in his late fifties with his hair greased back, nodded.

Can this fog have thickened? He shivered as the cab drove off and he dug into his pocket for his keys. He climbed up the five sagging wooden steps, blue paint peeling off in flakes with each footstep. He unlocked the door, stepping into the darkened passageway leading to the courtyard. A cracked birdbath with a naked cherub on its hands and knees stood in the center of the courtyard. Building materials lay in piles around it, the corners piled high with resealed paint cans, blue paint gummily dried down the sides. A wooden staircase stood in one corner, winding around in a squarelike pattern up to the fourth floor. His apartment was a tiny efficiency up on the fourth floor; an oven in the summer, always cold in the winter. He could hear sounds coming from the other apartments as he climbed the sagging wooden steps, one hand on the railing: televisions, stereos, laughter. About the third floor, his legs began to burn a bit, despite hours spent on the stair-climber at the gym. The stairs became rickety the higher he climbed, soft in some places, the railing giving beneath his weight a bit in others. Slightly out of breath when he finally reached the top, he lit a cigarette and stood there for a moment, waiting for the burning feeling in his legs to subside. He walked to the little corridor that led to his apartment. He slid his key into the dead bolt on his door.

"Hey."

"Jesus!" He dropped his cigarette onto the damp floor. "What the fuck, Rachel?"

Rachel stood in her doorway across the hall from his, her electric-blue hair hanging uncombed to her shoulders. She took a hit on the joint she was holding. She was wearing green camouflage army pants and a tube top that barely contained her large, heavy breasts. Her navel was pierced, as was her right eyebrow, and her nose. A tattoo of a sunburst surrounded her navel. She shrugged. "Sorry, man. Why you so jumpy?" She offered him the joint, and he took it, pushing his door open at the same time.

The little room was frigid. "Fuck," he said, turning up the gas heater mounted on the wall between the dormer windows, taking two hits off the joint. His lungs burned a bit, and he fought down a cough, blowing the smoke out. He shrugged. "You startled me."

She sat down on a tattered brown beanbag chair he'd bought for five dollars at a thrift store, pinching the joint out between her fingers. "Think I was a ghost or something?" She laughed. "Chill, boy. Where ya been?"

"Arthur's." He shrugged off his jacket. "How was work?" He worked afternoons at the Jazz Café.

"Slow." She made a face. "Cold as it is, you'd think everyone would want coffee, but the Quarter's deserted tonight."

"It was slow as fuck all afternoon." He shook his jacket off, dropping it on the bed. "Thank God Arthur called. I was down to my last five bucks."

She pulled a lock of blue hair in front of her eyes, staring at it like she'd never noticed it was blue before. "A weird old man came in, though, and hung out for hours."

He walked into the tiny bathroom. A broken tile crackled under his feet. He pulled the clear shower curtain open and turned on the hot water. It took about five minutes for the water to get hot enough. He pulled the curtain closed and stared into the mirror. "What was so weird about him?" he called back. There was a small, hard zit forming on his chin. Eyes a little bloodshot, maybe. He grinned at himself and walked out, sitting down on the corner of his bed, and started unlacing his boots. He grinned at her. "Come on, what creeped you out?"

"He looked like he was a thousand years old, for one thing." She let go of the hair, tapping her fingers on her knees. She shrugged. "Good-looking, if you're into the grandfather type."

"Only if they pay." He took his shirt off, shivering against the cold. He walked over to the wall heater and stood in front of it, letting the warm air blow against his skin. He turned back to her. "So?"

"Yeah." She shook her head. She relit the joint and took a long drag. "Anyway, he hung out there for hours, until I practically had to kick him out so I could close up, ya know? He just kept staring at me like I was from another planet, and then—get this—he tips me with a hundred-dollar bill, thank you very much."

"Fuck." He grinned at her. "So what's the big deal? A lonely old guy hangs out for a few hours, tips a pretty girl way too much. What's so weird?" He shrugged. "Arthur pays me three hundred bucks to beat off in front of him. At least you didn't have to get undressed." He laughed. "Must be doing something wrong—they won't pay me unless I get naked."

She grimaced. "Cute." She slid her hand into her right pocket and pulled out a business card. "He left this with the tip."

He took the card from her. It was a rich cream color, thick. In raised black old-English letters it read "Nigel Witherspoon, Nightwatcher." Below was a phone number.

"Nightwatcher? What the hell is that?"

"Maybe some kind of weird club."

He turned the card over. Written in spidery handwriting in red ink were the words "Your friend is in danger. Trust your instincts." He handed the card back to her. "Did you see this?" He felt a chill and turned the heater up another notch. "That's kind of weird." He read the words aloud, slowly, his scalp prickling. "What do you think it means?"

"Maybe it's some weird come-on." She rolled her eyes. "These old pervs'll try anything to get in a girl's pants."

"You didn't tell him you're a dyke?"

"Why get him all excited?"

Steam was coming from the bathroom. "Babe, I'm gonna get in the shower."

She stood up. "Going out?"

He nodded. "Wanna come with?"

She shook her head. "I'm working on a new poem." He was hardly an expert, but he thought her poetry was good. "See ya in the morning. Happy hunting." The door shut behind her.

He peeled off his pants and the jock, tossing them in a basket at the foot of the bed. He stepped into the bathroom, which was now full of steam. *Kind of like outside*, he thought, pulling the curtain back and stepping into the spray. He stood there for a moment, letting the hot water wash over him and take some of the chill out of his skin. He felt a little dirty, like he had the last few times he'd seen Arthur. *I can't keep doing this; I need to find a better job.* He was already, at twenty-four, too old for a longtime client. How long before Arthur started to think the same, saw some pretty young college student jogging shirtless down St. Charles Avenue, and pulled over, offering him what would seem like a fortune, for doing very little—actually, for doing something he would do later back in his dorm room for free? Then the calls would stop coming; the three hundred dollars he could count on every week, to pay his bills and buy his food and drinks and drugs, would be gone. Part of the reason he wanted to go out was to have someone find him attractive without money changing hands, to give himself up to his own pleasure.

He grabbed a bar of soap and began lathering his torso. There was stubble on his chest—he'd have to shave again soon.

I wonder if the blond will be out in the bars. His cock began to stiffen slightly, just thinking about him. He slid the bar of soap over it, under his balls, down through his legs and up the crack, then back up and around to his torso, soaping his torso, running it over his hardening nipples. He closed his eyes, thinking about the blond again, imagining his face, his naked body. His cock got harder, and he closed his right hand over it, sliding it back and forth, the soap making it slippery enough. His left hand came up and started pinching his left nipple, pulling and tugging on it, sending an electric current from it to the tip of his cock. He moaned a little as he felt his balls tighten, the dull ache in his lower abs that meant it would be soon, as his hand began moving faster and faster, each muscle in his body stiffening with tension, his breath coming in gulps, barely audible gasps, until a cry burst from his throat, his body convulsing and jerking with each eruption through the slit at the tip of his cock.

And he thought he smelled, for just a moment, roses and lilacs.

The poem wasn't coming right.

Rachel gnawed on the eraser of her pencil. She always wrote in pencil. She liked the way the lead would become softer as she wrote; she liked the clean, neat way the words appeared on the page. She didn't use ink, because scratching words out bothered her; it spoiled the way the page looked, and distracted her from the writing. If she wrote in ink and changed her mind about a word, a sentence, a phrase, she would have to start over on a clean sheet of paper. She looked over the line she'd just written. "Shit," she said, angrily erasing the entire sentence.

She put the notebook down, frustrated.

Probably should have gone out for a drink, she thought, putting the pencil down and reaching for the canister with her pot supply and rolling papers. She ground the pot up in her coffee grinder to a fine powder, which made rolling that much easier for her. She hummed to herself a Dixie Chicks song, "Goodbye Earl." She loved the Dixie Chicks. As she finished rolling, she realized the apartment was silent. She always listened to music when she worked on her poetry, getting so lost in thought that she often didn't notice when the CD ended. Lighting the joint, she hit the Play button on her portable stereo, and soon Beyonce's voice was filling the room again.

She sat on the edge of her bed, letting the mellowness of the pot take hold of her. She coughed a bit and then fell backward on the bed, staring at the water spots on the ceiling.

Your friend is in danger. Trust your instincts.

She bolted upright, shivering. The gas heater on the wall was blowing hot air right onto her, yet she felt cold; she reached for a blanket.

Can't be, she thought to herself. It sounded like the old guy was right there in the room with her, but that was impossible.

She wrapped the blanket around herself and put the joint out. *Don't need any more of that, obviously,* she thought, reaching for her notebook again.

Philip liked Thursday nights in the gay bars. The crowd was usually more relaxed and laid-back than it would be on the weekend proper. The crystal and ecstasy wouldn't come out until Friday; no one wanted to risk losing their jobs by showing up on Friday morning at eight coming down from a drug. Thursdays were more about getting tipsy or slightly drunk, maybe hooking up with someone. People were more relaxed on Thursday night—the desperate pressure to get laid, to hook up with someone, wasn't there the way it was on Fridays and Saturdays. Thursday nights were more about going out with friends to blow off steam.

He walked into Oz just as their weekly Calendar Boy contest was getting under way. Jambalaya Crawfish, a drag queen who towered over most of the bar boys, was standing on the stage with a microphone, braying with her thick parish accent. Her towering blond Dolly Parton wig added at least another foot and a half. She was wearing a black sequined evening gown over her massive bulk. She was a big girl—looked like she'd maybe been a linebacker in high school thirty years ago. Philip walked up to the bar and ordered a longneck Bud Lite, tipping the pretty blond bartender two bucks, and turned to watch the show, leaning back against the bar, tilting his pelvis forward. An older guy, maybe in his early fifties, walked by and stopped, staring.

Not if you paid me five hundred dollars, Philip thought as he turned his eyes away. *Go away, Gramps.*

"Are you ready to see some dick?" Jambalaya shrieked into her microphone. The crowd on the dance floor cheered. She consulted a napkin. "First up is Johnny!"

Johnny was maybe twenty, with long brown hair he liked to flick around as he danced. He peeled his clothes off in what he apparently thought was a seductive manner, but he couldn't dance to save his life, which was distracting. He just kind of bounced from foot to foot, wiggling his ass every once in a while, out of sync to the music. There was a cross tattooed on his left pec, and a sunburst around his pierced navel. He stripped down to his underwear, red-and-white-striped bikinis covering a very small dick. *No chance in hell of winning.* Philip yawned, finished his beer, ordered another. *What are these guys thinking?*

Philip had won the contest a few years earlier after getting talked into entering by Rachel. The shots she'd bought him to steel his nerve and loosen his inhibitions hadn't hurt, either. He remembered standing off to the side of the stage, watching the other guys, his stomach in knots, the liquor jumbling his mind a bit. When it was his turn, he'd gotten up. The music had been "Beautiful Stranger" by Madonna, and he started dancing. He'd always been a good dancer, and he figured, *The other guys might be hotter, but I can blow them away dancing.* He'd peeled off his T-shirt and eventually worked his shorts down until he was just dancing in front of the crowd in his white Calvin Kleins with the blue waistband. The crowd had cheered when they saw his semi-hard dick.

And when it was over, he was the winner and had two hundred bucks in his pocket.

Instead of watching the next few contestants, he scanned the crowds, looking for familiar faces. He recognized some of the guys, faces he'd seen in the bars before. Some of the guys he didn't recognize were hot: tight, round asses, broad shoulders, bulging arms. He made eye contact with a tall man, maybe about six four, standing in the corner by the stage, just off the dance floor. He was good-looking, maybe about twenty-five, with smooth skin and light brown hair. He was wearing a muscle shirt showing off his nice biceps and the obligatory tattoo around the right upper arm. His jeans hung loose and low off his hips. Philip allowed his line of sight to drift down to the crotch of the man's jeans. *Nice,* he thought, nodding and smiling at the guy, who started walking toward him, a friendly, eager smile on his face.

"Our last contestant is Gunther!" Jambalaya shrieked in her weird falsetto, and he turned his head to look at the stage.

It was the blond man from the corner of Napoleon and St. Charles.

Jambalaya towered over him, meaning he was maybe about five ten, maybe five nine. He was wearing a black leather jacket with a white ribbed tank top under it. His black jeans were tight, cupping the bulge under the button fly. Jambalaya moved away from the center stage as the blond began to dance. Philip stared, transfixed, as the blond shrugged off the jacket. The crowd cheered as he ran his hands up and down his hard torso, pinching his nipples.

"How you doing?" It was the tall man, standing next to him now, very close, almost touching him.

"Good." Philip nodded, unable to stop staring at the blond.

"I'm Steve."

"Philip."

The blond had undone his pants, kicking off his shoes. He slid them down, revealing a pair of tight white underwear over thickly muscled legs. He stepped out of the pants, kicking them off to the side, shaking his hips so the big cock flopped under the white cotton.

"Where you from, Philip?"

"I live here." Philip stared as the blond pulled the shirt over his head in one fluid motion. His torso was smooth as marble, carved and chiseled. The crowd cheered again. The blond turned so his back was to the audience; his back rippled with muscle, narrowing to the waist. Two dimples just above his round ass deepened as he leaned backward, then forward so his ass became rounder and fuller. He looked back over his shoulder, right at Philip.

Their eyes locked, and the blond smiled.

His eyes were blue, a pure, crystalline color.

The blond closed his right eye in a wink.

His eyes, Philip thought, staring back into them from across the room, *his eyes . . .*

He started moving forward, leaving Steve behind at the bar as he stepped onto the dance floor, pushing his way through the crowd. *Have to get closer; have to get right up there to the stage, get as close as I can to him; he's so fucking beautiful.* He edged around people, never losing sight of the blond, who was turning again to face the crowd, his hands coming down to cup his bulge.

Their eyes were locked.

You want me, the blond's eyes seemed to say to him. *Come with me and I'll make all your fantasies come true, forever and ever; I will take you places you never dreamed of going, give you pleasures you've never imagined, not even in your wildest dreams.*

Philip's cock hardened inside his pants, the crotch suddenly becoming tight and constrictive.

He reached the side of the stage.

The blond came over to him, kneeling down with Philip in between his legs. He grabbed Philip's head and pulled him forward. Philip reached up and touched the blond's legs. They were hard as steel, a thick dusting of golden blond down covering their whiteness.

His eyes, Philip thought as their lips came together.

He closed his eyes as the blond's tongue came into his mouth.

Time stopped.

The bar faded away.

He was on a large bed with satin sheets against his skin. Candles flickered, casting shadows.

Pleasure.

Gunther was between his legs, his long cock probing to find the entrance into his body.

Oh, yes, please fuck me.

Roses—he smelled roses, and yes, the lilacs too, their scent drifting over him, carried by a warm breeze.

He cried out as the huge cock found his entrance and pushed inward.

The blond was sucking on his lip, then bit into it. He tasted blood.

He opened his eyes as the blond began pulling him onto the stage. He didn't resist; he couldn't. He wasn't even aware of the cheering crowd, the sea of faces on the dance floor, wanting to see something different, something more exciting than the usual amateur-night strippers. It was like they weren't even there—there was nobody there, nobody around; it was just him and Gunther, the two of them alone. All he could hear was his heart beating as the blond turned him around and undid his pants, yanking them down, and then he was grinding his crotch against Philip's ass.

Oh, yes, fuck me, fuck me, fuck me right here; I don't care who's watching; fuck me, fuck me, fuck me . . .

He felt Gunther's mouth on the base of his neck, nibbling, quick little bites followed by flicks of his tongue.

Gunther's cock was huge as it pressed into the crack of his ass.

His body shuddered and trembled.

His balls ached.

I'm going to come, he thought.

No, you aren't.

He opened his eyes, looking back over his shoulder.

Gunther smiled.

He can see into my soul.

Gunther nodded. *You're mine, Philip.*

Philip nodded.

The music stopped, and Gunther let him go. He stumbled just a bit, aware suddenly that he was onstage.

The noise cascaded over him. The crowd was cheering, applauding, stomping their feet as Jambalaya teetered back onto the stage in her stilettos. "What'd you think of THAT, boys? YEAH." She grinned at Philip, her nicotine-yellowed teeth crooked underneath the garish red lipstick, the thick powder on her face barely hiding the blondish hairs along her jawline.

Philip brought his hands up to his head. Everything was so loud, the lights over the bar across the room so bright. A wave of nausea passed over him, but he fought it.

He reached down and pulled his pants back up. *Gotta get out of here,* he thought, *gotta get down from this stage; what the fuck am I doing up here . . . ?*

"What's your name?" Jambalaya shoved her microphone into his face, leering at him with bloodshot eyes beneath lashes coated with globs of mascara. Her breath smelled of stale liquor, and Philip staggered back a few steps; she looked almost demonic and frightening; why had he never noticed that before about her . . . ?

"His name is Maxi," Gunther said.

Philip stared at him, into those so-blue eyes. *Maxi? What the hell?*

I've been looking for you for so long, my darling Maxi, and now that I've found you at last, again, no one will ever separate us again.

"Let's hear it for Gunther and Maxi!" Jambalaya shrieked, her voice piercing his brain like a sharpened pencil going through his eyes. He winced as the crowd roared its approval.

The phone rang.

"Goddamn it!" Rachel threw her pencil across the room, cursing herself for not unplugging it. The poem was finally coming to her, and now her concentration was broken; maybe the poem was gone for good. *Must be the pot,* she thought. She always unplugged the fucking phone when she was writing. Shaking her head, she picked it up. "Hello?"

"Your friend is in danger, Rachel." The voice was low, heavily accented.

"Who is this?"

"Nigel Witherspoon."

"How did you get my phone number?"

"Does that really matter?"

"Look, you old freak—"

"Your friend is in mortal danger, Rachel. Philip?"

The hair at the nape of her neck stood up. "What do you know about Philip?"

"I know many things, Rachel." He coughed. "We need to talk."

"So, talk." *Hang up,* a voice inside her head screamed. *Just hang up the fucking phone!*

But somehow, she couldn't.

"I have many things to tell you. Come downstairs. I'm on the sidewalk in front of your building."

"Are you nuts?" she shouted. *How did you find out where I live?*

"No harm will come to you. If you care for your friend, you must come down."

"Okay, okay." She hung up the phone and grabbed for her coat. *I must be nuts,* she thought as she grabbed for her keys. *This creepy old guy is stalking me, and I'm going to go talk to him? That's crazy, just crazy; this is how you wind up on the front page of the paper and on the ten o'clock news, Rachel, this is the kind of thing you always get pissed off at in scary movies, the heroine doing something so unfucking-believably stupid . . .*

Then she noticed the cord curled up on the floor next to the nightstand.

She reached down.

She *had* unplugged the phone.

She felt the scream rising in her throat but fought it down.

She walked out her front door and headed for the staircase.

Chapter Three

Royal Street was deserted.

The mist swirled around them as they walked past parked cars covered with round beads of condensation, the windows fogged up on the inside. The street was silent except for the clicking of their heels against the cracked and tilted sidewalk. The trees they walked beneath dripped, the leaves rustling and swaying in a breeze Philip felt as a cold wet hand on the back of his neck. He shivered.

"Cold?" Gunther asked, squeezing Philip's hand tighter with his own, which felt cold and almost a little clammy. "Don't be nervous," Gunther said to him, smiling, his red lips parting. "You've done this before." He pushed Philip against a streetlamp, pressing himself between Philip's legs. Philip felt Gunther's hard cock through his jeans as Gunther moved his hips, pressing his lips against Philip's neck, his tongue darting out, twirling circles against the base of his neck. It tickled a bit, and Philip's own cock began to thicken and harden.

Philip's heartbeat pounded in his ears, his eyes closing and a growl beginning deep in his diaphragm. *Oh, yes, take me; fuck me right here in the street; nobody's watching; rip my pants open.* He pressed his own crotch against Gunther's, but Gunther pushed him back against the lamppost easily.

The satin sheets, the flickering candles.

Lilacs and roses, their heavy perfume clogging his nostrils . . .

"Come on," Gunther whispered, "it's not much farther."

Philip gulped air as Gunther pulled back from him, his cold hands enveloping Philip's as he smiled at him. Philip looked deep into those oh-so-blue eyes, feeling himself getting lost in them again, the blue seeming to draw him in even deeper as he gazed into their depths.

Gunther led him farther down the street, pulling gently yet urgently.

Something doesn't feel right, Philip thought, yet he followed willingly. His need was too strong to resist—the need to be naked with this beautiful stranger who might be a little dangerous, to feel Gunther's huge cock inside him, to be with a man who wasn't paying him, a man he wanted for something besides the cash in his wallet. Instincts finely honed from years of being a hustler were warning him, going off like sirens inside his head. *There's something not right about this guy; something's wrong here . . .*

They reached a carriageway, and Gunther let go of his hands to punch in the access code. The door buzzed, and Gunther swung it open, smiling at him. He held out his hand. "Maxi, come with me."

Philip closed his eyes.

The doors to the terrace were open, a gentle night breeze making the heavy red velvet curtains dance. He could smell the roses in the garden below. Gunther was on top of him, piercing into him, the pain becoming pleasure as he entered, thrusting into him, and he opened his mouth to let out a scream; but he couldn't breathe, the thrusts coming deeper and deeper, filling him, the pleasure, the thrill, the joy of it all coming in a rush; he'd never felt this way before, and his balls were aching, his own cock hard as Gunther drove deeper into him, his eyes coming open and looking up into Gunther's oh-so-beautiful face; and Gunther was smiling down at him, promising him eternity . . .

A cab went by, and Philip opened his eyes.

What the fuck is going on?

"You're remembering." Gunther smiled at him, pulling him close into a tight embrace, squeezing him until his back cracked and popped. "As I knew you would."

His eyes . . . Philip stared into their blueness and felt them piercing into his soul.

"Come on." Gunther pulled at his hand. "We're almost there."

* * *

Rachel could feel wetness under her arms as she pulled the door open. *I must be crazy,* she thought, fingering the switchblade in her jacket pocket. *This is by far the stupidest thing I've ever done; they're going to find my body in pieces in a swamp . . .*

"Ah, there's no need to be frightened," the old man said. His voice was soothing, calming. He was wearing a black trench coat with a matching fedora pulled down low so she couldn't see his eyes in the misty light thrown by the streetlamps. "You won't be needing your switchblade, but I am glad to know you are not so foolish as to venture out without some protection." He sat down on the steps, patting the space next to him with a black-gloved hand. "Here, sit with me, or we could go for a drink, if you'd prefer?"

"I'll stand, thank you." She didn't move out of the doorway. *Something about him,* she thought, *isn't . . .*

"You fear me?" He laughed, genuinely delighted by her fear. He smiled at her, patting the step again. "There is no need to fear ME, my pretty young girl. I'm harmless, nothing but an old man who wants to spend some time talking to a pretty young girl. Is there anything more innocent?"

Yeah, right, and my name is Courtney Love, she thought. "What do you want?"

"Are you sure you won't sit? Ah." He shrugged, holding his hands up. "I promise you will come to no harm from me."

"What do you want?" she repeated.

"I want to save your young friend's life, Rachel." He lit a cigar. "You don't mind if I enjoy this, do you? Surely you won't deny an old man one of his few pleasures."

"Save his life?" *This is crazy this is crazy go back inside . . .*

"It's a long story." He gestured with his cigar. "Are you sure you don't want to go someplace warm to talk? Someplace more public, where you might feel safer?"

"This is fine." She shivered. "You've got five minutes."

"Five minutes?" He pulled an old pocket watch from his coat pocket. "All right, five minutes." He puffed on the cigar, making a contented sigh. "Did you look at the card I gave you?"

"Yes."

"Do you know what a nightwatcher is, my dear?"

"No."

"Ah, how things change." He shook his head. "No nursery rhymes? About nightwatchers guarding the night, to protect small children from the evils that lurk in the dark? Ah, well." He shrugged. "The sun rises and sets, the world keeps turning, and things change."

"Four minutes," Rachel said, glancing at her watch.

"Ah, yes, a woman of her word—five minutes she offers, and five minutes exactly. Not a second more, not a second less." He gave her a smile. "In which case I will have to share with you the *Reader's Digest* condensed version; otherwise we would be here all night . . . and I fear we don't have that kind of time in any case." He put the pocket watch on the step beside him. "It doesn't surprise me that you—or anyone else, for that matter—have never heard the term 'nightwatcher' before; although at one time we were indeed the subject of a popular nursery rhyme. Very few know about us." He looked up at her. "We are a very ancient order, and it is our job—our mission, if you prefer—to protect the human race."

She raised her eyebrows. "What?" She took a step back. *Here he goes, off the deep end.*

"It is our job to protect the human race from what you would call vampires—well, not just the vampires, but a vampire is what concerns the two of us—and your young friend, Philip? Is that his name?"

"Vampires?" *That's it,* she thought, stepping back inside the door. *The man is obviously nuts; I'll go upstairs and call the police. And lock my door, forget this ever happened; this is crazy . . .*

"Come back!" he commanded.

Against her will she stepped back onto the steps, pulling the door shut behind her. She heard the lock click into place. *What am I doing? Get back inside!* She reached into her pocket for her keys, her hands shaking, not just from the cold—she was frightened, frightened of this crazy old man, however harmless he looked.

"You think I am mad, do you not?" He flicked cigar ash onto the sidewalk. "What do you believe, Rachel? Do you believe in God?"

"I—I guess." Her mind flashed back to her childhood: being dressed up and dragged to church; the priests in their fabulous gowns and hats droning on and on; the mass; the kneeling, up and down; the choir singing; the approach to the altar to take the wafer, the body of the Lord; crossing herself in front of the altar; lighting penny candles and saying prayers; wearing the medal of her patron saint around her neck; sunlight coming through stained glass. She'd stopped going when she was sixteen, when it all began to seem stupid and pointless to her.

"Then surely you must believe in evil."

"Evil? Like Satan?" She laughed, remembering the horned devils of Halloween just past, gay boys wearing red Speedos and black fishnet hose, plastic pitchforks in their hands, and little red horns attached to their foreheads.

"For there to be good, Rachel, there must be evil. It is the nature of all things. For every thing, there has to be an opposite, for balance. If there is good, there must be evil."

"I don't understand." She sat down beside him, curious despite her mistrust. "What does Philip have to do with any of this?"

"I am explaining myself poorly." He looked at his watch. "And I only have three minutes left."

"Tell me about Philip."

"Philip is in grave danger." He looked at her, patting her on the arm. "A vampire wants him—a very powerful vampire. A vampire who is evil."

"There's no such thing as vampires." It was an automatic reaction, one taught by rote, like "the sky is blue" or "the grass is green." *There's no such thing as vampires or ghosts or werewolves or witches.* She rubbed her arms and shivered.

"Oh, there are, Rachel. You can be sure of that. Vampires are not a creation of superstitious minds. They are very real, and when they are evil, they can be very dangerous. Most humans go their entire lives without encountering anything of a supernatural nature; others are not so fortunate. And your Philip has attracted the attention of one." He reached into his pocket and removed a golden locket. He clicked it open and passed it to her. "Does he look familiar to you?"

Inside the locket was a miniature photograph of a young man, wearing clothes from another period. His hair was long, curling gently at the shoulders. He was wearing a black suit with a white shirt underneath, open at the collar where a small cross hung at the base of his throat. At his neck. His face—she gave a little gasp.

"It's Philip." She stared at him, wrapping her arms around herself to keep from shivering.

He took the locket back and snapped it shut. "No, my dear, that is a portrait of Maximilian Hesse, the younger son of a German count before the Franco-Prussian War."

"He looks like Philip."

"Which is why Philip is in so much danger." He sighed. "Over a hundred years ago, a vampire by the name of Gunther von Gittelsbach fell in love with Maxi Hesse. And young Maxi loved Gunther in return. They lived an idyllic life together, loving each other the best they could. And when Gunther . . ." He paused, taking a deep breath before continuing. "When Gunther felt that Maxi loved him enough, he offered the gift of immortality, revealing his true nature to him. When that happened, Maxi killed himself."

Rachel began to shiver.

"And Gunther went mad with grief. He became a rogue, killing humans, torturing them, killing members of our order, who had been instructed to destroy him." He reached out with a gloved hand and took hers. "I've been trailing Gunther ever since. He has to be stopped, you see. It is our job—our holy mission, if you will—to protect the human race, not kill members of it."

"You've been after this guy for over a hundred years." *This is crazy,* her mind rebelled. *This can't be happening; this old man is a nutcase—probably should be locked up somewhere; this is crazy; I need to get back inside and away from this nutcase before . . .*

"And now he wants your young friend. He has never, you see, forgotten Maxi; it's actually quite sad, really." His voice trailed off, and he watched a cab go by. "Romantic and sad. Gunther wants to give him the gift of immortality, to make a companion for all eternity. He doesn't want to be alone, even though that's part of our existence—loneliness. Loving humans—mortals, if you will—is a mistake. Mortals die, you see, and we go on."

"This doesn't make sense."

"I assure you, I am not insane."

"Like you'd admit it."

He opened his mouth, pulling his lips back, baring marble white teeth. The canines . . .

. . . were long and pointed.

Gunther unlocked a black wrought-iron gate and pulled Philip inside. He pushed him up against the brick wall. He pushed Philip's arm up over his head, pinning him, bringing his mouth to the base of Philip's neck, kissing, licking, biting, taking little nibbles of the soft skin there.

Oh, yes, Philip thought, his body beginning to tremble, *take me now; take me here; I don't want to wait anymore,* as he brought up his left leg and wrapped it around Gunther's. His hands drifted down Gunther's back, cupping the hard, round ass, squeezing, his excitement growing.

Gunther tore Philip's T-shirt at the neck, ripping it down, shredding it, exposing Philip's hairless torso. Gunther's mouth hungrily moved down to Philip's nipples, biting them, teasing them with flicks of his tongue.

Philip closed his eyes and moaned. *Oh, yes, this feels so fucking good, yes . . .*

"My beautiful Maxi," Gunther whispered, "I've waited for you for so long."

Philip gasped as Gunther's teeth clamped down on his right nipple. He looked down, seeing the blond head, watching the tongue darting out and licking the blood bubbling slowly out of his nipple. He heard muffled voices, footsteps, two people walking by on the other side of the gate, the splashing of water from the other side of the dark tunnel they were inside, Gunther hungrily lapping at his nipple as though nursing. His body trembled. His cock and balls were aching, demanding release.

He heard his heartbeat pounding inside his head again.

He closed his eyes. And . . .

Candles, casting shadows.

"I love you," Gunther was saying, smiling down on him, sweat beading on his face, glistening in the flickering light. They were both naked, and he could feel the soft, silky sheets against his skin, sensuously ca-

ressing him, the softness of the bed shaping to his form. The windows were open, and the breeze coming through them was warm and soft, felt almost like gentle kisses on his skin.

What—what is happening to me? he wondered, opening his eyes, shaking his head to clear it. Gunther's tongue was trailing down his torso, licking at the faint trail of blood. The nipple had stopped bleeding, was healed. His entire body stiffened, and an involuntary groan escaped through his lips. Gunther smiled up at him, his mouth smeared with blood. *He's so beautiful,* Philip thought, *so beautiful; no one has ever made me feel like this before. . . .*

Gunther stood up and pressed his mouth to Philip's.

Philip tasted his own blood. Metallic and coppery, but somehow sweet.

His cock was aching, begging for release. He reached down and undid the top button of his jeans. His hand brushed against Gunther's crotch, the huge cock straining against the denim fabric and the buttons.

It was so big, porn-star big. *Can I handle that?* Philip wondered, imagining how it would feel inside him, sliding in and out with the urgent need to reach its inevitable conclusion, and he wanted it; he wanted to feel it inside him, feel it filling him with its need and size and girth; he wanted to put his mouth on it, to lick it, to nibble on the head, to run his tongue along its tender and sensitive underside, to suckle on his balls and make him crazy with desire, to make Gunther moan and cry out with pleasure.

Gunther cupped Philip's crotch, and Philip moaned again.

"*Liebchen,*" Gunther whispered, "I want to make love to you all night long."

Philip swallowed. "I'd like that."

"Come," Gunther said, taking his hand. "I don't know how much longer I can wait." He pressed his lips against Philip's again, his tongue darting into Philip's mouth, and Philip grasped it with his own mouth, sucking on it until Gunther began to growl low down in his throat.

He pulled Philip along into the courtyard beyond the carriageway.

"You—you're a vampire." *This is insane; this can't be happening to me,* Rachel thought, her mind reeling from the sheer unbelievability of it all. *It must be a dream; I'm dreaming all this; the pot put me to sleep and I'm just having some kind of weird dream caused by the weird mist and the darkness and my overactive imagination.* She started to rise, to get away, to go back inside and back to her apartment.

"You have nothing to fear from me." Nigel said, his voice soothing. "I am sworn to protect human life."

"You drink buh-buh-blood." She started shaking; she couldn't help it; even as she willed herself to stop, she couldn't; the chill from the mist seemed to have penetrated her soul, as though she would never be warm again.

"Yes, I drink blood." He patted her hand. "Please sit. I can compel you to do so, but I would so much prefer you choose to do so." He smiled at her as she sat back down. "Yes, our hearts are not capable of producing our own blood, our own life force, so we must borrow blood from your kind to live. That's all. It doesn't require much, you know—and we don't have to kill to get it." He shrugged. "It only takes a moment, and those we take it from don't even remember giving it. I could take some from you right now—although I don't need any at the moment—and all you would remember is having this conversation, uninterrupted by anything so crass as a giving."

"Giving?"

"That's our term for it. Come, my dear, relax. I can assure you, had I wanted to kill you, I would have done so already." He smiled at her.

"Comforting to know." She hugged herself, and the shaking stopped; she felt somehow calm.

"I wouldn't have revealed myself to you if I didn't need your help."

Rachel stared at him. "If you're so powerful, why do you need my help?"

"Alas, there is no such thing as 'all-powerful.' That is reserved merely for God, and God is very jealous of his privileges." He reached over and took her hand. His hand was cold as ice, yet she allowed him to keep hold of hers.

"So, there is a God?"

"Of course, my dear." He smiled at her again. "And there is a Satan—everything is in balance, remember? Lucifer Morningstar, the most beautiful of all the angels before the fall, God's favorite. His beauty surpassed all others—still does, I am sure."

"Uh-huh." She closed her eyes and took a deep breath. "And you need my help? Right. Like, what could I do to stop a—" She couldn't bring herself to say the word; it was all too nuts, crazy; there was no such thing.

"Gunther is powerful, Rachel, strong in his evil." Nigel stroked his chin. "I can sense him, but I cannot find him. He can block my mind from seeing him, from finding where he is. I know he is here, in New Orleans . . . but I cannot see where he actually is." Nigel sighed.

"So, why come to me?" Rachel shook her head. "I mean, none of this fucking makes sense, Nigel, but why me?"

"The other day, when I arrived, I saw you in the coffee shop, talking to a young man." He closed his eyes. "And I knew. I knew it was your friend he was coming for. I sensed the danger he was in—and then he turned and I saw his face, so like Maxi's, and I looked into his eyes . . . and saw into his soul."

"His—soul." She began twisting a lock of her hair in her hand, tugging it to make sure she was awake and not in a dream state.

"Yes, Rachel, his soul. The soul never dies; it moves from body to body, from life to life." He looked into her face. "You do not follow." He sighed.

"Reincarnation?"

"Yes." He smiled at her, and she avoided his eyes. "Yes, that's exactly it. Everything in balance, remember? There must be balance. God gave humans free will. Are you familiar with the concept?"

"Free will to choose between good and evil, yes." Sister Mary Angelique's voice came to her unbidden, from across the years, from Sunday school catechism classes: "And God gave us free will, to choose to either serve God or serve Satan. We always have a choice, to sin or to be true to God's will. To pursue earthly treasures, the pleasures of the flesh, or bow to a higher power and wait for the reward that comes when we go to heaven."

"You are Catholic, then? Good."

"I haven't been to mass in years." She shrugged. "The priests don't exactly approve of my lifestyle."

"Because you love other women." Nigel laughed softly. "Yes, the followers of God have never truly understood that all God cares about is the ability to love, rather than who you love. Perhaps someday—but the human race is still in its infancy. So you are familiar with the concept of Purgatory?"

"Yes."

"Another one of the errors of the church." Nigel swept with his hand, encompassing the street. "Earth is Purgatory, Rachel. The soul comes back, over and over again, trying to achieve a state of grace in order to be admitted into Heaven."

"So there's no Hell?"

"Other souls, Rachel, return and retain their evil; unrepentant—until anything that is pure and good is destroyed and they can be admitted to the gates of Hell." He shrugged. "Everything in balance, my dear girl. Just as a soul with the stain of sin on it cannot be admitted to Heaven, an evil soul with some purity, the ability to love, cannot be admitted to Hell."

"And you're saying that Philip is Maxi?" She stared at her hands. "Which is why this Gunther has come after him."

"Their souls are linked." Nigel folded his arms. "Only Gunther is a vampire who chose to serve evil."

"Linked?"

"Just as yours is linked to Philip's." Nigel sighed. "All souls are linked to other souls. Have you ever met someone you immediately were drawn to? That you felt you've always known, even though you just met?"

"Well, yes."

"Linkage."

"But if Gunther is a vampire, I don't see how—"

"Gunther was human once." Nigel sighed. "He was human, and he loved Maxi before he became a vampire." He rubbed his eyes. "It was one of my biggest mistakes, Rachel. I thought I had made Gunther understand that when he accepted the gift, by becoming a nightwatcher, he would have to let Maxi go. How was I to know? How was I to know that the only reason he wanted to become a nightwatcher was so that he and Maxi would be together for all eternity?"

"How did he become a vampire?" She knew the answer.

Nigel looked at her. "I created him. One of my greatest mistakes. Which is why it is my responsibility to destroy him."

Chapter Four

Gunther unlocked a door and pulled Philip inside. A massive chandelier hung over a staircase. Gunther kicked the door shut and pushed Philip up against the wall, their lips coming together again. Gunther lifted Philip up, and Philip wrapped his legs around Gunther's waist. *Oh, yes, fuck me; fuck me right here and now; fuck me on the floor; fuck me on the stairs; just fuck me . . .*

Gunther pulled back and smiled at him. "Not yet, *mein Liebe.*" He set Philip down, then pulled him up the staircase. There was another door at the top, and Gunther unlocked it and held it open for Philip.

Philip gasped.

The hallway beyond the door was lit only by candles, flickering and glowing through the darkness.

His mind swam.

He closed his eyes.

He remembered . . .

A room lit by candles; velvet draperies hanging over the windows, the sun shining, the scent of roses drifting through the windows, the sounds of people working in the garden, and—

It was gone.

He shook his head and opened his eyes.

"You still don't remember?" Gunther smiled at him, pulling Philip to him and pressing his mouth on Philip's.

Philip's head swam, his heart thumping in his chest, his stomach lurching. He tried to gather his thoughts, to get his head together. Something didn't seem right; something was wrong. . . . He felt Gunther tearing at his button fly, his jeans being pulled down, sliding down his legs. Gunther kissed each of his inner thighs softly, tracing a finger along the back of his legs. He shivered. Gently, Gunther lifted each of his feet and removed the pants. Then his mouth was on Philip's abdomen, licking and kissing, the tongue darting out and making circles on his skin, sliding into his navel, one hand grasping Philip's balls and squeezing lightly, and Philip's entire body stiffened again, his breaths coming in gasps. *Oh, it's so good; don't stop, Gunther,* mein Herr, *please, don't stop; love me; make love to me; fuck me hard; fuck me now; I want that cock inside of me, please,* mein Herr, *please . . .*

Philip moaned.

Then Gunther was tearing at his underwear like some kind of feral animal, pulling at it so the waistband was digging into his lower back, and then finally the elastic gave way, snapping apart, and the underwear lost its hold; but Gunther didn't wait for it to fall away. Instead, he tore at the cloth, tearing and shredding it, until Philip's aching cock sprang free, and then Gunther's mouth was on his cock, licking and kissing and moving his tongue up and down its shaft.

"Oh, God," Philip breathed as Gunther worked on his cock. He brought his hands down to the beautiful blond head, holding it as it moved. No one had ever sucked his cock like this before; he hadn't ever thought a blow job could feel like this, the warm, moist mouth lapping and licking and suckling with a sense of urgency and need and desire.

Philip wanted to be naked. He shrugged, dropping his shoulders so the leather jacket began sliding down his arms. He let go of Gunther's head, slipping his hands out of the sleeves and tossing the jacket over into a darkened corner. His T-shirt hung in tatters over his torso. He tore at the neck until it ripped, letting it fall off behind him, and then he was finally naked, offering his body to Gunther. He reached up and touched the nipple that had bled. He gasped, closing his eyes, pulling on it and pinching it, twisting it. It was incredibly sensitive, more so than ever before; just his fingers touching it sent a bolt of lightning through his body, making his cock ache and strain inside Gunther's mouth.

What the fuck? he wondered as Gunther began licking his balls. He touched it again.

Gunther's hands cupped his ass, squeezing and kneading, pulling the cheeks apart, and a probing finger went between them. Philip's body stiffened as the finger began tapping at his asshole.

Guttural noises escaped his throat.

The finger went in.

He cried out against the sudden invasion; then his body relaxed and welcomed the intrusion as it moved inside him in a small circle, slowly, gently, relentlessly. He leaned back against the wall, locking his knees, putting all his weight on his shoulders, and his pelvis moving forward, his cock aching to be touched, sucked, fondled. His eyes closed, and the finger probed inward, moving, stroking, finding his prostate and applying pressure to it. Heat seemed to radiate from the finger, warming him, his armpits getting damp, beads of sweat forming at his hairline, one running slowly down and along his jawline.

Oh god oh god oh god oh god . . .

Then Gunther spun him around, slamming him face-first against the wall, and then Gunther's tongue was there, between his cheeks, licking, probing, making circles, nibbling. He arched his back, pushing his ass back against Gunther's face. The warm, moist tongue went deeper inside him, moving in circles, lapping at him. Gunther began to nibble a bit on his portal, his teeth lightly touching the skin. Philip's whole body began to tremble, the pleasure sweeping over him in waves, his brain becoming lost in a single-minded ecstasy, an urgent need, the need to be filled up with Gunther, the need to give himself, to surrender to him completely, to give in to the pleasure . . .

Oh, God, fuck me, fuck me, fuck me; make me yours; make me your slave; just hold me down and make me your bitch, your pig, your slave; take me, Gunther, take me and fuck me and use me; ride me with that big cock; make me beg for it; make me beg for your love, for your cock; make me yours; mark me as yours; shoot a load all over me and make me lick the sweat from your armpits; make me taste your manhood; make me worship your body; anything you want, just fuck me fuck me fuck me; I'll do anything you want, anything you ask, anything you order; just take me and make me yours; fuck me, please; just fuck me senseless until I can't breathe, until I can't feel anything but your cock pounding away at me; make me sweat, make me tremble; fuck me fuck me, just fuck me, please, just make me yours and you won't be sorry; I'll do anything, just fuck me . . .

"You created him?" Rachel stared at Nigel. She wrapped her arms around herself.

"Yes, I created him." Nigel looked down at his hands. He flicked the cigar out into the street. "It was one of my biggest mistakes; much as I would like to think otherwise, I am not infallible."

Rachel pulled her wrap tighter around her shoulders. A cab went by, lighting the mist. "Why did you create him? Make him a vampire?" Make him a monster?

"A monster?" He smiled at her, delighted. "Inhuman?" He laughed, pulling another cigar from his inner jacket pocket. He sliced the end off and lit it, drawing on it till the end glowed red.

"How—h-h-how did you know what I was thinking?" *This is too much; go inside, you stupid fool; get away from this crazy man; this can't be happening; this kind of thing doesn't happen, damn it; this isn't possible.*

"As you thought, I'm not human." He bowed his head mockingly to her. "I can read your thoughts, pick them out of clear air." He snapped his fingers before her face. She started to stand, her face pale, but he grabbed her and held her down, without force. She wanted to resist but somehow didn't. "It's not magic, my dear young woman. You have the same capabilities as I, but you don't know how to make use of them." He laughed. "I can see by your face you don't believe me." He leaned his head closer to hers. "Have you ever heard that humans don't use more than one-tenth of their brain?"

"Yes." He was crazy, she told herself, yet was still somehow unable—no, unwilling—to get up and go inside. She'd heard it before, some college professor droning on and on outside her consciousness as she sat there in the lecture hall, bored out of her skull as all her courses had bored her, had failed to hold her attention.

"There's a lot of power inside your head, Rachel, if you only knew how to harness it." He tapped the side of her head. "But to harness and be able to use the power, you have to rid yourself of your humanity—or rather, what makes you human." He drew back, smiling and nodding at a young black man walking by. He was wearing a do-rag, pants hanging shapeless around the bottom of his ass, his plaid boxer shorts plainly visible, a loose-fitting army jacket. Once he'd disappeared back into the mist, footsteps fading into the distance, Nigel turned back to her. "And I need your help. I need you to find them for me."

Philip's body trembled.

Never had he felt such pleasure, such ecstasy.

His entire body was aflame. His skin felt everything; normal sensations were amplified to levels he'd never dreamed of. His lower back was arched, the muscles straining as he lifted his ass up, aching for Gunther's tongue and fingers to plunge deeper inside him. He was unaware of being up on his toes, all of his weight resting on his forearms and hands as they pressed against the wall. His head rested against the coolness of the plaster wall, and even that touch was erotic, exotic, pleasurable. Pleasure was sweeping over him in waves, faster and faster, the waves coming so quickly that he couldn't differentiate between one and the next; it was all so intense, almost too intense; it had never been like this before, his mind racing, unable to process and handle it all. His scalp was tingling, as though every hair on his head were an independent entity, sentient, alive, breathing.

Fuck me, fuck me, please, God, fuck me; I want that cock inside me; I want you inside me, please, please, please . . .

He shuddered as Gunther traced a light path with a finger up his spine.

His aching cock was filled with blood, almost as though it would explode. His balls felt as if they weighed ten pounds each, hanging between his legs, overly sensitive—the slightest touch would send him into paroxysms and spasms. His breath was coming in groaning gasps, panting as one wave of pleasure receded and another began building. He couldn't form conscious thought. Pleasure filled his brain, dominating it, reducing him to an almost animallike state, a state where all he cared about was the tongue and fingers playing with him like an instrument, rising into crescendos and falling away only to build again.

And then it stopped.

His mind swam back into reality, into awareness. His heart was thumping, pounding in his ears. His balls and cock ached. His feet lowered back down to the floor, but he wasn't able to do anything more than lean limply against the wall. He tried to catch his breath, but his racing heart couldn't slow down; he couldn't take deep enough breaths to stop the gasping. His body trembled, shaking.

Breath on his neck sent another delicious shiver through him.

"My sweet darling," Gunther whispered into his ear, the timbre of his voice sending a thrill through Philip, his jaw trembling as he gulped in air. "I've been waiting for you for so long."

Philip tried to speak, his mouth trying to form words, but nothing could come out—his mind still reeling from riding the waves, still anticipating the next to come rising from the swell of the last.

Gunther turned him around, and he gazed into those amazing eyes, their deep blue like pools of light beckoning him onward, and—

He smelled roses, and lilac, the soft breeze of a warm spring morning, the lazy buzzing of flies, and sounds outside, sounds he could barely make out; and he was looking up into those blue eyes, those oh-so-beautiful eyes, losing himself in them, wanting, needing to lose himself in them forever; for this was love, a love he'd never dreamed possible, a love he'd yearned for all his waking life, a love that would last for all eternity, until the sun burned out and time ceased; for love could never die, not a love like this, the kind of love others only dreamed of, couldn't in their wildest dreams fathom or comprehend, stronger than death, stronger than life . . .

And Gunther was gathering him up, lifting Philip into his arms as though he were no heavier than a small child, and he felt the strength in Gunther's arms, the coiled power in his muscles; yet he was gentle, caring, loving. His head tilted back, exposing his neck, and Gunther pressed his lips to the base of Philip's throat. Philip's body tensed as another wave crashed over him, all his breath rushing out of him in a guttural moan beginning deep in his diaphragm; and then they were moving, Gunther's tongue flicking out, licking and tracing small circles in the hollow where Philip's neck met his torso, pressing with an urgency, a need, a hunger, against his skin. Philip's heartbeat came faster and louder, and then Gunther was placing him gently down on a soft bed, a mattress filled with down and feathers, the velvet and satin of the coverlet feeling like a soft caress against his naked body. He opened his eyes. Long white tapers burned in sconces on the wall, casting flickering shadows into darkened corners.

It all looked familiar to him somehow, but his mind couldn't wrap itself around the thought, couldn't focus as another wave crashed over him. His body trembled and shook as Gunther's mouth moved down from the throat to the nipples again, licking and flicking and suckling on them.

Why did it all seem so familiar?

The thought nagged at his mind, even as Gunther's mouth moved farther downward, as his tongue wrapped itself around the head of his cock.

"*Mein Liebe* . . ." he muttered hoarsely as he began gasping again.

No one had ever made him feel like this.

No one.

He felt his orgasm rise in his balls, his body beginning to go rigid with the coming explosion, his back arching upward.

"Not yet, *mein Liebe,*" Gunther whispered, gripping Philip's cock with his hand, holding it tightly, tighter still as it tried desperately for release, pumping against the restraining hand, Philip's mouth open and moaning; and then the pressure lessened, the orgasm dying away, his body starting to relax again. He began trembling, trying to catch his breath.

My God, my God, this is too much . . .

Gunther stood up, smiling down at him, unbuckling his belt and the button of his jeans. Philip reached out and touched the hard-muscled abdomen, tracing his index finger around the navel, then tracing a path up to Gunther's right nipple, tugging on it. Gunther's eyes closed for just a moment; then he reached down and began sliding the black denim down legs carved from marble, each muscle visible beneath the skin, a light dusting of golden down on them. Black cotton underwear covered his huge, straining cock, which he grabbed and held for just a moment so Philip could get a good look at its size, and then he was sliding the underwear down, setting it free. It slapped up against his lower abdomen. Philip stared at the massive pink cock, longer and thicker than any he had ever seen before, and he wanted it; he wanted it inside him, wanted to feel it piercing him, feel it plunging deep inside to his very core. He wanted Gunther to ride him, to fuck him senseless, to make him his slave, his bitch, his pig, his slut. He wanted to run his tongue over the heavy pink balls, to take them into his mouth and suckle on them.

Philip reached a trembling hand up to it and touched it. It quivered in response, and a clear drop oozed out of the end.

Gunther stood over Philip, his legs spread, his hands on his hips. "You want my cock, *mein Liebchen*?"

Philip nodded. "Yes, please, may I have it?" He looked up into Gunther's eyes, those oh-so-blue eyes, and—

The scent of lilacs and roses swam up his nostrils, and he looked over to his left, seeing heavy tapestries moving in the soft, warm breeze. Daylight streamed in through the open doors leading out to a balcony. He could hear the sound of people talking, the sound of shovels and scythes as the fields were being worked. He heard a horse whinny, a dog barking. He was lying naked on a bed, a bed covered in smooth silk and satin and velvet. A mirror on the far wall reflected back light from candles on the opposite wall; there were candles everywhere, lighting the darkened corners of the room, where the gentle sunlight didn't seem to reach. The long white tapers flickered on the mantel, and just above the mantel hung a huge oil painting, framed in gilt wood. The painting was of a man with long, curling blond hair cascading down onto his shoulders. His clothes were from another time, another place: a miltary-looking uniform—he'd seen something like that before, once before, in a textbook in a history class, and the face belonged to—

"Gunther," he breathed.

What the hell . . . ?

He struggled to sit up, but Gunther pushed him back down against the mattress. Gunther was smiling, his oh-so-blue eyes—he looked into them again and felt himself lost in their blueness, as though he were being sucked into them, surrounded by blue and by magic and desire.

What the hell?

* * *

"You need ME to find them?" Rachel laughed. "Yeah, right. You're crazy."

"I trained him, you see." Nigel looked at her, reaching out a hand to brush a lock of damp hair from her forehead. "I taught Gunther how to use his mind, to develop the dormant powers everyone has locked inside their brain."

"By making him not human." She shook her head. *What is wrong with me,* she wondered, *sitting out here in the cold with a crazy old man? Get up and go inside, girl, and forget this ever happened; forget the old man with his crazy stories about nightwatchers and vampires, about Philip being in danger.* She should go inside to the warmth and back to her poetry; surely that would be a more productive way to spend the evening than sitting on her steps in the damp and the cold, listening to a crazy old man spinning ridiculous stories.

" 'Human' is a relative term," Nigel went on. "I was a human like you once, many years ago. Now I am a different kind of human, an immortal, one with powers unimaginable to most. But one needn't be an immortal to unlock the power within the mind; it merely helps because it affords the luxury of time. Time, as measured by those who die, means nothing to those like me. I trained Gunther for decades, trying to make him understand the meaning of power, the great responsibility that comes with it. But alas, for me and for many others, Gunther was unable to leave his humanity behind."

"His humanity." Rachel shook her head. "Look, Nigel, you seem like a nice enough old guy, you know? But I've really wasted enough of my night sitting out here with you, you know?" She started to rise again, and this time he didn't stop her.

She took a step up, turning her back to him. As she reached for the doorknob—

Music exploded in her head, intense, more intense than she had ever heard. It was as though a stereo had kicked on inside her mind, and the notes, the mix of the different instruments, each sound digitally remastered to perfection; and she recognized the lyrics; it was the poem she'd been working on, being sung by a woman who understood where the poem had come from; the poem turned into a song, as it would sound recorded and mixed with the best production values money could buy; and the sheer beauty of it took her breath away.

And then it was gone as quickly as it had come.

Her heart was thumping.

What the fuck?

She tried to catch her breath as her mind tried to recapture the ghost of the sounds, seeking them through the recesses and dark corners of her mind. It had sounded so beautiful, her poetry and the notes mixing together as though it had always been meant to be a song, meant to be sung and felt and experienced.

"It's a beautiful song," Nigel said pleasantly, his voice echoing distantly.

"How—how—" She stared at him. This didn't make any sense—none—and her brain was rebelling against it; he couldn't be telling her the truth; he couldn't be.

He tapped his right temple. "The brain, Rachel, the brain. Its potential is limitless."

Trembling, she sat back down, her hand on the railing for balance.

"To be able to use the true power of your mind you have to cut off what makes you human." He went on. "Rage, anger, jealousy, the darker emotions—those are what tether you to your primitive nature. It is those you have to divorce yourself from, train yourself not to feel, in order for your mind to be free. You don't have to be an immortal to be able to use your power—although it helps. . . . Immortality gives you the freedom to understand how little these things matter. But it also exacts a price—one that Gunther was unwilling to pay."

"What . . . ?" She struggled to form words. Her skin was tingling.

"We don't have much time." Nigel took her hand. "Gunther has blocked me—I cannot see into his mind. But he won't be guarded against you, Rachel."

"But—" She stared at him. "Why me?"

"Because you are connected to Philip. You can find Philip." Nigel sighed. "It is through you that I was able to find him. I know Gunther is here in New Orleans—that much I can sense. I sensed his exultation at finding Philip—the same exultation he felt when he first found him so long ago. I cast my mind out over the city, and it was through you that I found Philip . . . which is why I came to your little coffee shop."

"I can't—" She shook her head. "I—"

"But you can." He took a deep breath. "There is a way."

Somehow, she knew she wasn't going to like this.

"I have to drink from you." He gave her a sad look. "And while I drink, you draw on my power with your mind."

"No!"

"You have to trust me, Rachel. It's the only way to save Philip."

She stared at him, her mind racing, random thoughts coming and going.

This is crazy, this is crazy, this is crazy; the words went through her mind over and over again as another cab drove by, but the sound of its engine didn't break the spell or whatever it was she was feeling; none of this made sense, but somehow, in spite of herself, she found herself believing the old man; it all made a weird kind of sense somehow, something she couldn't define; it was almost too much for her mind to process, and yet she could sense the truth in his words.

If Philip is in danger . . .

Vampires? Nightwatchers?

No, none of this was real. It had to be a dream.

She closed her eyes and made her decision.

Trembling, she held out her wrist to him.

Chapter Five

Something wasn't quite right.

Philip struggled to get up to his elbows.

What—what the hell is going on here? He shook his head. Everything looked wrong—blurry, out of focus, like he'd been drinking too much. His head was aching—a dull pounding that felt like someone was stabbing an ice pick into his left temple. The pleasure was gone, as if it had never been there. *I need to get out of here; I'm in danger; something's wrong; something's very wrong here . . .*

Gunther dropped down to his knees and grabbed Philip's legs firmly, lifting them up and apart. Philip slipped off his elbows, lying flat on his back. His erection was fading away.

"No," Philip whispered, "no."

Gunther either didn't hear him or didn't care. He was smiling as the head of his cock found the passage to Philip, probing, pushing, forcing.

Philip forced himself to go rigid, to tighten, to close himself off to the intrusion.

Gunther smiled at him as he stopped. "So you want to play it that way, *mein Liebchen*? You want it to be rape?"

"No, I want this to stop." Philip shook his head. "Something's not right, something . . ." his voice trailed away as he looked up into Gunther's eyes, and he was drowning in the blue pools of light. "I . . ."

His voice broke off into a scream as Gunther forced his cock inside. Philip resisted, squeezing, trying to keep him out.

Gunther smiled. "Rape it is then, *mein Liebe.*" He reached down and slapped Philip hard across the face.

His ears rang, eyes filling with involuntary tears. "Please . . ."

"You cannot stop me," Gunther whispered, then forced himself deeper inside.

Philip's mouth opened and closed. It felt like he was being ripped apart, torn in two.

The pain, oh, God, the pain . . .

He felt himself losing consciousness; everything was swimming out of focus; all he was aware of was the pain—dear God, the pain, it hurt so fucking bad; it had never hurt like this before, not even the first time, with his high school English teacher, when all they'd had for lube was spit; this pain was unbearable; everything was out of focus and red, spinning out of control; everything was out of control . . .

And through the red haze of pain, he could hear Gunther laughing.

Nigel bit into her wrist.

She gasped.

The pain was excruciating at first, exploding into her consciousness like a firecracker. It was piercing, like the time she'd had her nose pierced, and her entire body shuddered at this invasion. For a brief moment she flashed back to when she was fourteen and she was with her then boyfriend—what was his name? You aren't supposed to forget the name of the one who takes your virginity—what was his name? She was naked and flat on her back, her legs spread, and he was entering her, and it hurt—*oh, God, Mary, Jesus, and Joseph, it hurts . . .*

And then the pain faded away and it began to feel better, her entire body relaxing, going with it, and ripples began going out, washing out over her body, ripples of tingling excitement; *oh, my God, this is better than ecstasy . . .*

Her wrist burned as though on fire.

She could feel the power surging through her.

Focus, Rachel; you have to focus, Nigel's voice echoed in her brain.

She let go of the pleasure.

Open your mind, Rachel; open your mind and reach out for Philip.

She wasn't at first sure what he meant, but then she began to relax, and she felt it—she felt her brain awakening, like it had never truly been awake before.

She felt like she was falling.

Falling.

Images crowded her mind, flashing past her consciousness like a crazed kaleidoscope, one scene blurring into another so quickly that all she could see were vague shapes and forms. Once she saw a woman, naked from the waist up, snakes wrapped around her forearms, standing before an altar with her arms outstretched to the sky. On the altar was a sheep with its throat slit, and the woman was chanting, and she could smell incense burning, and then the image was gone. It was replaced by the sight of naked images in a field under a clear, starry sky, a clearing in the forest, with torches burning. The naked forms were dancing together, lewdly, women grabbing their breasts, men cupping their genitals with their hands; and then just as quickly this was gone, and she glimpsed a naked man chained to a wall, a whip flicking out and raising bloody welts on his back. And then a woman, chained to a stake, piles of wood at her feet; and then the wood was set ablaze by a torch, the flames spreading, and the woman opened her mouth and screamed, a scream so primal and deep, it echoed in Rachel's soul . . .

Focus, Rachel; reach out to Philip's soul.

And she forced the images from her head, conjuring up Philip's face, his brown hair, his wide brown eyes, the smile with the even white teeth.

And then she saw—

A darkened room filled with shadows. Long white candles, burning in sconces on the walls, flickering. The scent of rose and lilac, mixed together into an almost sickening perfume. A bed covered in satin and velvet, surrounded by sheer white curtains that moved in the breeze. A man on his knees, golden curls tumbling down his naked back, his pelvis thrusting, two legs covered in curly, black hair wrapped around him, and she could see the young man on his back, sweat rolling down his face, his eyes closed in pleasure, raising up to greet the thrusts of the blond man as their bodies joined . . .

Philip.

Follow the trail, Rachel. You should be able to find them.

She looked at one of the candles, which seemed brighter than the others, burning stronger yet without giving off any smoke.

She focused on the flame, staring at it until it was the only thing she was aware of; there was no time or space or anything for her but the flicker of the yellow flame as it burned, melting wax flowing down the side, slight black smoke rising from it.

The room faded away from her consciousness, the colors blurring and running, the sunlight in the background melting, darkening, becoming night, eternal night, and then other shapes began to struggle to take form. It was a different room, she could tell; the breezes she was feeling against her skin were no longer warm and soft but rather cold and damp. The scent of lilac and rose was gone; she could only smell grease in the air, grease and fresh horseshit. The room began to take shape. Again there were burning white candles casting their sparse light. There was a gold-framed mirror on the wall. There was a large bed in the middle of the room, again with the satin and silk and velvet, and there were human forms on the bed. She turned her attention away from the candles and looked at them in the gloom, in the dim candlelight, and she heard a horse clip-clopping past outside.

She saw a man from behind, his buttocks clenching and unclenching as he moved his pelvis forward and back. His skin was like white marble, almost aglow in the light of the candles. She turned her attention to the other figure.

It was Philip, lying on his back, his legs spread, his eyes wide open as though in terror. His face was white, and he looked like he was gasping and trying to scream.

The man was between his legs, laughing, cooing to him like a baby in a guttural language she didn't recognize, and then he pulled Philip's legs up higher into the air and plunged deeper inside him.

Philip screamed.

Rachel winced as the sound exploded in her head, piercing her soul.

Go inside him, Rachel, she could hear Nigel urging her. *Go inside him; find out where they are, before it's too late.*

Inside him? What the hell do you mean by that?

Through his eyes, Rachel.

She willed herself to move in closer to them. Hesitantly she took a step, not sure if she was really there or not, afraid she might make a floorboard creak or make some other kind of noise. There was nothing, no sound, except for the fading of Philip's scream.

She took another step closer, but she still couldn't see Philip's eyes.

Another step.

The blond man stopped moving, cocking his head first to one side, then the other.

He senses me; oh, dear God in Heaven, he knows I'm here.

And she felt terror, beginning deep inside her mind, spreading to every part of her body, and she wanted to scream—

But even as she opened her mouth, Philip's head turned, and their eyes locked.

And then she was looking up out of Philip's eyes, up at the strong chest, the round, erect pink nipples, the trail of blond hairs leading from the navel to the thicker patch below, the blue eyes, the blond hair of the stranger, and she felt his enormousness inside her, ripping and tearing at her tissues, invading her, raping her; but it somehow felt so good, and she was beginning to lose herself into the rhythm, the rhythm of his entering and exiting, deepening with each thrust, each thrust going farther inside her; and she turned her head and looked out the window . . .

And she knew exactly where she was. . . .

Then it was all gone.

She was back, sitting on the steps in front of her building.

Her wrist itched.

She looked down at it, watching the two tiny holes slowly close until they were just pinpricks, and then even that was gone. Her skin was smooth, undamaged, like nothing had ever happened.

She looked at Nigel. She felt like throwing up.

"Excellent work, my dear." Nigel wiped at his mouth, keeping it hidden from her. He turned his head away from her and slowly stood up, holding on to the railing for help. "There's still time to save your young friend."

She grabbed him by the arm. "I'm coming with you."

"No." He wouldn't look at her, keeping his face in the shadows. "It's too dangerous."

"You need me, old man." She didn't even question it. Only a few minutes earlier she'd thought him crazy—now she believed. She didn't know what was different, what he had done to her, but the abilities she'd used, abilities she'd never known she'd been capable of—she wasn't about to let go now. "I know exactly where they are."

"It's dangerous." He moved out of the shadows, and she saw his teeth. The canines were longer, sharper than she remembered.

"All the more reason," she said, "for me to come with you. I can help you; I know I can."

He looked at her for a moment, then sighed. "I can see you're determined."

"Either I come with you or I follow you."

He held out his hand to her. "Then, come."

It hurt, oh, God, how it hurt.

"You are mine for all eternity," Gunther whispered as he continued to pound away at him. "All eternity."

Eternity.

The word echoed in his mind.

Lilacs. Roses.

He felt himself slipping away again.

You are mine for all eternity, Gunther was saying. They were lying, bathed in sweat, on top of the covers. Philip was resting his head on Gunther's strong chest, listening to his heartbeat through the skin and layers of muscle. The village priest had told him his feelings for the lord were sinful, but how could a sin feel so good? Surely God would not have made such pleasure possible only for it to be a sin. And the lord loved him; he knew it. Was he not wet from his kisses? Was he not covered in sweat from their love? It couldn't be wrong; it couldn't be sin; such happiness was surely his destiny. He was sated, with his lord's seed inside him, and relaxed, wanting to feel Gunther inside him again.

"Are you ready to join me for all eternity?" Gunther asked. "Our love will never die, mein Liebe. *All I want is to spend all eternity loving you."*

"Anything for you, my lord," he replied, raising Gunther's hand to his mouth and kissing it. "I will do anything you ask, my lord, my master."

And Gunther rose to his knees, a smile on his face, raising his right wrist to his mouth.

For a moment he saw Gunther's teeth—long, sharp, pointed, tearing at his wrist. And then the blood was flowing from the wound he'd made—bright red blood, trickling down over Gunther's hand, and the bleeding wrist was offered to him.

"Drink from me and join me for eternity."

He looked up into Gunther's smiling face, and saw—

The teeth.

Long. Sharp. Pointed.

Not human, oh sweet Jesu, not human.

He's a demon. The priest was right.

Philip moved away from him.

Don't be afraid, mein Liebchen.

Philip got to his feet, backing away from the bed, from the bed where he'd committed sin in the eyes of God, where he'd allowed a demon to take him the way a man takes a woman.

Gunther held out the wrist.

"Join me for eternity."

And Philip backed away from the bed, shaking his head, his body trembling with fear as he crossed himself, then turned and ran to the window, not thinking in his terror, fervent prayers rushing through his head, driven by terror.

"No, Maxi, no!" Gunther screamed, and sprang after him.

And he backed away and felt the back of his legs against the window frame, and he felt himself falling backward just as Gunther lunged toward him, his arms outstretched; and he was back and through the window, praying as he fell, fell, fell . . .

And then he hit the cobblestones . . . and as he felt his life leaving him, he kept praying, Forgive me, Jesus, for turning my back on you and committing a sin; forgive me; don't cast me down into Hell with creatures like this one. . . .

And everything faded to black.

He opened his eyes.

Gunther threw his head back and howled as his body convulsed with his explosion, and Philip's own long-delayed orgasm went, his seed splashing and spraying into his face, over his chest, his entire body rocking as his balls emptied. Then, both bodies spent, Gunther slowly removed himself from inside Philip. He smiled down at him. "*Mein Liebe* . . ." he whispered.

Philip slowly pulled away from him. "What—what are you?" he whispered. He slid off the bed and found his feet, wondering what he was going to wear, knowing his clothes had been ripped to shreds, just knowing it didn't matter—he had to get out of here.

Gunther reached over and stroked his cheek. "I offer you an eternity of love, my beautiful little one." His wrist rose to his mouth. "I offer you eternal life as my companion, my love, my life." Then he tore at his wrist, until the blood was flowing over his fingers again—dark red and rich, thick blood. "All you have to do is drink, *mein Liebe*, and then we will be together for all eternity."

"N-no." Philip backed away from him, away from the bed of nightmares, aware of his nakedness, aware of the bloody wrist being offered to him.

"DRINK!" Gunther shouted, leaping off the bed and pinning him against the wall, shoving the wrist into Philip's mouth.

Philip's eyes went to the balcony doors. *Heaven help me*, he thought as he struggled, as the blood filled his mouth.

It was strangely sweet.

"There." Rachel pointed to a balcony across the street. They were standing under a streetlight in the thick mist. She shivered. The street was completely deserted, lifeless. Flickering shadows danced on the curtains. The balcony doors were open. "That's where they are."

Nigel smiled at her. "Thank you." He kissed her hand.

"I'm going with you," she insisted, grabbing hold of his hand and squeezing. "You need me."

"No." He shook his head, effortlessly pulling his arm free from her grasp. "Too dangerous, my dear." He gathered himself and leaped gracefully up to the balcony in one motion.

Rachel stood for a moment and then crossed the street. The gate to the wide carriageway was open, and she ran inside, her shoes clicking on the pavement as she looked through the mist for the door that led inside the building. It was locked. She tugged on it, then pushed before giving it up. *I have to get inside*. She removed her shoe and smashed a windowpane, reaching in and unlocking the door from the inside, then opened it and ran up the stairs and into the apartment. She heard a scream from the end of the hall and headed that way, toward an open door. Flickering light came through it.

"There's no sense in sacrificing this young man, Gunther," Nigel was saying as she reached the door. He was standing in the balcony door. "This is between us, maker and creation. Let the boy go."

She glanced quickly into the corner Nigel was facing. The blond man was holding Philip in front of him. Philip was naked, eyes closed. His mouth was smeared with blood. He looked barely conscious.

"Leave me in peace, old man," Gunther sneered. "This is now between me and the boy. He drank willingly."

"Let the boy go."

"Never."

Rachel reached for a candle.

Philip swam in and out of consciousness.

He was vaguely aware of being held from behind, that he was standing and voices were swimming around him, but it was all just noise; nothing made sense; the noise wasn't being shaped into any words he could understand; his brain felt like it was short-circuiting. Images flashed through his mind . . . images that made no sense to him . . . He saw a woman, naked to the waist, snakes wrapped around her forearms, standing before an altar, her arms outstretched to the heavens. He saw a young man, wearing a loincloth and dirty, grimy, covered with welts and bleeding cuts, on his knees, his eyes swimming with tears.

He saw Gunther riding on a magnificent black horse.

The images came faster, too fast for him to see them as anything but a blur.

Voices.

Chanting.

His body felt like it was on fire, burning from the inside. The fire was pumping out of his heart, spreading through his veins. Sweat was pouring from him, his skin slick and wet and damp.

Fire—everything was on fire.

His mind, oh, God, his mind . . . The flames were there, burning through his brain.

What did he do to me?

And he could still taste the sweet blood, the sweet liquid . . .

God help me, I want more.

Rachel threw the candle and said a quiet prayer for her aim to be true.

It hit the wall behind the blond man, showering sparks onto his skin and hair. He screamed, letting go of Philip, who fell to the floor.

The scream shot through her mind, through her consciousness, into her very soul. It drove her back out of the room and against the wall, slamming her into it, knocking the breath out of her. Her eyes swam in tears, stars dancing outside her vision. She slid to the floor, pressing her hands over her ears to try to blot the scorching sound from her soul.

She smelled it, the burning, and its cloying sweetness gagged her.

She threw up.

Philip was vaguely aware of falling to the floor.

It burns, he thought, his entire body in agony. *Will it ever stop?*

In the far distance he could hear someone screaming, an unearthly sound that echoed in his brain, curdling his soul with its anguish and anger.

He tried to open his eyes, but the lids wouldn't obey his command.

The fire in his blood seemed to die down.

Is this, then, death? he wondered as he lay there, unable to move. *Am I dying? Is that what this is? Death? What did he do to me?*

He smelled scorched skin, the nauseating smell of burnt hair.

His canine teeth began to ache, his gums aflame with raw pain.

He slid his tongue over his canines.

They were longer, sharper.

Pointed.

* * *

Rachel crawled to the bedroom door.

She smelled smoke.

She looked inside.

Nigel was standing, blocking the balcony doors.

The blond man was engulfed in flame. He was screaming as he dashed about the room, trying to smother the flames by rubbing himself against the wall.

Tuck and roll, she thought, *how stupid are you?*

As though he'd heard her, he dropped to the floor and began rolling, and the flames went out as quickly as they'd begun.

He stood up.

"I will destroy you, old man!" he shrieked.

Nigel just stood, staring at him, his hands in his pockets.

With a cry, the blond man sprang at Nigel.

Nigel ducked to one side. The blond man reached the balcony and turned back to look at Rachel. She covered her mouth with her hands. His face was blackened, his hair burned away. He looked like something out of her worst nightmares. "You will pay, young bitch." One instant he was there; the next, he was gone.

Nigel began to weep.

"N-Nigel?" she whispered.

"I couldn't do it," he said, wiping the tears from his cheek. "For decades, I have tried to kill him, and I can't do it. I am a failure."

"Rachel?"

She turned her head as Philip stood up—although he didn't really seem like Philip anymore. She looked his nakedness up and down, her mind racing, trying to figure what was different, what was wrong with him.

The wall behind him burst into flame.

"We have to get out of here." Nigel beckoned to them both. When they didn't move, he said, "Hurry."

They followed him out onto the balcony. Black smoke followed them out. Nigel placed an arm around each of them. "Close your eyes," he said softly, and they did. Rachel let out a gasp when her feet left the floor, and then she landed gently on the sidewalk across the street. She opened her eyes.

The building was engulfed with flames. She heard sirens in the distance, the sounds of people shouting and running. "Let's go back to the apartment," she heard herself saying, her mind not really working out of anything other than instinct.

The sun rose outside her window, dissipating the fog. On her bed, Philip slept.

"He will sleep for several days while his body completes the change." Nigel lit a cigar.

"So, what now?" Rachel looked at his peaceful face. It seemed paler but somehow more solid to her than before.

"I can't leave him." Nigel shook his head. "He'll have to come with me."

Rachel looked at Nigel. "I'm coming with you."

"No, my dear, that I can't permit."

"You don't have a choice," she said simply. "You heard Gunther. He threatened me. And do you really think he won't come back for Philip?"

"There is always a choice."

"No. Not anymore." She gestured to Philip. "He wasn't given a choice. Neither was I. When you came here looking for me, you took away my choices." Her voice shook. "You have to make me one of you."

He shook his head. "No."

"You said yourself, you couldn't kill Gunther." She went over to the window and looked out. "He's out there somewhere, and he wants Philip. You said it yourself: he's a rogue, who kills. The three of us—together we can stop him."

"You don't know what you're asking."

"Yes, I do." She remembered the visions, the music in her head. "How do we know Philip will be able to do what you couldn't? Can you keep him safe?" She looked out the window at the gloomy sunshine. "And can you protect me?"

Tears spilled down Nigel's face as he bit into his own wrist.

He offered it to her.

And she drank.

Outside, the rain began.

Carnival

Michael Thomas Ford

Chapter One

The kid was doing it all wrong, but Joe didn't stop him. He just looked on silently as the boy tried uselessly to force the big metal pin into the hole. Frustrated, he was hitting it with the rubber mallet again and again, attempting to beat it into submission. The muscles of his thick arms bulged and relaxed as he swung the hammer over his shoulder and brought it down repeatedly in a rain of anger. His grimy white T-shirt was soaked through with sweat from his exertion, and his face was growing redder by the second.

Somewhere a radio was playing. The sound of the Jimmy Dorsey Orchestra floated through the hot August air. "Tangerine, she is all they claim," sang Bob Eberly over the sultry voices of the band's horns and woodwinds. "With her eyes of night and lips as bright as flame."

The song had been a favorite during that summer of 1942, and Joe found himself idly humming along as he watched the boy. Finally, when the kid looked like he would either explode or pass out, Joe stepped in. "Like this," he said, giving the pin a gentle turn with his hand and slipping it easily into the hole.

"How the fuck did you do that?" the boy said.

"You just have to know how it works," Joe said in his slow Texas drawl.

He turned and walked away, wiping the grease from his hands onto his work pants and laughing to himself. He'd been working the carnival for coming on twenty years, and in every new town they stopped in, it was the same. He had to hire a team of local boys to help him set up. Big boys, big enough to lift the heavy machinery and set it upright. He always got a kick out of watching the ham-fisted showoffs trying to force the rods and gears to do what they wanted, when he knew that all they had to do was ask nicely and the motors would be purring like kittens before a fire.

It had been different for him. Even when he was a kid, he'd understood what the machines were saying. He heard them calling to him, singing in their clickety-clackety voices of things no one else saw: worlds where time and motion whirled in an intricate dance, sweeping the stars along with them. And when they called, he was powerless not to answer. One night when he was about four, his mother had come to check on him, only to find his bed empty. After a frantic three-hour search, he'd been discovered in the basement, sitting next to the big old coal furnace with a faraway look in his eyes. They'd had to shake him to snap him out of it, and even then he couldn't remember how he'd gotten there. All he'd said by way of explanation was, "The box was talking to me, Mama."

The other kids decided he was crazy. They'd spy him lying next to the railroad tracks, his fingertips touching the steel as he listened to the engines rumbling somewhere down the line, or catch him leaning up against a spinning washing machine, a sweet smile on his face. "Dumb bastard," they'd say, pushing him into the dirt and laughing.

The worst was Billy James. "Joey's an idiot," he told the other kids one day when they found him behind McCane's Garage, gazing raptly under the hood of an old Ford and caressing the silenced pieces. "See that dent in his forehead? He's got that there 'cause his daddy fucked his mama while she was pregnant with him, and his dick poked old Joey in the head and made him stupid."

As he grew up, he moved more and more away from the world of people and deeper into the world of machines. His hands showed him the way, turning over the bits and pieces he found in garbage cans, tool boxes, and junk sales until he could tell just by holding a bit of iron in his hands exactly what it had once done and wanted to do again. He collected discarded motors and gears and took them to his secret place in the shed behind his daddy's house, where he fashioned them into deceptively simple machines that spun and whirred and surrounded him with their joyful cacophony.

He could have fit in, had he wanted to. He could have used what he knew to help boys like Billy James unlock the secrets of the cars they tried to make their own. But he didn't. Instead, he watched them try day after day to bend the engines to their will, to force themselves upon a world where they had no control. Sometimes he sat on the rise overlooking the school's auto body shop and slowly ate an apple while he observed the boys congratulating one another on some minor success, while in his head he had already figured out exactly what it was the sputtering car was trying to say in its own voice. He himself walked to school.

It had all ended shortly after his sixteenth birthday, when his father, enraged over Joe's refusal to be interested in football, hunting, or girls, followed him to the shed and spied on him as he sat among the machines he'd constructed. Bursting in, his father grabbed a can of gasoline, splashed it over the walls, and set the shed on fire. As the smoke rose up into the sky, and the voices of the machines turned to screams, Joe ran into the darkness.

When he stopped running, he found himself at the edge of a carnival. It had been in town for a week, but he had avoided it, knowing that Billy James would be there with his friends and the giggling, stupid girls whose tight sweaters and bright lipstick made Joe feel sorry for them. Now it was the last night, and the park was almost empty. Some of the rides were being taken down, and nobody noticed Joe as he walked among the towering machines.

When he came upon a group of men trying to disassemble the complicated gears of a carousel, he stopped to watch. Grunting and straining, they were attempting to pull it apart. The largest man was swearing and beating the nest of machinery as though it were a horse refusing to move. Joe, after listening for a few minutes, walked into the group of men, picked up a wrench, and effortlessly undid the knots of metal as the astonished workers looked on.

No one had ever asked his age, and when the carnival rolled out of town late that night, Joe had been asleep in the back of the truck housing the Ferris wheel, his thin body tucked into one of the gently swaying cars. He had been there ever since, the master mechanic who kept the rides spinning and the people laughing. Night after night, in town after town, he built his city up and tore it down again.

Now he walked through the maze of rides and attractions, surveying the work of his crew and hired hands. The skeleton of the Ferris wheel was nearly complete, its empty cars swaying as the men set another one into the circles of steel and tightened the bolts to hold it in place. Beyond it, the Whirly-Gig was being tested, its five cars spinning around as the men who worked it laughed and congratulated one another on having no leftover pieces. Joe nodded at them and walked on.

The carousel was still his favorite, and he saved it for last. Its interlocking wheels fascinated him as much as they had the first time he'd laid his hands on them. Each night after it was assembled, he stood in the center, watching the gears turn as an endless melody spilled from the music box hidden in the canopy decorated with roses and the faces of angels. The painted wooden horses, dogs, and mermaids circled around him, always laughing, always gay, rising up and slowly tumbling down again as tiny white and blue lights sparkled in the darkness. He knew the magic was created by cogs and pistons, electricity and grease, but it was magic nonetheless.

In a few hours the carousel would be filled with riders—children with hands and faces sticky from cotton candy, women in summer dresses and hats. There would be a few men, too, fathers holding on to little ones who balanced atop the horses, young men with arms flung protectively around skinny girls with shy eyes. They would pretend not to be enchanted by the magic, as if admitting to falling in love with the machine's song were an act of weakness. But Joe saw in their faces that they heard, saw the looks of longing that appeared when they thought no one else was looking.

"Is she going to be ready in time?"

Joe turned. Behind him Harley stood, his thumbs, as always, hitched behind the straps of his overalls. A cigarette, unlit, perched in the corner of his mouth. His dark eyes looked out from a face weathered by a life spent in the sun and wind, giving him an expression of perpetual weariness. In all the time that Harley had been managing the carnival, which was almost as many years as Joe had been part of it, Joe didn't think he'd ever washed those overalls or lit that cigarette.

"She'll be ready," Joe told him, nodding. "Has she ever not been ready?"

Harley paused a moment, then shook his head. "Not that I can recall," he said.

"Tonight's no different," said Joe. "She'll be ready for the good folks of whatever town this is."

Harley laughed. "Denton," he said. "Denton, Kansas."

"Denton, Kansas," Joe repeated. It didn't matter; he'd forget the name within the hour anyway. He always did. Where he was didn't matter to him. Kansas, Missouri, Tennessee—they were all the same. He'd set up his machines in hundreds of little towns all across the country, and he couldn't recall the name of a single one of them.

"Come on," Harley said, turning away. "There's someone I want you to meet."

Joe followed as Harley walked silently through the carnival. Although he seemed to be looking only at the ground, Joe knew the manager was registering every detail of the raising. If asked to, Harley could name every single person working to keep the show going, list every piece of equipment needed, and recite the take from every stop for the past seventeen seasons.

Harley opened the door to the trailer that served as his office, and stepped inside. Joe followed. As the power of the afternoon sun faded away and his eyes adjusted to the dimness, he saw that someone was seated at the lone chair in front of the desk where Harley kept the bits of paper that comprised the carnival's accounting system. The occupant of the chair—a man—turned and regarded him.

"Hello." Joe tipped his head in the stranger's direction as Harley took a seat behind his desk.

"Good afternoon," replied the man. "You must be the dependable Mr. Flanagan."

"That's right," Joe said. "And you are . . . ?"

"I am Mr. Star," said the man, standing up and removing the battered top hat that covered his head. Tall and thin, he had dark hair that fell several inches over the collar of his white shirt, and a trim beard and mustache of a matching blue-black color. His clothes had once been elegant—a suit and morning coat of the sort worn by gentlemen twenty years earlier. Now they were worn and patched, their fineness marred by age and dust. Mr. Star held out his hand.

Joe shook it, and when his fingers slipped away, he found he was holding a small card. It was decorated with an image of a moon and stars that hung above a circus tent, its flags fluttering in an unseen wind. The words *Tent of Wonders* appeared in script below the picture, and beneath that, *Mr. Star, Proprietor.*

Joe looked at Mr. Star. The man was seated again. "Nice trick," Joe remarked.

Mr. Star smiled and tipped his head slightly. "A simple sleight of hand," he said.

"Mr. Star is interested in maybe joining up with us," Harley told Joe. "Got a show of his own. Thought it might help us both to travel together."

"What kind of show?" asked Joe.

"Curiosities," answered Mr. Star.

"Freaks," Harley said in response to Joe's puzzled look. "Bearded lady. Midgets. Shark boy."

"Mr. Harley has put it more clearly than I perhaps did myself," Mr. Star said, laughing gently. "I have indeed collected a diverse number of oddities in my travels, and some may very well think them freakish."

"He's got Siamese twins," said Harley, looking at Joe. "Real ones, not like that pair we had a few years ago." He turned to Mr. Star. "Turned out they weren't even related—just two kids who looked a little alike and walked around pretending to be connected in the middle."

"I assure you, every one of my attractions is very much legitimate," said Mr. Star, "from Cannibal Mary to the Pretzel Man. You can, of course, see them for yourselves before making your decision, but I guarantee you that you've never seen anything like what I have to offer."

"Why do you want to team up with another show?" Joe asked him.

"Economics," answered Mr. Star. "There's a war on. People are reluctant to part with their money. If they think they're getting more for their nickels, they're more likely to open their pockets."

"Would you mind giving us a minute?" Harley asked, nodding at the door.

"Of course," said Mr. Star. "I'll be outside."

He moved past Joe and left the trailer. When the door had shut behind him, Harley looked at Joe.

"What do you think?"

"Why are you asking me?" answered Joe. "I just put stuff together."

"We both know you do more than that, Joe," said Harley. "You know as much about how this operation runs as I do. I want to know if you think this guy Star will fit into what we've got going."

Joe shrugged. "He's right about times being tough," he said. "But a freak show?"

"People love freaks," countered Harley. "Those Siamese twins pulled in an extra fifteen bucks a week for us before they split up and ran off."

"And you think he's for real?"

"Who cares?" said Harley. "Long as they look real and people pay to see 'em."

"What's Star want for pay?"

"Nothing," Harley answered. "Just what he brings in from his shows. Even has his own roustabouts and barkers."

"That kind of deal's hard to say no to," said Joe.

"My thinking, too," Harley said.

"So why do you sound unsure?" Joe asked.

Harley shook his head. "I don't know," he said. "I've been in this business a lot of years, seen a lot of strange folks and strange things. Something about this fellow just ain't quite right."

"You think he's trying to cheat you somehow?"

"Nah," said Harley. "Can't really tell you why I say that. Just something about him. The way he looks at you. Maybe he's a fairy. Sure dresses like one."

"Wouldn't be the first one in the circus," Joe told his friend.

"I just don't want any trouble, is all," said Harley. "Things are tough enough right now."

"So are you saying yes or no?"

Harley moved the cigarette from one corner of his mouth to the other, a sign that he was thinking hard. “I want you to go check out what he’s got,” he said finally. “See what these freaks look like. If you think they’re worth it, we’ll give it a try.”

Joe nodded. “I can do that for you,” he said.

“Good,” said Harley. He glanced toward the door. “I’ll let you give him the news.”

Chapter Two

The old Ford pickup rattled lethargically along the dirt road, in no hurry to get wherever it was going. The crack in the windshield was growing longer, Joe noticed idly. The warmth of the afternoon settled around him, whispering in his ear with sweet breath scented by the tall grass they passed through, and making him drowsy. But the jostling of the weary truck as it ambled over the road's bumps and dips kept him alert despite the best efforts of the world to lull him to sleep.

"It's just up here."

Star's words broke the silence. Joe nodded. The man had said almost nothing since they'd started their journey—making infrequent and inconsequential remarks about the weather, the passing scenery, and other mundane topics. Several times he'd asked Joe questions about the carnival, about its acts and its people, its routines and schedules. These Joe had answered without revealing anything unnecessary. He still wasn't sure what to make of the peculiar Mr. Star, and he resented more than a little being taken away from his carousel to go on Harley's errand.

"There," Star said, pointing toward a field that appeared as they rounded a turn.

Joe looked and saw a circle of tents pitched in what had once been a cornfield but was now a graveyard for a rusty tractor and the plow hitched to its backside. A few of the tents had faded red flags affixed to their center poles, and these hung limply in the hot air. No one was to be seen moving around the camp.

Joe pulled off the road and into the field, bringing the truck to a stop just outside the circle. He and Star got out. As they walked toward the largest of the tents, a face appeared in the opening: the small, round face of a boy. When he saw Star, he dashed from the tent and ran toward the two men. Only then did Joe see that the child's skin was thick and gray, and that from his back protruded what appeared to be a stiff, curved fin.

"Ranku!" Star said warmly, opening his arms and embracing the boy. He turned to Joe. "Ranku is the youngest of our family."

Joe looked at the boy's smiling face. In most respects he seemed an ordinary child, perhaps about seven or eight years old. His dark eyes looked back at Joe curiously as he pressed himself against Star's leg.

"How do you do?" Joe said, nodding.

"You'll have to forgive Ranku," said Star. "He does not speak. It's one of the conditions of the curse."

"Curse?" asked Joe.

Star nodded. "The same curse that gives him the skin of a shark." He ran his fingers over the boy's back, gently stroking the fin. "I found him in the Fiji Islands," he said. "I was told his mother had broken ancient taboos by falling in love with a shark god. Ranku was the result of her sin. The islanders had killed the woman but feared harming the child. They were only too happy to send him away with me."

Star ruffled the child's dark hair. As he did so, Ranku smiled, revealing a mouth filled with razor-like teeth. Joe turned away.

"You don't find him fascinating?" asked Star.

Joe looked at him. "Let's see the others," he answered.

Ranku ran ahead of them as Star led Joe toward the tents. As they stepped inside the circle, Joe realized that they were being watched. From each tent, faces peered out, as if assessing the risk of revealing themselves further. Some, upon meeting his gaze, disappeared again into the safety of the tents.

"Why are they hiding?" Joe asked Star.

"We are not always welcome in the places we stop," said Star. "People are not always kind." He stopped in the center of the circle and said in a louder voice, "You may come out."

All around them tent flaps were pulled back. Joe found himself looking from tent to tent, waiting to see who or what would emerge. He was still somewhat shaken from his encounter with the shark boy, and although he didn't know what to make of Star's explanation for the boy's unusual condition, he was nonetheless wary of what other surprises awaited him.

His fears were lessened somewhat by the appearance of a large, smiling woman whose chin was crowned by a thick beard that hung almost to her ample waist. He'd seen such a thing before, and while it was unusual, it was hardly upsetting in the way that the boy with the cold, black eyes was.

"Ah, Melody," said Star. "May I introduce you to Mr. Flanagan?"

"Pleased to meet you," said Melody in a girlish voice, flashing a smile that Joe was relieved to see was composed of perfectly ordinary teeth.

Arriving behind Melody were the Siamese twins Harley had spoken of earlier. Joe was surprised for some reason to find that they were girls. He'd only ever seen boys joined in that way.

"Eleanore and Sally-Mae Kittery," Star said by way of introduction.

The twins curtsied. They appeared to be joined somewhere in the middle, and Joe wondered if, beneath the blue and red gingham dress, their skin was truly shared, or if, like Tim and Tom, who had fooled Harley several years earlier, they simply walked with their arms about each other's waists.

"We have . . . ," said the twin on the left. ". . . One heart," finished the other. They giggled in unison, each clapping a hand over her mouth before running off, their pigtails flapping against their back.

"A miracle of nature," said Star dreamily as he watched Sally-Mae and Eleanore depart.

"This the one that's taking us in?"

Joe turned to see who was speaking. The voice was slow and thick, almost drunken. It was coming from a man whose appearance both repulsed and fascinated Joe. Dressed in black pants and nothing else, his skin was all over tattooed with gruesome depictions of torment: women and men twisted in agony as demonic forms danced about them. Not even his face was unmarked, the leering grin of a hellish creature peering out from one cheek, and the fear-filled eyes of a screaming woman from the other.

"Dwayne Upshall," Star said. "Our illustrated man."

"Reverend Dwayne Upshall," the man said, glancing at Star before holding a hand out to Joe. It, too, was covered in inky visions of death.

"Reverend Upshall received a vision from the Lord," Star told Joe.

"Revelations," said Upshall, closing his eyes as if in pain. "Revelations from Jesus Christ. Show them what's to come," he said. "Show them"—his voice dropped to a whisper—"what they sow."

He opened his eyes and grinned, revealing broken, blackened teeth. "The word of the Lord," he said.

He walked away, revealing as he did the work on his back. There Joe saw Christ on the cross, his body being ripped to shreds by long-fingered demons, who held his bleeding flesh aloft.

"Not one of nature's creations," remarked Star. "But an attraction nonetheless. What do you think of my children so far?"

Joe shrugged. "Doesn't matter so much what I think," he replied. "It's what the paying folks think. I suspect they'll find this bunch worth parting with a dime or two."

Star smiled. "And you've seen only a handful," he said happily. "There are so many more: Cannibal Mary, the pretzel man, the human lizard. Oh, and let's not forget Timpa."

"Timpa?" Joe repeated.

"Mmm," Star said. "Our zombie. Direct from Haiti. Would you like to meet him?"

Joe shook his head. "I've seen enough," he said. "I've got to get back and finish my work. I'll tell Harley you're the real thing."

"Excellent," said Star. "We'll join you tomorrow, then. It seems our lots have been cast together."

"Looks that way," said Joe.

"There's one more person I wish for you to meet before you go," Star said, taking Joe's arm.

"What's this one?" Joe asked him. "Midget? A fat lady?"

"Nothing of the sort," said Star. "In fact, he's completely uninteresting in that respect."

They walked through the tents until they came to a truck parked beneath a tree. From underneath protruded a pair of legs, and Joe heard the unmistakable sound of someone applying a wrench with great force to an unyielding piece of metal.

"Goddamn son of a bitch," the owner of the legs said forcefully.

"Derry," Star said, "come out from the belly of that beast and show yourself."

The man's feet scuffed at the dirt as he slid out from beneath the truck. The legs gave way to a naked torso, the skin golden from hours spent in the sun. This in turn was followed by a handsome face. The man squinted, covering his eyes with one hand to block out the sun.

"What do you want?" he asked. "I'm trying to fix this thing."

"Stand up and meet our new business partner," Star said, sounding, Joe thought, slightly irritated.

The young man pushed himself to his feet and faced Joe. "Hey," he said.

Joe pegged him to be about twenty or twenty-one. His body still possessed the leanness of youth, and although the stubble on his unshaved face was that of a grown man, beneath the sprinkling of hair Joe could see the boy he had only recently been. Derry gazed at him with a guarded expression.

"Derry is our chief mechanic," said Star. "He's a magician with machines."

"Really?" said Joe.

"I'm the only mechanic," Derry replied. "But, yeah, I keep things running."

Joe eyed the truck that Derry had recently been underneath. "What's the problem with her?"

"Cracked tie rod," answered Derry. "Leaky oil pan. You name it, it's gone or about to go. But I'll keep her alive for a while yet."

"We rely on Derry for so many things," said Star. "He's indispensable."

Joe saw Derry shoot Star a quick glance. He sensed a hostility between them and wondered briefly what the source of it was. But it was none of his concern. His job was simply to check out Star's show and report back to Harley. He'd seen enough.

"I should be going," he said. "It was nice meeting you," he added to Derry.

Derry nodded and turned his attention back to the waiting truck. As Joe and Star walked back toward the tents, Star said, "Derry has been with me since he was quite young. I took him in when his parents died."

"It must have been hard on him," Joe said.

"Hard?" asked Star. "In what way?"

"Growing up surrounded by freaks," said Joe.

Star laughed. "Why would that be hard?" he said. "We're all, as you say, freaks in one way or another, are we not? Even if it isn't visible to the outside world."

They'd reached Joe's truck. Joe paused, his hand on the door. "I suppose in some ways that's true," he said. He looked at Star. "I'll tell Harley to expect you and your people tomorrow noontime."

"I look forward to it," said Star, tipping his head.

Joe got into the truck, started it, and drove away. Without Star in the truck he felt more at ease. Yet still something was troubling him. And it wasn't Star but Derry. He couldn't get the young man's image out of his mind. As he drove, he kept picturing the lines of Derry's torso, the muscled skin streaked with dust and grease. He found himself imagining what it would be like to touch that skin, to feel it beneath the callused tips of his fingers.

"No," he told himself. He shook his head, scattering the vision, and concentrated on the road before him. But again Derry's face invaded his thoughts, and again Joe let himself feel the heat of the young man's skin against his own.

He pulled the truck over, coming to a stop at the edge of a field, where a disinterested cow glanced up at him and immediately resumed its chewing. Joe gripped the steering wheel tightly, resting his forehead against it. He'd promised himself he wouldn't do this. Not again. But even as he willed himself not to, he felt the telltale stirring in his belly.

Reluctantly, he let one hand fall between his legs. He felt the hardness there. His body was betraying him. Still keeping his eyes closed, he slid his hand beneath the waist of his pants, feeling hair and skin and heat. Pushing deeper, his fingers closed around his shaft, tugging it up and out.

He lay back against the seat, slowly stroking himself as he thought about Derry. He saw himself taking the other man in his arms, kissing him. He felt Derry's tongue enter his mouth as he accepted the embrace.

Joe pulled his T-shirt up and unzipped his pants, freeing himself.

He never once looked down as his cock stretched up along his belly, pressing itself against him. As his fist moved up and down the length of it, he told himself that it was Derry's hand holding him, Derry's fingers coaxing the pleasure from deep inside him.

He breathed in and smelled the scent of Derry's skin, an intoxicating mixture of sweat and oil and sun. He ran his hands over the curve of Derry's ass, allowed his fingers to dip inside and press against the warm center. Derry opened to him, taking his fingers into himself and moaning in Joe's ear.

A cry of release escaped Joe's throat as his stomach was splashed with a spray of wetness. His cock jumped in his hand once, twice, three times as his body tightened and the electric rush rippled through him. He squeezed himself, hard, wanting it to go on forever, but moments later it had subsided, and he was himself once more.

Now he did look down. The dark hair of his stomach was threaded with sticky whiteness. He lowered his shirt and wiped away the stains of his actions. Tucking himself back into his pants, he zipped up and started the truck. The cow, finished with its grazing, was looking at him accusingly. He avoided its gaze and turned the key. Ashamed, he pulled the truck back onto the road and headed for the safety of the carousel.

Chapter Three

They came in five trucks, each one pulling a long trailer painted black. The first to arrive was the one Derry had been working on the previous afternoon. He was driving it, and as he passed by Joe, he lifted his hand in greeting but didn't smile. Joe nodded in return, watching the dust kicked up by the truck's tires billowing in dirty clouds around his feet.

The caravan rattled and bounced to a clear area at the far end of the carnival grounds. There the trucks stopped, their motors shuddering to stillness. Joe watched as Derry opened the door of his truck and jumped to the ground. As his feet touched the earth, the doors of the other four trucks opened in unison, as if unlocked by the young man's steps, and four nearly identical drivers emerged. Young men all of them, they stood silently beside their trucks, hands thrust into the pockets of the overalls they wore. Their dark eyes watched impassively as Derry approached Joe and Harley, who had left his office when word of the new arrivals had reached him.

"Where shall we set up?" Derry asked when he grew closer.

Harley nodded in the direction of the trucks. "There's fine," he said. "Joe will get some men to help you."

"Don't need any help," answered Derry.

Turning around, he walked back to the trucks and the waiting men. At some wordless sign from him, they were set in motion, each going to the trailer pulled by his truck and unlocking a door set in the far side, away from the view of Joe, Harley, and the small crowd of carnival workers who had come to see the strangers.

"All them freaks are in those trailers?" Harley asked Joe.

Joe spit on the ground. "Unless Star keeps them in some magic box of his," he said.

Harley grunted. It was a sound he made when he wasn't sure someone was kidding him or not. "Well, you keep an eye on them for me. I've got work to do."

Joe returned to his own work, leaving Derry and his crew to do as they would. If they didn't want his help, he wasn't going to offer more than once. They could come to him.

They didn't. And the next time Joe went near their end of the grounds, several hours later, there were three large black tents set up. Over the entrance to one was a faded sign proclaiming, *Tent of Wonders*. The tents were connected, and Joe knew that somewhere at the side of the third tent was an exit. What lay in between the two doors, he'd glimpsed briefly during his visit to Star's camp, and wanted to see no more of.

"Would you like to journey through before the crowds come?"

Joe glanced to the side and saw Star watching him. He was dressed as before, in his black suit and top hat, only now he leaned on a cane made of black wood and tipped with the silver head of a crow. He gestured at the opening of the tent.

Joe shook his head. "No time," he said.

Mr. Star cocked his head and frowned. "No time for magic and wonder?" he said. "Have you forgotten what it is to be enchanted, to be a child once more? Were you afraid of the dark as a boy?"

The question took Joe by surprise. Why had Star asked it? What had it to do with anything? Yet he found himself answering.

"No," he said. "I wasn't. I liked the night."

"Because it brought dreams," Star said, his voice light as the wind. He walked closer to Joe until he was standing directly in front of him, looking into his face and smiling. "It took you away, the night. Wrapped you in its velvet arms and carried you somewhere wild. Where did it take you? Who were you in your dreams?"

Joe found his mind racing, filling with images, snatches of memory, half-remembered bits of song. "Sing a song of sixpence," a boy's voice cried out. "Olly, olly oxen free!" Who was calling? He recognized the voice, but before he could identify its owner, it disappeared.

"Who were you in your dreams?" Star's voice came to him again, coaxing, gentle. "Think back."

Joe closed his eyes. His head was spinning. He shook it forcefully, and the voices inside were silenced. When he opened his eyes, Star was looking at him curiously.

"I need to go," said Joe. "The carousel."

He left Star standing by the tent and hurried off. He wasn't sure what had happened, but he felt a need to get away, away from the peculiar man and his tent of wonders. The carousel, as always, would be his place of refuge.

He stayed there as afternoon turned to evening, and the sky from yellow to pink to purple. The first stars came out, and with them the carnival goers. It was Friday, and the looming freedom of the next two days filled the people of the town with thoughts of happiness. It was happiness they badly needed, as the war had taken from them a great measure of their joy, their belief in life. The carnival gave some of it back, even if its promises melted like cotton sugar in the light of morning and left them feeling slightly sick. At least for the night, they were lifted high.

Joe stood at the controls of the carousel, a magician spinning gold and starlight from the gears and motors hidden beneath the ride's painted facade. He took his passengers for a dizzying spin around and around, turning them for a handful of minutes into cowboys, princesses, lovers, and whatever else they wanted to be.

When the moon was nearly overhead, he decided to take a break. Handing control of the carousel over to one of the crew, he walked toward the midway. There he heard the sounds of the barkers enticing visitors to play their games and buy their wares. It was the sound of barking dogs mixed with the voices of a dozen preachers selling salvation. "Knock the bottles down and win a prize." "Popcorn and peanuts, three cents a bag." They were selling everything and nothing, and from the tone of their calls, Joe knew that they were succeeding mightily at it. Harley had been right: the town had been waiting for them.

He kept walking, coming to a stop only when he reached the perimeter of the carnival. At this crossing place between the golden world of the rides and the grayness of reality, a border had formed—a circle of torn ticket stubs, stained napkins, and the discarded remains of half-eaten sweets that were somehow swept to the very edges of the fairgrounds and surrounded it like a moat. It happened every night, this accumulation of worn-out glory. After years on the road, Joe had stopped feeling sad when he looked at the trashlands, had come to see them as he would the broken shell of a bird's egg, the bits and pieces signifying that something inside had broken free and flown.

He took a cigarette from his pocket and lit it. The end glowed firefly bright in the shadows, and when he exhaled, the smoke curled up around his face and kept rising into the night sky. He guessed that it was somewhere around half past eleven. The carnival would close at midnight, what remained of the crowds gently shooed away by men trained in the art of putting dreams to bed. Then the world would go to sleep.

A woman's laugh broke through his thoughts, and he turned to his left. There he saw a flash of light as a curtain opened against the dark and someone exited. He realized then that he was near the third of Star's black tents and that what he saw was the most recent visitor to the Tent of Wonders. The man stood for a moment in the darkness, as if letting his eyes—or perhaps his mind—adjust to the world around him. Then he walked toward the lights, slowly at first and then faster, until he was almost running.

Joe stared at the blackness where he knew the door to be. What, he wondered, had the man seen inside? The few freaks he'd seen at the camp had been enough to make him uneasy; what other surprises awaited those who stepped inside Star's house?

The tent flap opened again, and several young men tumbled out, laughing loudly. Their gaiety was overly bright, magnified beyond reason. Joe suspected it was a response to the knowledge that any day they could be called to war, to their deaths in lands they'd only heard of. Faced with this possibility, they demanded as much from every moment as it could give, wringing laughter from experiences that should quickly have been used up. At least, Joe thought, it would give them something to think about as they died.

The boys made their way back to the crowds. But as they broke into the electric light of the midway, one of them turned back. The others called to him, and he waved them on. Joe heard him tell them that he would catch up with them. Then he trotted back to the exit from which he and the others had recently emerged, and waited there, looking around nervously.

A moment later the flap opened, and a woman stepped outside. Joe could not see her features in the dark. She spoke something to the boy in a voice too low to be heard, then took his hand. Leading him, she walked into the shadows between the tents. Joe saw the boy swallowed up by the blackness.

From his years in the carny business, he knew there was only one reason a woman took a young man into the shadows of the tents. Although Joe begrudged no one a few minutes of pleasure, Harley had strict rules about whoring. It wouldn't do to have one of the newcomers getting into trouble with the locals should word of her services get out. And young men always talked. Joe had seen more than one carnival tart with a blackened eye and torn dress after a randy eighteen-year-old, boasting to his friends, had revealed her. Moved by beer and lust, the young men of dusty towns frequently turned into ugly, violent things.

Joe dropped what was left of his cigarette and ground it into the dirt with his heel. He would have a word with the woman, gently suggest that if she wanted to maintain peace she would find another way to relieve the customers of a half-dollar. He had no love for the denizens of Star's Tent of Wonders, but he wished no one ill. Besides, he didn't want to hear Harley bitch about it later.

He found the space between the tents and peered between them. The woman and the young man were still walking hand in hand. He followed, and soon their voices became audible.

"Where are we going?" the boy asked nervously.

"Not much farther," the woman replied. "Just back in here a ways."

"This better be what you promised," said the young man.

The woman laughed. "Don't worry," she told him. "It will be more than you ever imagined."

Something about the woman's voice was odd, raspy. She spoke as if she were underwater. Then she and her charge stepped into a patch of moonlight, and Joe faltered. Her face came into view: a horribly bloated thing. Her cheeks were impossibly round, her forehead domed. Her skin was all over slick with something, a moistness that shone wetly in the light.

She was obviously one of the many wonders contained in Star's tent, although Joe couldn't begin to imagine what her particular deformity was. It didn't matter. Was the boy really going to make his pleasure with her? Joe wondered, a shiver of disgust moving over him. Was he going to press himself into her misshapen body, close his eyes and kiss her twisted mouth? Joe couldn't even imagine the horror.

The pair slipped once more into darkness as they entered another circle of tents, these smaller than the larger three. It was, Joe realized, the encampment for the group. The girl, or whatever she was, was taking the boy to her private sleeping place.

"Here." The pair stopped outside a tent that resembled all the others. "She's in here."

The boy looked at the tent. So, Joe thought, he wasn't to lie with the girl after all. She was merely acting as an intercessor, a go-between for someone else. But who? Was it someone even more repulsive than she? What foul pleasure awaited the young man behind the tent's door?

The boy looked from the tent to the girl, as if trying to decide whether to enter or not.

"Go on," the girl said, coaxing him on. "There's nothing to be afraid of."

"I don't know," said the young man. "Fifty cents is a lot of money."

"You already paid up, honey," the girl said. "Now go on in and get what you paid for."

The boy reached for the tent flaps. Slowly he drew one of them aside and peered in. A pale light poured from the opening, flickering against the blackness. The young man stepped forward as the girl placed a hand on his back and urged him into the tent.

In the moving light, Joe saw the boy's expression change. He smiled broadly, like a child. Then he went into the tent, and the flap closed behind him, shutting away the light. The girl outside reached into the pocket of her dress, drew out her hand, and began to count the coins that lay on her palm. She giggled, the harshness of her laugh rough in the air.

The girl turned and skipped away into the night. Joe almost followed her, but his business wasn't with her; it was with the one who resided in the tent. He walked briskly to the flap and stood outside, listening for sounds from within.

At first he heard nothing. Then, faintly at first and growing louder, he heard the sound of someone humming. The tune initially seemed formless, a series of highs and lows sung in a woman's soothing voice. Then the notes grew into words, and a tune emerged. It was a lullaby, one Joe had heard his own mother sing many times.

"Hush, little baby, don't say a word . . . ," the woman sang. "Mama's gonna buy you a mockingbird."

He was puzzled. Who was singing, and why? If the boy had gone into the tent to find release in a harlot's bosom, it was an odd sort of release indeed. Joe had expected to hear the moans and cries of lovemaking, not the quiet singing of a mother to an infant. But that was exactly what was coming from within the tent. The woman's voice continued the song, telling the child of the diamond ring and horse and cart that would be his if only he would not cry.

Joe wanted to open the tent, but no longer for the purpose of interrupting a sinful act. He wanted to see the owner of the voice, to have her sing the words he heard to him. Suddenly he wanted more than anything to have the singer of the song hold him in her arms and rock him into the deepest sleep while her song filled his head.

Then, just as he was reaching for the black fold that would allow him entrance, the singing stopped. It was replaced instantly by silence so cold that Joe shuddered, as if an icy wind had swept across his naked skin. Fear flooded him, causing his mind to reel dizzily. He withdrew his hand and stood staring at the tent for a long, awful moment. And then, not knowing why, he turned and fled, running as quickly as he could from whatever had stilled the beautiful voice.

Chapter Four

The next day the rain came.

It was the first rain since summer had arrived, and they were caught by surprise. At first they looked up at the sky, startled. Then, as the drops came more quickly, dotting the ground with dark circles, they had run for the safety of the tents. Unused to wetness, it was as if they feared that remaining too long in the storm would cause them to dissolve.

Fortunately, it was a takedown day. Most of the rides had already been disassembled and loaded onto the trucks. The tents, too, were folded and stored. Only a few odds and ends remained to be packed before the overnight haul to the next town.

Having checked that the last of the carousel horses was safely in its place, Joe now sat in the trailer that served as his living quarters. There he had a bed and several boxes containing his clothes and the few memories he chose to carry with him. It was neither grand nor particularly inviting, but it suited him and he liked it.

He sat on the bed, the door to the trailer closed, and listened to the sound of the rain on the roof. He hadn't heard it in a very long time, and he realized that he'd missed it. The drumming of the raindrops filled the small space with its whispers. Normally Joe would have been surrounded by the noise of the carnival, but now all that was silenced by the rain. He knew that around the fairgrounds the others were in their own tents and trailers, perhaps looking out and wondering when the sun would chase the rain away, or, like himself, enjoying the unexpected visit.

He wasn't worried about getting to the next destination. There was time. Eventually the rain would stop, and Harley would give the command to move out. They would drive through the night, and when the curtain of dawn rose, it would be on a new stage. For now, though, there was time to rest.

Joe had said nothing to anyone about the events of the previous night. After some thought, he wasn't even sure what had occurred. He'd been frightened, that was all, and there had been no reason to be. Whatever had occurred in the tent did not concern him.

He shut his eyes and tried to sleep. But beneath the sound of the rain he heard a voice rising up.

"Hush, little baby, don't say a word . . ."

It was the singsong voice he'd heard emanating from within the black tent. Only now it was directed at him. He knew it, somehow, could feel it drawing him in.

"Mama's gonna buy you a mockingbird . . ."

He wanted to give in to it. He wanted to sleep. The voice seemed to promise him dreams beyond end, sleep without waking. He suddenly felt unbearably tired.

"And if that mockingbird don't sing, Mama's gonna buy you a diamond ring . . ."

The words floated around him, weaving a cocoon of warmth. He was safe inside, while outside, the world turned to water and washed away.

"And if that diamond ring turns brass, Mama's gonna buy you a looking glass . . ."

Joe was on the edge of sleep, staring out into a sea of endless stars. He longed to dive into them, to be cradled in the arms of she who sang to him.

A crash like the breaking of a thousand dishes broke through his thoughts, startling him awake. He sat up, rubbing his eyes and confused. Had he slept? For how long? His small room felt alien, unfamiliar and unwelcoming.

The crash came again, and he realized that it was thunder. The trailer shook with the force of it, as if the weather were deliberately trying to rouse him. Joe rubbed his eyes and stood. He had to get out of the trailer.

Opening the door, he stepped outside and into the rain. The coldness of it on his face immediately revived him. He stood there for a minute, letting it soak into his hair and clothes. The thunder rumbled again, this time followed by lightning strikes off to the east. Joe shook himself like a dog and walked as quickly as he could in the direction of Harley's trailer. When he got there, he knocked on the door, waited for Harley's call to come in, and entered.

Harley was seated at his desk, a cigarette in his mouth and a bottle of beer in his hand. Across from him was Madame Sylvie. Ostensibly a gypsy fortune-teller from the forests of Rumania, Sylvie was really Sylvie Ruskin of Weary, Arkansas. A thin, beautiful girl of twenty-three, she'd left her husband after one too many beatings and, with no family to take her in, had seen in the passing carnival her opportunity for escape. She had a talent for palm reading, Tarot cards, and clairvoyance, and these she offered to the public for a small sum.

Between Sylvie and Harley were a series of cards. Some were turned faceup, revealing images that Sylvie studied closely. The others remained facedown.

"Sylvie's reading my cards," Harley said effusively. From his tone, Joe could tell that the beer in his hand was not his first.

"Oh, yeah?" said Joe, shutting the door and running a hand through his wet hair to rid it of some of the rain. "And what does she see?"

"Pretty ladies and more money than I can spend before I die," replied Harley, laughing. "Right, Sylvie?"

Sylvie didn't look at him as she turned over another card. "The cards aren't something to joke about," she said.

"Right, right," said Harley, winking at Joe over Sylvie's bowed head. "We don't want to get the spirits angry or nothing. Joe, why don't you have Sylvie tell your fortune? Come on."

Sylvie turned and looked at Joe. She was a beautiful girl, with long dark hair she let fall wildly around her shoulders, and a face that, while not pretty, reflected an unearthly beauty. Despite the rain, she wore a thin cotton dress of pale blue, and her feet were bare. She regarded Joe coolly, then swept the cards up and began to shuffle them.

"Okay," Joe said, coming to take the chair beside Sylvie. He'd come to Harley's trailer to tell him about the strange happenings of the night before, but now that he was here, he found that the memory of them was once more fading and that they didn't seem so important after all. Still, he was happy for the company, and if allowing Sylvie to tell his fortune kept him from being alone, he welcomed it, even if he didn't believe in such things.

Sylvie pushed the stacked cards toward him. "Cut the deck," she said.

Joe picked up half the cards and set them aside. Sylvie once more stacked them and began to lay them out on the table in a pattern.

"Sure you want her to tell you what's going to happen to you?" asked Harley, grinning. "You might find out you're going to die."

"We're all going to die," said Sylvie as she set the unused cards to the side. "The cards don't waste time with inevitabilities."

She turned over the first card and looked at it. "The Queen of Cups," she said. "A woman of mystery and sadness."

"Got a lady friend you're keeping to yourself, Joe?" asked Harley, laughing.

Joe ignored his friend, watching as Sylvie went to the next card. "The Knight of Pentacles. A hardworking man who is useful to those he serves."

"Sounds just like you, Joe," Harley teased.

"The Eight of Swords," Sylvie continued as the third card was revealed. "Inability to get out of a difficult situation."

Harley whistled. "Uh-oh, buddy. I hope you didn't knock nobody up." He took another swig on his beer and, when nothing came out, tossed it into the garbage and reached for another in the chest behind his desk.

The fourth card was turned. "The Lovers," Sylvie said, smiling slightly.

"I told you!" crowed Harley triumphantly.

Sylvie shook her head. "The card is about making choices," she said. "Choosing between different attractions."

"So there are *two* women," Harley said. "That's even better. Joe, you've been hiding a lot from your old friend. I'm hurt."

Sylvie took the final card and looked at it. "The Devil," she said softly. She glanced quickly at Joe, and for a moment he saw something troubling in her eyes. Before he could tell if it was fear or pity, it was gone, and Sylvie regarded the card with her usual detachment.

"What's that one mean?" asked Joe.

"It means you're going to hell for your sins," said Harley. "So you might as well enjoy them as much as you can."

"The Devil is the representation of our most depraved selves," Sylvie told Joe. "See the people chained to him? They're his puppets, doing as he commands. The card symbolizes the loss of our souls."

"So what does all this say?" Joe asked her, indicating the five cards spread before them.

"It can mean many things," she answered. "What do you see here?"

"Isn't that your job?" said Joe.

Sylvie shook her head. "The cards reflect the influences surrounding you," she replied. "I can tell you what these influences are, but only you know who or what might be behind them."

"Then what do you see?"

Sylvie looked at him. "Pain," she said. "And love. That's all."

"Can you believe the rubes pay her two bits to hear this stuff?" said Harley.

Joe ignored him. There was something Sylvie wasn't telling him, something he knew she saw in the cards but didn't want to reveal. He was tempted to try to get her to tell him more, but he wasn't sure if he wanted to hear it, and was even less sure that he believed any of it anyway. After all, there was no woman in his life. There was no love, no difficult choice to make. Perhaps, he thought, the entire reading meant nothing at all.

"Thanks," he said. "I guess I'll be going now."

"What?" cried Harley. "No. No. Stay and have a cold one."

Joe held up a hand. "That's okay," he said. "I have some things I need to do."

He left the trailer, thankful that Harley was drunk enough that he hadn't asked why Joe had come to see him in the first place. It was still raining, harder now, and he walked quickly through the deserted fairgrounds, back toward his own trailer. Already he was pushing Sylvie's Tarot card reading from his mind.

As he neared his trailer, he caught sight of someone else walking ahead of him. Whoever it was moved quickly, with purpose. Through the rain it was impossible to tell who it might be, and Joe wondered who would be out in such weather if he didn't need to be.

He followed the figure as it moved past the last of the trailers and headed out into the empty plains that surrounded the encampment. Here the rain was swept in sheets by the wind. Joe bowed his head against the storm and soldiered on, determined to find out who was walking ahead of him and why he would venture into the teeth of the storm.

After some minutes, the quarry came to a stop. Joe paused, ducking behind some scrub and watching as a bundle was lowered to the ground. He saw then that the person also carried a shovel. The spade was thrust into the earth, and a clump was turned over. As the figure turned, Joe realized with surprise that it was Derry.

He watched as the young man dug a hole, seemingly oblivious to the rain that fell around him and turned the normally dry ground into thick mud. Again and again the shovel bit into the plain, until a small mound was built up at Derry's side. Joe, cold and confused, could only stare and wonder.

Derry stopped and dropped to his knees in the mud. He was tired, Joe could tell, exhausted from digging. The young man knelt for a minute before reaching for the bundle at his side. Without picking it up, he slid it through the mud and shoved it into the hole. Then, using his hands, he began pushing the dirt over it. The earth had turned to mud, and Derry scooped it up in his hands, pouring it over the bundle in dripping handfuls.

Joe was tempted to go to him, to offer his help. Derry seemed weary, defeated. Whatever he was burying beneath the prairie's skin, it was something he wanted very much to be rid of. Why else, Joe thought, would he come out in such a storm? What could be so hateful to him that he would want to bury it with his hands?

Derry was finished, the last of the dirt smoothed into place. Using the shovel to help him, he rose to his feet and stood looking down at the ground as rain dripped from his face. His clothes clung to him, stained the deep red of the prairie. Above him the sky grumbled and spit out bursts of lightning.

Joe ducked low as the boy turned and made his way back to the carnival. As he passed by the scrub, Joe saw that his eyes were empty. Life appeared to have been drained from him, and he walked with the slow purposelessness of a man with nowhere to go and no reason to get there. Then he was swallowed up by the rain, a shadow growing fainter and fainter until Joe could no longer distinguish him from the storm.

Joe stood and went to the spot where Derry had been. The rain had pounded his handiwork down, erasing the seams of the hole so that it was difficult to see where it was. But there were still some irregularities in the earth, and when Joe plunged his fingers into the dirt, it came away easily.

He didn't have to dig very far. Derry had gone just deep enough to ensure that the bundle and its contents were hidden from view. Within minutes Joe was able to grab hold of the cloth. He pulled at it, trying to lift it from the ground, but the mud resisted him, sucking it back down. Finally he contented himself with working at the knot that held the material closed. His fingers were cold, and the wetness of the cloth drew the knot tighter, but eventually he loosened it and pulled the bundle apart.

Looking up at him was a skull. It sat atop a pile of bones, a grotesque egg cradled in a nest of human remains. Joe stared at it, disgust rising up in him as he became aware of the blood and bits of skin clinging to some of the bones. Even the teeth were still there, grinning at him as if rejoicing in some great joke.

He turned his head and retched, his stomach cramping and his mouth filling with the metallic taste of sickness. He couldn't look at the bones again. He'd seen enough to know that they were not old, that the flesh had only recently been stripped away and the life drained out. The thought made him heave again, not just from the horror of such thoughts and the nearness of the bones, but also because Derry was somehow connected to them and because Joe was almost certain he knew who it was that had been buried in the hole, and when his death had come.

Chapter Five

He said nothing. He didn't know why, except that somehow he understood that no one would believe him. Even if he produced the bones, which he'd left in the hole, he knew that they would prove nothing. They were only bones, and bones were not an uncommon relic of the prairies. Men died, and what were the bones of one when across the oceans thousands of men were dying every day?

Besides, there was Derry. Joe didn't know what the young man's role was in the events surrounding the bones, but he could not believe that the boy was capable of anything so sinister as murder. He'd met murderers in his life, and he knew that they carried within them a darkness that blotted out all feeling, allowing them to commit their acts with steady hands and detached amusement. He saw no such blackness in Derry.

He carried the secret for three days, as the caravan outran the thunderstorms and left them behind for the farmlands of Nebraska. During this time he busied himself with his machines, talking to almost no one and avoiding everyone connected with the Tent of Wonders. The crowds were large in this part of the country, and he had much to do, so it was easy to keep his mind distracted until he almost began to think that he'd imagined the whole thing.

If not for the dreams, he might eventually have forgotten entirely.

But as soon as he closed his eyes at night, the voice came to him, singing.

"Hush, little baby, don't say a word . . ."

It always began the same way, with the command to quiet. Then came the promises, the litany of rewards for his continued silence.

"And if that looking glass gets broke, Mama's gonna buy you a billy goat . . ."

It was from the voice that the dreams bloomed, nonsensical images that he could never recall in the light of morning. But always there was the voice, hanging over all like a fog. And as if in a fog, he wandered through his dreams, lost, looking for something to guide him to safety from whatever it was that pursued him. The voice, he knew, would only lead him deeper into danger. It was not to be trusted.

It was when he found himself humming the tune to himself while working on the machinery of the Ferris wheel that he knew something had to be done. The song had emerged into his waking life, and that was intolerable. It was time to unravel the mystery of Derry, the bones, and the voice that tied them all together.

He found the boy in his trailer. He was seated at a small table, an open bottle before him and a half-filled glass in his hand. Joe entered the trailer and pulled the door shut behind him. He had never visited any of Star's band in their homes before, had in fact stayed as far from them as he could. Now, standing before Derry, he felt his heart pounding.

"What do you want?" Derry asked, looking up at him but remaining seated.

"I know about the bones," said Joe.

Derry took a drink from his glass. "What bones?" he asked, wiping his mouth with his hand.

"The ones you buried," Joe explained. "Three days back. I saw you."

"You saw nothing," answered Derry, pouring more whiskey into his glass.

"I saw you," repeated Joe. "And I held the bones in my hands."

Derry slammed his glass on the table and glared at Joe. "You saw *nothing*," he said firmly.

Joe darted forward and grabbed the young man by his T-shirt. Half lifting him, he pressed his face very close to Derry's until he could smell the alcohol on the boy's breath.

"Tell me," he demanded. "Tell me where they came from."

Derry looked into his eyes. "They came from no one," he answered. "They came from nowhere."

"Damn it," Joe said, shaking Derry. "You're going to tell me."

He pulled Derry up and pressed him against the wall of the trailer. Derry smiled drunkenly.

"You don't know anything," he said, and began to laugh.

Infuriated, Joe slapped the young man across the face hard, leaving a mark that quickly flamed to red. Derry glared at him for a moment; then his eyes softened. One of his hands slid up Joe's back and came to rest on his neck. He pulled Joe closer.

"Isn't this what you really came here for?" he asked softly.

Joe resisted. Then, as Derry's lips parted, he surrendered and allowed himself to be pulled in. He felt Derry's tongue enter his mouth. He closed his eyes, tasting heat and warmth. His hands found Derry's body and held on tightly.

Derry pressed into him, and Joe felt the hardness below his waist. He pushed Derry's T-shirt up and ran his hands over the smooth, muscled skin. Derry lifted his arms, and Joe slipped the shirt off. He bent his mouth to one of the boy's exposed nipples and bit gently. Derry groaned.

Derry fumbled with the belt at his own waist and quickly undid it. His pants fell to his feet, and his cock sprang forward into Joe's hand. Joe closed his fingers around it, stroking its length slowly. He fingered the head, and his hand came away sticky.

Derry stepped forward and leaned over the table. His ass was spread out before Joe, firm and round and waiting. Joe hastily undid the buttons of his pants and freed himself. Spreading the cheeks of Derry's ass, he revealed the darker center and spit into it. Then he pressed himself against the opening and thrust forward.

Derry cried out as Joe entered him. The heat of the young man surrounded Joe's cock, and for a moment he thought he might empty himself before he'd even begun. He paused a moment, steadying himself, and then began to move in and out.

Derry moaned as Joe fucked him. His hands gripped the edge of the table, which shook each time Joe's body slapped against the boy's. Joe held Derry by the waist, pushing deep into him with every return. It had been a long time since he'd been with a man this way, and the wanting he'd built up during those long nights coursed through him.

"Hush, little baby, don't say a word . . ."

The words whispered in Joe's ear. At first he thought perhaps Derry had said them, but he quickly brushed aside that thought. It was a woman's voice he heard.

"No." Beneath him, Derry was pushing his body back toward Joe, who had ceased his movements at the sound of the song. "No. Don't."

"Mama's gonna buy you a billy goat . . ."

"No!" Derry said again, more loudly.

Joe didn't know who the young man was speaking to, or if he could hear the voice singing, but he responded to the urgency in his voice. He began to pump with renewed force, and Derry in turn tightened himself around Joe's shaft. Joe closed his eyes, feeling the approaching climax begin.

"And if that billy goat won't pull, Mama's gonna buy you a cart and bull . . ."

"I said no!" Derry cried out. "Leave him alone! He's mine."

Joe came, filling Derry with burst after burst of heat. Joe bucked against the boy, moans of relief escaping his throat as his body shook with the force of release. He fell forward onto Derry's back, still not drained, and lay there as he finished. The young man's skin was covered in sweat and warm with the heat of the night, and Joe kissed it gently.

"Mama's gonna buy you a cart and bull . . ."

The voice was fading, barely audible. Thankful for its leaving, some moments went by before Joe realized that beneath him Derry was shaking. Then he heard the sounds of muffled sobs.

He stood up and pulled the young man to his feet, turning him around. Derry's eyes were wet with tears.

"Did I hurt you?" Joe asked, worried.

Derry shook his head. "No," he whispered.

"Then what is it?"

"Nothing and no one," said Derry. "Nothing and no one."

"You heard it," Joe said. "You heard the singing. Didn't you?"

Derry looked away. "You need to go," he said.

"Not until you tell me you heard it," Joe demanded.

Derry said nothing, slumping against the table and looking down at the floor. Joe put a hand under the young man's chin and forced him to look up.

"Tell me you heard it," he said. "I know you did."

"I heard it," said Derry softly.

"Then tell me who it is."

Derry shook his head again. "I don't know who it is," he told Joe.

"But you spoke to it," Joe insisted. "You told it to stop."

"I know nothing else," said Derry.

Joe looked into his face and knew that whether he was telling the truth or not, the boy had said everything he was going to say. He released him and pulled his pants up. Derry remained where he was, naked and beautiful.

"I won't ask you again," said Joe. "If I have to, I'll find out by myself. But I won't ask you again."

Derry nodded silently. Joe watched him for a long moment, hoping he would speak, then left the trailer. Outside, the night was filled with the familiar sounds of summer, laughter and music and a hundred voices all running together in a senseless jumble. One of his mechanics had completed the repair on the Ferris wheel, and he could see it turning against the moon.

Joe turned and looked back at the trailer. Part of him wanted to go back inside and take Derry in his arms. Another part wanted to run as far away as he could, away from the boy and the voice that taunted him. Whatever mystery Derry was a part of didn't concern him, and perhaps if he left the boy behind, he would leave behind everything else as well. It was a comforting thought.

But he knew he wouldn't, if for no other reason than that he had nowhere else to go, no one else to go to. The carnival had become his world, and he could not leave it. He would stay, whatever doing so brought him.

"A lovely evening."

Joe saw Mr. Star emerge from the shadows of the tents and step into the light. He smiled and regarded Joe with interest.

"Yes, it is," Joe replied.

Star raised his cane toward the sky, indicating the multitude of stars glittering in the darkness. "Orion the hunter is out tonight," he remarked. "I wonder, Mr. Flanagan, what it is you yourself are hunting for."

"I'm just walking," Joe replied.

"Just walking," repeated Star. "As a fellow wanderer, I understand the compulsion. Sometimes I feel almost as if something, someone, is calling me to venture out into the unknown. The voice of the universe, perhaps." He laughed. "Sometimes that voice sends us on a fool's errand, I think. It's wise to be careful."

"I'm afraid I don't follow you," Joe said. "I just enjoy being out."

"Yes," Mr. Star said. "No harm in that, I'm sure. And since you are out, my friend, would you like to walk with me?"

Joe wanted to do anything but spend another moment with Star, but he sensed that refusing the invitation would invite more suspicion than would agreeing to it. He nodded at Star and followed him as he began to walk through the tents.

"I can't help but notice that you have yet to visit my Tent of Wonders," he said. "May I ask why not?"

"I'm busy with my work," Joe answered.

"A very polite excuse," said Star. "But not, I think, the true one."

Joe began to protest, but Star held up a hand to stop him.

"You needn't spare my feelings," he said. "I am well aware that what I have to offer is not to everyone's liking."

"It seems to be to a lot of people's liking," Joe commented. "You always have a crowd waiting."

"The curious, the daring, and the unbelievers," Star said. "They come to prove me a charlatan and my children fakeries."

"And how do they leave?" asked Joe.

"Ah," said Star. "That is an excellent question. Some of them leave convinced that they are correct; others, that everything they have ever believed is a lie. It depends on how open their eyes and minds are to what they see."

Joe said nothing, and the two of them walked in silence for a minute. Then Star said, "A word of unasked-for advice. I would be wary of Derry Stroud."

"Derry?" said Joe.

Star continued. "He is a lovely young man, and I am very fond of him. He does, however, harbor certain peculiarities."

"I don't understand," said Joe.

"He has been known to become infatuated with certain gentlemen," Star said carefully. "Several times it has led to unpleasantness."

"He seems like a nice enough kid," said Joe.

"Until his attentions are rebuffed, yes," Star replied. "Then he can become, well . . ." His voice trailed off, the sentence left unfinished.

"Can become what?" Joe prodded.

"He has been known to become violent," said Star. "Unpredictable."

"Are you saying he's hurt people?" asked Joe.

"I am saying that it is best not to get too close," Star said. "Nor to believe too much of what he might say."

He stopped and looked into Joe's face. "Do we understand one another?"

Joe shrugged. "I suppose so," he said.

Star smiled. "Good," he said. "As I say, I am very fond of Mr. Stroud, and I believe I am very fond of you as well. I would not like to see anything happen to either of you."

"I don't think you have to worry about that," Joe told him.

"I'm sure none of us have anything to worry about," said Star. "Now, if you will excuse me, I have some unbelievers to convert." He gestured at the long line of visitors who waited outside the Tent of Wonders.

Joe looked at them all. They were mostly young men, some not yet fully grown. Each was willing to pay to see what amazements were contained in the three tents. And what would they find? Joe wondered. What had the boy he'd seen led from there by the hoarse-voiced woman seen?

He didn't know what to make of anything: the voice that came to him, Derry, the bones, and now Star's warning. Somehow they were all tied together, but he had no way of knowing where to begin to untangle the truth from the lies. Had Derry killed someone? Joe couldn't imagine it. But he had seen him with the bones. Perhaps Star was correct and the bones' owner had been a victim of Derry's rage. If so, Joe thought, had he placed himself in danger by going to the young man?

Suddenly he recalled something that Derry had cried out in the trailer. "He's mine," he'd said. The importance of the words struck Joe with a force like a thunderclap. "He's mine."

He looked back in the direction of Derry's trailer, a new fear enfolding him in its black wings.

Chapter Six

"Those freaks are the best thing that ever happened to us."

Harley was sitting at his desk, the cash box open and a wad of dirty bills in his hand. Several piles of neatly stacked bills were lined up before him. He was counting. When he finished, he slapped another pile on the desk and laughed.

"Nearly doubled our usual take this week."

It was Monday morning, and like clockwork, Harley was figuring the accounts from the weekend. How he managed to keep them straight, Joe never knew, but somehow he did, even hungover and bleary-eyed, as he was now.

"Here's to Mr. Star and his sideshow," crowed Harley, raising a glass and taking a drink.

"Isn't it a little early for that?" asked Joe.

"Ah, it's just water," Harley said, grinning.

Joe looked at the money on Harley's desk. It was more than he'd seen there in a long time—a lot more. And he knew Harley was right. It *was* the freaks who were bringing them in. Every night the crowds outside the Tent of Wonders were larger and more excited. News spread quickly in the small towns, and by the second night the carnival was open, curiosity seekers from miles around were handing over their hard-won money to see what all the fuss was about.

"What's the matter?" Harley asked his friend.

Joe shook his head. "Nothing," he said. "It's just that I don't see why folks are so excited about what's in that tent."

Harley laughed. "Makes 'em feel normal," he said. "Makes the things that really scare 'em seem pretty in comparison. Cannibal Mary and Pretzel Man are things they can look at. A war isn't. So they come to see the freaks and leave feeling better about everything."

Joe regarded Harley curiously.

"Don't look so surprised," Harley told him, guessing what Joe was thinking. "You spend enough time in the carny and you learn a thing or two about people. I may not be a genius, but I know some truth. You been in that tent yet?"

"No," Joe answered.

"Go," said Harley. "Tonight. Take a walk through there and look at the people. You'll see what I mean."

Joe looked down.

"Go," Harley repeated. "Ain't nothing in there that's gonna bite you."

"All right," said Joe. "I'll go."

Harley nodded, satisfied. "Now, get out of here," he said. "I want to be alone with my money."

Joe smiled as he stood. He waved good-bye to Harley and went outside. It was too early for most of the carnival's residents to be up. They were still in their tents and trailers, snoring and dreaming. Around noontime they would begin to emerge, stretching, yawning, and blinking at the sun. He would have much of the day to himself.

He spent it going over the machines, oiling and greasing and inspecting everything for needed repairs. Losing himself in the engines and mechanisms kept him from thinking too much. Certainly it kept him from going over the events of the past days. He'd done too much of that, getting nowhere. He hadn't seen Derry since the night in his trailer, and his sleep had been untroubled by nursery songs. Still, however, there remained the mystery of the bones. His conversation with Star had introduced new doubts regarding them and regarding Derry. But was Star to be believed? That, too, was in question.

Joe pushed all questions from his mind. The gears and pistons became his sanctuary, and he occupied his thoughts solely with them.

These things he could understand. They behaved in predictable ways, their actions controlled by their purpose. Never did they surprise him, and never were their intentions in doubt. This was why he loved them.

He worked on the machinery until afternoon arrived and the fairgrounds came to life once more. He gave each ride a final check and then retired to his trailer for a rest before the real workday began.

When he awoke, it was evening. The heat of the day still lingered, and he found it hard to shake the sleep from his head. When he went outside, he found the carnival bustling quietly, as if the heat muffled the sounds of merriment. There was no breeze to break the spell, and even the calls of the men who worked the midway sounded weary.

Remembering his promise to Harley, Joe walked in the direction of the Tent of Wonders. Only there was the buzzing of the crowd in full force. The people formed a dense thicket around the tent as they waited for entrance. In the middle of them, standing on a wooden box, was Star. He presided like a minister in black, his hands outstretched to his congregation as he enticed them.

"Such wonders you have never seen!" he cried joyously. "Such miracles await you!"

The throng thrilled to each new promise, clamoring excitedly as they handed their money to Star, who took it and placed it in a bag at his waist.

"Come see the Sargasso mermaid," Star called. "Come see Sheba, the half-man–half-woman. Come see all the Tent of Wonders holds."

Listening to him, Joe was tempted to leave. He didn't want to be part of the madness he saw in the eyes of the waiting customers. Their fervor, their eagerness to see the oddities in Star's tent, disturbed him.

He was turning to go when Star, seeing him, called out above the crowd. "Mr. Flanagan!"

Joe faced the man, who was smiling and beckoning. The crowd, not looking at Joe, seemed to part, allowing him passage. When he arrived at Star's pulpit, Star leaned down.

"I knew you would come," he said happily. "Enter and be amazed."

He gestured to the tent flap. Joe moved forward, pushing aside the black curtains and stepping inside. Almost immediately the noise of the crowd seemed to disappear. Although the tent was crowded, an awed hush pervaded the space. People spoke in whispers, an occasional laugh breaking the stillness.

The freaks were scattered throughout the tent, each on an individual platform designed to highlight her or his particular uniqueness. Visitors wended between them, gathering around particular favorites before moving on in a progression that, Joe saw immediately, was carefully designed to push them through to the next tent to make way for those coming behind them.

The first few attractions were only slightly out of the ordinary, beginning with Melody the bearded lady and the tattooed Reverend Upshall. Each was entertaining a sizable crowd, Melody by allowing a child to pull on her beard, and the Reverend Upshall by exhorting his listeners to return to God. Joe passed them quickly, pausing briefly to watch Eleanore and Sally-Mae Kittery display their talents at a small piano on which they performed a duet, their four hands working in unison as they took turns singing verses of "Don't Sit Under the Apple Tree."

Beyond the Siamese twins, things grew more unusual. On a small stage, the shark boy, Ranku, ate live fish from the hands of gawkers who paid an attendant a nickel each for the privilege of putting their fingers near his forbidding teeth. Gasps of amazement erupted each time the boy took another fish and chewed it, displaying the shredded innards before swallowing.

In the space beside him was the promised Sargasso mermaid. She sat in a large tank, her tail beneath the water, and her torso above. Her breasts were exposed, and it was at these as much as her tail that the crowd stared in wonder. She combed her long hair and sang, seemingly unaware of the onlookers. Behind her a painted drop cloth depicted sailors throwing themselves from the deck of a ship into the waves as she looked up at them, smiling.

As if proving the power of the mermaid's song, a young man dashed forward, holding out his arms to embrace her. At the last moment he was pushed away by a sturdy, ruddy-skinned fellow who stood in front of the tank, arms crossed and with bits of cotton stuck into his ears, presumably to make him immune to the siren's song.

Joe had seen mermaids before and knew that their tails were generally rubber and painted scales. Still, the Sargasso mermaid was lovely, and whether she came from the sea or not didn't seem to be a question her guests cared about. Joe left them gazing at her and walked on. Beyond the mermaid was the entrance to the second tent. He ducked through and found himself standing before the famed pretzel man, who was in the process of entwining his legs and arms in an intricate knot.

The second tent housed also a man who consumed fire and glass, a snake woman, whose rough skin and forked tongue were said to be proof of her descendance from the reptiles of the Amazon, a brother and sister whose reputed psychic powers were displayed by having them guess the contents of randomly selected audience members' pockets, and the promised hermaphrodite, Sheba.

It was Sheba who interested Joe the most. Seated on a red velvet couch and smoking a cigarette, Sheba wore a dressing gown of black silk embroidered all over with Oriental designs in silver thread. She appeared in every way a woman, with long dark hair and a beautiful face. When she opened her dressing gown, she revealed a pair of breasts that only further convinced Joe that she was indeed female.

But when she spread her shapely legs, he saw between them a man's parts. The penis was large and unmistakable. Joe watched as Sheba patted it briefly with one red-nailed hand before closing her gown. When Joe looked up, she was gazing intently at a smoke ring she had just blown from between her lips, a small smile playing across her face.

He hurried on into the third and last tent. Smaller than the other two, it held only a handful of exhibits. The mood, too, was different, more subdued. It was as if the wild excitement that suffused the first tents had been used up by the time patrons reached the end of their journey.

The freaks contained in the tent, too, were different. There was a gruesomeness to them that Joe immediately found troubling. The first he encountered was the Haitian zombie he recalled Star mentioning to him at their first visit. A skinny black man with wild hair and wilder eyes, the zombie was restrained with a rope about his neck. The other end was held by a man who addressed the crowd, waving a burning torch he held in his other hand.

"The zombie does as he's commanded by his master," he said. "If I were to tell him to, he would work himself to death or destroy anyone I set him upon."

The zombie wailed, causing the crowd to gasp and fall back. The man yanked on the rope and thrust the torch at him, making the zombie cringe in fear.

"No, Timpa!" he cried. "You will obey me!"

Joe was not interested in seeing more of the zombie. Whether it was theater or not, it upset him. This feeling of disease was not lessened by the next attraction. Cannibal Mary was nothing but a girl, but a girl with a most grisly appearance. Dressed in a blood-spattered dress, she sat in a cage surrounded by bones. From time to time she picked one up and gnawed at it, rubbing the bleeding flesh over her face and lapping at it.

"Mary was born of Christian parents," a barker standing beside the cage told the gaggle of onlookers. "Missionaries. They took her with them to deepest Africa. There they were set upon by cannibals, who killed the parents and forced Mary to partake of their flesh. The act drove her insane, and she became as you now see her."

Joe looked at the girl. She couldn't, he thought, be more than thirteen years old. Was she truly insane? Her mannerisms suggested as much. And the way in which she savaged the bones that were presented to her by her keeper appeared genuine. She tore the meat from each one eagerly.

"We feed her horseflesh," the barker told the crowd. "It does little to quench her desire for human meat, but it sustains her."

Joe couldn't bear to see any more. Nor did he want to see what other perversions were on view in the tent. He wanted to be out in the night air, free from the smell of rotting meat and from the sickness that was stirring in his belly.

He saw the exit and made for it, turning his eyes from whatever else might be waiting to distract him. As he pushed his way through the last of the crowd, however, he heard a voice that made him pause.

"You've never seen anything like her."

It was the hoarseness that was familiar. He turned around, looking for its source, and saw a young man talking to a girl. They were standing in a neglected corner of the tent. The girl wore a blue dress with white polka dots, and her blond hair was neatly curled. When she lifted her face, Joe saw that it was the girl he'd seen before, the one with the bloated face. He saw then that she stood near a poster proclaiming the marvels of Lizzie, the frog girl. The portrait showed her with tongue extended, in the process of devouring a fly.

The young man shook his head. "I don't know," he said. "It's a lot of money."

Lizzie took his hand, and Joe saw the boy cringe a bit. "Too much for seeing the devil's mistress?" Lizzie asked.

The young man hesitated. Joe crept nearer.

"She's beautiful," Lizzie said. "And she can show you things you've never dreamed of."

The boy hesitated another moment, then nodded. Lizzie gave a little croak of delight and led him toward the door. Joe followed, anxious both to have the horrors of the final tent behind him and to see where Lizzie was taking the boy.

As before, she led him down the corridor between the tents and into the area where the performers were housed. And once again she stopped before a tent, where the young man handed over his money.

"She's inside?" he asked.

Lizzie nodded. "Go on in."

The boy, like the one before him, pushed aside the tent's door and stepped in. Lizzie watched him go, then melted into the darkness. Joe waited a moment before once more moving to stand before the tent.

He felt as if he had stepped into his own nightmare. Everything was the same as it had been on that first terrible night, only now he knew for certain to fear whatever it was that sat inside the tent. When the singing began, he had to force himself not to run.

"Hush, little baby, don't say a word . . ."

The fogginess reached out for him, and he fought it. This time he couldn't allow himself to become bewitched. He had to find out what was inside the tent, even if it meant the end of him.

"Mama's gonna buy you a mockingbird . . ."

He grabbed hold of the tent flap, pulled it aside, and entered.

Chapter Seven

The interior of the tent was bathed in candlelight, but still it was dim. Pale yellow light flickered against the black walls, fluttering like moths and throwing shadows that obscured the scene within. Joe felt at first as if he were trying to see underwater. Everything was out of focus, hazy and distorted. Then, too, there was the overwhelming smell of blood. It filled Joe's head, threatening to make him sick.

He shook himself, trying to clear his mind, and looked for the source of the stench. He found it in the form of the young man he'd seen enter minutes earlier. He was stretched across the lap of a beautiful young girl who sat on a chaise. A smile of sweetest happiness was on his face, and rivulets of blood trickled down his neck and fell in fat, red drops to the dirt floor.

The girl was wearing a dress of deepest red. Her hair, too, was the color of flames. It fell down her back in curls and framed her face in graceful tendrils. She regarded Joe with a bemused expression, her eyes unblinking. One hand fell across the young man's chest while the other stroked his hair, like a mother comforting a sick child. Her mouth was stained with his blood.

Unable to comprehend what he was seeing, Joe stood and stared in shock at the grotesque tableau. He couldn't tell whether the boy was dead or merely wounded. The gashes on his neck seemed insignificant, yet the quantity of blood that covered him suggested otherwise.

The boy groaned, his eyes fluttering. Immediately the girl bowed her head to his neck. Joe saw the boy arch his back, shudder, and then lie still. When the girl raised her head, fresh blood dotted her lips and stained the teeth she revealed to Joe. Her eyes had lost all humanity, and in them Joe saw only unending darkness.

"What are you?" he asked, his voice trembling.

The girl cocked her head to one side and smiled. Her tongue darted out, washing the blood from her lips. She let her victim's head fall back, lolling on what seemed to be a neck emptied of all strength. The boy lay like a broken doll across her.

"Hush, little baby, don't say a word . . . ," the girl sang. "Mama's gonna buy you a mockingbird . . ."

Joe clapped his hands to his ears as the haunting voice tugged at his senses. He knew that to listen to the words would mean his death, and he tried to drive them away by singing words of his own.

"Four and twenty blackbirds!" he screamed as he rushed toward the girl. "Baked in a pie!"

He grabbed her by the throat and began to squeeze, determined to destroy her. He knew nothing about what she was, but he knew that she was responsible for bringing death to more than one man, that she would bring more death if he allowed her to go on living. So he squeezed with all his strength.

"The king is in his counting house, counting out his money!" he raged. The ridiculous words of the rhyme fell from his lips in ragged gasps.

"And if that cart and bull turn over, Mama's gonna buy you a dog named Rover . . ."

Somehow the girl was still singing, her voice as calm and wheedling as ever. How was she doing it, with her throat surely crushed? Joe closed his eyes and screamed.

"The queen is in the parlor, eating bread and honey!"

A violent force tore him backward, and he felt his grip on the girl falter. He hit the ground hard, the breath knocked out of him. The girl remained seated, watching him, while strong hands encircled his chest.

"You cannot destroy her," a man's voice whispered in his ear. "She's not human."

Joe struggled with his captor, but the arms were strong, and he knew he was bound. Finally he ceased his thrashing and collapsed against the body behind him.

"And if that dog named Rover won't bark . . ."

Joe convulsed at the sound of the voice in his head, and once again the one holding him tightened his grip.

"Enough! You will not take him!"

The voice paused. Joe looked and saw the girl staring at him. The boy who had been in her lap now lay on the floor, his lifeless face peering into Joe's. The girl seemed to be weighing choices in her mind. She looked from Joe to the man holding him. Then she folded her hands in her lap.

The arms that were keeping Joe still relaxed, and Joe shrugged them off. Turning his head, he saw Derry getting to his feet. Derry looked at him.

"Leave now," he said. "This is over."

Joe jumped up. He pointed to the girl. "Who is she?"

Derry shook his head. "Please," he said, "this doesn't concern you."

Joe pointed at the body on the floor. "And does this not concern me, either?" he demanded.

Derry said nothing, looking at the dead young man for a long moment. Then he looked back at Joe. "She's my sister," he said.

Stunned, Joe stared at Derry in disbelief. "This . . . thing is your sister?" he said. He turned back to the girl, who was watching him coolly, unconcerned.

"She wasn't always like this," said Derry. "He made her this way."

"Who made her?" Joe asked. "Satan himself?" He remembered suddenly the frog girl's words. "The devil's mistress," he said to himself.

"Not the devil," Derry said. "But one of his children. Star."

"Star?" Joe repeated.

At the mention of the name, the girl gave a slight hiss, like a cat warning its intended quarry before a strike. Joe stepped back.

"Don't fear her," said Derry. "As long as I'm here, she will do as I say."

He went and sat beside the girl, who took his hand in hers and held it tightly. Derry looked at her lovingly, then turned to Joe.

"Her name is Emma," he said. "When she was nineteen and I was fourteen, Star brought his show to our town. Our parents took us to the carnival. I begged to be allowed into the Tent of Wonders. Emma didn't want to go. She found the freaks repulsive. But finally I persuaded her. That's where Star saw her and fell in love."

Emma looked away, and for a moment she looked to Joe like any beautiful young woman. But then he saw the blood that still stained her cheek, and he remembered the eagerness with which she had drunk her prey's blood.

"He wanted her," Derry continued. "And he stopped at nothing to have her. Later that night he came to our house and killed our parents while they slept. He drained Emma and left her near death."

"And what about you?" Joe asked. "What did he do to you?"

"Nothing," answered Derry. "He let me live."

"Why would he do that?"

"To make her stay," Derry replied. "He knew Emma would never love him. But she does love me."

Emma looked at her brother, and Derry avoided meeting her gaze.

"As long as I live, she won't leave."

"Why can't you both leave?" asked Joe.

"If we do, he'll find us and kill me," said Derry. "And so we stay together."

Joe looked at the brother and sister, sitting together on the chaise. He found Derry's story unimaginable. Yet he'd seen Emma's handiwork, and he found it impossible to believe that anything with a soul could do what she had done.

"What is he?" he asked finally. "What is she?"

"Vampires," Derry said. "Creatures drained of life but still living. They need the blood of others to stay young."

Joe nodded. "I know what they are," he said. "But they're just stories. Legends."

"No," Derry said. "They're as real as you and I. Star is one. He's lived for a hundred years or more. Look at Emma. She hasn't aged in the six years since he made her what she is."

"Nothing can do that to a human," said Joe stubbornly.

"He can," said Derry. "He can do that and more."

"They're crazed," Joe said. "They kill because their minds are rotted by some sickness. And you cover up their crimes."

"You've heard her voice," Derry said, interrupting him. "She puts her thoughts into yours. She invades your sleep and calls to you. You can't deny that."

Joe started to answer, then stopped. Derry was right. He had heard Emma singing. But that had nothing to do with evil magic; it was simply his mind replaying a moment of shock, allowing it to grow into something more than it was.

"She can't speak," said Derry, before Joe could make his argument. "She's mute."

"But I've heard her," Joe rebutted.

"Yes," Derry said. "You've heard her thoughts, but not her voice. He took that from her when he stole her soul away. He took almost everything she was."

"Then why don't you kill her?" Joe asked.

Derry shook his head. "That wouldn't stop him," he said faintly.

"But it would stop her killing," said Joe. "It would stop the deaths of these innocent young men."

Derry glanced at the body of the boy on the floor, then looked away. "Their deaths are quick and painless," he said. "They go to sleep dreaming of her beauty."

"You make excuses for her," said Joe. "She is not to be pitied; she is to be destroyed."

"Then destroy her," Derry said.

He stood up and moved away from Emma, leaving her alone on the chaise. She looked at him with a bewildered expression.

"Go on," Derry urged Joe. "Destroy her if you will."

Joe looked at the girl. He took a step toward her. Emma turned her gaze on him, and he saw her eyes go dark once more. His body was gripped by an unseen force, and he could move not even his mouth to scream as Emma stood and began to come for him.

"Enough," Derry said, and Emma paused. Joe felt the invisible bonds around him fall, and he collapsed to the floor, gasping for air. Emma returned to her seat, stepping neatly over the corpse she had so recently created.

"Now maybe you understand a little," said Derry. "This is not a parlor trick. It is real."

"You say Star made her," said Joe. "Everything made can be unmade."

Derry came and knelt beside Joe. He took Joe's head in his hands and kissed him. When he pulled away, he looked into Joe's eyes.

"What is one missing man now and again?" Derry asked him. "We send tens of thousands to die in war. What are a handful of others?"

"And what is one dead girl?" Joe countered, flashing a look at Emma.

"Please," said Derry. "I've kept her from harming you. I didn't have to."

"Then why did you?" Joe asked him.

Derry bowed his head. When he looked up again, his eyes were wet with tears. "I thought maybe you would understand," he said. "I saw something in you that is also in me."

Joe closed his eyes. How long had he hidden himself away? How long had he not dared to let himself dream about the things he'd done with Derry, the things he wanted still to do with him? How long had he, like Derry and Emma, been ruled by a dark secret? No, he didn't believe their story. It wasn't possible. But part of him wanted to believe it was true, wanted to believe that Derry was simply doing what he had to for himself and for Emma.

"I know you don't believe everything," said Derry, as if he shared his sister's talent for invading the mind. "But you must believe something or you would have told someone about what you saw."

Joe nodded. It was true. And several times he almost had revealed Derry's actions. Yet he hadn't, and he knew that meant something, even if he couldn't admit the reason to himself.

"Why does she try to seduce me if she knows your feelings?" he asked Derry.

"There is part of her that acts on its own," said Derry. "She does what she's been created to do. She means you no ill will."

Joe looked at the body of the dead boy. "And what about him?" he said. "Did she mean him no ill will either?"

"They're instructed to bring her only those who will likely not be missed," Derry explained.

"Then they know?" said Joe.

"Some of them," Derry told him. "Not all. Many of them are tied to Star as we are."

"Vampires?" asked Joe.

Derry shook his head. "Emma is the only one like him. The others are . . . something else." His voice trailed off, and Joe didn't press him for more. He couldn't imagine a horror worse than the one Derry had already described, and if such a thing existed, he didn't want to know.

Behind them Emma made a noise, a small cry as if she were in pain. Derry looked at her.

"She needs more," he said. "She needs to finish him. If she doesn't, the wildness will overtake her, and then I can promise nothing as to your safety."

Joe glanced at Emma. She was looking at the corpse at her feet with a hunger in her eyes. She looked at Derry, who nodded.

Immediately Emma was on her knees beside the boy, her mouth at his neck. Joe listened as she tore at him, her mouth sucking as she fed on the last of his blood.

"Don't watch," Derry told him, but Joe refused to avert his eyes.

As Emma's mouth did its work, the boy's skin began to wrinkle. Very quickly he aged a span of years, until his flesh shriveled and dried. It fell from him like dust, leaving his bones bare. Even his innards were reduced to nothing, and after a moment Emma was left kneeling over a skeleton. She touched it lovingly before standing and throwing herself once again on the chaise. Her hair hung about her, and her eyes fluttered and closed. Within moments she slept.

"I need to bury him," Derry said.

"What about her?" asked Joe.

"She will sleep for a time," Derry answered. "Later he will come to her."

"Star?" Joe said.

Derry nodded. "Even after all this time he still tries to make her his," he said bitterly. He hesitated, then asked, "Will you help me?"

Joe looked at the sleeping Emma, and at the pile of bones on the floor of the tent. He closed his eyes and remembered Derry's mouth against his. He breathed deeply.

"Yes," he said.

Chapter Eight

Time came and went, and Joe soon lost count of what day it was, or even what month. His nights were spent with his machines, and his days with Derry. He cared about nothing else. Every third night or so, he and Derry would wait in the shadows outside Emma's tent until they were needed to remove the evidence of her latest feeding. Joe had come to see the grisly bundles they dragged away and buried as nothing more than waste, bits and pieces of refuse to be cleared away.

His growing love for Derry allowed him to do this, made it possible for him not to look at the faces of the young men who were led by Lizzie as lambs to the slaughter. Any remorse he felt was washed away later, as he and Derry lay entangled in each other's arms in Joe's trailer. Derry's kisses cleansed his conscience. He was doing what he did for the boy.

They were careful not to let Star see them together, avoiding each other in public and touching only when doors were locked and window shades drawn. Even Lizzie knew nothing of their partnership. Only Emma ever saw them together, and the secret remained locked inside what was left of her mind.

In his daydreams Joe imagined murdering Star. He invented a thousand ways to do it, all of which he knew, from what Derry told him, were impossible. Slowly he'd come to accept the idea that Star and Emma existed in a kind of living death, although the notion repulsed him so greatly that he rarely allowed the thought to linger long in his head. It was too enormous for him to comprehend, too vague and insubstantial. Unlike with his machines, he couldn't point to a failing part and blame it for the actions of the whole. He simply had to believe what he was told, and he was not a man who believed easily.

Derry, though, made it easier. In his kisses Joe found the ability to accept what he couldn't understand, and in their lovemaking, impossibilities no longer mattered. The touch of his fingers was real. Joe could feel, smell, and taste him, and when he emptied himself into Derry, holding him tight and pressing his face to the boy's neck as their bodies shook, he believed everything.

He lost count of how many young men he saw enter Emma's tent. They moved through a dozen towns, saw thousands of faces and immediately forgot them, created a dream world for most, and brought death to a few. The summer rose to fullness and then began to fade out as the days shortened and the night came earlier and stayed longer. Harley's cash box overflowed, and it looked to be the best season of their lives. They talked of wintering in Florida and recovering their spirits under the gaze of a never-ending sun.

Then, on a night in August, everything changed. They were camped outside Jolesville, Ohio. It was their second day of a three-day stay. Emma had fed the previous evening on a traveling preacher who had been enticed by the promise of meeting Satan's whore face-to-face. As he'd died, he'd repeated his favorite Psalm, and Emma had drunk his soul with particular vigor. Joe and Derry had thrown his bones into a nearby river, then made love in the grass beneath the stars.

The next night, after the close of the carnival, Joe was returning to his trailer when he found his way blocked by Star. The man stepped in front of him and stood, both hands on the head of his cane. He looked at Joe for a moment, then smiled thinly.

"I think, Mr. Flanagan, that it is time for us to have another talk."

Before Joe could answer, he found his arm gripped tightly in Star's hand. He gave a jerk, trying to free himself, and Star tightened his grip painfully.

"I think you know that won't work," he said pleasantly. "It is best if you don't try it again."

Star escorted him to the Tent of Wonders. Once inside, he led Joe through the first two tents and into the smaller third tent. There Joe discovered a small group of Star's freaks waiting, including the shark boy, the frog girl Lizzie, the tattooed Reverend Upshall, and Sheba, the hermaphrodite. They were gathered around a chair to which was tied a young man whose mouth was stuffed with a rag and whose eyes darted wildly from place to place, like an animal seeking escape. Star walked over to the chair and placed his hand on the boy's shoulder.

"It has come to my attention that you have involved yourself in my affairs," Star said, addressing Joe.

Joe said nothing. He hoped Star knew nothing and was just testing him. Even if he did know the truth, Joe wasn't going to give him any confirmation of the fact.

"You needn't answer," said Star. "I assure you that I do know everything. Emma has become quite adept at concealing her thoughts from me, but even she has her weaknesses."

Joe immediately thought of Derry. Had Star done something to him? His heart began to pound as he thought that perhaps he'd lost his lover.

"Mr. Stroud is quite well, I assure you," Star continued. "He does not know about our little visit. Nor will you tell him. In fact, you will do nothing further with him at all."

"Why not?" Joe asked, finally getting his voice.

"Why not?" Star repeated in a mocking tone. "Because I have asked you not to."

"And if I refuse?" demanded Joe.

Star smiled broadly. "That is why we're here," he said. He indicated the young man in the chair. "I would like you to meet Mr. Samuel Brown."

At the mention of his name, the young man began to squirm. Star patted his head. "I'm afraid Mr. Brown is a trifle stagestruck," he said.

The assembled freaks laughed at the joke, and Star laughed with them. Joe looked from one distorted face to another, wondering how they could tolerate such a monster. The sight of such ugliness rejoicing in the fear of the boy tied to the chair sickened him.

"Mr. Brown came to our Tent of Wonders earlier this evening," Star said when the laughter died away. "He showed quite an interest in our little family. Apparently he has no family of his own. Isn't that right, Mr. Brown?"

Star leaned down and peered into the face of the terrified captive. Samuel shook his head violently.

"I thought not," said Star, nodding. "His parents were killed in an auto accident," he told Joe. "It's really quite tragic."

He walked around behind the boy and placed his hands on Samuel's shoulders, looking over his head at Joe.

"He would make a lovely meal for Emma, wouldn't he?" he asked.

Joe remained silent. Star's game was wearing on him, and if it weren't for the presence of the freaks, he might have considered risking an attack on the vile man. But outnumbered as he was, he chose to let events play out as they would. He knew that whatever else happened, things would go badly for Samuel Brown; he could do nothing for the boy.

"Mr. Stroud has told you something about who I am," Star continued when Joe refused to answer him. "But he has not told you everything. I am not, as he suggests, simply a crude angel of death. No, I am much more than that." He held up his hands and indicated the freaks around him. "I am a transformer of souls."

Joe didn't understand. What was Star trying to say? He risked an insult. "You collect freaks," he said. "Nothing more."

Star wagged a finger at him. "Now, now," he said. "You do all of us an injustice. I do not collect. I make."

Joe's confusion showed on his face, and Star laughed at him. "You still don't understand. Very well, I will show you."

Moving more quickly than Joe thought possible, Star bent his head to Samuel's neck. The boy tensed, and his eyes widened. He strained against his bindings and failed. Star's fingers gripped the boy's leg tightly.

When after a minute Star lifted his head, his lips were stained crimson. Two small punctures appeared on Samuel's neck, with only tiny smears of blood to indicate what had been drawn out of him. Star wiped his lips daintily with his finger.

"You see, he is not dead," said Star.

Joe looked at the boy's face. His terror had settled into a kind of shock, his eyes glazed over but still seeing. His chest rose and fell raggedly.

"Draining a body of life is a crude operation," Star said. "Even the youngest of us can do it easily. But there are those of us who possess a far greater talent."

Samuel Brown began to convulse. His eyes rolled up into his head, his body twitched violently, and his neck snapped to the side. Star clapped his hands.

"And so it begins," he said.

"What are you doing to him?" Joe asked.

Star indicated the creatures standing around him. "Some of us become what we are naturally," he said. "Others of us must be made."

Sheba laughed, startling Joe. Beside her, Ranku, the shark boy, regarded Joe with his black eyes, his razor teeth glinting wetly. Star nodded at Samuel. "Untie him," he ordered.

The Reverend Upshall stepped forward and, with a knife he produced from his pocket, severed the ropes holding the boy to the chair. Samuel fell to the ground, where he writhed in the dirt.

"We all have inside us another self," Star said, ignoring the young man at his feet. "Most of us keep that self hidden forever, taking it with us to our graves. But a lucky few are reborn into this world in a new guise. For those I choose, I provide this entry."

Star glanced down at Samuel Brown. Joe followed his gaze. The boy was changing. His skin had turned an ashen color and was becoming leathery, and his fingers were shriveling, drawing in on themselves and becoming gnarled claws. His ears, too, were changing, elongating. He was curled in a ball, crying softly.

"He's coming back," said the Reverend Upshall, who looked down at the boy along with the other freaks.

Samuel threw back his head. His face had been transformed, the human features pinched and remolded into something that filled Joe with revulsion. His eyes were round and impossibly large, his mouth reduced to a small hole filled with needles. His nose had disappeared into his skull, leaving only a mangled remnant of the original.

"Very interesting," Star said calmly as the boy clawed at his new face with his tiny, crippled paws.

Samuel continued to change. His shirt ripped, falling away from him and revealing arms grown thin as rails. From them hung flaps of skin like impotent wings. His torso, too, was now misformed, sunken and sheathed in more thickened skin. Samuel opened his mouth and let out a series of squeals.

"What have you done?" Joe said. He wanted to run, to leave Star and what had become of Samuel Brown behind. But something compelled him to stay, to look at the boy who had now become something else, something not of the earth.

"I've made him what he is," Star said. "I've helped him to cast off his human costume and reveal his true self." He knelt beside Samuel, who was looking around confusedly, as if he'd just woken from sleep. "Welcome home, my little one," Star said.

"He's some kind of bat," said Lizzie, croaking gleefully as she peered over Star's shoulder at Samuel.

"Indeed he is," said Star. "Thank you, Lizzie. The bat. Recovered, I think, from the caves of some remote place and brought into the light for the first time by my good graces. I think that will do nicely."

Star looked up at Joe. "You see now what magic I am capable of."

"That's not magic," Joe told him. "What you do is evil."

"Call it what you will," Star replied. "Would you care to find out what lives inside you, Mr. Flanagan?"

Joe looked at Samuel, now a bat creature, and shuddered. Did the boy know what had happened? Did he remember who he was? Joe looked at the other freaks, some of whom stared back at him, and some of whom looked at the latest addition to their family. How many of them had been created from the poison that coursed through Star? Who had they been, and what price had they paid for being transformed?

"I wonder," said Star, standing up and walking toward Joe. "I imagine something fascinating lies within you. Shall we find out what it is?"

As Star drew closer, Joe backed away, his heart beating wildly as panic bloomed in his mind. Did Star intend to do to him what he'd just done to Samuel Brown? He couldn't bear it.

Star closed his eyes and sniffed the air. "There is so much hidden inside you, Joe," he said softly. "So much I could bring out. Would you like that?"

Joe shook his head. "I'd rather die," he said.

Star opened his eyes. "I'm afraid that would be too simple," he said. "But perhaps we can strike a bargain."

"What do you want?" said Joe.

"Your promise to stay away from Derry," Star answered.

"I don't understand why," said Joe.

"Because it suits my purposes," Star snapped.

"And if I don't agree?" Joe asked, mustering the last traces of defiance within him. "Are you going to turn me into one of these . . . things?"

"No," said Star. "I will turn Mr. Stroud instead."

Joe's blood ran cold. "Emma would leave you," he said, remembering what Derry had told him.

"Emma will never leave me," Star snarled. "And if she somehow managed to, I would find another to replace her. But you would live the rest of your life knowing that you were responsible for the death of what the boy was. Could you live with that, Mr. Flanagan? Could you see the one you love turned into something like what you see behind me?"

Joe looked beyond Star, where Samuel Brown was crawling to his knees. He was staring at what were once his hands, and Joe saw on his face a dawning realization that he was looking at himself. In a moment, Joe knew, he would understand that he was not in the midst of some nightmare that would end with the rising of the sun, but changed forever into something hideous.

He couldn't let that happen to Derry. He knew that without question. He had to accept Star's bargain, even if it meant tearing his heart in two.

"I'll stay away from him," he said flatly. "He's yours."

Star laughed. "He always was," he said.

Chapter Nine

He packed hurriedly. He had little, so it took him only a few minutes. He would be gone before anyone awoke. He would leave Harley a note. Not an explanation or an excuse, just a good-bye. It would come as a surprise, he knew. Harley would be angry, at least until he washed away his resentment with a bottle and a girl. Then he would find someone else to care for the machines, one of the men who apprenticed under Joe. None of them were ready; none of them had Joe's all-encompassing love for the mechanical, but they would allow the carnival to continue.

He took his one bag and left the trailer, closing the door for the last time. The world was bathed in moonlight, iced with the pale silver of the hours between midnight and dawn. Joe made his way toward the truck that would take him away from the carnival forever. He still had no idea where he would go, but that didn't matter. He would find a new place to call home, a new life to replace the one he was giving up to Star. All that mattered now was that Derry was safe.

He couldn't say good-bye. Even if he didn't fear what Star would do should he find out, he couldn't bring himself to face Derry. It was cowardly, he knew, but he didn't trust his heart. The boy was the first man he'd allowed himself to love, and Joe knew that should Derry ask him, he might find it impossible to leave. Then he would bring destruction on them both. At least this way Derry would live.

Passing through the sleeping attractions, he came to the carousel. The moon's light glinted off the golden paint of the horses' bridles, turned the mermaids' skin to alabaster. Joe paused, struck as always by the ride's beauty. It was, besides Derry, the one thing he would miss.

He walked to the carousel and stepped up onto the circular platform. His hands touched the wooden head of a dog, its tongue extended in glee. How many times had he assembled the carousel and taken it down again? He couldn't count. He knew each of the pieces by heart, could probably put them together in his sleep if need be.

He climbed astride a black horse and sat, his hands clasped around the pole that extended from the horse's back. He closed his eyes and played in his head the familiar music that accompanied the turning of the wheels beneath him. The tune came easily, and he lost himself in it as he imagined the horse carrying him up into the sky.

"Hush little baby, don't say a word . . ."

The words cut through the music of the carousel. Joe opened his eyes. Emma stood not a dozen feet from him. Her hair fell around her shoulders, and her skin was white as milk. Her mouth was closed, but still Joe heard words coming from her throat.

"And if that dog named Rover won't bark, Mama's gonna buy you a horse and cart . . ."

Joe turned his head, looking for Star. If Emma had left her tent, surely he would be with her, or at least close behind.

"He's not here."

Joe felt the words in his mind.

"I came alone. He sleeps."

He looked at Emma. "What do you want?" he asked out loud.

"Stay," Emma answered. "For Derry. He loves you."

Joe shook his head. "You know I can't," he told her. "Star will kill him."

"There is a way."

Joe waited for her to continue. Did she really know of a way to kill Star? His heartbeat quickened, although he dared not believe her.

"Star can be destroyed," she said.

"How?" asked Joe.

"Become like him," Emma replied. "Like me."

Joe felt as if she'd struck him. Anger roiled inside him, mixed with fear and loathing at the thought of what she had suggested.

"He can only be undone by one of his own kind," Emma said. Her voice in his head sounded desperate.

"Then why don't you do it yourself?" Joe said.

"I can't," came Emma's answer. "Alone I am not strong enough. But together we could do it. Together we could bring an end to him."

Joe shook his head. What she was asking was impossible. He couldn't allow himself to become what she and Star were.

"I'm not asking for myself," Emma told him, cutting through his thoughts. "Do it for Derry."

He wished he could block her out, keep her from toying with his mind. His thoughts were tangled up in her words, and he felt exposed. Was Emma telling him the truth? Could Star really be destroyed? He had no reason to trust her. After all, she had been trying to entice him into her embrace from the beginning—would likely have killed him already had Derry not stopped her. Who knew how much of her mind had been destroyed by Star's transformation, how much of her was controlled by him?

"He will change Derry by force. When you are gone, he will change him. To spite me for not loving him."

Joe looked into her face and saw there hurt and fear. Perhaps, he thought, she was telling him the truth.

"Then we will all leave," he said.

Emma shook her head. "Don't you think we have tried that?" she said. "He will find us and make it worse for us. There is only this way."

He didn't want to believe her, but he did. What she said rang true. But what sacrifice would it mean for him if he agreed to help her destroy Star?

"I would become a blood drinker?" he asked simply.

Emma hesitated before answering him. "Yes," she said when she spoke. "It is how it must be done."

"And then we would be able to kill Star?"

For the first time Emma avoided his gaze. "I believe so, yes."

"You don't know?"

"Nothing is certain," Emma answered. "Nothing except Star's hatred for my brother and his fear of you. There has to be some reason for this fear. I believe he sees in you someone who could be his match. Otherwise he would have tried to kill you already. He fears what you might become."

Joe's mind reeled, emotions and questions and fears swirling together in a storm that made it impossible for him to think clearly. Could he do what Emma was asking of him? Could he damn himself to a life lived as hers was? It was unthinkable. Yet if he said no, what might the consequences be for them all?

Suddenly he imagined Derry, instead of Emma, standing before him. If Derry asked him to do such a thing, would he hesitate? If Derry asked him for his soul, would he give it up? Thinking on these questions, he chose.

"What do I do?" he asked Emma.

She stepped closer, coming to stand beside the horse.

"I must feed from you," she said. "You will sleep. And when you awake, you will be changed. Are you ready?"

Joe nodded. Emma reached up a hand and placed it behind his neck. She drew him toward her. Joe closed his eyes and tightened his grip on the pole. It was now his only connection to the real world. He felt Emma's breath against his skin, then a sharp slice of pain as her teeth entered him.

Immediately he was plunged into dreams. It was as if he were falling. His body was weightless, and he drifted through the air like a leaf tumbling from a tree. All about him beings of incredible beauty sang, reaching out their hands and calling to him. The words of their song were impossible to make out, melting away before he could comprehend them.

Down and down he went, through an endless sky filled with stars. Then he realized that he was growing cold. The breezes that surrounded him were no longer warm but chilled his skin. He shivered, longing for the comfort of a fire. Above him he saw a far-off sun, growing dimmer and dimmer as he fell away from its light. He reached for it but was snatched away by unseen hands.

The beings around him, too, had changed. Their beauty had been replaced by faces hidden in shadow. From time to time he caught a glimpse of a twisted visage peering out at him from the darkness. And always there were the voices, no longer soothing but mocking. They laughed as he continued his descent, filling his ears with cruel cackling that he couldn't block out.

Then something inside him was torn asunder. His chest heaved, and it felt as if something were being pulled from within him. He felt his heart explode, and pain seared his thoughts. He opened his mouth to scream and was met with silence, the sound strangled in his throat as the taste of blood filled his mouth. It seemed as if every atom that made up his body was being wrenched away, eaten by the blackness and the cold in which he was sinking.

Again his chest was racked with pain, and this time a tiny light, like the pale glimmer of a firefly, flew up from inside him and exited his tormented lips. He watched helplessly as it soared up and away from him, racing for the light and leaving him to whatever awaited him when his fall came to an end. He saw pale, withered hands reaching out to trap it in their grasp, but the light evaded them and continued its ascent.

When it was gone, he lost all hope. He knew that whatever soul he possessed had fled him. He was alone. He closed his eyes and surrendered to his fall. Within moments he was lost in total blackness.

When he again opened his eyes, he was still seated on the black horse. Emma stood beside him, looking into his face. When she saw him gazing at her, she gave him a smile that was both welcoming and pitying.

"You survived," she said.

Joe shook his head to clear away the dizziness that buzzed in his mind like a bee. "Did you think I wouldn't?" he asked.

Emma steadied him as he slid sideways on the horse. "Keep hold," she said. "It will take some moments to get used to the feeling."

Joe did as she said. "I feel light," he told her.

Emma nodded. "You are no longer human," she said. "The lightness will pass as your body completes the change."

Joe looked at his hands, felt himself all over. Except for the two small wounds he felt in his neck, he seemed the same.

"How do you know it worked?" he asked Emma.

"I saw your soul depart you," she answered.

Joe recalled the light in his dream. Was it true that he was now without a soul? He laughed at the thought. Had he ever really had one?

"Already you despise your former humanity," said Emma. "You feel the power of immortality."

Joe laughed again. He felt nothing but the dizziness. Was this what it meant to be immortal? It seemed nothing, a trifle. Why, he wondered, had he been so afraid of the notion?

"There will be pain," said Emma. "Later, there will be pain. You will need to feed. But not now. Now you must hide."

"Hide from what?" said Joe. "I feel as if nothing could harm me."

"You are vulnerable," said Emma. "Until the transformation is completed, you cannot protect yourself. Come with me."

She helped Joe get down from the horse. His first steps sent him stumbling, but he quickly righted himself. Emma took his arm and held him as he stepped off the carousel platform and onto the ground.

The world seemed brighter, the darkness only a faint twilight. Joe could make out everything as if it were daylight. The calling of the night birds sounded to him like the screams of children, and even the wind that ruffled the flags atop the tents was like a roaring gale. When he took a step, the grass beneath his feet bent like trees felled by an ax. Joe put his hands to his ears to quiet the noise.

"Everything is alive," he told Emma.

"Because you see the world through the eyes of death," she said matter-of-factly.

Joe looked up at her, pain twisting his features into a grimace. Emma read the question in his eyes.

"Yes, you died," she said. "But my gift brought you back."

"I think I would prefer death," said Joe as a new wave of pain coursed through him.

"Think of Derry," Emma said. "It will help."

Joe tried. He pictured Derry's face, imagined kissing his mouth. He had done this for the boy, he told himself, given up his soul in order to save him. Now he looked to that knowledge for healing. But he found nothing but greater pain.

Emma aided him as he staggered through the encampment. He let her lead him, not knowing where they might be going. All around him the brightness that suffused the world dazzled him. He prayed that it would end. But who, he asked himself, would hear his entreaties? To whom did the dead pray?

They left the carnival behind and walked through the surrounding fields. Joe slowly grew accustomed to the light, but even the twinkling of the stars was enough to blind him if he looked up. When finally they came to a railway car sitting on rusted tracks, he gratefully climbed into the open door and collapsed. Emma climbed in beside him and helped him into a corner, where the shadows wrapped around him like a comforting blanket.

"How long will this last?" Joe asked.

"Just a few hours," Emma said, taking his hand and holding it. "Then you will want to feed."

Joe couldn't think about that. "Feed," she called it. He called it killing. The idea that he would soon need to take the blood of a living thing was almost more than he could bear. He pushed it from his mind.

"And Star?" he asked.

"I must return to him," Emma told him. "When you are strong again, we will make our plan."

"Will you tell Derry?"

Emma squeezed his hand. "I will tell him that you love him."

"I'll tell him myself," said Joe, smiling despite the throbbing pain in his head. "When I see him."

"I will visit you later, when I can," Emma replied. She released his hand. "Stay here until I return."

Joe nodded. He was tired. He wanted to rest. Already he felt himself slipping into unconsciousness. Through closed eyes he felt Emma move away from him, leaving him alone. He would sleep, he thought. Yes, he would sleep. And if he was lucky, he would not dream.

Chapter Ten

He awoke screaming.

Pain clawed at his belly, and his throat was on fire. His first thought was that he wanted water. But as his mind cleared, he understood that it was life he wanted—warm, wet life to slake the burning within him. It demanded a sacrifice, and it would not be satisfied with anything less.

It was day. Joe saw light spilling from beneath the closed door of the train car. The car was hot as an oven, warmed to almost unbearable temperatures by the heat of the sun. Something about the light frightened him, made him recoil instinctively. He drew himself deeper into the shadows of the corner, where the cool blackness soothed him.

"It will take time to get used to being in the light again."

For the first time Joe noticed Emma. She was sitting on an overturned crate, watching him closely. Her thought-speak filled his mind.

"I'm so thirsty," he told her.

Emma stood, and Joe saw that lying on the floor beside her was a child. It was a girl. She seemed to be asleep. Joe looked at her, a hunger growing inside him. He could feel the beat of her heart from a dozen feet away, smell the blood that ran in her veins. He knew what she had been brought here for.

"I can't," he said to Emma. "She's a child."

"A child with nothing to live for," Emma replied coolly. "A child who is beaten every day of her life and who prays for death."

Joe shook his head. "No," he said.

"You must feed," said Emma. "And soon, or you will be overcome by madness."

Joe looked at the girl. Even in sleep she seemed troubled, her eyes moving rapidly beneath the lids and her limbs twitching. He knew she dreamed badly, chased by something that meant her worse harm than he might do to her.

He forced himself to crawl to her. Kneeling beside her, he saw that her skin was covered in blue and purple roses, the marks of cruel hands. Her dress was thin and torn, her nails ragged and dirty. She had not been loved.

"Take her," Emma instructed.

Joe put his arms beneath the sleeping child and lifted her. She weighed nothing, filling his arms like feathers. He cradled her to his chest and looked into her face. His fingers stroked her short blond hair.

Holding one thin wrist in his hand, he raised it to his mouth. The skin was mottled with dirt and bruises. He kissed it gently, then felt the skin break beneath his teeth. Blood splashed over his tongue, and he drank eagerly despite himself.

For a moment the girl stirred, her dreams interrupted, and he feared she would open her eyes and look at him. But quickly her expression became calm. Her breathing deepened, and the worry in her face began to fade, replaced by something close to peace. The blood flowing into Joe's mouth slowed as the fierceness in the girl's heart ebbed away.

"You do her a great favor," said Emma.

Joe drank deeply. The blood revived him, and with each passing minute he felt himself growing stronger. When finally the girl was dead, he released her wrist and gently laid her on the floor. He tried to feel remorse for his actions but found that he instead felt only relief. The pain inside him was diminished, and his body radiated power and vitality.

"The worst is over," said Emma. "Now, with each new feeding, you will become stronger."

"And what if we don't feed?" asked Joe.

"We die," Emma told him. "But it is a death that takes years. Hundreds, perhaps thousands. Little by little, everything that is still human about us is torn away, leaving only decay."

"What else can kill us?"

"Some say fire," Emma replied. "Some say water. I have proof of neither. Star has told me almost nothing. He knows I would use it against him."

"But you said that together we could destroy him," said Joe.

Emma nodded. "Yes. I believe there is a way. We must drain him."

"And what good will draining him do when he has no life to lose?" Joe demanded.

"It will weaken him," said Emma. "And when he is weakened, we will imprison him. Without food he will slowly wither away."

"After a thousand years!" Joe exclaimed.

"Perhaps," Emma agreed. "And until then we will watch over him."

Suddenly the full meaning of what he had agreed to came to Joe. He sank to the floor, looking up at Emma. Was he really to spend a thousand years or more as the watchman for Star? Would he see many lifetimes come and go?

"It has to be done," said Emma. "There is no other way."

Joe fought the rage that was threatening to consume him. He felt tricked, but he knew he had chosen freely. If Emma had failed to tell him all of her plan, it was also his own fault for not asking.

"And how will we drain him?" he said quietly.

"I will give him the one thing he has always asked of me," Emma answered. "I will let him lie with me tonight. Afterward, when he is spent, we will take him."

Joe looked at her. Her face was cold, and he knew she was thinking of what she would be giving up to bring about Star's end. He was not, he saw, the only one who was to sacrifice something dear to him. They had made a bargain, the two of them, and both were paying dearly for it.

"Come to my tent tonight," Emma said. "After midnight. When you hear me singing, it will be time."

She left him with his thoughts and with the corpse of the little girl.

The girl he dragged into the corner farthest from him, where he couldn't see her. But still he smelled her, smelled the sweet scent of death that surrounded her like a flower. Soon, he knew, the smell would be replaced by the stench of rot. But for the moment it intoxicated him, and he spent the hours until nightfall breathing it in and familiarizing himself with its potent effect.

When finally darkness descended, he opened the door to his hiding place and jumped to the ground. He was no longer unsteady on his feet, and the brightness of the night before was now only a glimmer that shone over everything. Beyond the field he saw the lights of the carnival and headed for them.

It did not feel like returning home. The tents, the attractions, the trailers that had been his home for so many years—all of them felt changed. But he knew it was he who was changed, and that he was for the first time seeing the world as it would look to him for the rest of his days.

"Joe!"

The voice startled him. It was Harley, emerging from his trailer. He was drunk. Joe could smell it in his blood. He felt a longing begin to stir in him, and he willed it away. Harley approached him.

"Where the hell have you been?" he asked Joe. "We've been looking for you all day."

"I wasn't feeling so good," said Joe.

Harley eyed him quizzically. "You weren't in your trailer."

"No," Joe said, fumbling for an explanation. "I was . . ."

"You dog," Harley said, breaking into a grin. "You found yourself a girl, didn't you?"

"What?" Joe said. "No. I mean . . ."

"You did," said Harley. He laughed. "I knew you wasn't queer after all. Goddamn. Sylvie's cards were right."

Joe had forgotten all about Sylvie and her cards. Now that Harley had reminded him, he realized that they had been correct. He had met his Queen of Cups and been forced to make a terrible choice. And now he was soon to face the devil.

"Hell, I won't begrudge you a twenty-four-hour screw," Harley said. "But next time let me know. We thought you'd run off and died or something. I hope she was worth it."

"She was," said Joe. "And next time I'll be sure and let you know. Maybe I'll even share."

Harley walked away, still laughing to himself. Joe immediately put him out of his mind and continued on his path to Emma's tent. When he reached it, he paused outside, listening. Rough grunts reached his ears, the sounds of flesh against flesh. He knew Star was taking pleasure not only in Emma's body but in at last conquering her will.

Emma herself was silent, no thoughts flowing from her mind. She had closed it off, Joe thought, sealed herself in some protective circle where Star's lust couldn't touch her. What was it like for her? he wondered, to have those hands caressing her, those lips pressed against hers. What must it feel like to be invaded by him in such a way? His hatred for Star grew, and he came near to entering the tent, stopping himself just as he heard Star cry out, not in joy but in triumph.

Then all was silent. There were faint rustlings from within the tent, and then Emma's voice came softly out of the darkness.

"Hush, little baby, don't say a word . . ."

Joe wasted no more time. Slipping into the tent, he stood looking down on Emma and Star. Emma was naked on her chaise, her body covered by Star, who lay unclothed between her legs, with his head on her breast. His bare skin shone with sweat, his black hair plastered against his neck.

"We must do it quickly," Emma said. "While he still sleeps."

Joe knelt beside the chaise and looked into Star's face. Then, without pause, he bent and sank his teeth into the flesh of his neck.

Immediately Star awoke. He tried to push himself up and away from Joe's bite, but Emma, too, had begun to feed, her mouth tearing at Star's wrist. Pinned between them, Star could do little more than twist like an insect pierced by a pin. His mouth opened in a hiss, and his free hand tore at Joe, scratching wildly.

Joe held on, feeling the strength in Star begin to waver. The taste of Star's blood sickened him, as if it were diseased. Time and again his stomach tried to rid itself of the poison, but Joe continued to feed. Finally, he sensed that the fight had gone from Star, and he risked releasing him.

What he saw made him fall back in terror. Star had been drained not only of blood but of substance. Lying against Emma was something that resembled a mummy more than a man, with browned skin and twiglike limbs. Joe turned and spit up the contents of his stomach. Star's blood seeped into the ground, staining it black.

Emma pushed Star away from her and grabbed something to cover herself with. Star was still, no movement from his body. For a moment Joe thought that they may have succeeded in bringing his existence to an end. Then the eyes opened and fixed themselves on Joe. The shriveled mouth opened, and Star spoke.

"It is not finished."

"We must secure him," Emma told Joe.

"Where?"

"We will lock him inside a trunk for tonight," Emma said. "But tomorrow you will have to build him a prison, a casket with locks that cannot be undone by anyone but us."

She had grabbed hold of Star's feet. Joe helped her, taking the creature's shoulders. Between Star's legs, his sex had withered to nothing. Joe couldn't believe the body held any more power, yet he had seen too much not to believe Emma.

Together they put Star into a wooden trunk that until then had housed Emma's dresses. The body folded up like a piece of paper, the legs tucking up like a child's as Joe put what remained of the vampire into its prison. With the lid shut, Emma produced a padlock and secured it.

"Are you sure this will hold him?" Joe asked.

"For a time," answered Emma. "Enough time for you to go to Derry. If he stirs, I will summon you."

Joe nodded. Giving the trunk a final look, he left Emma's tent and ran through the fairgrounds to Derry's trailer. Already in his head he was planning the box he would build to hold Star. Its doors would be sealed with steel bars and intricate locks, the designs of which he sketched in his head. It would be his greatest machine ever, a machine built to house the creature for as long as it took him to return to the earth.

But first there was Derry. Joe reached the boy's trailer and opened the door. Inside, Derry was stretched across his bed. A white sheet covered his lower body, and one arm rested across the expanse of his stomach. The other was thrown over his head.

Joe stood for a long time, watching him sleep. Then, slowly, he removed his clothes and dropped them to the floor. When he was naked, he went to the bed and, lifting the sheet, slid in beside Derry. His sleep disturbed, Derry stirred. Rubbing his eyes, he peered at Joe sleepily.

"I thought you'd gone," he said.

Joe shook his head. "I could never leave you," he said. He kissed Derry gently.

Derry kissed him back. Then he turned and pressed his back against Joe. Joe put an arm around him and drew him in closer. His face pressed against Derry's neck. He closed his eyes and imagined staying that way forever, sleeping every night with Derry in his arms.

But Derry wouldn't live forever. He would grow older and someday would die, while Emma and Joe continued. Then Star would have succeeded in separating them, and Joe would have ages to spend grieving his loss.

He couldn't allow that. He'd given up too much to keep Derry, to lose it all to something as insignificant as death. No, he would not allow it.

Cradling Derry in his arms, he kissed his neck.

"Hush, little baby," he sang softly. "Don't say a word."

The Vampire Stone

Timothy Ridge

Prologue

Paris, 1583

"Just take the boy and leave, Favreau," Margaret said, turning toward the rumpled bed.

Favreau had his arm slung over the boy's right shoulder and bent around the boy's neck. The boy looked to be in his late teens; his dark eyes were moist with tears and filled with fright. He looked at Margaret as if she had betrayed him. He could not struggle in Favreau's grasp; he was overpowered physically and mentally.

Favreau was tall but solidly built. His movements were elegant and light. He seemed to shimmer in the air, as if he were only a dream briefly visiting the earth. His long black hair was pulled back in a ponytail, held in place by a simple red silk ribbon. His skin seemed like parchment, but he looked ageless.

"What are you so worried about, *my dear*?" he said, drawing out the last bit in a mocking tone.

"If Henri, *my husband*, comes in and finds the two of you here, I'm finished."

"Catherine was not nearly so timid," he taunted, speaking of Margaret's mother. "She would have told your father to find a mistress and call it even."

Margaret screamed and grabbed for the object closest at hand. The ivory comb whirred through the air and fell at Favreau's feet as if it had hit an invisible wall. Favreau leaped toward her, dragging the boy behind him by the neck. He pushed Margaret onto the bed and forced his free hand under her jaw. He snapped her head back and exposed the softest part of her neck. He could see the artery pulsing beneath her delicate skin. She breathed heavily, terrified to be in Favreau's grasp. He was suddenly monstrous; his greenish eyes flashed. His lips became pink and parted slightly. He leaned down. Margaret could feel his cool breath on her neck. She whimpered. He heard footsteps approaching along the stone hallway floor, toward the chamber door. He raised his lips to Margaret's ear.

"I won't forget your insolence, but someone is coming and I can't be seen here."

Favreau released Margaret as if she were a rag doll. She turned over and pressed her face into the pillow. She was crying. Favreau pushed the boy against the wall by the open window. A gentle breeze fanned the velvet drapery inward. Favreau reached into his coat pocket and removed a small object.

"*Ma chere,*" he called lasciviously to Margaret, "a trinket for a trinket."

Favreau tossed a small wooden box onto the bed beside Margaret. It was a gift, in exchange for the boy, who had been one of her many lovers. He had been her favorite lover, in fact, the bastard son of a German lord, born to the now-ostracized Comtesse Rocerres. As Margaret looked at the box, which had been carved on the top with the letter "V" surrounded by vines, the chamber door swung open with a violent crash against the wall.

"Who was in here?" demanded Henri, Margaret de Valois' husband and king of France. He looked around the room, now empty save for Margaret.

"No one," she protested.

"Liar!" he screamed, and rushed toward her, snatching the box from the bed, then shaking it in her face. "It was that bastard again. I heard voices."

Henri dropped the box back onto the bed in disgust. He spit on Margaret as she sat up to face him. Favreau's defaming words stuck in her head; he had accused her of being weak. She stood from the bed, taking the box in her hand. She felt a sudden rush of power move through her body. Before she knew what she was doing, she slammed the box on the side of Henri's face. He fell backward, catching himself on the edge of the vanity by the door.

"You must leave Paris at once. Be a whore in some other town."

"You will regret this, Henri. I will prevail."

Favreau now had the boy back in his chambers on the other side of Paris. He held the boy at arm's length and looked at him, admiring his soft beauty. He wanted the moment to last: he did not want to rush this one. He did not want simply to kill him and leave him for dead. For the gendarmes to find him and wonder about the small wounds in his neck. He wanted to keep this boy with the auburn hair forever, as if he were a porcelain figure. He stroked the boy's head.

"Don't be afraid, Monsieur Rocerres. It will be a little painful at first, but you'll get used to it. Eventually, you'll feel nothing at all, except fully and completely alive."

Tears gushed from the boy's eyes and ran down his face. Favreau lowered his head as he pulled the cotton shirt down over the soft shoulder. He pulled the shirt quickly and effortlessly away from the boy's body, revealing a firm torso that quivered at Favreau's slightest touch.

"Please," the boy begged.

Favreau looked into the boy's eyes again and put his lips to Rocerres' moist cheek. He felt the sting of salt. He hungered violently. He ran his hand down Rocerres' back, feeling every muscle tighten as he followed the path of the spine. Then, the unexpected.

Rocerres suddenly pushed against Favreau with all his might. Favreau reeled backward, arms flailing, but never completely losing balance. He floated above the floor for a second. Rocerres made a dash for the window and leaped through it, breaking the glass as he went down, landing just feet below the window. The boy took off down the cobblestone street.

Favreau moved to the smashed window and looked out, smiling. He was now utterly infatuated with the boy. He needed him and was even more aroused by the fact that he fought back. Even a vampire loved a challenge. He reached out to a shard of glass that stuck out of the side of the window frame. It was dripping with Rocerres' blood. Favreau covered the tip of his finger with the blood and placed the finger in his mouth. He was wild. He bit down on his own finger and groaned. He closed his eyes and concentrated on the boy. Flashes of the boy's life filled his vision. He saw him doubled over in ecstasy with men and women of the court. He had been the lover of many, not just Margaret. The longer Favreau concentrated, the closer he came to Rocerres' present, until he could see where the boy was at this moment.

In the next arrondisement, Rocerres ducked down in an alleyway behind a tavern. He was doubled over, breathless. He pulled pieces of glass from his shoulder and arm. He winced as a large piece came free from his right side. He thought he was going to pass out from the pain, and from the stench of human and animal offal decomposing in the gutters.

Then he froze in absolute terror. A voice spoke inside his head. It was Favreau.

"My precious, precocious boy. Come back to me, my love. Let me show you a magnificent life."

Rocerres began to sob. He knew at that moment that he was doomed, and as every second passed, he felt himself giving in. The decision was no longer his own.

He walked out of the alley and into the dark, cloudless Paris night and headed east toward Favreau's manor.

Chapter One

The naked man in the daguerreotype appeared stiff and uncomfortable. His head faced slightly away from the camera. His right arm and right leg were extended. His lazy, uncircumcised cock hung straight down. His body was toned but not muscular, typical of mid-1800s men. The lighting made his skin look like silk: inviting and smooth. I was nearly in a horny rage from staring at this old collection of naked men. I turned the plate over and stuck a small sticker with a number on the back, then wrote the number in my ledger. Next was an eighteenth-century etching depicting two men of godly stature holding tight to each other as a battle raged in the background. I cataloged this one as well, then pushed away from my desk.

The desk was loaded down with a private collection of valuable erotic art, which belonged to my client, Clive Tarry. Most of it was rather tasteful, but I'd stumbled upon a few pieces that would, even by modern standards, be considered snuff. There was no denying that they were the most valuable, due to their rarity. So far, the collection filled six pages of my ledger. Unfortunately, I would not benefit from a sale, only from what he was paying me to appraise and catalog for his insurance. His collection of books also loomed over me from behind, gingerly packed in boxes by the doorway of my office.

The office was a model of organization. I'd built great metal-and-glass cases into the wall to the left of my desk to temporarily house items of value. The last case held my private collection of books, the only antiquities that held real value to me. Generally, I was hired to track down rare pieces of furniture, art, and occasionally books, which were really my forte. Appraising, though, was my favorite task. I got lost in the research; sometimes an entire day would pass and I wouldn't stop to eat or smoke.

Unfortunately, business had been rather slow, and the bills piled up. I did not lead an extravagant life. My social circle was very small, and my family and I barely spoke. When we did, it was cold and terse conversation. I lived alone in a house that had belonged to my uncle in the town of Irvington, New York. It sat rather mournfully on the shore of the Hudson River. I could barely afford the upkeep, but I was determined not to let it slip out of the family. I was convinced that someday, hopefully soon, I would make the sale that would change my pauper-like existence. Most of the furnishings came with the house. My uncle had had exquisite, if dark, taste.

The office was just as I had found it, aside from the metal cases and the computer, which hummed monotonously on the corner of my desk. The dark burgundy drapery, the behemoth mahogany desk, and the Oriental rug were as they'd been when I inherited the house. I knew that I would be set for some time if I sold the house and its trappings. The last time it had been appraised, the figures made my jaw drop. Selling it was out of the question, though.

I stood and walked out of the office and into my bedroom. The French doors that led onto the balcony overlooking the river were open, and I stepped outside. I lit a cigarette and propped my tanned arms on the iron railing and admired the graceful vine pattern that led from the brick on which I stood to the six flower bud finials that ringed the iron railing. I inhaled deeply and watched as a barge moved lazily downriver toward Manhattan. The sound of the commuter train whooshing past from the other side of the house barely reached my ears. It was muted and somehow comforting.

There was a slight knot in my stomach because today marked the last day that Kyle and I would spend together. I anticipated his arrival, but not with excitement. It was a somewhat anxious feeling. My only friend from this town was about to depart for Westport, Connecticut.

Of course, this wasn't so far away, but it meant that there was one less person in my nearly empty social circle.

Kyle was much like me in that he led a rather reclusive lifestyle. It was a wonder to most people why he would be so antisocial. He was a good-looking man, with dark hair and large, brooding blue eyes—not sky blue, but more like the deep blue of indigo ink. It was unsettling to stare into his eyes for too long; they were almost unnatural. I adored his body, especially in the winter months when he became pale, as if his skin were vellum stretched over taut bundles of rope.

While I was rather dour of mood most of the time, possessed of a macabre sense of humor, Kyle was all lightness, no deeper than a puddle after a rain shower. Despite that, he never failed to put me in a good mood with his childlike sense of humor and refreshingly naive view of the world. He was a house painter by profession but longed to be an artist, or rather, fancied himself to be one. I'd seen the canvases he had stacked in his cluttered little apartment, but found few of the abstractions aesthetically pleasing, preferring the realists and impressionists. None of this mattered to our relationship, if it could be called that. We merely enjoyed each other's presence and satisfied our desire for sexual contact. By no means were we romantic.

I snubbed out my cigarette, nearly burned to the filter. I heard the squeal of brakes to the right of the house, then an engine cutting off and a door slamming shut. I knew it was Kyle, playing out the routine we'd developed whenever he came over during the months when it was warm enough to keep the balcony doors open to the world. I caught a flash of his white shirt in the gap between the giant cypress and the rear of the house. In a few seconds Kyle came bounding down the garden path, then stood beneath the balcony. He looked up at me with a giant grin on his face.

"Hallooo!" he called, as if the distance between us were much greater than it really was.

He then moved out of sight beneath me, and I felt the balcony vibrate as he climbed the iron trellis to where I stood. He appeared suddenly just in front of me on the other side of the rail. He grabbed me by the back of the head and planted a smacking kiss on my lips. I smiled at this youthful gesture—even though he was almost ten years my senior—and stood aside to let him hop over to me.

"Hello to you, too."

Kyle waltzed into the bedroom and flopped down on the grand four-post oak bed. He bounced up and down on top of the down comforter, kicking off his shoes, which landed with a thud on the hardwood floor. He propped himself on his elbows and grinned at me. His white button-down shirt pulled away from his tight stomach, revealing the delicious, sparse treasure trail of hair. I sauntered to the bed and sat next to him, then leaned back on my side, resting my head on my hand and looking at him. I used my other hand to unbutton his shirt. The white cloth fell away, button by button, revealing his tan lines, made by the wife-beater he wore when he painted outdoors. Once the shirt fully opened, Kyle sat up and pulled it from his torso, tossing it haphazardly over the arm of the dark green velvet overstuffed chair near the doors to the balcony. He then pushed me onto my back and pulled off my T-shirt with one swift tug.

I'd lost track of how many times this exact scene had replayed. It was like watching a favorite movie for the thirtieth time. I appreciated it for what it was, never tired of it but never craved it either, knowing it would always be there for me to enjoy. I'd thought this last time would be different, that it would have a sacred air. It didn't feel that way, but I wanted to continue when I saw the plump outline of Kyle's cock.

As if reading my desire for spontaneity and a new sexual experience, Kyle grabbed me in his powerful arms and turned me onto my stomach with a willfulness he'd never before displayed. His hands grappled with my belt and, with a deft flick of the wrist, unbuttoned my jeans. They were soon tossed to the floor, followed shortly by Kyle's. The entire length of his warm, smooth body surrounded me. I could feel him throbbing between my legs.

He kissed the back of my neck while pushing my face down into the pillows, pinning me down. I panicked and bucked against him. He thrust against me in return, pushing his pulsing erection against the rim of my hole. I spread my legs and relaxed, eager for him to be inside me but knowing I would have to wait.

Kyle moved down my back with his tongue. I turned my head and gasped for air. I inhaled the sweet perfume of our mingled scents—his was almost the smell of oranges; mine was musky and deep. I salivated, wanting to taste him, to taste his cock, but even as Kyle made his way to my plump ass, he held me down so I could not move. I raised my hips just as his tongue found my hole. He covered me in spit, slowly relaxed me, massaging the muscles with his tongue. One finger slid in, and my cock responded with a jump. I pushed against it to the second knuckle. Kyle reached under my body and grabbed me by the shaft, slowly stroking me. One finger slid out of me, and then two slid in. He pumped with those two fingers, going deep until I felt as if it were his cock. As Kyle stroked my cock, I felt myself getting closer to cumming. I didn't want to, not yet. I pulled away from Kyle and flipped onto my back. I sat up and pulled him down on top of me. I grabbed the back of his head and reined him in to kiss me deeply. I tasted my sweat in his mouth. I groaned as he brought himself in between my legs, his hard cock resting against me, teasing me. His hips gyrated. I ran my hands over his taut arms, then over his shoulders and down his back. I reached around until I grabbed his ass and pushed him nearly inside me. He gasped. I reached into the nightstand drawer and pulled out a condom, ripping the package open with my teeth. I rolled the condom onto Kyle. He slowly worked into my ass. I grunted; he was so thick, I could barely take it all. Sweet pain shot through my body as I gripped Kyle's arms. He stopped. I could feel him looking at me. I looked into his eyes as he leered at me. My hole began to conform to his size and shape. Kyle pulled out slowly, then just as gently slid back inside me. I reached around his back and crushed him to my chest. I wrapped my legs around him and wrestled him so close, his pelvic bones crunched against mine.

As Kyle built up a rhythm, images of a savage dance flashed into my head. Four naked men were spread out, writhing on a bed. I saw sharp teeth puncture taut skin. These four wiry young men were laughing, leaping on top of one another and drawing blood from each other as if it were a game. My heart beat faster, at once thrilled and disgusted by the images.

It could have been the result of physical exertion and the thrill of being invaded, but the impression on my mind felt as if it came from someone else. I cried out, and Kyle worked more furiously against me. I tightened around his excited manhood. He, too, groaned out. In one quick movement, Kyle turned me onto my side, I reached out with my arms and grabbed a pillow and bit down. I was electrified, and Kyle was dripping as he worked away on my sore but hungry ass. Unable to withstand any more and fearing more gruesome images, I grabbed my cock and pumped up and down. Kyle responded with even faster and harder strokes until I felt like I would break in two. I felt the entire world shake as I shot and collapsed beneath Kyle. His hard and sweaty chest slapped against me as he came to rest, gasping, on top of me.

We finished without the ceremony of holding each other as lovers would do. I stood up immediately, breathing hard, satisfied and shaken, and made a break for the bathroom. I composed myself, not wanting to tell him what had gone on during our passionate entanglement. Kyle followed me on tiptoe. The black and white bathroom tiles were warm from the sun shining through the giant window over the tub. I pulled the shower chain; streams of water beat down on the metal tub. I jumped in; Kyle was soon to follow. We took turns beneath the water, as if we were brothers forced by our mother to bathe together. When we were done, we toweled off and, with the towels wrapped around our waists, went onto the balcony.

The sun had begun its late afternoon descent, casting a yellow light on the smooth surface of the river. I tapped a cigarette out of the pack and handed one to Kyle. He took it absently while he stared at the river. I admired his body. His skin was bejeweled. Tiny water droplets that he'd missed with his towel caught the sunlight like small diamonds. With his wet hair slicked back, he reminded me of a Hollywood actor from the fifties.

"In a way, I'm going to miss this sleepy town," he said, turning his head toward me.

"You know, Westport's not much bigger."

"I just need a change. I'm bored. I've spent my entire life here."

"What are you going to do there that you can't do here?" I asked.

A pensive look washed over Kyle's face. His eyes appeared to be searching the placid surface of the river for an answer. I stepped closer to him until my shoulder was touching his. It was comforting to have him so close. There were no sparks or fireworks; it was more like the soft, even heat of a forty-watt lightbulb.

"I figure that by discovering a new town, I may get the kind of inspiration and jump start I've been looking for. Not to mention a better chance of finding someone to love." He paused and looked down at his wrist, which was absent a watch. "What time is it?"

I turned around and squinted at the clock on the nightstand on the far side of the bed.

"Seven," I replied.

"I guess this is good-bye, old friend," he said with a smile.

I watched him dress, admiring his body, knowing this might be the last time I would ever see his beautiful form. I was surprisingly moved, possibly by my own fear that my life was stagnant. Maybe Kyle's easy availability had kept me lazy in terms of finding a lover. It could have been that he was just what I'd needed for the past two years: good sex and good companionship, no complications or worries.

Kyle lingered in the bedroom doorway and looked around. He suddenly pulled me close to him, then grabbed the back of my head and pushed my mouth against his. He parted my lips with his tongue and kissed me more passionately than he'd ever done in the past two years. I kissed him back with equal fervor until he pulled away.

"Remember," he said, "I'm only forty-five minutes away. I'll give you a call after I settle in."

He disappeared down the hall, sinking into the darkness that slowly overtook the rooms as the sun set behind the hills. I closed the bedroom door and heard the roar as Kyle's truck came to life. As the sound of the truck faded, a bittersweet feeling settled in my gut. Instead of dwelling in the emotion, I dressed and returned to my desk to catalog the rest of the antique porn.

Chapter Two

The images became indistinct as I flipped through the remaining items in the first folio of erotica. I couldn't focus and knew it was time to stop. I looked from the window in time to see the last ribbons of pink sky fading into the deep blue of night. I stood and stretched. The view of the river and the smell of cut grass wafting through the window lured me out of the house.

I walked up the street, over the train tracks. The air smelled sweet from the copious rose garden in front of my neighbor's home. The musty, wet smell of the river complemented the flowers' scent.

I turned right onto Main Street, then walked down an alley toward Aster's Coffeehouse. It was a bohemian hideaway, unknown to nearly all out-of-town visitors. The bell above the door tinkled when I entered. The air was thick with smoke despite the smoking ban. The sound of softly playing jazz accented the quiet murmur of the patrons engaged in hushed conversations. The walls were lined with books. A sign above the bookcases read, *Aster's Lending Library Employs the Honor System, Please Return All Books When Finished.* I smiled to know that someone in the world still trusted humanity. The hardwood floor was worn and darkened by years of heavy foot traffic.

I waved at Aster, who was behind the counter, busily steaming milk for a cappuccino. The long, floral print silk scarf that held her dark gray hair in place hung down perilously close to the cap of foam rising in the metal steamer. I moved to the end of the line and looked at a man in a tight white T-shirt who appeared to be in his late twenties, like myself. He looked back at me after lowering the copy of *Transcendence of the Ego* he'd been reading. The corner of his full mouth rose in quiet appraisal. I gazed with appreciation at his thick arms and thighs, the worn denim stretched over muscle. Brawn *and* brains, I assessed. Lurid thoughts danced through my mind as I played out a possible night with him in my bed. I imagined the two of us reenacting positions and situations depicted in the etchings in the folio of erotica.

The reverie was broken as Aster called my name: "Roland!"

I ordered my latte to go. I wrapped my hands around the warm cup and exited into the alleyway. As I reached the street, I was somewhat disappointed that the young man of brawn and brains had not at least made an attempt at conquest and capture. I weighed it in my mind and concluded that it was probably for the best that he hadn't.

I wasn't sure what I wanted: a companion as Kyle had been, a true lover, or just a chain of vigorous, unknown encounters. I knew it was not the time to seek out any of those. As the end of August drew near, it was imperative that I finish entering the erotica and book collection into my ledger so I could bill Mr. Tarry.

The fading vision of the boy in the coffeehouse dissipated completely as I approached the oak trees standing like two grand guardians on either side of the entry to my driveway. The driveway sloped down toward the side of the house, where a single-car garage had been built separate from the house. I passed by the driveway and continued to the flagstone walkway, lined on either side by waist-high shrubs, that led from the road to the front porch. I froze when I realized that a long black limousine was idling in the drive. I hopped the hedge and approached it slowly. When I reached the rear door of the limo, the tinted window lowered with a mechanical whine. I could just make out a pale face, obscured by the shadows of the car's dark interior. I tensed from head to toe.

"Roland Weir, I presume," a stranger spoke from the back of the car.

"Yes," I answered hesitantly.

"I apologize for arriving unannounced after business hours, but my schedule does not always allow for propriety. I have something to discuss with you."

I hadn't realized I'd been holding my breath until I exhaled heavily. I hoped the stranger didn't notice or, if he did notice, that he didn't take offense.

"Fine," I said, dropping my guard only slightly.

"Only, we shouldn't discuss it here."

"Right," I spoke, hoping he didn't hear my nervousness. "Won't you come in?"

I turned away and walked to the side entrance. Originally, it was used as a servants' entrance. I unlocked and opened the door and started up the stairway that led directly into the kitchen. At the top of the stairs, I pulled a chain to turn the light on. I had an odd notion not to turn around. I knew I was being rude, but I couldn't stop myself. I heard the side door close at the bottom of the stairway. I passed through the spacious kitchen, which had a slate floor and hardwood cabinetry. Though it had been fully modernized, my uncle had been careful to preserve the colonial design.

From the kitchen, I passed into the foyer. The grand staircase led up to a landing, which then split off into two narrow corridors. I proceeded past the bedroom door. My office had a second entrance from the hallway. I opened the door, flicked on the light, illuminating the office with an unobtrusive glow, and walked to the two leather chairs that faced a small fireplace opposite the metal cases. I turned toward the door and stood, resting my hand on the back of the chair farther from the door.

The stranger appeared at the doorway and entered. He seemed to float rather than walk. His skin was opalescent and smooth, as if devoid of pores. His eyes nearly glowed in the light. *Or were they lit from within?* He was almost unbearable to gaze upon because of these unexpected qualities. *Were the eyes green or amber? Or both?*

He towered above me. His shoulder-length hair was the color of rust, but the sheen was silky. His tresses swayed in a breeze that wasn't there. His clothing was elegant and seemed to be a part of him. His jacket fit snugly to his thin body. Brocade of black vines wound in and around the front panels of deep blue velvet. A billowing white cotton cravat was tucked seamlessly into the frills of his white shirt. Tight pants of blue velvet tapered down to delicate ankles. Staring at him alarmed and excited me. He was a walking mystery who left no clues to his origin.

I knew that I was being rude again, examining and appraising him as if he were an item up for auction. When I spoke, it took all my faculties not to stutter.

"Would you like to sit? May I offer you a drink Mr. . . . ?" I prompted.

The man moved around the chair and sat. He looked up at me from the chair.

"Rocerres." He paused for a beat. "Holbrandt Rocerres. Thank you for the offer, but nothing for me at the moment."

I took the chair opposite him and turned it slightly to face him. His voice was like thick vintage wine: musical and bold, rich and intoxicating. When he spoke, it poured heavily over me. I felt it beneath my skin.

"I understand that you deal in antiquities." I nodded. "I've been informed that you are extremely resourceful at acquiring rare and valuable objects. That is not the reason I've come, though."

He paused. I couldn't read his countenance at all. It seemed, though, that he was giving some thought to what he was about to say to me.

Now that he was in such close proximity, I realized he had a distinct scent, both seductive and frightening. He smelled of earth and ripe fruits. I wanted to reach out and touch him, just to have his scent on me after he'd gone. I didn't dare make a move. We seemed to share an unspoken understanding that he was in charge. I would have surrendered anything for him, given the chance. Somehow, my own will was slipping away by the minute. It was not anything that he did; just his presence was awe-inspiring. He commanded attention. I knew I was dealing with an individual of great power and influence.

He picked up a black satchel from the floor beside his chair. I hadn't even noticed that he'd been carrying anything when he entered. When he opened the satchel, the air around me seemed electric. My skin tingled. I felt flushed and warm, nearly breaking out in a sweat. My heart raced. Rocerres held a small wood block in his hand. I assumed it had come from within the satchel. I was so distracted by the sudden and arousing sensations that I hadn't seen him remove it.

Rocerres turned toward me, the small block resting in the palm of his hand. He looked directly at me. I was overwhelmed. My hands clenched my chair arms. A low hum filled the room. My insides were shaking, but I was frozen and held my breath. An amused smile spread across Rocerres' face. Suddenly, I heard a voice inside my head. It spoke, *Calm, calm.* I heeded the command. All tension in the room cleared away and it was just me and this strange, enticing man holding out a small square piece of wood.

I focused on the object, cocking my head as I peered at it. I was amazed at the minute details carved into the top. All around the edges, an intricate pattern of leaves and vines spiraled inward. In the very center was a raised script letter "V." Delicate flourishes surrounded the letter. The sides of the block were deeply rubbed with vertical indentations, as if fingers had been pulling on the block from the top and the bottom. Although it was commonplace for such markings to appear on old letterboxes and wooden containers, I found it odd that those markings would appear on the side of a solid block of wood. I offered a questioning look to Rocerres.

"You are very observant," he said.

I pushed myself back into the chair. My eyes widened in disbelief and vexation. Had I spoken out loud and not realized it? Was this man some sort of psychic? Had it been his voice in my head that had told me to remain calm?

"You are right; this is not simply a solid wooden block. There is very little known about its creator"—Rocerres turned the box upside down—"but he etched a signature and date onto the bottom of each of his creations that has surfaced over the centuries: 'J. Favreau, 1583.' "

I leaned in closer, nearly falling from the chair in my excitement. The name meant nothing to me, but I had always been mad for mysteries. I could already picture myself pulling at threadlike clues, driving myself to the brink until I unraveled the history of this box, its previous owners and supposedly enigmatic creator. I reached with my hand as if to relieve Rocerres of the box.

"Just a moment," Rocerres scolded. "There is a trick to this box, as with all of Favreau's creations. Each one was designed with a unique release mechanism. That will be part of your fun, or total frustration: figuring out how to open this box. Many have tried, which explains the wear on the sides. Legend tells us that those who could not figure out how to open these little mysteries were driven completely mad."

"Tell me, now. What else do you know about Favreau?"

For me, this was like Christmas, had I ever celebrated it. I'd come from a family of godless intellectuals. They spurned religious holidays, viewing all dogmas with the same amusement and interest with which most contemporary people viewed the Greeks and their pantheon of gods. I, on the other hand, was willing to believe that gods and devils existed. I was unconvinced that Rocerres himself was not some sort of otherworldly being.

"Honestly," Rocerres said, his voice deeper and more penetrating, "I know little of Favreau. Most of what I do know is unsubstantiated legend and is fraught with contradiction and implausibility. It's told that he was a favorite guest of Catherine de Medici, but also rumored that he was intimate with her daughter, Margaret de Valois, who was exiled from Paris in 1583 for promiscuity by her husband and king of France, Henri the Fourth, and her brother, Henri the Third. What I hold in my hand now is said to have belonged to Margaret, or Queen Margot, as she was known."

"You sound as if you know all of this for a fact," I braved.

"I know only what scholars and legends tell me. I also know the value of this little *trinket*," he said, putting a strange, almost bitter emphasis on the last word. "I know that if you can find a buyer, take nothing less than a half million."

My heart raced at the figure. I would not have to worry about my financial situation for quite some time. Then again, that seductive little box in Rocerres' hand seemed to call to me. I saw it clearly in my head; the little treasure resting upon a velvet pillow as part of my private collection. *As if I could ever afford it*, I thought to myself, forgetting that Rocerres seemed to have telepathic abilities. As if on cue, this exquisite man spoke.

"If you decide that you need to use this box for yourself, I ask only one thing." Again his words left me taken aback. "Make sure that when you are finished with the box, you pass it on to someone who needs it."

Utterly confused by what he suggested, I sat forward and said, "I don't understand."

Rocerres stood. I gazed up at him. He smiled at me, bemused. He set the box on the chair where he'd been sitting moments ago, plucked the satchel from the floor, and swiftly made his way to the door.

"Pardon my sudden departure, but I really must move on to my next appointment. I'll check in with you soon. Don't let the mysteries of the box take up too much of your time. It really will drive you mad."

Chapter Three

The air absolutely crackled in Rocerres' wake as he left. The room seemed dull without his presence, until the box caught my eye again. I gingerly lifted it from the chair, as if I might spring it open and release some evil into the air the way Pandora had done in the myth. The small details were truly astounding. The craftsmanship involved in carving such smooth and delicate lines was nearly beyond my comprehension. The fact that the design was intact stumped me when I turned the box to look at the deep wear on its sides.

I took the "trinket," as Rocerres had called it, to my desk and flicked on the bright halogen desk lamp. I pulled a silver-handled magnifying glass from the top left drawer and searched for a seam along the side of the box. Under magnification, I could see that there was indeed a seam that precisely followed one line of the grain. As I rotated the box, I heard the tiny clink of metal against wood inside. I squelched my excited urge just to pull on the box. It was obvious that hadn't worked for the many who had tried to open it before me. Instead, I would turn to the wonders of modern technology to see if I could drum up some possible explanations or, at the very least, some clues to its maker or perhaps the box itself.

* * *

My eyes watered. I stretched my arms above my head and stared at the computer screen and then down at the sparse notes I'd scribbled on a legal pad. After hours of searching the Internet, I had unearthed a few bits of information. A search for "Favreau" had yielded only family trees and numerous Web sites referring to actors with the same surname. There had been only one lead from that search: an entry in a book titled *Toy Makers of Europe,* dated 1789. Unfortunately, the book seemed to be located solely in the Library of the Arcane, in Boston. I made a note to call the library in the morning. Of course there were tons of sites referring to Margaret de Valois and her mother, Catherine de Medici. One mention of Favreau did surface in conjunction with Margaret. They had both attended a soiree in Paris, according to an original list of invitees that was being sold in an antique shop in New York. It seemed that I had my work cut out for me.

I turned off my computer and took up the box once more. I turned it over in my hands and studied the name and date on the bottom. As I did so, my finger slid over the top of the box, feeling the fine edges. As I brought the box closer to my eyes to look at Favreau's name and date, a click sounded within the box. I set the box faceup on the desk. I had inadvertently found the release mechanism. The letter "V" had been depressed, allowing the box to open.

My heart raced as I grabbed the corners of the box. It was tempting to let it sit on my desk until morning. I feared disappointment. I feared that the container would be more interesting than its contents. I took a deep breath, lifted the cover from the box, and set it aside. Inside, resting on deep crimson velvet, sat a necklace. A gem the color of blood was set into a small, shining silver disk that resembled a coin. The disk was attached to a glittering silver chain with no clasp.

My heart slowed and sank. I knew that I shouldn't have been disappointed. I was looking at a necklace that more than likely had been made for Margaret de Valois, former queen of France.

Open your eyes, Roland, I thought, *this piece is museum-worthy.*

I retrieved the magnifying glass and bent closer to the sparkling red gem. Too dark to be a ruby, it was probably a garnet. As I studied it, I lifted my hand to remove it from the box. As I did so, I thought I heard a deep groan. I whipped around and peered at the room. I half expected to see Rocerres lurking in the dark corners by the door. I stared into the hallway . . . I saw no movement. Satisfied that it was the old house settling on its foundation, I returned to my scrutiny of the necklace. I reached out to touch it again.

A tingling sensation rushed up my arm as my fingers nearly grazed the top facet of the gem. I pulled away. I thought I heard laughter this time, but realized it was inside my head. The drapes over the window billowed inward. I leaped back from the desk, standing and whirling around as if something were about to attack. I shook my head vigorously, trying to shake off my anxiety. I looked at the clock. It was late. I put the lid back on the box and decided to go to bed.

I stripped down to my boxer shorts and climbed under the sheet. The cool night air brought in the slight scent of flowers from below the balcony. I could barely hear the quiet lapping of the river against the rocks on the bank. I began to fade.

I felt it before my eyes adjusted to the darkness of the room around me. Two white hands had pulled the sheet from my chest. The contrast between the hands and my tanned skin was alarming. I could see no other features of the intruder, only the fingers with their long nails working their way up over the small ridges of my abdomen. My own hands clenched the edges of the bed as I fully realized what was happening. *Someone else was here with me.*

I couldn't move. I saw no shackles or fetters, but I felt them. I could move my head, but when I tried to speak, no words issued from my lips. My heart pounded, and a thin film of nervous sweat broke out on my skin. I didn't want to be restrained, and the presence in the room terrified me.

The long white fingers were topped with unusually shining nails, resembling carefully cut pieces of glass. When the tips of the fingers touched my stomach, an alarming sensation swept over my skin. I fought against it, refusing to recognize it as pleasurable.

The hands began to caress me, as if the being was trying to calm me. I felt as if the bed beneath me were slipping away. I tried to turn my body away from the hands; they pressed down on me with greater force.

No, I thought.

Yes, a voice hissed inside me.

I was astounded.

The hands inched their way up to my chest and came to rest over my heart. I whimpered internally, but was flooded with inexplicable warmth. My head shot back in response, and I heard mocking laughter in my head. An image flashed through my mind, much the same way it had happened during my last session of lovemaking with Kyle. This time, however, I was in a softly lit garden, sprawled upon a bed of flowers. A man was on top of me, and I welcomed his weight. His hands ran the length of my arms, and I felt hot breath on my neck.

The beautiful image was cut short as I was reminded of where I really was. The hands had moved from my heart. The left hand cradled my head and turned it to the left, exposing the softest part of my neck. I felt the veins and arteries pulsing, as if offering to be cut and drained. The right hand gripped my neck; the thumb forced under my jaw, pushing my head back until I was looking at the wall behind the bed. A mysterious weight lay over my body. I was breathing so fast, I thought I would explode. The being's skin felt like smooth marble. I thought I would be crushed. Again I was whisked away to a fantasy garden; blood red petals rained down from impossibly tall trees. I found myself begging for mercy, then for something else. I wanted this creature to take me away.

"Tell me that you want this, Roland," a deep voice said aloud.

In my heart of hearts I wanted to say no, but I felt the word "yes" forming on my tongue—yet I could say nothing.

I pushed my neck toward the creature until I felt its lips, soft lips that grazed my skin. I writhed against the weight, forcing myself harder against the lips. The mouth opened and covered my pulsing vein. I was in the garden, not in my bedroom. Something sharp touched my skin. I groaned as I felt fangs sink into me. My eyes widened. I couldn't breathe. Tears welled up.

I was crushed against the being, and the shackles and fetters fell away. My body was rising in the air with the creature. It was an exotic sensation. Instead of feeling fear and resistance, I was giving in to its will. I still saw no part of the creature except the hands, which fell away from my head and gripped my back. I was cradled in its arms as it drew away my blood and my spirit. A smile formed on my lips.

Roland, you're dying, said the part of me that was still in reality.

Finally, I was able to scream.

As my voice resounded throughout the room, I shot up in the bed. The room was flooded with light, and the bed was completely soaked in sweat. I felt a dull ache in my chest. My heart raced. I collapsed on the bed and sobbed. I didn't know why, but I felt cheated. It was as if some glorious treasure had been offered to me and I'd refused it.

I tried to convince myself that it had been a dream. I'd just had a lucid dream. I thought it was somehow connected to the box resting on my desk in the next room. I threw the sheets aside and let my bare feet hit the cool wood floor. I looked around the corner into my office. The box, seemingly innocent, remained closed and unmoved on the desk. I laughed at myself. Had I let my imagination run wild?

I took a shower, made a dark brew of coffee, and settled at my desk. The box seemed to stare at me. I lifted it from the desk and placed it inside the top drawer. As I did so, I would have sworn that the box projected a feeling of betrayal toward me. I slammed the drawer shut. I reached behind me and lifted the last folio of erotica from the pile of books.

I had only four more etchings to go through before I finished appraising Mr. Tarry's collection. I stopped short at the second to last. I could barely believe my eyes when I stared at the piece. Two men appeared to be arguing. They were in some sort of parlor. One of the men was standing imperiously over the other, who looked as if he'd been pushed back on the settee beneath him. His shirt was undone, and one hand was draped over the back of the settee. It was what was in his hand that astounded me. He was holding a small box.

I whipped out my magnifying glass for a closer look. The box was identical to the one in my desk drawer, except that, instead of a letter "V," the box in the etching was adorned with the letter "K." I swore I heard the object in my desk rattling, as if begging to be released.

I was obviously still disturbed by my dream from the night before; my imagination pumped up. I opened the desk drawer. The box seemed to stare back at me. It was wedged between the side of the drawer and my business checkbook. I didn't want to believe that there was really anything supernatural about the box. I didn't want to think that it had any influence over me or my dreams.

I pushed the folio off to the side of the desk. I didn't care that a few of the etchings fell to the floor with a sound like a disgruntled whisper.

I centered the box on the desk and assured myself that I was the one making it seem to possess importance. It did not have its own volition. I removed the lid and withdrew the necklace without a wince, refusing to give it the power that I felt it wanted. The chain snaked over my hand and brushed the hair on my arm as I lifted it. The gem caught the sunlight. I closed my eyes, and for a split second a woman's face flashed through my mind.

"What the hell?" I said aloud.

I stood up from my desk and strode into the bedroom, holding the necklace aloft as if it would rear and strike out at me any second. I stood in the dim shaft of light filtered by the drapes, and looked in the mirror. My white shirt was unbuttoned to my midriff. The necklace would look handsome hanging between my pecs.

Wouldn't it be too girlish? I wondered.

"Put it on," a deep voice said.

I almost lost my balance as I twirled around. It seemed the voice had come from everywhere at once. I was shaking and breathing hard, and I felt as though my hands were guided by an unseen force. I felt something around my wrists, but when I gazed at them, nothing was there. I wanted to cry; I wanted to rebel. Instead, I faced the mirror and myself. I gritted my teeth, unwilling to be played like some marionette.

My eyelids slammed down, and for a second I was someone else. I was not a man and I was not alive; I was not dead, either. I opened my eyes, and I was confused. My surroundings looked unfamiliar for a minute, and I burned from head to toe as if I had a fever, yet when I exhaled, steam shot from my mouth.

It's the end of summer, I thought.

I watched my reflected hands lift the necklace above my head. Then I felt the gem graze my forehead as my hands lowered the chain around my neck. The stone fell over my Adam's apple, then over the divot below, across the pronounced collarbone, coming to rest on my sternum, which was framed by the muscular chest I'd barely worked to achieve. Then . . . the world fell apart.

Chapter Four

For a moment I was standing in a double exposure. Two realities overlapped. I could still see the furnishings and paintings of my own house, but they were faded and slowly morphing into something resembling eighteenth-century France. It wasn't long before the new reality took hold completely, and I was standing in a parlor whose windows overlooked the twinkling lights of a city.

This can't be real, I told myself.

But my surroundings didn't flicker as they would in a fantasy. I tugged on the necklace, then touched my chest. I turned slowly and gazed upon an ornately carved mantel over a fireplace. My eyes fell greedily on the bookcases lining the far wall, filled with leather-bound volumes. The jacquard-upholstered chairs filled me with childish delight. My insides were a cauldron of glee and fright. In a way, this was what I wanted. I'd always dreamed of traveling back in time to see objects that I admired in their original setting.

I was not alone. In this strange place that was out of time, I could sense the very movement of molecules and displacement of air. I didn't know if he had always been there or if he had simply materialized, but across the room from me stood another being. I knew in my heart of hearts that this was the same creature who had invaded my dreams the previous night. I recognized the white hands with the slender fingers. The being smiled at me. He knew I recognized him.

He had dark, sumptuous hair and sullen green eyes. He moved toward me, but it seemed as if it were the room that moved around him, bringing him only a foot from me. He had the same delicious smell that Mr. Rocerres had possessed. He didn't speak at first but merely looked at me. I felt heat and light pierce my mind. I felt his presence inside my head. His mouth turned upward in a lusty smile. He closed his eyes and drew my own scent into him. He sighed as he exhaled. I couldn't move and couldn't resist him.

"Finally," he began, "a man after my own heart."

His voice was rapturous. I felt my eyebrows rise in anticipation of more words, more of him. My impulses felt sexual in nature but altogether different and indescribable. I had a dark need to be completely drained. I wanted to serve him, not love him.

"Roland, you have been chosen for me, and I accepted. You do know what I am, do you not?"

The fact was, I didn't know, and at that moment I didn't care if he was an angel or a demon, devil or saint, as long as he wanted me. I shook my head. The creature laughed and extended his arm toward me. He perused my body with his eyes as his hand came to rest on my naked forearm. I gasped as a pulse jolted through my body, radiating out from the point of contact.

"Do you not have the slightest guess as to my name? You've heard it. Think," he commanded.

"You are a vampire," I said weakly, feeling as if I'd already been drained of blood.

The creature laughed quietly, as one laughs at a child's innocent realization that he doesn't disappear when he covers his eyes.

"Yes, a vampire. My name? You are wearing the necklace that I created from my own blood."

I looked at him questioningly as the answers flooded my brain.

"My name is Julius Favreau, toy maker, jewelry maker, seducer of queens and princes, killer of men, women, and children. I am a dream and a nightmare. A child of Lilith. You see, I am one of the first vampires.

"I have been here since the dawn of mankind as we know it. When Lilith was cast into the valley of darkness on the shores of the Dead Sea and copulated with demons, she bore the rotten fruit of evil. The creatures who are her children are now of myth and legend. I do not know who named my race 'vampire,' but I know that I am not human and I am not a demon. I am somewhere in between, existing in two planes of reality. My father was an incubus, a demon with the power to seduce women into despair, the power to forge pleasure out of pain and death. Do you understand?"

I nodded my head in awe. I gazed upon Favreau as if he were an ancient relic, an icon of some dark church.

"When I drink the blood of humans, I take part of them with me. When I feed, I possess them to satisfy my demonic genes. The blood is nourishment for my strange body. I am immortal, but forever conflicted by my two halves. The human will is weak, overpowered by the demonic force of rage and need to commit to evil. I am not so conflicted, though, as a certain vampire we both know. Rocerres is convinced that he can find an angel to change him back or possibly transform him into a different being. He is sure that he can be unmade. I tell you, I have traveled the world over millennia and have not seen angels in this reality."

"Favreau the beautiful nightmare," I wanted to call him. He moved ever closer to me, by small degrees. His hands reached for me and removed my clothing slowly, deliciously. He placed his full hands on me; I convulsed gently, feeling his own being intermingling with mine. He closed his eyes. His mouth fell open slightly, and his long fangs were exposed and glittered like pearls. They dripped with a clear liquid. He spoke softly into my ear as he pulled me close to him.

"When I touch you, I can feel every vein and artery pulsing with your energy. I crave you more than I have craved anything. Your spirit awaits me, but I have better plans for you, my sweet one. I want you to join me, to see the world as I see it. I want you as a companion, as Rocerres could never be. Do you accept? Tell me that you accept, and I will come to you full-bodied and make it so."

My mouth opened to speak. I wanted so badly to answer affirmatively. I wrapped my arms around his body. A golden light burst into my closed eyes.

I fell forward. As I hit the floor, I heard a faraway scream of frustration. I shook my head as I pushed myself from the hardwood floor. Early morning light flooded the bedroom of my house. I was back in my own time. The necklace was no longer around my neck but lay on the bed. If I'd removed it, I had no memory of doing so. I was shaking from head to toe. As I tried to adjust to my return from wherever I had—or had not—been just a moment before, I realized that the telephone was ringing.

I bolted to my office.

"Hello?"

"Roland, it's Kyle. You sound out of breath. I hope I didn't . . . disturb you," he said, insinuating that I had someone with me. I laughed internally because he wasn't far from the truth.

"No, I was just rearranging my office," I lied lamely. "Are you all settled in?"

"Yes."

"Care to elaborate? Is Westport all that you thought it would be and more?"

"It's barely been a week," he sighed as he spoke, "but so far it's not that different from Irvington."

"It'll get better as you settle into the town and get to know people."

"I don't know, Roland. Maybe it's just me. You know the old saying, 'Wherever you go, there you'll be.' I think I finally get what it means."

"Give yourself some time."

"Hey," he said with the impish tone that I knew well, "I miss our trysts already."

"Me, too," I lied.

"Nah, you were ready to move on to something more fulfilling. You were always much deeper about stuff than me."

Kyle had a way with words. Not a great way, but his simplicity was endearing. Endearment was not enough for me, though. I had expected this call. Kyle was a stranger in a strange town, and I'd known he probably would reach out to me, his only friend, for the first few months. After he was acquainted with the ins and outs of Westport, Roland Weir would completely disappear from his brain.

"You're experiencing separation anxiety, aren't you?" I teased.

"What?" he asked, but received no response. "Never mind. You're probably busy, so I'll let you go. I'll give you a call in a few days. Maybe you can make the drive out here?"

"Sure, Kyle. Give me a call. I'll see if I can get over there sometime."

Almost immediately after hanging up the phone I was struck with a premature nostalgia. My memories of Kyle were pleasantly tinted, as if they had occurred in a much more distant past. I thought of him affectionately. Sadly, ours was the most significant relationship I'd ever had with another human.

Maybe if we were vampire companions, it would be different, I mused. I brushed the thought away and turned from the desk.

Chapter Five

I had finished all my work for Mr. Tarry and called him to let him know. He came to pick up the ledger and gave me a check before he left. I could finally have a few moments to myself as the sun began its descent over the hills on the western bank of the Hudson River.

I made coffee, adding a hint of whiskey to it before making my way out of the back door of the house, walking between the cypress trees and following a path of stone steps overgrown with grass. I made a mental note to call my neighbor, whose son cut my lawn for a small fee. My uncle, a fantastic landscaper, had built a small circular stone patio on the river's edge. Two wrought-iron chairs faced the water. A treated wood table sat between the chairs. I set my coffee cup on the table and lowered myself onto the iron chair. It was more comfortable than it looked.

I wanted to be as far away from the necklace as possible. I had seemed to disappear for an entire day when I'd worn the necklace the day before. I shuddered, thinking of my meeting with Favreau. I didn't fully know what to make of it. I felt the way I imagined a person who'd been possessed might feel after the invading entity had left his body—I felt violated and more guarded now. Yet there still lingered a curiosity about the life of vampires, particularly the life of Favreau and Rocerres. As mental images of the day before flipped through my mind, I found myself somewhat aroused.

I ran my hands over my chest, where the gem had rested, feeling the warmth of my skin. Overall, I felt drained, as if I had orgasmed nonstop for an entire day. I wondered if I would ever meet Favreau in my own reality, or if the meetings would be confined to some alternate time-space continuum that he was able to create. I was in awe of the powers he must possess. I thought of myself touching him, feeling his inhuman skin, tasting it. I ran my tongue over my teeth and fleetingly wished that I had those great and terrible fangs. I fantasized briefly about Kyle. I didn't think about our sexual interludes, instead exploring something much darker. I put myself in the preternatural shoes of a vampire. Made my mental self into a vampire. I pictured Kyle's head snapped back, his eyes full of fear and longing; the same emotions I had when Favreau or Rocerres was near me. I would lower my fangs to Kyle's neck and tease him with the possibility of death, the overwhelming sensation of being drained.

But what would it be like to be refilled by the strange blood of the vampire? I wondered.

I sat back and closed my eyes for what I thought was only a minute. My eyes shot open, and I jumped from my seat when I felt someone's hand rest on my shoulder. I then realized the sun had gone down. I turned on the stone to face whoever had touched me. I raised my fists—as if I had ever been in a fight. When I saw that it was Rocerres who stood behind the chair, I lowered my hands but kept my distance. He spoke first.

"I understand you've met Favreau," he said gravely.

"I suppose I have, in a way," I replied.

"Then I'll wager he told you his opinion of me."

"Somewhat."

"I want to tell you my side of the story. Rather, show you."

Rocerres leaped in front of me and put one hand on either side of my neck. He tilted my face upward until I was looking directly into his eyes. I was disarmed. His face moved closer to mine until his lips were nearly touching mine. He bit his lip. A drop of blood bubbled to the surface. He pushed the blood onto his tongue. I didn't know what was going to happen, and I was anxious. My breathing quickened, and I felt tears rising in my eyes, which were fixed tightly on Rocerres'. I felt something cold and wet against my lips, then tasted a coppery liquid.

He had forced his tongue into my mouth. I resisted the urge to bite it. As the taste of Rocerres' blood began to fade, he pulled back from me a few inches. I felt my muscles stiffen for a moment, though not with tension; it felt as if they had died then been revived. I had to shake my head because I suddenly had a memory that was not my own. Taking Rocerres' blood inside me had caused a memory of his to be transferred, or copied, to my own mind.

The few people still on the streets of Paris stepped away from Rocerres as he made his way back to Favreau. He had every appearance of a madman. His eyes were wide, and he shook his head every few feet as if his ears were clogged with water. His internal battle was great, but he was losing. Favreau's telepathic hold over him was akin to twelve horses pulling an empty cart.

When Rocerres finally reached Favreau's domain, he stopped outside the gate and steadied himself against the stone column at the entrance. He looked toward the window he had burst through earlier. A dark figure stood there, arms outstretched and long hair flowing outward. Rocerres clung to the column, resisting with his last bit of strength. He dug into the stone so hard that he bled from beneath his fingernails. He gasped, then cried out.

Favreau seemed to materialize in front of him. He held out his hand to Rocerres. Rocerres turned his face away; tears streamed down his cheeks. He felt his arm reach out. Favreau had full dominion over him. He felt the cool touch of unnatural skin and the strength of a hundred men in the hand that touched his own. Favreau effortlessly pulled him from the column.

Once they had entered Favreau's lair, Rocerres was led up a marble staircase to a lavishly furnished bedroom. The bedposts reached almost to the high ceiling. Favreau looked at Rocerres with a tender yet hungry expression. He led Rocerres to the bed and gently laid him down. He removed his silk cravat, then grabbed his wrists. He sucked the blood from Rocerres' fingertips, then tenderly bit down. Rocerres let out a cry as Favreau's fang pierced the surface of his index finger. Favreau groaned, then pulled away.

"You are delicious, as sweet as I imagined," he said, grinning lewdly.

Rocerres yanked his wrists away from Favreau's grasp and kicked his legs out, attempting to scamper off the bed. Favreau leaped with the prowess of a tiger and gripped Rocerres by the shoulders. He let his hands trail down Rocerres' stiff arms. Rocerres breathed hard and stared defiantly as Favreau bound his wrists together with the cravat, then tied them securely to the headboard.

"There will be no impish escapes this time, my boy."

Rocerres turned his head away in a final attempt to break the mental bind Favreau had over him. It seemed useless now that his hands were tightly locked together. He felt a fingernail trace his collarbone, then scrape his sternum. The fingernail traced the underside of his pectoral muscle, then moved up, just below his left nipple. He winced as he felt the skin break at the bottom of the areola. Favreau bent down and flicked his tongue over the nipple, which sent a shock through Rocerres. He gasped with unwilling pleasure. Then Favreau ravenously sucked from the puncture. Rocerres turned his face to watch with morbid fascination. Favreau's dark hair was splayed out, and his head moved back and forth as he suckled. Rocerres' face grew pale, but Favreau's face, when he looked up, had become flushed. His eyes were electric as he snarled.

Rocerres bucked against Favreau and once again tried to kick him from the bed, to no avail. Favreau laughed at his efforts. He leaned down close to Rocerres, who looked up, terrified. Favreau bit down on his tongue, then forced Rocerres' mouth open with it. Hot vampiric blood flowed into Rocerres' mouth; he let out a muffled cry as his muscles tensed in reaction to the enchanted blood. As painful as it was at first, it was all too pleasant as it began to work its magic on Rocerres' mortal body. For a moment, the world was more vivid than it had ever been. Rocerres heard voices of people miles away; the colors were bright, and the sensation of Favreau's weight on top of him filled him with glee. Their skin seemed to grow together. Rocerres felt as if he were penetrated; he grew rock solid instantly. He wanted Favreau, wanted the darkness, more of the ferocious blood. He opened his mouth and instinctively bit down on Favreau's neck, but his blunt mortal teeth could not break the skin. He convulsed beneath Favreau, frustrated and excited. He clenched his legs together as a shiver welled up at his feet and worked orgasmically up his entire body.

Favreau pulled away, delighted by Rocerres' reaction. He watched as

Rocerres stretched out his body, enjoying the new sensations. While his victim was charmed, he took the opportunity to taste Rocerres once again. He bit down on Rocerres' bound wrist. Rocerres gasped and pleaded.

"Another kiss."

Favreau pulled away and gave Rocerres a frightening look, then grabbed him fiercely by the shoulder. Favreau snapped his head back. He leaped on top of him and sank his fangs into the pulsing jugular vein. Rocerres could feel his life slipping away by degrees, and he welcomed it. The lights became hazy, and all thoughts abandoned him. In his last few minutes of fuzziness, he saw two figures burst into the bedroom and rush toward the bed. He heard a single thought of Favreau's in his own mind: It seems that we will have to make a new life in the New World.

"So you see now," Rocerres said to me when I snapped out of the trance, "it was not by choice that I became what I am."

"But you came to America with Favreau anyway?"

"He kept me weak. We went to England from France. I cannot recall how long we remained there before we set sail for America. It could have been a century, but it wasn't until we reached what is now New York City that Favreau fully filled me with vampiric blood.

"I am not as Favreau is, though. I've never taken life or reproduced. I am determined to find a way to escape this life and become human."

"How do you resist?" I asked.

"It isn't easy. There are times when the lust for blood nearly blinds me. Though Favreau warns me that I will wither away if I do not feed, I'm willing to take that risk if it means remaining pure in some sense."

"And the necklace. How did it get here from Europe?"

"I can't answer that, but I have my suspicions that Queen Margot did not die as history books would have you believe."

I shook my head in disbelieving comprehension. Rocerres went on to warn me about the necklace and about Favreau. He explained its many uses: to lure victims to Favreau's manor, to drive those who possessed it to insanity, to serve as a link to a ghostly plane where vampires and other dark creatures existed, and to be a telepathic link to Favreau. He pleaded with me to give up the necklace, to sell it in hopes that it would disappear forever into the collection of someone finally able to resist its call.

I wasn't sure why the temptation was so great for me to become like Favreau. Perhaps I longed to be a permanent part of mythology, to watch time pass into history. It was exciting despite the darker side: taking human life.

Rocerres stroked my hair affectionately before he left. His scent lingered on my skin for hours after he departed. I avoided entering my house, content to watch the barges move lazily down the river toward the sea. It wasn't until the last train of the night pulled out of the Irvington station that I went indoors.

Chapter Six

I undressed and slipped into bed as an internal war raged inside my head. The cautionary words of Rocerres battled with the seductive memory of Favreau. I looked at the lamp on the nightstand beside the bed, where I'd hung the necklace from the switch. The gem caught the light and hypnotically threw sparks in my eyes. *You're not helping matters,* I said to the necklace in my thoughts.

I reached to turn off the light. My fingers grazed the cool links of the silver chain. The glittering gem and the powers it held as a link to Favreau were like a drug. Maybe my addiction was to Favreau.

Instead of turning off the light, I removed the chain from its perch and held it in front of my face, completely surrendering to my need. The battle in my head was drawing to a close. I closed my eyes and envisioned the reactions of both Rocerres and Favreau. I imagined Rocerres turning away in disappointment, abandoning me and feeling as if he had failed to save me from a fate that he feared.

It's my decision, I thought.

Favreau, as I pictured him, would smile with delight and welcome me into his arms. He would kiss me into darkness with his thirsty teeth. He would welcome me as his new companion. What, then, would be the fate of Rocerres? I wondered. Would he be cast away from Favreau's side? Why did he stay around Favreau? That point bothered me, but I reasoned that there were probably few other beings of their sort and—though Rocerres hated what he was—like any other creature, he needed to feel some sort of solidarity with a group.

I didn't even realize the passing of time. As the thoughts in my head were tossed back and forth, the sun had begun to rise, casting a pink glow over the surface of the river. I gingerly dangled the necklace from the switch and went out to the balcony, feeling the cool, moist morning air on my skin. I watched as the sky became lighter by degrees.

When the sun had risen and the sky turned pale blue, I turned back to my bedroom with the resolve and enough exhaustion to sleep through the day. I woke, almost too perfectly, just as the sun touched the tops of the hills across the river. I suspected that it would be the last sunset I beheld.

I stood on the balcony, then turned to the iron trellis that extended upward. I climbed up to the slate tiles and made my way to the peak of the sloping roof for a better view of the changing sky. I had already forgotten the life that had led to this moment. It was not a life well lived; at least I was trying to convince myself of that. I had cut myself off from my family and had almost no friends. I wondered if maybe I'd known that this moment would come, if I'd been holding out for something better. *I'll still be Roland Weir when I'm a vampire*, I thought.

I shook my head and slid slowly down the roof until my feet were dangling over the balcony. I laughed, thinking that if I became a vampire, I'd be able to leap from the roof without a trace of worry. Then again, what did I really know about vampires except that they'd really fucked with my head?

Maybe I was asking the wrong questions. I probably should have been asking myself what I knew of Roland Weir. I looked around the bedroom as I entered it. There were very few traces of my past or myself anywhere. I had inhabited the life of my uncle. The only possessions that were truly my own were the books in my office and the painting given to me by Kyle. When I'd left my parents' house, I threw out any sign that I'd even gone through the public school system. I kept no yearbooks, school literary magazines, prom pictures, or anything to remind me of where I'd come from. I had even thrown away my own journals. I threw them away as I wrote them, in fact.

What was important to me was a larger scheme. I was enamored of the great events of European history, of the deeds of heroic men and women. The work of artists held me in awe. My own life was all that I was capable of, and I accepted it for what it was and had no aspirations to change the course of the world. As an immortal, though, I hoped to have a better understanding of the present world as it slowly became history, and I would witness those people and events with the power to withstand obscurity.

I stood by the nightstand, looking at the necklace as it swung gently from the switch. I pulled it from its perch and held it in front of my face. I held the chain in both hands, ready once again to slip it over my head. I wanted to contact Favreau, to tell him that I was ready for him. I wanted to call him to kill me and revive me in my own bed. I closed my eyes. I slipped the chain over my head and let it fall around my neck. The stone came to rest on my sternum.

Nothing happened.

"Favreau!" I called out.

I was answered only by the sound of the train approaching in the distance.

I pulled my jeans from the chair and slipped them on, then my shirt. I did not remove the necklace but kept it on, hoping that Favreau would come to me on his own. I didn't know what to do in the meantime. I had nothing to occupy me. All I could think of was to go into my office. I pulled the carved wooden box from my desk and turned it over in my hands, concentrating on the name carved into the bottom. It remained with me as I strolled to the bookcase and turned on the interior lights. All my fabulous books stared back at me, their spines glowing softly in the artificial light. I flicked off the switch and paced the floor, holding the gem in my left hand. Just as my frustration was becoming unbearable, I felt an electric tingling move over my skin. My hair stood on end, and I shook. My eyes watered. I groaned and collapsed on the floor. The entire world fell into darkness.

When I returned to consciousness, I couldn't open my eyes right away. I was lying on what felt like earth, leaves, and twigs. I felt the ground with my fingers and touched something wet. I lifted my head and, with great difficulty, opened my eyes a sliver. My fingertips were covered in mud, and my hands clutched wet leaves.

When I tried to push myself up, my muscles resisted. My body was as exhausted as if I had climbed a mountain. Everything in my vision beyond my hands was blurry. I mustered enough strength to roll onto my back. The sky was bright, but looked fractured. I breathed deeply and let my eyes close again. I relaxed my muscles, and the grogginess floated away.

I fully opened my eyes and had to blink away the fuzziness. When I looked up, I could see that I was surrounded by trees. Branches, resplendent with leaves in the midst of changing their colors, cut the sky. I looked down the length of my body. My clothes were soiled. Twigs and leaves stuck to me. I pushed myself up on my elbows. The ground in front of me sloped downward. I pushed myself up farther to see if I could look over the edge. I squinted my eyes. Far below, I could see water. It caught the sunlight in small flecks. I shook my head.

"What the hell?" I said out loud.

I had expected no response, and none came. I turned my head and was astonished at what lay in front of me. I was startled and jumped up; my muscles burned as I stood erect.

I was standing in front of a large stone Italianate house. It had fallen into disrepair but was still startlingly beautiful. Vines crept up the walls but did not cover the iron-framed windows. Most of the panes appeared to be intact. The double doors at the front of the house were closed. The metal around the doorknobs was completely rusted.

On the right side of the house, a tree grew out of a curved sunroom. Most of the glass was missing from the panes, and nature had taken over. Tips of fern fronds peeked out of the windows. I could make out the edges of a fountain through overgrown bushes about ten feet away from the sunroom. What had once been a garden was now a jungle of vines and tall, unruly cedar trees.

The shutters on the upper floors were askew, a few hanging on by only the bottoms of rusted hinges. Stone had fallen from the rim around the top left of the house, leaving a dark hole open to the elements. Birds flew in and out, twittering excitedly, probably at the sight of a human—perhaps something they'd never seen here, at least during the daytime.

I began to walk toward the fountain with hopes that it still held water, even after close to a century of abandonment. I knew what this house was. In the mid-nineteenth century, great manor houses had sprung up along the banks of the Hudson River on both the east and west sides. The fortunes of the families who built them on the western bank of the river dwindled, and the mansions were left to rot. The great houses were too far from civilization at the time, and the cost of maintaining them had been staggering.

My mind reeled. My home in Irvington was on the east bank of the river. If this house I was looking at was on the west bank, then I would have had to swim across the river, which was nearly a quarter mile wide at Irvington. The swim explained why my clothes were soaked, but how had I managed it?

I pushed aside the overgrown bushes surrounding the decrepit fountain and peered down at the water. It was still clear, but dense algae reached from the bottom like great tresses of green hair. I sank my hands in the water and watched as the dirt and leaves swirled away from my skin. I cupped my hands and brought the cold water up to my face. I felt immediately refreshed. I removed my shirt and washed my arms. I then dared to stick my entire head in the fountain. As I twisted my head back and forth, I felt something hit my crown. I pulled out of the water, shook my head, ran my hands over my eyes, then peered down to the water.

I was frozen in place. The algae released a stiff body from its swaying green prison. The body floated upward from the bottom, rolling over as it did so. When the face came to the surface, I had to turn and release what little I had in my stomach. I recognized the face. It was my former client, Mr. Tarry. My eyes were bleary. I stumbled from the bushes surrounding the pool and wanted to run, but I didn't know in which direction. I started to hyperventilate, and I doubled over until my breathing returned to normal.

I turned toward the house and called out, "Why him?"

There was no answer, of course, except for the fluttering wings of frightened birds as they took flight from the roof and the exposed interior of the mansion. I stomped heavily to the front doors. The necklace, still around my neck, responded as I drew closer to the doors. A jolt went through my body. I shook out my shirt and slid it back over my body. I grabbed a doorknob and turned. The door creaked open.

Before I entered, I had to let my eyes adjust to the darkness that waited inside.

The first thing I noticed was the smell. I knew the smell of abandoned houses, and that scent of mold and decay was not present. As my eyes adjusted, I could see outlines of objects in the dark. I could tell that the house was, unbelievably, still furnished. I looked to my left by the door. There was a shelf with two oil lamps on it. I pulled down one of the lamps. When I brought it into the light, I could see that it was still filled with oil. I ran my hand over the shelf and knocked a box of matches to the floor. After I picked them up, I removed the glass chimney from the lamp and struck a match to light the wick. I remembered my cigarettes, which were a soggy mess in my pocket. I took them out of the pack and set them on the shelf beside the remaining lamp so they could dry. I raised the wick to cast more light. I did not close the door behind me as I took a few steps farther into the house.

I turned to my right and walked through an archway into a room scarcely lit by the dim light filtering through drawn drapery. A thin shaft of light fell on a settee and two facing chairs. I raised the oil lamp and scanned the walls, which were nearly covered by large paintings. I stepped closer to these and realized I was not mistaken: all the paintings were priceless. The furnishings would have fetched a great deal, as well. An impossible thought danced through my head. I imagined getting out of here, going back across the river, renting a truck, and fighting my way back to raid the place during the day. I could leave the necklace here and take everything else.

As that thought flashed through my head, the reality before me seemed to flash as well. I blinked my eyes as the vision became something different. For a second, I saw the furniture as tattered, moldy pieces, the paintings falling away from the frames. The ground was covered by leaves and moldering carpets. Then the vision returned to the splendid delight I'd had at first. I shook my head and tried to calm my heart, which had begun to beat quickly.

The sitting room led to a marble floor. Light flooded in, and the lamp was unnecessary, but I kept it lit. Marble steps led down to the sunroom I'd seen from the outside. In the middle of the room was a small fountain; water still fell musically into the pool. Trees grew out of the roof, and perennial flowers had grown to monstrous proportions. Vines tangled themselves in and among fallen logs, choking bushes and tree trunks.

I turned the corner away from the sunroom and went into a dining room; doors on both ends of the room were thrown open. Eight chairs surrounded a large table, which appeared to be pristinely polished. A chandelier dangled above the table, and again, paintings covered the walls. These were portraits, which, I assumed from the style of dress, were from the late nineteenth century.

From the dining room, I passed directly through the kitchen and into a hallway. Stairs at the far end led upward. I went past the stairway and into a library. The walls held built-in bookshelves from floor to ceiling, which were filled with books. I was entranced and studied the books closely, awed by the editions I saw. When I finally turned around, I realized the remaining daylight had faded. I walked to the window and pushed the velvety fabric aside to peer outdoors. I could barely see the outlines of trees. Anxiousness crept into my stomach, as did pangs of hunger. I left the library and walked back into the foyer, finding one of my dried cigarettes and lighting it from the lamp's flame. The tobacco tasted as if it had been cured in swamp water, but I didn't mind. I was immediately light-headed after not smoking all day. It felt wonderful.

I finished my cigarette on the porch and listened to the night sounds. Crickets chirped, and unknown animals scurried among the trees. I didn't feel frightened as I sometimes did at night when I was alone and let my imagination get the best of me. I had now met the real creatures of the night. Instead of finding them frightening, I found them fascinating. Enticing.

A familiar sensation—an internal pull—came over me. I knew that the necklace was working as it had before. I fought it—or him—even as I turned to go back inside. I was astonished by the transformation of the house as I looked into what had once been complete darkness. Wall sconces in the foyer were suddenly aglow, and I noticed a double doorway that I hadn't seen before. I walked through it to find a grand ballroom, its walls lined with glowing candles. Above me, a gigantic chandelier twinkled with small candles, illuminating statues of Italian design that were placed into recesses in the upper part of the walls between windows. Frame molding held lavish paintings depicting scenes from Roman and Christian mythology. I gawked for a moment, then came to a dead stop.

Four figures slowly emerged from the dark corners at the far end of the ballroom. They swayed as they walked, as if dancing to music I could not hear. They were four men with pale, naked torsos, wearing only loose-fitting, ratty brown linen pants. All had dark brown hair and were about the same height, so similar that they looked like brothers. They whispered to one another in soft, hissing voices. Their graceful steps, liquid arm movements, and beauty transfixed me. As they waltzed closer, I could see they were not entirely human, yet they lacked the glow that Favreau and Rocerres had. They smelled of earth but did not emit the sweet, almost winelike scent of my vampires. Perhaps I should have run, but they were too enchanting. After a moment I could make out what they were saying.

"He must be the one," said the one closest, his eyes locked on me. He had a wolf tattooed on the left side of his muscular chest. I speculated that he was in charge of the other three.

"He was promised to us," hissed another, whose hair was pulled back in a ponytail rather than close-cropped like his companions' hair.

"I knew he would come," said the one to my left. He was probably the most beautiful of them all. His eyes were light, gray-green as chrysoprase.

Soon the four of them circled me, each one staring into my eyes. They began to touch my face and the back of my neck. They gasped and groaned and began to chant, "He will be sweet. . . . Let us feed him. . . . Who will go first?. . . His skin is soft. . . . Feel his veins. . . ."

The one with the tattoo moved in front of me. He bent his head down until his nose nearly touched me. He parted his lips slightly and placed them over my own. He sucked my lower lip into his mouth a little. Then there was a quick pain as he sucked on my lip. He groaned; then the others protested.

"Why did you do that? . . . Wait your turn. . . . Feed him first! . . . Is he sweet?"

"Delicious," said the tattooed one as he whirled away from me.

Soon the four of them began to dance out of the ballroom, holding me aloft by their invisible force. As they walked, they continued to caress me, then began to kiss my arms and hands. The one with long hair pulled the index finger of my right hand into his mouth. He sucked on it gently and lightly grazed my flesh with his fangs. He looked me in the eye with a devilish expression, then nipped the end of my finger and sucked out a drop of blood. The others scolded him.

"You'll scare him. . . . He's hard to resist, isn't he? . . . He's so soft."

They took me into the dining room, where the lamps and candles were at full blaze. The table was set for one, with fine china, silver, and crystal. Two candelabras illuminated each end of the table. They sat me down to a mouthwatering feast. The smell of the meat was intoxicating; a glass of wine tempted me with its deep-purple body. I began to eat without question, feeling light-headed and dreamy as the four boys began to shiver excitedly. They took turns caressing me as I gorged, hunkering down and laughing with delight when I lifted the fork to my mouth over and over again.

"He's enjoying it. . . . Now he'll really be irresistible. . . . He's a superb gift. . . . Should we tell the others? . . . No."

When I'd eaten the last mouthful, I pushed away from the table. A gold cigarette case appeared beside my plate. I popped it open, removing a cigarette and lighting it from the candelabra closest to me. I reclined in the chair and smoked. The four beautiful monsters moved away from me as the smoke I exhaled rose up and played with the light. I felt powerful and masterly. I looked at the four boys and narrowed my eyes. They gazed back with seeming adoration. It could have been hunger. I smoked the cigarette down to the butt and extinguished it on the empty plate. I suddenly noticed spots of blood up and down my arm. These creatures had been nipping at me the whole time without my notice. My anger flared for only a split second before some other force seemed to squelch it. It could have been the wine but was more likely their crafty use of telepathic powers.

"He is ready. . . . Shall we take him? . . . He's seen the blood."

They gathered around me once more and lifted me high above their heads, walking in line beneath me to carry me through the house and up a stairway. The halls were dimly lit. I marveled at the intricate details of the house, forgetting that I was in the hands of four vampiric men. Circular tin plates embossed with floral patterns surrounded every overhead light. Cream-colored walls rose up to meet a hand-painted border that stretched the length of the hall. After we entered a doorway, they set me down. I looked around the room and saw a large bed, its covers crumpled against the footboard. The monsters pushed me forward.

"To the bed. . . . It's our turn to feed. . . . Remove his clothes; taste all of his skin. . . . Take from every vein."

I lay down on the bed and invited them. I wanted to touch them. I reached out as they bent over me, and I ran my fingers over their bodies. Their skin was smooth and felt as if it were clay that could be sculpted. The tattooed boy undid my pants. The boy with the longer hair moaned as he pulled my pants off from my ankles. I started to feel slightly uncomfortable, recalling bits and pieces of what seemed like distant memories of Rocerres. I could barely see who I was. My heart started to pound as if trying to beat away a fog that had blown over my vision. I tried to sit up. Once again I knew this wasn't right, and I wanted to fight it.

"He's going to struggle now. . . . Clear his mind. . . . Make him forget. . . . Make him want us."

With a snarl, the tattooed boy moved around to my shoulders and roughly flipped me onto my stomach. His hands held me firmly to the bed by my shoulders. He pulled the top of his pants down until his throbbing erection poked my face. He moved it to my lips. I turned my head away. One of the other boys grabbed the back of my head and made me face the huge cock. I couldn't struggle or move, or maybe I didn't want to.

I then felt long hair tickling my ass as a third boy climbed onto the bed. I felt a cold tongue force its way to my constricted hole.

"He can please us. . . . We can give him pleasure, too. . . . Take us all in."

My lips parted, and the tattooed monster slid his cock over my tongue. It was hard and smooth and smelled of spices. I groaned as he pushed it to the back of my throat. He allowed me to reach up with my hand. I stroked him slowly as the long-haired boy plunged his tongue far into me, then pulled out and teased me with the flicking end of his tongue. I groaned as the tattooed one put the monstrous cock back into my mouth. I devoured it, licked it until it was drenched in spit.

With movements too quick for me to see, the creature pulled out of my mouth and was behind me. I reached out to the youngest-looking one and ran my hand over his face. He sneered as I clenched the sheets. The tattooed boy rammed inside me. I cried out. I pushed against him. He stretched out over my back, and his hips made rhythmic movements. He pulled my head up and exposed my neck. I felt his breath, then his teeth. Tears welled up; he did not have the sharp fangs that Rocerres had. He bit down again, barely breaking the skin as he continued to pleasure me from behind. The other boys stood in my line of sight. They stroked each other as they watched.

Part of me still struggled, but not physically. My body belonged to them, so great was their power over me. I wanted their bodies on top of me, one after the other. I invited them with beseeching looks. They moved closer until I could touch each one individually. They were all smooth gods—or demons. Their movements were anything but cold as they kissed each other, stroked my head, and reached out to their brother who continued to dive furiously into me. I was incredibly hard and wanted them to jerk me off.

Without warning, the tattooed boy turned me onto my back and continued his assault on my ass. The long-haired boy grabbed my erection. His hand was soft and warm; my back arched as he got me closer. I wanted to scream; he had me so close but would not let me release. I punched his shoulder and begged for him to make me cum. He snarled at me and nipped my hand. The tattooed boy threw my legs back and fell on top of me, once again biting down on my neck; this time his teeth broke the surface. I tried to push him away, but he was too strong. He ripped at my shirt to get more of my skin. When the shirt fell away from my chest, the boys leaped back as if I were the monster. They held their hands over their mouths and looked around at one another. The tattooed creature leaped from the bed, his erection still throbbing. The youngest began to cry. Instead of tears, thin streams of blood flowed down his pallid face from his eyes.

"He wears the stone! . . . He belongs to Master! . . . He's not the one for us! . . . Master will be furious with us! . . . We shall be punished! . . . Master will starve us! . . . Hide him! . . . Master will know!"

I was dizzy as they continued their rant. I felt nauseated, as if slightly hungover. I gazed at the four boys, all the illusion gone. They were still beautiful, but they'd lost the sheen and grace they had exuded earlier. They all appeared to be terribly frightened, especially when a familiar voice bellowed from the doorway.

"Have you boys had your fun?" Rocerres demanded, his eyes blazing orange. He looked incredibly angry and larger than he'd ever looked before.

Chapter Seven

Rocerres stormed into the room. He pushed the four boys out of the way as if they were dolls. They stumbled over one another as they tried to regain their footing, then ran out of the room, clinging to one another like one creature with eight legs.

Rocerres approached me. His foul mood evaporated, and he seemed to return to his normal size. He sat on the edge of the bed and ran his hand over my forehead, then stroked my head. He smiled at me, yet I had the foreboding sense that all was not completely well. Rocerres then held out his hand, as a gesture to help me up.

"The brothers are a ghastly lot. I don't know why Favreau keeps them the way he does. I find it to be cruel."

"They are different from you," I ventured curiously.

"Oh, yes, they are. We call them vamplings. They are still human, never drained of their mortal souls, yet Favreau feeds them his blood to keep them young and alive. The effect, however, drives the boys mad. I imagine that if they stopped taking Favreau's blood they would live but would be completely and utterly lost mentally. Most likely, they would kill themselves.

"They cannot drain another human the way I could or Favreau does. They are so obsessed with the idea that they try over and over. For Favreau, it is a malicious game. He often brings men and women here and allows the boys to play with them, as a cat plays with a mouse before he kills it. Ultimately, Favreau will chase off the boys and finish their game for them."

I winced at the idea that it could have been me. It was no wonder Favreau had chosen them. In the mortal world, they would have been a hit, a feast for the eyes. They were somehow childlike, yet frightening. I wanted nothing more to do with them and was glad that Rocerres had come. I knew it made no sense that a creature who should have seemed much more dangerous than the boys had put my mind at ease.

I looked down at my body again and felt faint when I saw the crimson-stained sheets beneath me. I had lost blood, just enough to make me feel dizzy, but not to the point of losing consciousness. I pulled my bloody shirt back over my skin and slipped into my pants.

"Come, you must bathe before meeting Favreau. If that is why you came here," Rocerres said.

"I'm not sure why I'm here. I don't remember getting here."

"Roland, you know why you are here. It is not only the necklace but also the desire you have to be immortal. I know about your wish to watch the present fade into history. Your overwhelming . . ." He paused as if looking for the right word: ". . . ennui with the world."

As Rocerres spoke, he led me down the hall and into a large bathroom. Torcheres along the wall cast a romantic golden light across the sand-colored walls. By the windows on the far wall, I could see a large bath. It was rectangular and deep and, like a Greek bath, was made of decorated tiles. As we neared it, water began to pour into it. Rocerres reached into a closet and pulled out a towel and a large glass bottle that appeared to be filled with flower petals and leaves in a thick liquid. He upended the bottle over the bath, and the liquid flowed into the water, gathering at the bottom. Immediately I was hit with the sweet, fresh scent of floral essences. Rocerres set the towel on a marble bench next to the bath, then turned to me.

"You are a delight to the eyes. It is no wonder Favreau wanted you the first time he saw you by the river."

An eerie feeling passed through me. I wondered when Favreau had seen me by the river. I now doubted that I'd ever had the privacy I thought my home offered.

"It was not terribly long ago, Roland. At the beginning of the summer, you sat reading by the river while Favreau was nearby. You read by the light of a simple lantern. You had a sheet wrapped around you, and the soft lantern light made you look like an angel in corporeal form. He sent me every so often to check up on you and find out about you, to discover some way that we could meet you without raising your suspicions about our macabre lot."

As Rocerres' words spilled over me like fine oils, his hands gently undressed me. Childlike, I lifted my arms for him to remove my shirt. He was careful not to touch my wounds or allow the shirt to stick to the drying blood. He kissed my forehead and looked into my eyes as he reached down and undid the clasp of my pants. They slid off effortlessly. He slipped his fingers between my skin and the elastic band of my boxers and tugged them down my legs. He leered at my jutting erection. I gasped when he reached out, enclosing it in his cool, hard hand. He began to stroke gently. I looked down at him as he knelt next to me. I wanted this.

I wanted him, above all others—more than the four terrifying boys and definitely more than Kyle. As his hand moved up and down my shaft, I felt the familiar telepathic invasion. My senses were heightened. I grabbed his auburn locks in my hand, they seemed to be alive. His tresses wrapped themselves around my fingers. I felt warmth all over my body. I shuddered, then gasped as his mouth engulfed my cock.

He teased the head of my cock with his fangs, nibbling but not penetrating the skin. I was fearful, but more aroused by the danger. His mouth warmed with the friction of moving over me. He grabbed my buttocks and pushed me farther inside his mouth. Every push brought me closer to letting go. I leaned back against the wall for support.

Rocerres pulled away and covered his hands with sweet-smelling oil. He grabbed my erection again and worked furiously at it. He teased the head with his palm, making circular motions that sent a shock up my spine. I longed for his grip and moaned for him to bring me off swiftly. He complied with a demanding hand, but each time I got close, he slowed his movements. I couldn't take it anymore. I grabbed a handful of his hair and pulled forcefully. He responded by grabbing my hip with one hand while continually stroking my cock. My muscles tensed and released, tensed and released, my mouth was dry from panting. I burst, sending streams of white across the marble floor. I collapsed on top of Rocerres.

"I thought that vampires didn't do that sort of thing."

"There are many misconceptions," he replied. "Though we do not generally engage in human pleasure, remember that most of us were human at one time and do remember what it was like to hold hot bodies, to sweat in acts of carnality."

Rocerres led me to the edge of the bathtub. I slid into the flowery, oily water, soothed by the heat. Rocerres pushed up his sleeves as he moved to the side of the bath. He caressed me with a sponge, running it down the length of my arms and legs. He looked into my eyes and smiled as he ran the sponge over my tight chest. I was ready again, but the release would not come to me in the same manner as before.

I shivered as he moved the sponge down my stomach and then around the base of my erect cock. He plunged his other hand into the water and grabbed my balls. He moved the sponge under me, not caring that his sleeves were now submerged. He circled my hole with the sponge; I jumped. He slowly massaged me; my sphincter loosened. His wet fingers slipped easily inside me. He turned his head impossibly and bit my lower lip. He growled as a drop of blood passed from me to him. I heard singing in my head. His hand that had been around my balls grabbed the sponge and then, with the sponge, began to stroke me while still fingering and kissing me with sharp little bites. I was brought off quickly. Hot, white streams of semen swirled in the water. Rocerres stood up.

He pulled me out of the water and held my hand as I stepped onto the cold marble floor. I stood shivering for a moment while he took the towel from the marble bench and massaged my head, then dried me from head to toe. Rocerres then put a robe over me and wordlessly led me from the bathroom to a grandiose bedroom. I stood in awe of what lay before me. Every inch of the walls was hand-painted fresco. Cherubs teased Boticelli-style women. Naked men stood in gardens overlooking sprawling ancient Roman cities. The sky was so blue—it was my immediate understanding that this was the only blue sky a vampire would ever see. I looked at the ceiling. A vast bronze sun looked down upon Rocerres and me as he waited for my eyes to be satiated by the room's magnificence. Below the sun was a large round bed covered in layers of differently colored silks. The golden light from the torches played with the silk, making it appear like the ocean at sunset. I moved without thinking toward the bed, desiring the cool softness of the fabric. I lay in wait, watching Rocerres.

Before I knew what was happening, the room darkened. Soft fabric covered my eyes, bound around my head. My arms and legs were free, and I did not panic. I felt the weight of Rocerres' willful mental intervention. Then, a new sensation altogether. An aroma akin to exotic Eastern spices filled my nose. I felt hands on my skin, gingerly touching my wounds. Hot liquid was poured onto them, one by one. Hands massaged my muscles, massaged the hot liquid into the wounds. Though I could not see, I had visions—or delusions—it was hard to say.

One hundred naked men stood around me. I was in a different time, a far more delightful place. I heard singing in the distance, echoing over a valley. I saw the valley stretched out below a window set in a wall across from me. I was in a dust-colored room, wrapped in the finest of fabrics: velvets, satins, silks, and rich cottons. The men were angelic, smooth, young and golden-skinned. They attended to all my needs.

Two of the youths sat at the foot of the bed and engaged in long, passionate kisses, aware that they drove me to distraction. Another two golden-haired men sat on either side of me, their sun-bronzed skin glistening with powdered silk. They massaged my shoulders with warm hands but paid no attention to my cock as it rose beneath the cool sheets.

I began to fully realize the other activities around the room. It was a scene from a Greek bath. There were men everywhere, in every sexual position imaginable. I could not move from the bed but was meant to be a voyeur to it all. I paid particular attention to two giant young men in the far corner. Their rippling masses working furtively together in a mad rhythm of pleasure. The larger of the two was standing behind while the one in front was doubled over, taking in an enormous cock. I shook my head in disbelief and slowly drifted out of the spell.

"Where . . . ?" was all I could muster.

"Sshh, my precious one."

I froze. Rocerres had spoken, but his words and inflection reminded me of someone else. Some mental block kept me from getting to the answer. Just as I felt on the edge of discovery, the fabric was pulled from my eyes.

"Look," said Rocerres.

I gazed at my skin, which had earlier been ripped, nicked, and cut. I was now whole, and my skin seemed to vibrate where the wounds had been. I looked at Rocerres and smiled. I felt tears come to my eyes. He responded in a like manner, except his tears were pink: water mixed with his strange blood. I watched as a cut on his wrist closed within a matter of seconds.

He sat next to me and touched my healed skin. His fingers were cold, but I invited them. He put his face close to mine and licked the tears from my face. I saw two sharp teeth exposed beneath his upper lip. This was too much for me to see, and my heart began to beat madly within my chest. Rocerres caressed me, and I felt him inside my head again, soothing away worry, fear, and, yes, anticipation.

Rocerres removed his shirt, revealing pale skin stretched over muscle and bone. He gracefully stretched out on top of me so I could feel his cool, hard weight. I wrapped my arms around him as if he were a lover instead of a creature who had materialized out of myth and lore. Rocerres looked at me with his strange eyes, they seemed to spark and shimmer. His hands cupped my face while his elbows pinned me down. His lips met my brow, then my nose; finally he rested his chin against my forehead and spoke.

"You don't know what you're asking for. This is not life. It is not a game, not something you can play at, then return to normalcy."

I want it, I cried internally.

"I cannot let you have it."

An image flashed through my head. I knew what Rocerres intended to do. I saw him against my neck. I knew he meant to end my life or save it; it came to the same end.

If you kill me, then you are damned.

"I am already damned. For you there is hope."

Lightning fast, his mouth was against my neck. I gasped as his fangs punctured my skin. Tears streamed down my face. My heart seemed to shiver. A wave of nausea passed through my body. I felt my own ghost seeping into Rocerres' body. Another shiver. My arms shot out; I clenched Rocerres' hard shoulders and felt for his skin. I grabbed his neck. The skin was smooth, and I felt it growing warm by degrees. I pushed his fangs deeper into my neck, and the world faded for a split second. He pulled away from me. His face, once pale, now radiated a pink light, as the Virgin Mary is always portrayed with a soft glow. He looked holy. His lips were no longer pale. Not a drop of blood appeared anywhere. Blood tears streamed down his face. He mouthed, "I'm sorry," then dove into me again. I cried out, never having known any sensation like this. I was dying and living at the same time. It was a heady, high feeling, as if I'd been drugged. The world became cloudy. I could hear my own heart slowing down in my ears. I was not yet dead when I heard a familiar and frightening voice speak.

"He is mine." Favreau's voice filled every corner of the world. "At last, he is given to me."

Chapter Eight

The world flickered like a movie from the 1920s. Flashes of Favreau's face filled the palette of my sight. His hands roamed my body. He massaged my thighs. Even near death, I was aroused. He seemed to be inspecting every inch of me. I wanted to move, to cry out, but it was as if a hundred silk ropes were holding me to the luxurious bed. Death bed.

I looked at the bronze sun on the ceiling and tried to imagine the real sun. Then I felt a drop of warmth on my lips. My tongue reached for it desperately. I barely tasted it. It was sweet and spicy and seemed to caress my tongue. I groaned as it electrified my throat. I saw that Favreau held his arm over my mouth; a small gash dripped blood onto my tongue. It took the little strength I had to grab the arm and pull the gash fully against my mouth. I sucked greedily at Favreau's exotic blood.

My stomach burned from the liquid. I knew I was dying. Some dark being ravaged me from inside out. My own blood receded from my skin and veins like water from the shore, overtaken by the new, demonic blood. New knowledge filled me; Favreau's memories, too. I was learning the truth of him.

* * *

In a garden of dark flowers and wet, black trees that oozed a clear, viscous substance lay a woman of extraordinary beauty. She was ravished again and again by translucent figures who howled and grunted. After each demon finished with her, a new creature emerged from her body, covered in black liquid and a film of thin membrane. The being inside the amniotic sac would burst into the dank air. The dark creatures of the world were brought forth: vampires, werewolves, walking dead, and devils incarnate. Lilith writhed on the ground, crying out, cursing God, her black hair in a spray around her like an obscure nimbus. The clouds above whirled in madness; a great lightning bolt struck the earth and scattered her grotesque offspring across the globe, and Lilith perished, and the demons screamed.

Upon the death of his mother, Favreau wandered the world. For centuries, he had the innocence of a child who does not know his mother, questioning his beginnings, yet killing men because his devilish spirit demanded the souls of humans to live, and his body the blood of men to survive. He soon lost all hope of discovering his identity but, millennia later, stumbled upon the civilization of men in Europe and made his home there.

It was in France that he adopted the name Favreau and learned to walk among humans and fool them with his deceiving powers. He fell in love with men and women alike but was drawn to the fragile power of young, beautiful men. He would get close to them, learn their histories, until his natural bloodlust overcame him, and instead of making love, he would kill and regret. His fury and malicious side were born with the death of Rocerres.

How he was enchanted by the boy with reddish hair. The innocent boy with the soft skin, who trembled at his every move, too precious for the world, too beautiful to play whore to the royal court of France. Favreau had meant for Rocerres to become a vampire, to spend the rest of eternity by his side, feeding on humanity until humanity's end.

He had drained Rocerres of blood, but Rocerres still lived. He was as pale as the white cotton beneath him on the bed in Favreau's manor.

Favreau, convinced he was to lead a lonely life, had never made one of his kind before. His knowledge of creation was an instinct that only surfaced late in his existence. He knew that his own blood was a tonic for the dying. He was a fountain of dark, eternal life. Favreau bit into his own wrist, prepared to feed Rocerres and bring him into the macabre world of strange vision, preternatural power, and insatiable, unnatural hungers.

There was a rumbling outside the chamber door. Favreau whipped his head around and was face to face with two heavily armed and armored guardsmen from the palace. He threw up an invisible and impenetrable wall. The guardsmen's armor clanged against the barrier. Favreau grabbed Rocerres' limp body and fled from the room, bursting through the window, falling lightly to the ground. Rocerres paled, impossibly, even whiter than before. Favreau felt the hot blood-tears streaming down his face. He sobbed as he ran for the secret entrance to his own chamber. He burst into the room and laid Rocerres on top of the stone lid of the sarcophagus. Favreau sliced his wrist again, as it had already closed. He let his blood drip onto Rocerres' blue lips. As the blood trickled into the slight opening of the mouth, a horrible gurgling sound came from Rocerres. His body heaved; his chest shot upward. He collapsed on the stone. Favreau gathered the auburn head in his hands and screamed into the night. His precious boy had died.

Favreau had taken Rocerres' soul. He could assume his appearance and his voice at will. He had the boy's memories. He fled from the tomb, furious at the human world and man's mortality. He blamed one person for the death of Rocerres: Margaret de Valois. He would not seek his revenge immediately. In fact, more than a decade passed before he finally sought his justice. He had all the time in the world, after all. It was late one night, after Margaret had successfully carried out her own revenge on her brother and former husband and had been admitted back to Paris, when Favreau took her mortal life and gave her the life of a devil. Then he left her without explaining what she was or what she would have to do to survive. To the present day, he neither knew nor cared if she had endured.

I knew Favreau as I had never known anyone else. I saw everything he had ever experienced, thought, or dreamed. When my visions faded, I burst back to reality with a thudding in my ears and chest. I was covered in my mortal sweat, as one who is at the very fading end of his life. Yet I was becoming more alive as well. I still felt weak as I pulled the dark blood from Favreau.

He pulled his wrist from my mouth and stood over me, smiling. He backed away from the bed.

"I haven't had enough," I growled.

He laughed, as if I had told an evil joke.

"You will have to come to me," he teased.

I pushed myself up with my elbows. My body felt lighter, as if I were only half attached to it. I gathered my strength and leaped from the bed. I landed only a foot from Favreau and collapsed at his feet. I gathered what could have been the last of my energy and made another desperate attempt. This time my hands found his shoulders, and with all my force and weight, I landed squarely on Favreau. He fell backward. On top of him, I instinctively went for his neck. I had new, sharp little fangs. They pierced his skin. I locked my legs around his hips and bit deeper until a gush of spicy heat entered my mouth. Favreau called out:

"Take me, my precious one."

I let the liquid rush into me and burn me more, hotter and hotter. Favreau writhed beneath me. I began to suck so that the fluids pumped harder into my mouth. He maneuvered his arms beneath me and pushed. I was flung from his body. I landed, laughing, on the bed. I was thrilled and delighted. I knew that I was not fully made. I was not done. I had to have more. As I thought this, Favreau flew through the air. He tackled me on the bed. We wrestled amid the silk, satin, and velvet. We turned over and over until he surmounted my will. It was then that he dove into my neck with his sharp teeth. I wanted this. I needed it. He must have all of me. I let it happen but did not feel my death coming on as before. I was light-headed and lighthearted. As he pulled the blood from my neck, I reached out with my free hand and wrestled his wrist to my lips. I bit down. Our blood circulated from one to the other. I took him in until I could take no more.

We collapsed on top of each other. Our wounds healed as if they had never existed. I knew then that I was what he was. The world was altogether different. I could see the colors in the room as if it were daytime. The frescoed walls were more detailed than my mortal eyes could ever have perceived them to be. I saw the truth of this villa. It was not run-down, as I had thought when I was human. That had been a vampire's trick. The manor was fully intact and well maintained.

I sighed, feeling a new kind of hunger. I was naked and newborn. I was taken by surprise as my body gave up its last mortal stand and released its dead organs. My heart still beat strongly. Favreau looked upon me as a father would look upon a son. He lifted me from the bed and took me to the bath.

He set me gently in the warm water that he drew into the bath, and sponged me as he had before, when he wore the mask of Rocerres.

Rocerres. In some way I had grown attached to that image, that being. Anger flared up in me as I looked at Favreau, who was looking at me. Bloody tears ran down his porcelain white cheeks. He smiled as well. I felt pity for him even as he infuriated me. I was too weak to do anything about it.

"Why did you come to me as Rocerres?"

"Because I am too frightening for mortal eyes in my natural state. We all are. You will find that if you stay in contact with one mortal man or woman for too long, they will soon hate and fear you. They won't know why until they are in your grasp and you are taking their life from them."

"Why have you not made others, aside from Margaret and me?" I asked as he finished washing away all signs of my human self.

"It is not something easily done. It is not easy to find a mortal who truly wants it. I have tried. The others went mad and burned themselves up in the sunlight. It was too horrible."

Favreau had new clothes waiting for me in the room where the four boys had taken me. I slowly put them on. They seemed to have no weight on this new body of mine, but I could feel every thread of the woven cotton shirt and pants. I touched my own skin, amazed that it was becoming hard and slowly losing its color.

"You must feed," Favreau said.

It seemed that even before he had finished speaking, the boy with the tattoo glided into the room. I could smell the blood pounding in his veins. My teeth ached for him. My cells cried out for the warm blood that mixed with Favreau's in his veins. I did not yet know the mental tricks to call my victims to me.

I advanced toward the boy. He didn't make a move to get away. He smiled at me; he invited me with his eyes. He smelled delicious. I let one hand rest on his muscular chest. The other I slipped behind his head, tilting it to expose the pulsing vein in his neck. I drove my teeth into his flesh. I could feel Favreau watching me, smiling when I took my first hot mouthful of the boy. The boy gasped as I sucked.

I was startled and pulled away when I began to receive flashes of his life. My desire for his blood overrode the shock, and I went back to the wound. I licked a stream of blood that had escaped onto his naked shoulder. I enveloped his wound with my mouth and sucked gently. I could feel his heart beating, slowing almost imperceptibly with each gush of hot liquid that filled my mouth and ran down my throat. My entire immortal body tingled with the new life it was receiving, and I realized that my victim was eighty years old. Favreau's blood had kept him in the shape of a twenty-year-old. He had been taken by Favreau when his parents had perished in a fire. The last thirty years of his life were a blur. He'd been driven mad by his own existence. He was not vampire, nor was he human, and his psyche couldn't bear it. He had become a simpleton, but he was still sweet and nourishing.

As his heart convulsed, nearing the end of his life, the blood tasted different.

"You must stop now, and let the body die naturally and release the soul. If you feed until your victim dies, that soul will stay with you. No good for immortals," he smiled, proud of his fledgling vampire who had made his first kill. "Would you like another?"

I couldn't deny it. I would. "Yes."

"I think I will dine with you," he said with a malicious smile.

The three remaining boys appeared in the doorway, entered the room, and stopped, all three standing in a subordinate manner, heads bowed and hands clasped in front of them. They were a sight to my new vision. Gorgeous specimens, they positively glowed. It was no wonder Favreau had kept them for so long, as one might collect dolls.

The boy with the ponytail saw his brother's drained body and looked at Favreau with a scowl on his face. He broke from his stance and rushed at Favreau. With a ferocity that I had only glimpsed in Favreau's memories, he grabbed the boy by the neck and lifted him off the ground. He gashed the boy's throat with his teeth and pulled him close. The boy struggled and beat on Favreau's back with his arms. Favreau pulled the boy even closer. The boy cried out, then went limp.

The other two boys gazed on, expressionless. I didn't have Favreau's rage. I merely held out my hand to the eldest of the boys. He took one gingerly step toward me. I pulled him gently against me and took in his deep brown eyes and his slightly musky scent. I flicked my tongue over his Adam's apple and licked the skin over his pulsing vein. I gently tore open the skin. The blood trickled out. I sucked the small hole, teasing myself. He groaned in my ear. I bit down until he gushed inside me.

I could feel my preternatural strength grow stronger as I fed. When I finished with the boy, I moved to the last. I would not be able to finish him off. I'd had nearly enough and could take no more. My vampiric hunger was satiable, despite what I had always read and believed in my mortal life. As I took from the boy, I heard him gasp. Favreau took the boy's wrist. We fed on him together, and as he took his last mortal breath, Favreau and I dropped him.

"You have fed well, my young one. Now come; the sun is almost upon us, and we can't be found by its rays."

I awoke the next evening in the cellar of the manse. Row upon row of vintage wine concealed the door to Favreau's lair. A modest wooden door that mortals would regret opening was all that protected Favreau from the outside world while he slept the sleep of the dead.

I was immediately starved for blood and looked toward the exit. I heard Favreau rise from behind me and felt his eyes on my back as if they were two hot pokers. Already I despised him, yet I relied on him to teach me the ways of our kind. I then felt his hand on my shoulder. It moved down and around to clutch the gem, which still hung around my neck. He pulled the necklace over my head and held it in front of him. He kissed the stone, then spoke to it.

"You have brought me my greatest gift."

I was not his gift. I had made the decision to be what I'd become.

Hadn't I? In truth, I didn't really know, and it was far too late to puzzle it out, and I had only blood and flesh on my mind. I raced out of the cellar, ecstatic with my newfound supernatural strength and speed. I knew that I would never be a match for Favreau. He had millennia on me. He spoke as if reading my mind.

"I have not even begun to display my full abilities. I have no need, either. You will hunt with me."

"I will do as I wish," I braved.

Before I knew what was coming, Favreau's impossibly hard fist glanced across my face. I flew back and through the wall of the hallway and landed in the foyer. I heard a snap, then felt the strange and immediate sensation of my vampiric blood gathering at whatever bone had snapped. I was instantly repaired. I rubbed my jaw, which still stung.

"You will hunt with me!" he roared.

Favreau disappeared for a few moments, then returned with the carved box in his hand. He wore a long black coat, looking every bit the walking myth that he was. I didn't dare speak but followed him outside. He grabbed me roughly by the arm. He enveloped me in the coat and looked down at me. He smiled, and his eyes went soft. I was terrified by his emotional shifts.

We took to the air, Favreau holding my body tightly to his. I once again felt safe, and relaxed.

"Where are we going?" I asked.

"You have a friend who I would like to meet someday." Favreau held the carved box in front of me while he said this.

"Kyle?"

Favreau laughed. Then, to torment me further, no doubt, he shifted his form. I saw, for half a minute, the one I would love to have known: Rocerres.

When Favreau returned to his normal state, his sadness was written deeply on his smooth skin. He was mad, completely insane. He had been tormented for centuries by what I knew he considered his greatest failure: allowing Rocerres to perish.

Suddenly, we were on the ground outside a large white house. I was overwhelmed by the sound of voices and thoughts flying at me from every direction. I nearly doubled over. I adapted quickly, however, and instinctively filtered out the telepathic signals. I homed in on a strong wave of images from the house. I knew then that we were already in Westport and that in that house, on the second floor, Kyle was fast asleep. As I started to move away, I felt Favreau slip the carved box into my hand. I looked down at it, then at Favreau. The look on his face and his willful mind told me that I must take it. I hated that I had no control.

I walked to the house. Kyle's bedroom was on the other side of the French doors that led to a balcony, much like in my house in Irvington. I easily scaled the trellis and hopped onto the balcony. I moved to the window and peered in.

Kyle, in all his human beauty, was sprawled across a thin mat on the floor. Stacks of canvases three feet deep leaned against the far wall. He looked angelic. His full lips were parted slightly, and with my powerful hearing, I knew the sound of his breathing. I could read his dreams. He dreamed of Irvington with a yearning to be back there. It had not been such a long time, though much had happened to me to make me forget that it had been mere days since I last spoke to him.

I pushed the doors. They caved in easily. There was a crunching sound as I broke the lock, but Kyle was a deep sleeper. His dreams were a thick barrier separating him from the conscious world. I knelt beside him and stroked his head. He wriggled beneath my touch. His brow furrowed. Then, frighteningly for me, he opened his eyes and looked directly at me.

He smiled at me and spoke, "Roland."

I said nothing as his eyes closed again. The smile remained on his face. He thought I was part of his dream. It was a good thing, too, because I would not have been able to control myself. It was something I did not expect. I wanted to tear into him, not caress him. I wanted to have his blood, his soul, racing inside my own body. My human side, though, did not want this. I stroked his head and kissed the soft space between his eyes. I feared what would happen if I set the carved box beside his bed, knowing that Favreau himself would call Kyle to the manse, to become his toy or a victim.

With more tenderness than I had ever displayed for Kyle during our human time together, I touched his face and began to push it away from me. He smiled yet again and moaned softly. His hand closer to me clutched my arm. He pulled me down, as if he thought I meant to kiss him. I did kiss him, lightly on the lips.

"Thank you for coming," he said in a sleepy voice, now conscious that I was there, but not knowing what I was.

I said nothing but moved my mouth to his neck. I hesitated before leaning closer, softly breaking his unsuspecting skin. He laughed quietly, as if this were a new game for us. I felt overwhelmingly saddened by what I was about to do. This was a much better fate than what Favreau would have planned.

As Kyle's blood trickled into my mouth, then flowed freely, I saw his life lived out. Astonishingly, I realized his true emotions toward me. He felt much more strongly for me than he'd ever let on over the past few years. He'd feared my reaction. I shuddered as I took in the blood and love. I clenched him tighter to my body as his heart revolted. I sobbed as I sucked. He gasped as his life slipped effortlessly away from his body. One last beat of his heart sounded in my ears, and I released him. I collapsed on top of him, too shocked to move. *Is this what it will be like, forever?* I asked myself.

I was furious as I realized that Favreau had meant for this to happen. Once again I had played into his cruel game. I would not stay by his side for long. I vowed to myself to return to my own home in Irvington.

When I regained my composure, I gazed at Kyle's lifeless body one final time before turning away, torn between wanting to be what I had become and wanting to be what I had been.

Vampires, Inc.

Sean Wolfe

Thanks and Acknowledgments

Thanks to the great guys in my writers group: Lake Lopez, Matt Kailey, Jerry Wheeler, Drew Wilson, and Peter Clark. Your input and commitment to helping make me a better writer are much appreciated. Thank you for your willingness to accept my unconventional ideas on vampirism—even if it was reluctantly.

Thanks to my earthly angel, Jane Nichols. You are always there for me, whether it's to encourage me to continue writing and to keep dedicated when it was hard, or to remind me I am loved and to be my shoulder to lean on during the most difficult year of my life. I love you more than words could ever say. And that means a lot, especially coming from a writer.

Thanks to my editor, John Scognamiglio, for your unending patience in extending my deadlines during very difficult personal circumstances, and for going the distance for me. You're the BEST—don't listen to what those others are saying about you. <grin>

A very special thank-you to the love of my life, Gustavo Paredes-Wolfe. Gustavo was my life partner for thirteen years and passed away on September 4, 2003, one month before this novella was originally due to my editor and publisher. He never saw the completed work. But Gustavo always encouraged me to live my dream of writing, and provided invaluable feedback on all my work. He is truly my inspiration for all that is good and right and love in this world, and I miss him terribly. Te amo, *babies.*

Chapter One

No one paid any attention to the storm when it rolled in. There was no reason to, really. Nestled between the enormous Rocky Mountains to the west and the dry and dusty plains of eastern Colorado, the city of Denver had seen its share of thunderstorms, certainly.

Midafternoon June showers are common and, for the most part, welcomed. Temperatures hover in the mid-nineties to the lower one hundreds for most of the summer, and residents of the city revel in the precipitation and the cool breezes the thunderstorms usually bring with them.

This particular storm began as a low rumble among some scattered gray clouds scooting in from the west and across the foothills. This was a pattern the residents of Colorado's largest city were familiar with, and most did not even look toward the mountains to acknowledge the approaching storm. It started a couple of hours later than most did, just as people were arriving home from work and settling in for dinner. But other than that, it was as predictable as what they knew they would inevitably be having for dinner that night. The ground shook, and windows across the city rattled as the winds picked up and the clouds became darker and thicker in the sky above. The temperature dropped from ninety-six degrees to seventy-four in less than an hour. When the tiny drops of rain began to fall, people ran out to roll up their car windows or to raise the tops of their expensive convertibles to protect the leather upholstery.

It had been an unusually hot and dry summer, as had the previous one. The ground was bone dry and cracked in amazing spider-web patterns across the entire Denver metro area. The area-wide water restrictions caused the lawns to wither and die. Instead of lush green lawns and bright, colorful flowers, homes were surrounded by dried, brown dead grass and withered, lifeless weeds. The entire state was in the middle of the worst drought in state history, and the capital city was thirsty for a good wetting.

So when the storm first made its presence known, it was welcomed with open arms. No one looked up into the sky and pointed with confusion or wonder. Instead they looked up and smiled with relief. No one cried out in horror or sought shelter from an unknown danger. In fact, some of the more colorful citizens dropped their briefcases or backpacks and danced a little jig in thanks to the rain gods.

As far as anyone was concerned, this was just another midsummer, midafternoon, midsize Denver thunderstorm. The kind they'd known and loved all their lives. These storms had abandoned them for the past couple of years and now had returned like prodigal parents.

Though it had been almost twenty-four months since they'd experienced the pleasures of the thunder and lightning and cool rain, there was no reason to be afraid of this storm. As far as the people of Denver were concerned, this was a wonderful and most welcome gift.

Sure, it had suddenly appeared out of nowhere, without any advance warning. The forecast for the day had predicted a record high of 103 degrees, and cloudless skies. But everyone knew the weathermen here could do little more than hope and pray they were anywhere close to an accurate forecast. The weather in this region was as fickle and unpredictable as it came. Even the weathermen themselves joked about their inability to deliver an accurate forecast most of the time.

So the residents of Denver felt there was no reason to believe this storm would be any different from all the thousands of others the fine people of this fine city had seen in the many years they'd lived here.

They were wrong.

* * *

Christiano Montez glided through the darker clouds that were concentrated in the center of the large storm. Here the thick mist that made up the ominous clouds was dark enough and solid enough to filter out almost all of the little sun that was left. Sundown was still a few minutes away, and he was aware of the danger he'd put himself in. But the urge to keep moving was too much for him to ignore, and he'd decided to trust the instinct in his gut that told him he'd be okay.

Christiano had been blessed with the gut instinct from a very young age. Though it had most likely been with him much earlier, he'd first really paid attention to it on his first solo feed, almost 180 years ago. He was seven years old then, as all young vampire boys were when they ventured out on their first feed without the aid of their fathers or mentors. He was just about to pounce on a middle-aged woman exiting a small corner store in Barcelona when he stopped in his tracks. Though all his training urged him to jump on the woman's back and sink his teeth into her neck, something held him back. A quiet whisper in his ear convinced him to sit back and wait. A few moments later a young boy, probably ten or eleven years old, stumbled out of the same store and glanced from side to side in the thick fog of the evening. His little fists were filled with candy, and he looked lost.

Christiano crouched behind the tree in the dark and watched the young boy.

The boy called out for his mother a couple of times, and then sat on the edge of the curb just a few steps from the store. He tore the paper wrapper from the candy and began eating hungrily.

Christiano stared at the boy and couldn't tear his eyes from the kid's lips and tongue as they licked and chewed at the candy. His heart raced as conflicting thoughts flashed through his mind. The boy was only a child, and he shouldn't feed on such an innocent. Yet he couldn't help but wonder how thick and warm the blood would feel on his own lips and tongue. How thick and sweet it would taste as it slid past his tonsils and into his throat.

He looked back in the direction the woman had walked, and thought briefly about chasing after her. But the fog and the dark of the night had enveloped her, and she was nowhere to be seen. He glanced back at the boy, and that's when his gut instinct first spoke to him in a loud and clear voice.

Go for the boy, it said. *Everything will be all right. It will taste and feel better than anything you can imagine.*

And so he did. He stood from his crouched position behind the tree and walked slowly over to the boy. When he was but inches from the child, he crouched down and wrapped his own little arms around the back and neck of the boy, tilted the head slightly to the right, and sank his teeth into the sweet and supple neck of the boy who was only slightly older than himself.

The blood was as sweet and warm and deliciously bitter as he'd dreamed and known it would be. The young boy struggled slightly, but Christiano's extraordinary strength proved too much for the mortal boy. Christiano felt the kid fight back, felt his muscles tighten and struggle against his own smaller body. He heard the boy whimper and felt the cool tears as they dropped from the boy's chin onto his own cheeks.

As Christiano drank from the young boy's neck, he sniffed the air around him. He could smell fear, yes, but there was something else as well. Something he'd never smelled or sensed when he'd accompanied his father on feedings. He could smell the sweet, clean odor of the boy. The aroma wafted up past the cold, soft throat and into Christiano's nostrils. As the boy's struggling began to weaken, the smell became stronger and more alluring.

Christiano's heart raced harder. As he breathed, the sweet smell filled his nostrils, and he sank his teeth deeper into the boy's neck and sucked more blood into his mouth. The small body lost all signs of life and struggle, and Christiano knew he should stop. It was one of the first lessons his father had taught him. When the body is dead and the blood begins to run cold and bitter, it is time to stop feeding.

But he couldn't stop. He tried, but the smell of the young boy and the feel of his body lying limp and lifeless against his own were more than the young Christiano could resist. He kept drinking blood from the cold, clammy neck until no more was coming out, and he found himself almost chewing at the torn and nasty flesh of the boy's neck.

When he finally pulled himself from the lifeless body and stood up, he was surprised to notice that he had an erection. He wasn't yet old enough to know exactly what that meant, but he knew it felt good, and knew he wanted to feel that way again.

It had been the gut instinct that told him not to go for the middle-aged woman but to go instead for the young boy closer to his own age. And from that moment on, he'd learned to trust that instinct and to go with it.

And now, all these years later, he was still trusting it. Trusting that he would be okay to fly inside the dark clouds, even a few moments before dusk. And he'd been right. As he glided in the clouds above the city, he felt his blood grow warmer and flow easier through his veins. He felt energy begin to fill his body. He knew without seeing that the sun was now dropping below the outlined crest of the Rocky Mountains. He was safe, and he opened his eyes and flew down through the middle clouds closer to the lower levels.

When the sun was completely gone and the air around him was bathed in darkness, he descended from the clouds and landed on his feet in the middle of the city. The night around him whispered to him. It told him he would be safe here and that he could stay as long as he wanted.

Christiano smiled as he strolled through the dark streets. They were almost empty because of the rain. He sniffed the cool, damp air and looked around him. He liked the infusion of old architecture and new, and instantly felt at home in the strange city. He'd felt that way a couple of times before, in Paris and in San Francisco, and knew at once that it was a mixed blessing. Feeling at home was always nice, and both Paris and San Francisco had offered that. But in both instances, tragedy had struck and ultimately led him to leave the cities he'd grown to love.

Denver might also offer itself as home to Christiano, if he gave it the opportunity. But he didn't plan on doing that. This city was only a stopover on his way to Chicago. The only reason he'd stopped in the middle of the storm that was heading slowly toward the Windy City was because he was hungry and feeling weak. He was already two days late in feeding, and he knew he wouldn't make it to Chicago before he'd be dangerously weak.

A short layover in Denver for a couple of evenings wouldn't hurt anything. There was nothing waiting for him in Chicago anyway. The lure of anonymity and the ability to get lost in the largest vampire community in the United States was the only force driving him there. He wanted desperately to get lost in the crowd and to lose himself somewhere in the process.

Once Christiano descended from the clouds, the storm dissipated quickly. It rolled out of the Denver metro area, rising and losing form and strength as it went. Christiano knew that in another hour it would disappear altogether. He was the only reason it had had any strength to begin with. Now there was no reason for its existence.

As the winds died down and the rain trickled to a few sprinkles, the city began to come back to life. Streetlights flickered on, and people ventured into the streets. Christiano watched them as they greeted one another and laughed and hugged one another while slowly getting back to the business of living.

He stood on the corner of Colfax and Broadway, in the very center of the city, and looked around him. East on Colfax, just a few blocks away, stood the Cathedral of Immaculate Conception. The massive white structure stood like a sentinel over the city. Bright white lights reflected over the stone building and made it shine like a spotlight against a mirror.

Christiano walked toward the building. His steps were slow and deliberate at first. Then his heart began racing in his chest, and he found it more difficult to breathe. He quickened his pace and struggled not to break into a run. He needed to settle into his temporary home for an hour or so before venturing out into the Denver night. He couldn't wait to reach the cathedral and find his way into the dark depths of the basement he knew would be there. Of all of the dwellings he'd called home over the past 187 years, none was more comfortable and homelike than the basements in the centers of the various cities' most revered Catholic cathedrals. They were quiet, solitude could always be guaranteed, and when the shit hit the fan—as it always did—the cathedrals could always be assured to be the one place police and vigilante citizens never stormed and searched. They were safe.

He strolled around the side of the building, making sure no one was watching him, and then crawled over the fence that surrounded the back of the building. Sure he was not being observed, he smashed his elbow against one of the bottom windows near the ground, and reached inside to unlock it.

It slid open easily, and Christiano slipped inside quickly and unnoticed. Once inside, he closed the window and taped a piece of cardboard over the small hole he'd made. His eyes instantly adjusted to the darkness, and Christiano walked around the spacious basement. There were a few statues and old pieces of furniture that had long ago been discarded.

He walked past the dusty furniture and deeper into the darkness of the basement. In the corner farthest from any of the windows, he noticed it. On the floor beneath a large and heavy statue of the Virgin Mary was a door. It would have been unnoticeable to the human eye, but Christiano saw it clearly. He moved the five-hundred-pound statue effortlessly out of the way and reached down to pull the door open. It opened with barely a trace of a squeak, even though Christiano was certain it hadn't been used in over fifty years.

Christiano stepped through the hole in the ground and found the steps. He climbed down about thirty steps and reached the dirt floor. It was much darker at this level even than the basement had been, but Christiano adapted to the darkness quickly. It took him only a few moments to locate the candles and get them lit. He smiled as he looked around the small room and saw the casket. It was lying in the far corner, a heavy coating of dust covering it.

He walked over to it and carefully wiped the dust away before opening the lid. Inside, the casket was lined with immaculate white silk. It was plush and perfectly maintained. Christiano stroked the soft, smooth material and sighed deeply. He couldn't wait to slide inside and fall into a deep, dark sleep. He knew without ever having slept in this particular casket that his sleep would be complete and without disturbance. Tomorrow he'd wake up refreshed and ready to meet another evening.

But tonight he had business to tend to. He was hungry and needed to feed. He slowly closed the casket lid and blew out the candles. Then he climbed the steps and reentered the basement. He was careful to put everything back in its place, and then he cautiously opened the window and climbed back into the cool Denver night.

* * *

The evening was just coming alive. The storm had deluged the city; so much rain had pounded the streets, they'd quickly flooded, pouring over the curbs and saturating the lawns. By now, however, the streets were cleared again and people were streaming into them. The rain had cooled the air, but just slightly. More than anything, it made the evening humid.

Prostitutes of both genders sauntered along the Colfax sidewalks, barely dressed. Some of the women had their breasts completely exposed. Young men leaned against buildings and lampposts with their legs hiked up against the walls, and grabbed their crotches as Christiano walked by them. Several of them followed Christiano for a block or two, assuring him they were the best of the bunch, and lowering their prices the farther he continued to walk without looking back at them.

Up Colfax Avenue, just a few blocks from the cathedral, Christiano noticed a bar with the brightly colored rainbow flag painted across the outside walls and windows of the place. "The Detour" was painted above the door, and Christiano thought it was the perfect omen, and a good enough reason to stop in for a few moments.

It was dark inside the bar, the only light emanating from the dim swinging overhead lamp above the pool table and from the neon signs above the bar advertising various brands of beer. Smoke wafted up from brightly lit tips of cigarettes dangling from the lips of several heavyset women with short, spiky haircuts, who were draped in oversize flannel shirts and dirty, torn jeans.

Christiano noticed that the whispered conversations grew even quieter as all heads turned toward him. He walked slowly toward the bar, nodding silently at some of the women closer to him as he passed. He was quite aware that he had drawn the attention of every woman in the bar. His black jeans, black button-down shirt, and knee-length black leather trench coat probably made it even harder to be inconspicuous than it would otherwise have been. But the fact that he was well over six feet tall, with creamy-white skin and a head full of dark black hair that was slicked back, probably didn't help, either.

There were probably thirty women in the bar, and they all watched him in silence as he approached the bar.

"Good evening," he said as he leaned against the wooden bar.

"Can I help you with something?" the woman behind the bar asked. She was short and stout, with bleached blond spiked hair. She chewed on a piece of gum and puffed on a cigarette at the same time. The sleeves of her flannel shirt had been ripped—not cut—off, exposing several large and elaborate tattoos on her well-muscled arms.

Christiano considered ordering a drink and then thought better of it. "I seem to be lost," he said, and smiled at the bartender.

"You think?" The woman leaned in closer to Christiano and blew smoke into his face. "I never would have guessed."

The other women in the bar laughed and slowly returned to their own conversations.

"We're not impressed with your fancy clothes and your arrogant walk here, mister. I doubt seriously we have what you're looking for here. Maybe just moving on might be a good idea."

Christiano glanced around the room, taking stock of the number and size of the women present. He guessed it might take him about ten minutes to kill them all. He'd save the bitch behind the bar for last, of course, making her watch as he flew through the room, snapping some of the women's heads, stabbing his dagger through the hearts of others, and strangling the rest. As for the bartender, he'd wait until she was paralyzed with fear, and then he'd sink his teeth into her neck and suck every last ounce of blood from her body. It'd take a couple of minutes—long enough for her to realize what was happening, though she would be unable to do anything about it.

But that would cause a scene. One of the women might escape through one of the two doors that led outside. And even if that didn't happen, someone could walk in right in the middle of the massacre and could run for help. Then it'd all be over. His first night in Denver would end disastrously, with a barrage of police and reporters. No, that wouldn't do at all. Besides, he didn't have a taste for women anyway.

"Perhaps you're right," Christiano said. "You wouldn't happen to be able to point me in the right direction, would you? Perhaps an establishment with a larger . . . male clientele."

"Couple blocks just up the street. A little pansy bar called Charlie's. Plenty of nicely trimmed weenies and shaved white asses there, if that's what you're into."

"Precisely. Thank you for your assistance."

Christiano turned around and walked toward the back of the bar, to the door he'd entered. Several of the women snickered as he passed by them. When he got to the door, he turned and looked back at the woman who'd disgraced him. Even from this distance, a good fifty feet, and through the dark and the smoke, he could read her name tag. Sheila was her name. If he didn't find what he was looking for at Charlie's, he might just come back here and feed on her even though he didn't like the taste of women. It'd be worth it to kill her just for the joy of it, and for her being such a bitch.

Christiano tipped an imaginary hat toward Sheila and exited the bar.

Charlie's was a little better but, from what Christiano could see upon his arrival, not a whole lot better. It, too, had a small-town, honky-tonk feel to it. It seemed Denver thrived on that particular atmosphere. The wooden decor and smoke-filled entry were unpleasant. To the left of the entry were a couple of pool tables, and to the right was a coat check. Just beyond the door was a large bar that greeted customers as soon as they passed the entry and the staff members who checked your ID and made sure you weren't carrying a weapon.

Beyond the bar and to the left was a small dance floor and another, smaller bar. This dance floor was filled with young yuppie guys in various states of dress and undress, dancing maniacally to a loud bass beat. Sweat poured from their faces as they jerked their heads from side to side and jumped up and down. From his vantage point several feet away, Christiano could see their faces clearly. Most of them had their eyes closed and were smiling deliriously. The rest had their eyes open and were staring with empty gazes ahead of themselves, into thin air.

Christiano thought for a moment about choosing his prey from the group of skinny young men who were sweating and dancing in this bar. But the taste of their blood would be bitter and acrid from all the drugs. He decided to move on.

To the right of the main bar were a glass partition and a glass door. Beyond them Christiano could see another bar, packed full with a slightly older and slightly more dressed crowd of men. He walked past a group of men who watched his every move, through the glass door, and into the larger, less smoky room. This part of the bar was filled past its legal capacity with guys dressed in jeans, button-down shirts, and cowboy boots. Country music blasted from large speakers spread throughout the room. A mirrored cowboy boot disco ball hung from the ceiling over the center of the larger dance floor. The air reeked with a mixture of various sweet-fragranced colognes, sweat, and alcohol. The men all stood tall, with their chests puffed and pushed out in front of them. They scoped one another out with an eagle's eye. It didn't take long for Christiano to feel hundreds of eyes boring in on him.

He walked to the back of the room and leaned against the door that led out to the patio. Several men in their late thirties or early forties approached him and tried to strike up small talk with him. Christiano was not attracted to middle-aged men with thick mustaches or chests filled with matted hair, and so he dismissed them politely.

After an hour, Christiano was just about to give up and move on. Then he noticed him. The boy couldn't have been more than twenty-four or twenty-five years old. He was standing in a group of similarly aged and similar-looking young men on the far end of the dance floor. He and his friends were drinking and laughing and watching the older men dancing two-step on the dance floor a few feet away.

Christiano focused his vision on the young man, and the friends around him blurred into Christiano's peripheral vision. The young man was tall and thin, with wavy blond hair and sparkling blue eyes. When he smiled or laughed, his entire face lit up, and giant dimples popped out on either side of his full, pink lips. He'd been wearing a white T-shirt earlier but had taken it off and stuck it inside the waist of his blue jeans. His torso was thin but well-defined. He sported a marble-smooth and perfectly proportioned chest with dime-sized nipples that were hard and dark brown. The washboard abs drank in the sweat that dripped down his chest and tummy, and flexed involuntarily as the young man laughed.

From where he stood, easily fifty feet away, Christiano could smell the kid's scent. It was sweet and clean and strong. And it made Christiano crazy with lust. His heart raced, and his cock stirred in his pants. Christiano knew at once that he had to have this young man.

His eyes bored in on the blond guy across the room, and then he waited. It didn't take long. A few seconds later, the young man turned his head in Christiano's direction. Christiano raised his glass and smiled. The kid smiled back and brushed several stray strands of hair from his face. His movements seemed to be in slow motion, and when he raised his arms, Christiano noticed the flexing biceps and dark brown patch of hair under the kid's armpits. Again he could smell the boy's scent: strong and masculine and confident.

Come here, Christiano whispered in his own head, without moving his lips.

The boy cocked his head to one side and looked perplexed. He glanced around him from side to side and then behind him. He shrugged his shoulders and then returned his gaze to Christiano.

Come to me, Christiano repeated.

The blond kid set his drink down and excused himself from his friends. He began walking toward Christiano, stopping only a couple of times to stop and kiss one guy on the cheeks and to shake hands and chat for a short moment with another acquaintance. Then he set his eyes on Christiano and walked steadily to him.

"Good evening," Christiano said as the boy approached him.

"Hey," the kid said, and stuck his hands into the back pockets of his jeans. "What's goin' on?"

"Just trying to get my bearings," Christiano said. "It's my first night in Denver, and I'm afraid I'm a little lost."

"Lost, huh?" the blond boy said. He looked around him to make sure their conversation wasn't being overheard. "What exactly is it that you're looking for?"

"A little company."

"Company, huh? Like an escort?"

"Not exactly," Christiano said. "I don't usually pay for the company of another man."

"I don't blame you. I wouldn't, either. But I'm not really a man, now, am I? I'm really just a boy." He tilted his head to the side and grinned sheepishly as he blinked his eyelashes seductively. "A boy who is willing and able to do pretty much anything you want. Do you get my drift?" the young man whispered. He looked around him again, nervously.

"Yes, I believe I do. And just how old are you?"

"How old do you want me to be?"

Christiano looked down at the kid and raised his eyebrows.

"All right, all right. I'm twenty-three. But keep that between you and me, okay? Some of the guys in here like to believe I'm seventeen or eighteen."

"Just between us," Christiano said as he crossed his heart. "And also just between us: twenty-three makes you a man and not a little boy."

"I get it. So you're not going to pay?"

"No."

"That's cool, I guess. Wanna get outta here anyway? I've done pretty good tonight. I suppose I could give it up for free just this once. Just for you."

"How thoughtful," Christiano said. *As if you had a choice,* he thought to himself. *As if you ever had a chance. You poor boy.*

"Let me go say good-bye to my friends," the boy said as he started to walk away.

"No," Christiano said, and grabbed the boy's arm. "They will get the idea when you don't return."

The kid looked up into Christiano's eyes, and for a brief moment he looked afraid. Then his eyes softened, and he nodded his head.

Christiano smiled and led the boy to the front door.

"Do you have a place we can go?" The boy was anxious and looking around him in every direction.

"No," Christiano said. "I mean, I do, but it's not very convenient."

"I hear ya," the boy said. "Wife wouldn't be real thrilled with the idea of watching another guy fuck her husband, huh?"

"You are quite crude, aren't you? Maybe this isn't such a good idea."

"I'm sorry, man. I don't mean to be such an ass." He squeezed his crotch and danced around Christiano. "I'm just horny as fuck. And you're really turning me on."

"You've already had sex a couple of times tonight, and you're still horny?"

The kid smiled. "I'm twenty-three."

"Right."

"So what do you say? We could go to my friend's car. It's just right over there," he said, and pointed to a car at the end of the parking lot. He jingled the keys in front of Christiano's face.

"All right. Let's go."

Once inside the car, the young man wasted no time in unbuckling

Christiano's belt and unbuttoning his jeans. He began unbuttoning Christiano's shirt as well, then became impatient and ripped the shirt open, popping buttons in every direction. He leaned Christiano's seat back and pulled Christiano's cock out of his jeans.

"Wow, dude," he said as he wrapped his fist around the girth of Christiano's quickly hardening cock. "This is fucking awesome!"

"I'm glad you approve," Christiano said as he felt the warmth of the kid's mouth surround his cock.

"Approve?" the kid said as he pulled his mouth from the now swollen dick. "It's outta this world. I don't think I can take it all."

"Try," Christiano said as he held the young man's head in one hand and pressed slowly downward.

The young blond boy sucked Christiano's cock for several minutes. Several times he had to stop and take a couple of deep breaths.

Christiano thought the sloppy cocksucker might not be able to finish, but before too long, he felt the inevitable signs of his pending climax. His balls began to shrink up, and the familiar tingling started at the base of his cock and worked its way slowly up his hard shaft.

"That's it," Christiano said as he panted and held the boy's head deep onto his cock. "I'm gonna shoot."

The kid moaned loudly and sucked harder on Christiano's cock. He wrapped his hand around the thick cock and slid it up and down the veiny shaft.

A couple of seconds later, Christiano's body tightened up, and he moaned. The young guy sucking his cock also moaned, and his grip on Christiano's throbbing cock tightened.

Christiano's body convulsed for several seconds and then lay limp on the passenger's seat.

"How was it?" the blond asked as he shifted himself in the seat and wiped at his mouth.

"Incredible," Christiano said. He leaned forward to kiss the young man on the lips.

The boy leaned back. "Sorry, I'm not really into kissing strangers."

"That's all right."

"But my cock is fucking harder than a rock. I gotta get off, man. Will you suck me, too?"

"Oh, I will definitely suck you," Christiano said. "Lie back."

The young man shuffled around in the seat and switched places with Christiano. He lay back in the seat and shoved his jeans down his legs and to his ankles. His cock throbbed against his belly.

Christiano looked at the dick for a moment and deliberated with himself. It was long and thin. White skin stretched across it and highlighted the thick, blue veins that snaked around it. A tiny drop of precum leaked from the head and glistened there a moment before dripping down the hard shaft. It was a nice cock, and Christiano wanted to suck on it until it was spent.

But he was hungry. As much as he wanted to enjoy this young man, he needed to feed even more. Time was running out.

"Come on, dude. Suck my dick," the young boy said as he repositioned his body in the front seat.

"Later," Christiano answered. "First I want to kiss your neck."

"Look, dude, I told you I'm not into kissing. I just want you to suck me."

"Don't worry. I will. Just lie back and relax."

The kid sighed deeply, then relaxed in the seat.

Christiano leaned forward and kissed the cool, sweaty neck. He licked it for several moments and then clamped his mouth across the jugular vein. The boy moaned loudly, and his body twitched a couple of times. Christiano knew the kid was getting into it, and smiled to himself. As much of a fight as they initially put up, they always eventually begged for more. He knew it wouldn't be any different this time.

"Oh, man, you're fucking getting me all hot and shit," the young man said as he bucked underneath Christiano. "Keep sucking my neck, dude. It feels incredible."

Christiano sucked for a moment longer and then opened his mouth enough so that the lips around his now protruding teeth could slink back. He took a deep breath and then sank his canine teeth deep into the kid's neck and across his jugular vein.

"Owww!" the kid yelped. "What the hell?"

Christiano sucked hard as his teeth pushed deeper and deeper into the kid's neck. The first wave of blood that flooded into his mouth was warm and sweet. Christiano moaned loudly and sucked more of it into his mouth. He closed his eyes as the warm sweetness slid past his tonsils and down his throat.

"Stop it, man," the boy yelled, and tried to push his hands against Christiano's chest and push him away. "That hurts, dude. Stop it!"

The feel of the young man's hands against his chest and the struggle the boy was putting up only fueled Christiano's desire. The boy bucked up against Christiano, wiping his sweat against the smooth skin of Christiano's own naked torso. Christiano could feel the cool sweat against his skin, and his own cock began to throb back to life. The boy's cock, which was long and hard and throbbing just a moment ago, was quickly shrinking and losing its hardness.

"Please don't," the boy pleaded as he realized he was nowhere near strong enough to overpower this man on top of him. "I'm sorry."

Christiano continued sucking the blood from the boy's neck and wondered what the boy was sorry for. Not that it mattered. The body beneath him began to lose its strength, and the struggle became much less powerful. Christiano reached between his own body and the boy's and pinched the boy's nipples. Another moan escaped the boy's mouth, and Christiano smiled to himself. Even in a moment of pain and confusion, the young kid recognized his own arousal.

"Don't . . . ," the kid pleaded quietly as his arms grew limp and fell to his sides. "Please don't . . ."

Christiano increased his sucking on the boy's neck as his hands tickled across the kid's chest. The kid's skin was cooling down quickly, but his nipples were still hard. Christiano wanted to lick at them, but that would mean he'd have to stop feeding, and that was not an option at this point. He could still enjoy the young man, though, and reached down to squeeze the soft cock lying between the boy's legs. A couple of tugs on it, and Christiano felt it try to fill with blood and grow hard again. That meant he still had another couple of minutes before the boy was dead and his blood became rancid.

It was at this point that the blood became thicker and sweeter. It was what Christiano considered dessert, and he drank the thick blood thirstily. The boy lost consciousness a moment later, and Christiano reluctantly let go of the half-hard cock in his hands and stopped massaging the boy's nipples.

When the blood flow began to thin and taste like tarnished brass, Christiano took one last mouthful and then slowly pulled himself from the limp body beneath him. He looked down at the boy and noticed that his eyes were still open. He closed the kid's eyelids and lay back on the seat next to the dead boy. He took a couple of deep breaths and then wiped the quickly caking blood from his lips.

"Sorry, kid," he said as he looked over at the white, lifeless face next to him. "Nothing personal."

After catching his breath for a few moments, Christiano got out of the car and buttoned up his jeans and shirt. He walked around to the passenger's door and opened it. The dead boy's body slumped across the seat and halfway out the open door. Christiano reached inside and lifted the lifeless body effortlessly. He walked over to the Dumpster a few feet away and tossed the heavy body over his head and into the Dumpster. Then he walked back to the car, shut both doors, and walked out of the parking lot and down Colfax toward the cathedral.

Back inside the cathedral, Christiano quickly found the statue and the trapdoor. He climbed down the stairs more quickly this time, since he was more accustomed to them, and lit three of the candles in the small dungeon room. He looked around himself and sighed deeply. Already, after just one feeding and a couple of hours in this strange new town, he felt more at home than he had in years. It was a good feeling.

Christiano opened the door to the casket and looked inside. It was calling to him. He stripped his clothes and folded them neatly and laid them on the chair against the wall opposite his casket.

Standing naked in the cool, damp room several feet below the ground, he caressed his body. He felt alive, and his cock stirred back to life quickly. It was a good sign. He wrapped his fist around his long, thick cock and slowly stroked it for several minutes. It didn't take long for him to shoot his second load of the night. Thick, white streams of semen poured from his cock and onto the dirt floor beneath him. His knees buckled beneath him as he unloaded himself, and he reached out to steady himself on the side of the coffin.

When he was completely spent, he shook the last remnants of his seed from his shrinking cock and climbed into the casket. The silk pillow and sheets were soft and cool on his naked skin. He closed his eyes and looked forward to the deep sleep and the dreams he knew would come. They were almost always good dreams, comforting and most welcome. He loved the dreams, even the ones that weren't quite as colorful and comforting as most.

He took a deep breath and looked around the room one last time before he closed his eyes and relaxed his muscles. He was asleep in less than ten minutes.

Chapter Two

"Christy, if I've told you once, I've told you a thousand times. You simply cannot argue with me anymore about this." His mother looked down at him, her eyes filled with gentleness and love as she stroked his soft, smooth skin. "Bedtime is absolutely no later than five o'clock. We can't risk being awake when the sun rises. You know that. Why do you insist on arguing with me?"

"Probably because you insist on calling him Christy," his father whispered as he sneaked up behind her and kissed her softly on the nape of her neck. "If I've told *you* once, I've told *you* a thousand times not to call him Christy. How is he ever going to grow up and become a strong, virile vampire if his mother keeps calling him a girl's name?"

"Oh, for crying out loud, Stefan. He's only three years old. I seriously doubt that my calling him Christy is going to traumatize him in any way. He's my little baby, and I need to hold on to him for as long as I can. In a couple more years he'll be accompanying you on feedings, and before you know it, he'll be going solo. He'll grow up fast enough. But for now he's still my little boy, and I will spoil him if I want."

"Yes, dear. Just don't come crying to me when he's sixteen and still sucking on these beautiful breasts of yours," his father said as he leaned into his mother and cupped her ample breasts in his hands and kissed her passionately on the lips.

"Stefan! Not in front of the boy."

"Come on, Marguerite. It's 1814. Get with the times, will you? Kids today are growing up faster than ever. He's going to have to get used to it sooner or later."

"And later it will be. Now get out of here and leave us alone. I have to sing Christy to sleep now. I'll be in, in just a few minutes."

"But . . ."

"Go on."

"Oh, all right," Stefan sulked as he turned and walked toward the bedroom door. When he reached the door, he looked back and blew his wife a kiss, then exited the room.

Christiano looked up at his mother's beautiful, creamy-white face and giggled as she began her lullaby that always put him to sleep immediately.

Stefan had been right, of course, but as much as he might get upset that Marguerite was overprotecting their son, and as much as he worried that she was overnurturing Christiano, he could not bring himself to stand his ground and force her to let go of their son and allow him to grow up. The few times he'd tried, she'd broken into tears and become faint with hysteria. Stefan was a strong vampire and a natural-born leader. But the one thing that could bring him to his knees in agony was to see his beloved wife racked with pain and crying. Those giant drops of water that cascaded down her delicate white cheeks were more than he could stand. More than he had ever been able to stand. And so he stood back and let his wife raise their son as she saw fit.

By the time Christiano was ten years old, it was obvious he was very different from the other little vampire boys. While other boys flocked together and wreaked havoc and mischief wherever they went, Christiano preferred wandering the fields alone beneath the moonlight and composing songs and poems under his mother's watchful eye. While other boys begged to accompany their fathers on nightly feedings and rendezvous even when they were not hungry and did not need to feed, Christiano preferred to stay home and brush his mother's hair as he read her his latest composition.

From as far back as he could remember, Christiano had been an outcast among everyone save his mother. He had very delicate features that distinguished him from the other boys: soft, silky skin that, though white from the lack of sunlight, shined with a little more color than any of the other vampires, boys or girls. His light hazel eyes sparkled with life and joy and hidden secrets aching to be told. The twin dimples that graced either side of his full, pink lips gave him a doll-like appearance, and made it all that much easier for other vampire kids to ridicule him.

And they did. Sometimes they forgot and made fun of Christiano in front of the adult vampires. They would always get scolded and reprimanded and pulled by the ears by their parents. The older vampire parents reminded their children that of all living beings, vampires should know what it felt like to be different, to be scorned and ridiculed. They should never make another vampire feel ashamed or embarrassed about who he was. They should be proud to be vampires and always support one another, despite their differences. They should embrace their uniqueness and celebrate the diversity of every individual vampire.

The other kids would sulk as they were dragged away by their parents. The parents always spoke eloquently and loudly, making sure everyone, especially Marguerite and Stefan, heard them. But behind their words was always a note of sadness and patronization. They would look back as they dragged their own kids into the houses and, upon meeting the eyes of Stefan and Marguerite, would drop their own to the ground.

If anyone had told Christiano his life would forever change on his eightieth birthday, he would have laughed. There was no reason that particular day should have been any different from any other day in his life. He was young and just entering into the prime of his long life. For every seventy-five or eighty years of life, a vampire only aged physically about ten or fifteen years, and so Christiano was still a beautiful young vampire. He wore his hair a little longer back then, the natural black waves flowing almost to his shoulders. His twin dimples stayed with him and caused everyone who looked at him to fall in love instantly.

And when he met Bernhardt, that's exactly what happened. He was in Germany, taking a couple of years to travel and learn the language. His mother had been adamant in not wanting her only son to venture so far from home, but Stefan had met Christiano's proposal of three years' travel experience in Germany with open arms. For the first time in their lives, father and son formed an uncomfortable alliance, and much to Marguerite's dismay, Christiano set out for a new life in Germany.

On his birthday, Christiano had made plans to meet some friends at a bar. He arrived first and, after waiting for them for almost half an hour, was beginning to lose patience with them. They were always tardy, and he, for one, had had enough of it. Were they not adults? Did they not fathom the importance of responsibility and being on time? He was fairly new to the country and had so far only made a handful of friends. Could they not be on time just this once to celebrate his birthday?

When Bernhardt walked through the door, Christiano turned to see if the newcomer was his friends. His eyes met Bernhardt's, and he immediately felt the breath escape from his lungs in a sigh. Even halfway across the room he was struck by Bernhardt's beauty, and the energy between the two of them was ecstatic. Christiano forced his mouth to produce enough saliva to allow him to swallow, and tried unsuccessfully to draw his eyes away from the stranger's.

Bernhardt kept his own eyes fixed on Christiano's as he walked past him and made his way to the back of the bar. Once there, he ordered a drink and returned his gaze to Christiano.

"Take a deep breath and remain calm," Christiano whispered to himself. He tried to do so but ended up coughing loudly as the harsh, dry air forced its way up his throat and into his nasal cavity. He looked over at Bernhardt again and felt his cock harden as he watched the handsome stranger take a sip of his beer and then lick his full, red lips seductively, his eyes boring deeper into Christiano's soul.

Come here, he heard whispered deep inside his head. It was a voice he was not familiar with. He looked at Bernhardt again. *Come here,* the voice repeated. Christiano was certain it was Bernhardt's voice, but he was equally certain the handsome stranger's lips had never parted to speak any words.

Bernhardt raised one eyebrow, and raised his mug ever so slightly. *Are you going to play coy and make me come to you?* he said without moving his mouth again.

Christiano swallowed hard again and walked over to the high table where his new friend stood. "How do you do?" he managed to squeak out as he reached the handsome stranger.

"I do very well, thank you."

"My name is Christiano."

"I'm Bernhardt."

"Today is my birthday," Christiano blurted out and then immediately regretted having said it.

"Congratulations! Happy birthday, Christiano," Bernhardt said as he smiled and held his mug up in a toast. "To many more birthdays. And to many happy years. Together."

"Huh?" Christiano asked, not sure he understood the German correctly.

"I'm a man with very good intuition. And I have a feeling we'll be getting to know one another very well, and spending many years together."

"You are? I mean, you do?"

"Yes."

"How did you do that earlier?"

"Do what?"

"Talk to me without opening your mouth."

"It's an old trick. I will try to show you sometime how to do it."

"Would you? I'd like that."

"Of course. But first I have to know something. As I said, I'm fairly intuitive, so I believe I am right. But I must know for sure."

"What is it?"

"Are you a night owl?"

"I beg your pardon?"

"I'm sorry. I really don't know how to say this. I'm not accustomed to meeting new friends in this . . . environment."

"What environment is that?"

"Here, out in . . . well . . . the general public. What I mean to say is, if I asked you to meet me tomorrow morning, say at nine o'clock . . . for breakfast . . . yes, that's it, for breakfast—what would you say?"

Christiano dropped his gaze and focused on his glass of beer on the table. He shuffled his feet and cleared his throat. "I'm afraid I'd have to decline."

"Oh?" Bernhardt said, and gently reached over and cupped Christiano's chin in his hand. He lifted Christiano's face up until they were looking into each other's eyes again. "Why is that?"

"I'm not really a morning person."

Are you a vampire? the voice inside Christiano's head asked again. Bernhardt's hand was still holding Christiano's chin, and his lips never moved. Neither did his eyes, and Christiano knew without a doubt where the question came from.

"Yes, I am."

"Oh, good," Bernhardt said as he dropped his hand from Christiano's chin and took another large sip of his beer. "I thought you were, but I wasn't quite certain."

"Is that a problem?"

"No, no. Quite the opposite. I am also a vampire, and if you were not . . . well, we'd have a little problem."

"And what problem would that be?"

"Well, I'd have to kill you, and then I'd have been completely wrong about the whole 'many years together' thing, now, wouldn't I have been?"

Christiano laughed. "Yes, I suppose you would have been at that."

I abhor this place, the voice said again. *What do you say we leave and go back to my apartment?*

"Only if you promise to show me how to do that," Christiano said as he set his glass on the table and reached down to take hold of Bernhardt's hand.

"I'll show you that and so much more," Bernhardt replied, and led Christiano out of the bar and into the dark, cool night.

"You are the most beautiful creature I have ever laid eyes upon," Bernhardt said as he forced himself to pull his lips from Christiano's.

"Really?" Christiano said as he licked his lips. It was not the first time those particular words had been said to him, but every time someone spoke them, it felt new and exciting to him. "What is it you like most about me?" he asked teasingly.

"Where do I start?" Bernhardt asked. "Is it your bedroom eyes that speak volumes of untold secrets? Or is it your milky, smooth complexion that taunts me into believing you're still a child? Or maybe those adorable dimples on your cheeks that exude an aura of false innocence?"

"False?" Christiano said, pouting.

"Or maybe it's that strong jawline that defies that innocence and says that you are truly a man."

Christiano giggled and pulled away from Bernhardt to sit on the bed.

"No. No, I don't think it's any of that," Bernhardt said.

"You don't?"

"No. I think it might be this beautiful chest of yours, so smooth and hard and begging to be kissed," he said as he ripped the shirt from Christiano's chest and leaned in to nibble on Christiano's nipples and then kiss his way down to the taut stomach and belly button.

Christiano gasped for breath as he felt Bernhardt's tongue dart its way down his belly and around the sensitive navel.

"Or perhaps it's the lure of what lies beneath these skimpy pants," Bernhardt whispered, and then unbuttoned Christiano's pants and slid them off his hips and legs in one swift move.

Christiano swallowed hard and squirmed as Bernhardt slid his hands up and down his smooth, muscular legs, and then lifted his hips off the bed so that he could slide the underwear off as well.

"Or could it possibly be this most beautiful ass I have ever laid eyes upon?" Bernhardt said as he rolled Christiano over onto his stomach and lowered himself to his knees on the floor so that he could more easily access Christiano's marble-smooth ass.

Christiano let out a low moan as he felt Bernhardt's wet tongue tickle the outside of his ass and then slide ever so slowly inside. His cock grew hard instantly, and he was afraid he'd spend himself too quickly. He tried to think of something, anything to take his mind off the sensation that traveled through Bernhardt's tongue and into his ass and up deep inside him.

"Stop," he managed to squeak out as he pulled himself from Bernhardt's tongue and rolled over onto his back.

"What's the matter? Don't you like it?"

"Of course I like it. I love it. But you're getting me so close so fast. I want this to last. I want to taste you, too."

"That can be arranged," Bernhardt said, and quickly began removing and discarding his own clothes.

Christiano watched as Bernhardt removed each item of clothing. He squirmed with delight as Bernhardt threw his shirt on the floor, revealing a large, muscular chest that was dusted with thick curly patches of hair that snaked down past his navel and got lost in the waistband of his pants. He reached up and pulled Bernhardt's pants off in one clumsy move, and gasped when Bernhardt's long, thick cock popped out the top of the pants and swung heavily in front of his face.

"You're not wearing any underwear!" Christiano shrieked.

"No. They are a bit binding. Is that a problem?"

"Definitely not," Christiano said, and leaned forward to lick the head. He moaned as the slick, salty precum slid across his tongue and down his throat. He wrapped his lips around the head of Bernhardt's cock and tried to tell himself to play it cool and to take it a little at a time, but was completely unsuccessful. He took a deep breath, and in one fell swallow, Bernhardt's massive cock was deep in his throat.

"Dear God," Bernhardt moaned as he slid all the way inside Christiano's hot throat, "how in the world did you do that?"

Christiano sucked on the giant cock for a few seconds, then let it slip out of his mouth. "I'm talented that way."

"Yes, you are, indeed."

Christiano licked at the salty head again and then swallowed the cock back into his mouth, past his tonsils and deep into his throat. His throat muscles gripped the hot shaft and massaged it as his lips tightened and slid up and down the last couple of inches of Bernhardt's cock outside his mouth.

Being careful not to withdraw his cock from Christiano's mouth, Bernhardt repositioned himself so that his face was in front of Christiano's cock while his own dick plunged deeper into Christiano's mouth. He reached out tentatively with his tongue and licked on Christiano's cock for a moment, and then took a deep breath and deep-throated the entire length.

As much as Christiano would have loved for this to continue forever, it didn't take long before both men had reached the point of no return. He felt Bernhardt breathing heavier and sliding his cock deeper and deeper into Christiano's throat. When it was completely buried,

Bernhardt stopped thrusting and simply let his cock lie in the wet warmth of his throat. Seconds later it spewed shot after shot of warm cum into Christiano's throat. Christiano swallowed each shot, relishing the sweet warmth as it settled into his belly. Then he took a deep breath and tightened up his entire body as he released his own load into the warm mouth and throat of his new lover.

When they were both finished, they lay on top of each other, catching their breath. Christiano was just about to drift to sleep when he felt Bernhardt slip his cock out of his mouth and roll him over onto his stomach.

"What . . . ?"

"You didn't think we were done, did you?" Bernhardt asked. "We are just getting started."

"But I thought . . . ," he gasped as he felt Bernardt's huge cock slide effortlessly inside his ass. He immediately tightened up and grabbed the sheets with his hands. "Bernhardt . . ."

"Shhh . . . ," Bernhardt whispered as he licked the outside of his ear and kissed it softly. "Just relax. You're going to like this, I promise."

"I already like this," Christiano whispered back, and tightened his ass muscles even more as he arched up to meet Bernhardt's thrusts.

The deeper Bernhardt stabbed himself inside him, the more Christiano moaned and begged for more. The sweat poured off both men as they brought each other closer and closer to ecstasy. Christiano swore he could feel Bernhardt's cock grow thicker and thicker as he pounded inside him. And Bernhardt knew he was not imagining the sensation of Christiano's ass muscles wrapping themselves around his big cock and squeezing it as if milking a cow. Both men bucked against each other with uncontrolled passion and soon reached the point again where there was no turning back.

"Not inside me," Christiano moaned as he struggled to roll over onto his back.

"What?"

"I want to feel you all over my face."

"Are you sure?" Bernhardt gasped as he already slipped his cock out from the tight confines of Christiano's ass.

"Yes! There will be plenty of time to feel your hot seed inside me. But right now I want to feel it bathe my face."

"Okay, here I . . ." And with that, Bernhardt sprayed his load all across Christiano's stomach and chest and face. It seemed to go on forever, and when he was finished, he looked down and saw that Christiano was covered with his load.

A second later Christiano moaned loudly, and Bernhardt felt a massive load of thick, hot semen shoot all over his back. He collapsed on top of Christiano and hugged him until they both caught their breath. Then he leaned up and kissed his lover long and deep. They fell asleep in each other's arms.

And that is how they stayed, for eighty years. Christiano and Bernhardt were madly in love and never once regretted their decision to spend eternity together. They were partners in every aspect of their life, and defied anyone to challenge that love. No one ever did. Vampires don't really distinguish between gay and straight, like humans tend to do. Some were a little skeptical at first, not knowing what to think of the two strong and handsome men who were so devoted to each other. But it didn't take long for their love and devotion to become legendary, and soon they were welcomed and even celebrated in most vampire communities.

Bernhardt was truly the love of Christiano's life, and their relationship was the one thing he was proudest of. For eighty years they loved and supported each other, and as far as they were concerned, it would last forever.

But that was not to be.

They'd stayed in Germany for another ten years and then decided to move on. They visited London, Prague, Moscow, Rome, and even stayed in Barcelona, Christiano's hometown, for a few years. But they eventually ended up in Paris, and that was where they felt most at home. They lived there happily for over fifteen years. And then the dream came to an abrupt end.

It was a cool evening in April, 1970. It had been storming outside all afternoon, but by the time the two lovers woke just an hour after sunset, the storm had weakened considerably. They could still hear the tinkling of raindrops on the large glass windows that looked out onto the streets, and the low rumbling of thunder as it crawled across the dark sky. Bernhardt had always loved a good storm, but Christiano had never particularly cared for them. He also wasn't feeling well, and decided to spend the evening at home. Bernhardt had woken extremely hungry and needed to feed, and so they agreed he would venture out into the storm alone. It wasn't something they did very often at all; they usually hunted and fed together. But every once in a while one or the other of them wouldn't feel up to it, and the other would feed alone. This was such a night.

Bernhardt had been gone for nearly three hours, and Christiano was beginning to wonder where his lover was. In the few times they fed alone, they always made short business of it and returned to be together. He was reading a book by the fireplace when he heard a commotion outside in the streets below. At first he thought little of it, thinking the bars had just let out, and that they were probably just some rowdy youngsters heading home after a night of drinking. But then the noise grew more heated and angry, and he realized there was a mob moving slowly down the street.

He got up and walked to the window. The thunder had returned about an hour earlier, and the raindrops tickled the windows once again. Christiano's heart dropped in his chest, and a lump in his throat prevented him from swallowing. He parted the heavy drapes from the window. Outside there were maybe a hundred people, yelling and screaming and waving long wooden poles. Some of them carried lighted torches that struggled to stay lit in the light rain but somehow did. They all crowded around something in the center of the crowd and were all trying to get closer to it.

Christiano's heart stopped beating for a moment, and he fell to the floor as his heart constricted in pain. "Bernhardt," he cried out, and crawled on his knees over to the door of the apartment. He took a couple of deep breaths and forced himself onto his feet. Then he walked out into the hallway and into the street below.

By now the crowd had moved several blocks down the street, and Christiano struggled to catch up with them. The cold rain pelted down on the crowd, but they didn't seem to notice. By the time he reached them, they were at the plaza, almost half a mile from their apartment. The crowd was now chanting and moving to form a circle around the center of the plaza. Christiano pushed his way through the crowd, fighting back tears and the pangs of pain from his heart.

When he reached the front of the crowd, he fell to the ground. There, on top of a long wooden pole, was Bernhardt, pinned to the pole with a long wooden stake hammered through his heart. His eyes were open, staring blankly ahead. They looked frightened. His mouth gaped open, and blood trickled down the corners of it. His white shirt was stained bright red.

Christiano wailed out loudly and beat his hands against the ground. Other members of the crowd must have thought it was a ritual, because several of them threw themselves to the ground as well and began beating it as they chanted and yelled undecipherable phrases in French, Italian, and English. The more Christiano cried and hit the ground, the louder the swell of chants grew, and the more the crowd around him danced and laughed and sang.

Christiano stood up weakly and stumbled backward through the crowd. The tears mixed with the rain and streamed down his face and kept him from seeing anything too clearly. He finally reached the edge of the crowd and ran to a nearby alley, where he vomited. When he caught his breath, he looked over at the crowd and spat at them.

It took only a moment for the rage inside him to take over. His eyes grew red and glowed in the dark of the night. He felt his canine teeth grow and distend at an alarming speed, and the blood flowed through his veins with an intensity that he'd never felt. Before he could realize what was happening, his feet were off the ground and he was flying through the air. He'd known this was possible, and Bernhardt had even spoken of experiencing it a few times. But it had never happened to him before, and he was unable to control it.

He floated about fifteen feet above the ground for a few moments and then rose a few feet higher and began flying toward the crowd. With each passing second, he felt himself gaining more control over the flying, and it didn't take long before he'd mastered his balance and his mastery of this newfound skill. The closer he came to the mob, the angrier he grew, and the faster he flew. When he was over the center of the crowd, he whooshed down and grabbed the first person he saw. It was a young woman, and he grabbed her by the hair, pulled her face to one side, and sank his fangs deep into her neck. She tried to scream, but barely a moan escaped her throat as he bit into her neck and ripped it open. He didn't even bother drinking her blood but instead threw her to the ground and left her alone to bleed to death on the street.

He was back up in the air in seconds and continued through the crowd. The mob was so frenzied and caught up in their partying that they didn't realize at first what was happening. It took a couple of minutes and at least three dead mob members for the crowd to realize they were being massacred, and when they did, they began to scream and run. Christiano was able to reach several other people and rip into their necks before the majority of the crowd dispersed screaming into the streets.

When they were all gone, he lowered himself to the ground and looked around him. He counted fifteen people on the ground, covered in blood. Not nearly enough. He stormed through the plaza, kicking the dead as he passed them on his way to Bernhardt. When he was just a few feet away from his lover, he kicked one of the people on the ground and was startled to hear a moan.

"Please help me," the young man cried.

Christiano stopped and lowered himself so that he was inches from the young man's face. His eyes still burned red, and his teeth were still protruding and very sharp, dripping in blood.

"No, please . . . ," the young man cried again.

Christiano grabbed him by the hair and slowly brought the man's face to his own. "You will pay for this," he said, and sank his teeth into the cold, wet neck of the young man.

The blood was thick and sweet, and had Christiano not been so overwrought with grief, he would have enjoyed this young man very much. But instead he sucked the blood from the jugular vein just past the point of its turning sour. Stopping here meant the man would forever roam the earth, neither dead nor alive but somewhere in between. The term that was currently popular was "zombie." Had he stopped a moment earlier, the young man would have died. Had he kept drinking until the blood became sweet and warm again, the young man would have lived an eternity as a vampire himself. But Christiano didn't do either of those. He stopped and spit out the last mouthful, and threw the young man's head back to the ground.

"Now you will know," Christiano spit at the young man. "Now you will know."

He kicked the man in the side again and walked over to Bernhardt. He slowly lowered his lover off the wooden pole and removed the long wooden spike from his heart. In the distance, he heard the sirens as they quickly approached the plaza. He wrapped Bernhardt in his arms and ran quickly down the street toward their home. Raindrops streamed down his face, washing away his salty tears. He looked up into the sky and cursed the storm that had brought death to his home that evening.

Every evening when he woke, Christiano prayed he would die. He knew he would not, of course, and cursed the gods and the fates that had borne him into this eternal life, but he prayed anyway. He'd wake up early in the evening, shortly after the sun dropped, with tears in his eyes and a dull, aching pain around his heart. For a few weeks after Bernhardt's death, Christiano sulked around the apartment, crying and spending hours looking through the memories of their life together. In the eighty years they'd loved each other, they'd accrued many priceless souvenirs of their time and their life together. It took Christiano almost a month to go through them and pay them homage. When he was finished, he found himself bitter and angry again at the mob that had taken his lover from him. And he vowed to avenge Bernhardt's senseless killing.

Up until this point, feedings had been only a matter of survival. Christiano needed fresh blood for his nourishment and to give him strength to spend his evenings with the man he loved. But now things were different, and when Christiano finished looking through his photos and souvenirs of his life with Bernhardt, he was a new man. He woke that evening with a hunger he'd never known. It was a hunger not just for blood but also for violence and pain and revenge.

These were feelings foreign to Christiano, and ones that he'd often prayed never to experience, regardless of how long his eternity would eventually be. But when he woke with them that evening enveloping his body and vibrating through every fiber of his being, he found himself embracing them and looking forward to their collective experience.

It was early June, and a welcome cool breeze wafted through the Paris evening. Christiano walked the streets, taking note of the various bars and restaurants and sidewalk cafés that were filled with people laughing and drinking and smoking and eating. Laughter and conversation filled the air with a rancid stench that caused his stomach to wrench in painful knots and forced him to hold back the overwhelming desire to vomit.

He found himself at a club that he and Bernhardt had visited a couple of times. It had only opened several months earlier, and so they hadn't made it a habit yet to frequent the bar. Certainly they were not known as a couple there yet. But the young college men who frequented the club very much appealed to both Christiano and Bernhardt, and they'd enjoyed the couple of visits they'd had. And so Christiano smiled as he walked into the club, and the smell of wine and cigarettes and overcharged libidos smothered him as he slowly walked though the crowded room.

He didn't feel like playing games tonight. His cock had become fully hard even before the front door clicked shut behind him as he walked into the club, and his heart pounded and his skin tingled with the desire to feed and to kill. Sometimes, in the past, he'd enjoyed engaging in the games the mortals played when they were on the prowl for sex. He'd found them interesting and exciting, and they'd heightened the sexual experience for both him and Bernhardt. But tonight was not one of those nights, and he leaned against the wall and focused his attention on two men playing pool a few feet away from him.

One of the men was short of stature, with well-developed and overworked muscles that he showed off by wearing cutoff denim shorts and a bleached white muscle shirt. His blond hair was a little long and tussled and kept falling down over his eyes, which caused him to brush it away absently. His skin was tanned and smooth and glistened with a light sheen of sweat from the heat in the club. His baby blue eyes sparkled even in the dark of the room and were lined by long, black eyelashes.

His boyfriend was tall and thin. He was strong and well muscled as well, but it was obvious that his were developed from natural hard work rather than a few too many vanity-filled hours at the local gym. He had short black hair that looked like it was cropped to be as easily maintained as possible. His red and black flannel shirtsleeves were rolled up to reveal hairy, muscular arms, and his black jeans clung to powerful legs that carried him with an air of confidence. He had a thick shadow on his cheeks and jaw that caused Christiano's cock to flex again involuntarily.

Christiano noticed both the young men staring at him intently, and locked his eyes on to theirs. When they smiled at him, he returned the smile and reached down and slowly groped his crotch and squeezed it several times. He felt it grow harder with his touch, and when he looked down at it, he was happy to see the long, thick outline stretch several inches down his leg.

This is what you want, he whispered to the two boyfriends several feet away, without moving his lips. *Why don't you come over here and get it?*

He smiled as he watched the two young men look at him, bewildered, and then stare at each other as if they were experiencing the same dream.

Don't think about it too much, he whispered again as he took a drink and smiled. *Because the offer won't be on the table for long. There are plenty of hungry young men here who will be happy to take it if you continue to contemplate.*

Christiano grinned as the boyfriends set their pool cues down and took a step forward in unison. He noticed they both had hard-ons straining to be released from the confines of their jeans. As they got closer, he could smell their hunger and their desire hanging thick in a cloud around them, and when they were only a couple of steps away, he could also smell a faint trace of fear. That was good. They were not completely stupid, then. It would be all that much more fun if they weren't completely stupid and might be able to comprehend what was going to happen to them.

"Hey," the shorter, blond man said as they approached. His smile was bright and friendly. It exuded confidence and let Christiano know at once that he was the one accustomed to approaching other guys and convincing them to join him and his boyfriend for a night of fun. "How's it goin'?"

"Not too badly," Christiano said, and smiled before he took another drink of his wine. "I can't complain too much. Especially now."

"Excellent," the blond said again. "I'm Jacques." He extended his hand and accepted Christiano's handshake.

"And I'm Gerard," the taller brunette said, a little clumsily. "I'm his boyfriend."

Christiano forced himself not to laugh at the awkwardness that dripped from Gerard's words and his movements.

"Christiano," he said as he shook hands with the men and pulled them closer to him in one movement.

Jacques was all over him in seconds, kissing him on the ear and mouth and rubbing his body against Christiano's seductively. Gerard was a little slower in getting started but, with Jacques' encouragement, was soon rubbing his crotch against Christiano's leg as he opened his mouth and accepted Christiano's tongue.

It didn't take long before the trio was drawing a crowd. There was no doubt that Jacques would have enjoyed staying and performing for the eager group of onlookers. But Gerard was growing uneasy and soon suggested they all go back to their apartment and continue with a little more privacy. Christiano was quick to agree, and the three men situated their cocks back inside their pants and exited the bar.

Back at their apartment, Jacques and Gerard made quick business of getting Christiano undressed and in their bed. When all three men were naked, the boyfriends flanked Christiano on either side and devoured him with their mouths. Gerard kissed Christiano on the mouth tenderly and caressed his chest and stomach while Jacques immediately went for his crotch and licked his cock a few times before swallowing it deep into his throat.

Gerard was gentle and loving as he kissed and caressed Christiano and rubbed his thick, uncut cock against Christiano's leg. Jacques was intense and extremely talented in the art of cocksucking. As he swallowed Christiano's big dick, he thrust his naked ass into the air, moaning with delight as his throat expanded to accommodate the thickness of Christiano's cock. Though total opposites as far as looks and behavior were concerned, it was obvious how the two lovers could complement each other very well in bed, and that they were very much in love.

That was good, and Christiano was pleased with his conquest. Gerard's tongue tasted sweet and delicious in his mouth, and his big cock was hot and slick with precum as it slid against Christiano's legs. Jacques' mouth was hot and strong as it sucked on Christiano's throbbing cock. It was not long before he could hold back no more, and he moaned loudly as he tightened his body and thrust his cock deeper into Jacques' throat.

Jacques whimpered with delight as Christiano's cock spurted shot after shot of warm, thick cum into his throat. He reached down and squeezed his own cock at the same time, and seconds later he sprayed his own load all over Christiano's feet and on the bed. Gerard pulled his tongue from Christiano's mouth and balanced his body on his knees as he steadied himself above Christiano's body. He pointed his dick at Christiano's face and beat his cock ferociously until he splashed his load all over Christiano's face and chest.

The two young lovers lay down on either side of Christiano, and all three men took several minutes to catch their breath. When it seemed as though the boyfriends were about to drift to sleep, Christiano reached over to both of them and took their heads in his hands. He gently brought their faces together above his chest and in front of his face.

"Kiss," he said to them.

"It's getting late," Gerard said sleepily.

"Kiss," Christiano said again.

The boyfriends kissed, and it wasn't long before Christiano felt both of them begin to harden against his legs again.

"I want to see you make love to one another."

"But it really is getting a little late," Gerard said again, a little less convincingly this time.

"Shut up and fuck me," Jacques said to his lover as he smiled and rolled over onto his stomach next to Christiano.

Christiano moved out of the way as Gerard spread his lover's legs wide apart and lay between them on his stomach. He spread Jacques' ass cheeks and licked around his ass. Jacques moaned and lifted his ass higher so that Gerard's tongue could enter it more easily.

Christiano's cock throbbed and bounced in front of him as he watched the two lovers. Jacques' ass was smooth and whiter than the rest of his body and seemed to glow in the semidarkness of the room. Gerard's thick black hair and heavy stubble were a stark contrast to the milkiness of Jacques' ass, and it excited Christiano to watch the two move in perfect sync with each other. This was an act they were obviously very familiar with.

Gerard lifted himself from the bed and positioned himself directly above Jacques' ass. He spit on his cock a couple of times, then placed the head of it between the cheeks of his lover's ass. Jacques took a deep breath, and then Gerard pushed his hips forward and slowly entered Jacques' welcoming hole. Jacques let out a small cry of pain and gripped the sheets as his lover entered him. Then he smiled and tilted his head backward so that he could kiss Gerard on the mouth as Gerard slid in and out of his ass, slowly at first and then with more speed and rhythm and passion.

A large drop of precum dripped out of the tip of Christiano's cock head and slid down the veiny shaft until it reached his balls. He moaned as he watched the boyfriends make love, and then he could not control himself any longer. He positioned himself behind Gerard and began humping his cock against Gerard's ass.

Gerard moaned when he felt the heat of Christiano's big dick sliding against the outside of his ass, and pounded himself deeper and harder into Jacques' ass. That only drove Jacques even madder with desire, and he thrust his ass backward harder onto his boyfriend's dick.

Christiano felt it building up and smiled. He didn't give a second thought whether he was going to go through with it. He'd known since he left his own apartment that this night was going to be different, and he looked forward to it with much anticipation. When he felt his skin begin to tingle and warm up, he smiled. A moment later his gums began to ache a little as his canine teeth pushed forward and grew sharp. His eyes began to burn, and when he looked over to his left at the mirror that hung from the bedroom door, he saw they were fire red and seething with desire.

He spit on his cock and spread Gerard's cheeks as he placed the head of his dick at the opening of Gerard's ass.

"No, wait a minute," Gerard moaned as he continued to slide in and out of Jacques' ass. "I don't do that. I don't get fucked."

"You do now," Christiano said, and slid the head of his cock just inside the tight sphincter.

"Owww!" Gerard cried out.

"Oh, Jesus," Jacques moaned as he thrust his ass up and deeper onto Gerard's cock. "You should feel how great this feels, baby. Your cock just got so much thicker and harder when he went inside you. Try to go with it. You'll like it, I promise."

"No, really," Gerard moaned, and tried to wriggle off Christiano's thick cock. "I don't get fucked. It hurts. Pull out."

"Not a chance, my friend," Christiano said, and shoved every inch of his cock deep inside Gerard's hot, gripping ass. His teeth hurt now, and his skin was burning hot, and his eyes itched.

Gerard moaned and tried to protest some more, but Christiano pushed his face against Jacques' back so that his mouth was covered with the sweaty skin of his lover's shoulders.

Christiano left his entire cock deep inside Gerard's ass for a moment and then began sliding slowly in and out. Gerard was still trying to protest, but his ass gripped Christiano's cock and twitched around it, bringing him more pleasure than the shy young man would have liked to know. Christiano slowly slid his cock all the way out and then, when Gerard gasped a sigh of relief, shoved it back in all the way to the balls in one move.

"Please, stop," Gerard cried out as Christiano fucked him deeper and harder. "I can't . . ."

"Shut up!" Christiano said as he slammed himself relentlessly into Gerard's ass, and forced his face back into the shoulders of his lover.

The bed bounced with the efforts of their sex, and Jacques was oblivious to what was happening behind him. He closed his eyes and moaned with animalistic lust as he felt his lover's thick cock sliding in and out of his ass, and imagined what it must feel like for Gerard to be taking a big dick up his ass for the first time.

Christiano grabbed Gerard by the hair from the back of his head and tilted his neck to one side. He noticed that Gerard was crying at this time, but paid no attention to it. As he shoved his dick deep into the hot tightness of Gerard's ass, he leaned forward and bit deeply into Gerard's neck. Gerard let out another cry, a little louder this time.

"That's it, honey," Jacques moaned, mistaking Gerard's cry for one of immense pleasure. He lifted his ass higher again, trying to take more of Gerard's cock inside him. "I told you you'd like it."

Christiano clamped down harder on Gerard's neck and sucked the blood deep into his throat. It was thick and sweet and warm and tasted like spiced nectar as it slid across his tongue and down into this throat. Christiano couldn't remember having had such a sweet and delicious meal in a very long time. As he sucked more blood from Gerard's body and drank, he continued fucking him.

"Fuck me, baby," Jacques said with much more animation than he'd previously exhibited. "I'm getting really close just thinking about Christiano fucking your sweet little ass as you fuck mine. Does it feel good, Geri?"

Gerard's blood was beginning to thin and become cooler, and Christiano knew it wouldn't be long before he was finished with him. He fucked the young man harder and faster and struggled to keep his dick inside the man for as long as he could before stealing his last breath from him.

"Gerard, what's wrong?" Jacques moaned beneath Christiano and Gerard. "Your dick is getting soft inside me. Aren't you enjoying this?"

A loud animal growl escaped Christiano's throat before he could stop it.

"What's going on?" Jacques cried out, trying to maneuver himself off Gerard's now limp cock and from underneath Gerard's motionless body.

There were still a few breaths left in Gerard, and so Christiano knew it was time to pull out and move on. In a single move he slid his cock out of Gerard's ass as he took one last swallow of his blood. Then he grabbed Gerard by the hair with one hand and tossed him effortlessly off the bed and halfway across the room. Gerard's body landed with a dull thump against the far wall, where Christiano watched him take several deep breaths and then witnessed his last breath escape him and his eyes close.

"What the fuck is going on?" Jacques screamed as he tried unsuccessfully to get to his knees so he could face his lover's killer. When he noticed the blood still dripping from Christiano's lips, and the red glow emanating from his eyes, he whimpered and cowered against the headboard of the bed. "Please don't hurt me," he begged.

Christiano grabbed him by the back of the head and pulled him roughly down to his crotch. "Suck my cock," he growled in a voice even he didn't recognize.

Jacques cried and tried to resist, but it was futile. Christiano was overpoweringly strong, and his large hands against the back of his head left no alternative but to open his mouth wide and take the large cock. He sucked it deep into his throat, but couldn't take it all because he was still crying. He tried once or twice to relax his throat and open it to take the big dick, but only succeeded in scraping the thick cock with his teeth.

"You useless cocksucker," Christiano spat out. "You can't even take it like a man." He pulled Jacques off his cock, and rolled him back onto his stomach.

"Please don't . . ." Jacques begged.

Christiano roughly pulled Jacques' ass cheeks apart and slammed his thick cock deep into his ass in one move. When Jacques cried out in pain, it only spurred Christiano to fuck him harder. When he felt his balls begin to tighten, he leaned down and sank his teeth deep into Jacques' neck.

"Oh, God, no," Jacques cried out, and a moment later his body began to convulse and then went limp.

Christiano knew the young man was not dead but had only fainted. Jacques' heart still beat strongly, and he was breathing normally. Christiano sucked the blood from his neck and savored the warm, thick fluid as he drank it. It was not as sweet as Gerard's, but every bit as delicious in a uniquely different way. He fucked Jacques as he continued to drink, until he knew that the boy only had a couple of minutes left.

He pulled his cock out of Jacques' ass and roughly rolled him over onto his back.

"This is for Bernhardt," he said as he straddled Jacques' stomach and chest. He pointed his big dick directly at Jacques' face and leaned back as he sprayed his load all over Jacques' smooth chest and his face.

When he was finished, he looked down at Jacques. He was still breathing, though it was labored, and was staring at Christiano with a dazed look of confusion. Cum dripped down his face and mixed with the blood on his neck. For a moment Christiano looked at the boy, and a pang of guilt and remorse flooded over him. This had been a young and innocent man who had loved someone deeply and passionately. He hadn't deserved this at all.

And then, as quickly as the feeling came, it also went. Christiano smiled down at Jacques' cum-smeared face and kissed him on the lips. Then he grabbed the young man by the head and twisted it roughly until he heard the bones break and heard the last breath of life escape from the boy's mouth.

Christiano, too, had once been a young and innocent man who had loved someone deeply. He hadn't deserved losing his Bernhardt to a crowd of senseless and stupid mortals.

He stood up and dressed quickly, then walked out the door without looking back.

Chapter Three

Christiano woke up and looked around him dazedly. It took his eyes a couple of minutes longer to adjust to the darkness than usual, and he was disoriented. What was that musky, dusty smell? And why didn't he hear the sounds of traffic and bustling evening street life outside?

And then he remembered. He was not in San Francisco anymore. He wasn't at home. He sat up in the coffin and stretched as he looked around the dark room. Denver. He was in Denver now, in the subdepths of the basement in the cathedral. He'd fed on the crass young man, the prostitute, just yesterday. What had his name been? He struggled to recall, because he was always so good with names. Then he remembered he'd never asked the boy his name. It didn't matter. He hadn't been that savory anyway. His blood hadn't been all that sweet.

Christiano crawled out of the coffin, very much aware of the aches and pains in his joints and muscles. He was starting to feel his age. That couldn't be good. He wasn't even two hundred years old yet, and already he was squeaking and creaking like an old rusted door. He felt much older than two hundred, that was for sure. Most vampires his age didn't feel this old or this tired. But most vampires his age hadn't gone through the pain and misery he had.

He walked around the room naked, getting used to the dark and taking mental stock of his surroundings. The room was sparsely furnished, but Christiano remembered having seen a sofa and some chairs upstairs in the basement the previous night. Without getting dressed, he climbed the stairs and opened the trapdoor, then crawled out of it and into the basement of the cathedral. It wasn't quite as dark here, and it was warmer. He rummaged around for a few minutes until he found some old rags and some cleaning supplies. Then he stepped back down into the trapdoor in the floor of the basement and deep into the dark dungeon below.

He began wiping down the coffin and the chest that lay next to the door. He pulled some candles down and dusted them as well. Then he stopped in the middle of the room and stared at the coffin. Why was he dusting and cleaning up this small room? Was he really planning on staying here in Denver for more than a couple of evenings? Was he really contemplating the idea of settling here for a while?

After Bernhardt's death, Christiano stayed in Paris for a few more years and then spent the next couple of years moving from one country to the next, never settling down for more than a year at a time. He stayed just long enough in one place to grow comfortable and then found it necessary to move on.

It was always for the better, anyway. Once he'd been known all over Europe for his legendary love with Bernhardt. Anywhere they went they were celebrated and treated as royalty. He stayed in the homes and castles of kings and dignitaries. But that had been years ago, before Bernhardt had been senselessly slain. Since then Christiano had become bitter and angry and mercilessly vicious. Almost every night he ventured out and fed, whether he was hungry or not. He found his prey wherever he could. Sometimes they were weak and helpless, and sometimes he intentionally sought out the strongest and most highly visible persons to kill and leave whimpering for mercy.

He'd become careless and drew attention to his killings wherever he went. People were talking again about vampires and believing they lived among common folk. It made the other vampires nervous and didn't take long for vampire communities all across Europe to blacklist Christiano. He was no longer welcomed into the homes of kings and dignitaries. He was no longer asked to join even the common vampires for a drink or for dinner. In fact, he was soon asked to leave the community altogether and never to return.

Fuck them all, he thought. He didn't need them to live his life the way he wanted to anyway. They didn't understand him. They didn't know what it was like to lose the love of one's life. They didn't know what it felt like to have one's heart ripped out of one's chest. Fuck them.

Eventually he left Europe and found his way to San Francisco. He'd lived there for several years and then became bored with it. Being a vampire in San Francisco was nothing novel. Many people there claimed to be vampires and even walked around in broad daylight wearing the dark clothes and makeup that made them appear to be what mortals thought vampires looked like. They were ridiculous. On the few occasions that real vampires became sloppy and left behind evidence of their killings, it was always mortals who took credit for the kill and got all the press coverage. Of course, they eventually withdrew their confessions and issued apologies and were never charged. It wasn't right and it wasn't fair. A few of the real vampires in San Francisco had attempted to strike up conversations and become friends with him, but he wanted no part of it. He had no intention of getting too close to anyone here in San Francisco or anywhere else. He didn't need their friendship, and he didn't need their approval, and he didn't need their sense of community. He didn't need any of it.

So he'd left San Francisco with the intention of ending up in Chicago. There was a large vampire community there, and he could get lost easily. They were well known for their violent nature and their unwillingness to compromise or blend in with mere mortals. They were defiant and mean and excessively destructive. And they were proud of their reputation. Christiano thought he would fit in there easily, and was actually looking forward to arriving.

And so why now, after only one full evening, was he contemplating staying here in Denver and settling in for a while? What was that feeling deep in his stomach that caused him to pause and reconsider his decision to move to Chicago? Could it be that he was actually afraid of moving to Chicago? Might he be getting into more than he was capable of dealing with? No, he really didn't think so. Prague had been even more violent and dangerous than Chicago was reported to be. In Prague vampires were at war not only with mortals but with one another as well, and they were exceptionally violent. Yet he'd thrived in Prague and had enjoyed living there. And Budapest was especially known for its aggressive community and the wars among vampires there. He'd found his place there as well, and was respected as one of the fiercest warriors there. So what was it, then, that caused him to doubt his decision to move to Chicago, and to stay here in Denver?

Christiano shivered in the cold darkness of the dungeon. He had no idea why he was entertaining the thought of staying, but by the time he found his breath again, he knew it was not only an entertainment but a fact. He was settling here. At least for a while.

He smiled and looked around the room again. If this was his new home, he'd have to do a little shopping. These old chairs and old chest just would not do. And he'd have to get some new clothes, too.

Chapter Four

It was a large, nondescript building far from downtown and in the middle of one of Denver's older industrial areas. There was nothing special about the building at all, and most passersby undoubtedly thought it a warehouse, filled with old oil-caked tractors and machines and probably abandoned for at least the past ten years, as were most of the other buildings in this part of town.

The building itself was huge and covered two-thirds of an acre that was set far back from the onetime paved but now long since dirt road that brought close to a thousand partygoers every weekend. The other third of the property provided a massive parking lot.

All the windows were boarded up, and most of them also had thick plastic black tarp draped over them. The door was a colossal wooden structure that slid across a large, wide steel rolling trolley. Standing outside the door were two men who could easily have been mistaken for large oak trees. Their arms remained crossed across their immense chests, and they seemed never to flinch, even as they checked the IDs of the long line of people waiting to get inside the club. The guards wore black tank tops that strained to contain the immense muscles beneath them, black jeans, and stylish dark sunglasses, even though it was pitch black outside at eleven in the evening.

Christiano smiled and walked confidently toward the two sentinels. No matter what continent he was on or what era he was currently in, this scene never varied at all. For over 150 years he'd been visiting the large underground clubs just like this all over the world. He was amazed that the mortals could never see through the facade and recognize these clubs for what they really were. But then again, mortals never stayed in one place long enough to make the connections, and didn't have the luxury of seeing the various clubs in other countries and continents.

He walked up to the door, never slowing as he approached the two guards. The bigger of the two men reached out and grabbed Christiano by the arm.

"Slow down, Tonto," the guard growled as he grasped Christiano's arm and squeezed it tightly. "Not so fast. There's a fifty-dollar cover charge tonight. And I need to see some ID."

Christiano glared at the man behind the glasses and smiled. *"El Papa Dominici vive y bendice a vosotros."* He lifted the long shirtsleeve a couple of inches, revealing a small red tattoo over the river of veins along the inside of his left wrist.

The guard immediately released his grip on Christiano's arm and took a step backward. "I'm sorry, sir. I didn't know. I haven't seen you here before."

"It's okay," Christiano said, and patted the large man's shoulder. "This is my first time here. But hopefully not my last. You couldn't have known."

"Enjoy your evening, sir," the big man said with a quake in his voice.

Christiano could tell the guard's eyes were staring downward at the ground, and that he was afraid he might not see the light of morning. He enjoyed the power but had no intention of killing the guard for doing his job.

"Relax," he said as he smiled again. "I told you, you couldn't have known. It's all right."

"Thank you, sir," the guard said, and visibly relaxed. "I appreciate your kindness."

Christiano turned and took a couple of steps to the door of the club. The other guard, who had not spoken to Christiano, took a step toward the door as well and reached out to open it. Christiano glanced at him just as the first guard grabbed his partner and pulled him back quickly.

"He'll get it," the first guard said.

"But he can't . . ."

"Yes, he can."

Christiano looked again at both guards and slid the heavy door across the trolley with no effort whatsoever. He smiled at the guards and noticed the second guard's stunned expression just before the door slid shut behind him.

A ten-foot-tall blue neon sign welcomed him just inside beyond the door: *Club Suque.* Christiano sidled up to the sign and ran his hands along the cool, smooth glass. He felt the tingling surge beneath the glass massaging its way through his skin and deeper into his muscles. He felt his cock stir inside his pants and closed his eyes and took a deep breath.

He pulled his hand away from the sign and walked several steps to the left. Though he hadn't been to this particular club, he knew exactly where he was going. They never deviated from one another. If he'd visited one club, whether it be in Prague or Berlin or Moscow—or Denver—he'd visited them all.

A few steps ahead, he parted the heavy black curtain and stepped inside the main floor. Close to a thousand young people crowded the large dance floor on the main level and the railings overlooking the dance floor from the upper two levels of the building. It was completely dark inside, the only flashes of light coming from the deep purple ultraviolet ray that scanned the dance floor and from the observation posts on the upper two balconies above the main floor. Every once in a while the beam would chance upon someone wearing a white shirt, and they'd glow like a firefly in the crowd of otherwise black-clothed patrons.

The music was so loud inside the club that the steel girders shook and rattled loudly enough to compete with the music. Christiano could hear the metal beams moan and cry out with agony as they struggled to hold the building together and not collapse onto the overpacked crowd below.

Christiano stopped walking and looked around him. He'd only just stepped foot into the building, and already he smelled it: sex, lust, desire, heat, and a little fear. It was a very distinct odor that he'd smelled often before. It was, in fact, his favorite odor. Sex with the carrier of that particular odor was always most satisfactory. And when the meeting of that carrier was at one of the clubs, then the sex was even more satisfactory, because that person was usually much more open to the experiences of vampire sex, and Christiano did not have to pretend to be nothing more than an exceptionally gifted mortal.

He walked across the dance floor and passed three large bars along the way. The one he was looking for would be located at the back of the bar and would have two guards, similar to those outside, making sure that only a select few passed through the velvet-roped area that gave access to the smaller bar a few feet back.

"You got your card and password?" the overly muscled man asked as he stepped in front of the thick red velvet rope and prevented Christiano from walking through.

Christiano smiled. This club was better protected than many he'd been to. He rolled up his sleeve again and showed the tattoo. *"El Papa Dominici vive y bendice a vosotros."*

The guard stepped to the side and motioned Christiano through. He didn't smile or lose his composure in the least. "Have a good evening, sir."

Christiano raised his eyebrow at the guard, an unspoken acknowledgment and appreciation for his strength and professionalism, and then walked through the small crowd of eight or ten people milling about the ropes, looking out into the crowd. He noticed everyone looking at him, though they tried noticeably to be inconspicuous. The more experienced glanced at him only out of the corners of their eyes, while two or three of the lesser-trained people turned around and watched him as he walked past them and up to the bar.

"Welcome, sir," the bartender said as Christiano approached the bar. He laid down a tiny square satin napkin and slid it toward Christiano. "What can I get you?"

"I'll have a ruby Cuervo nectar, please."

"Certainly, sir," the bartender said.

Christiano watched as the young man aimed the spigot and pressed the tiny red button on top of it. It took several seconds, but soon thick red liquid poured from the spigot and slid slowly into the miniature silver goblet. When it was three-quarters full, the bartender switched and hit another of the buttons on the spigot. The light yellow tequila flowed much more easily and quickly through the plastic gadget and into the goblet. The bartender stopped the flow just short of filling the goblet and finished the drink off with a small splash of pineapple juice.

"Please make sure it is to your liking, sir," the bartender said as he set the silver goblet on the satin napkin and slid it toward Christiano.

Christiano lifted the goblet and brought it to his nose and inhaled deeply. He smiled as the smell embedded itself along the membranes inside his nose and sinus cavities. His heart raced and his cock grew noticeably more plump as he allowed the smell to ingrain itself in his tissues. Then he brought the goblet to his lips and took a sip. He rolled the thick liquid around his tongue and savored its rich, coppery taste and cool, slick texture before swallowing it. As it slid down his throat and into his belly, Christiano moaned as his cock grew completely hard and ached within the confines of his pants.

"It's perfect," he said as he opened his eyes and smiled at the bartender.

"Thank you, sir," the bartender said as he smiled back. "Your first time at Club Suque? I haven't seen you before."

"Yes, it is."

"Well, welcome. I hope you find it pleasurable."

"I'm sure I will," Christiano said. "But perhaps you can help ensure that will happen."

"I'd be more than happy to help in whatever way I can, sir. What is your pleasure?"

"Male," Christiano said as he stared into the bartender's eyes. "And young. Spirited."

"Knowledgeable or ignorant?"

"That is not as important as appearance. I am fond of both the knowledgeable and the ignorant. But he must be young and spirited and exceptionally beautiful."

"Yes, sir. Well, there are many to choose from, then. Lyle, over there in the corner, is quite popular. He's knowledgeable, and very much agreeable to most any scene."

Christiano looked over into the corner and spotted Lyle immediately. He was a couple of inches taller than six feet, with broad shoulders and a tapered waist. His dark, spiky hair was tipped blond. His copper skin had a natural sheen to it, and when he smiled, his bright white teeth sparkled.

"Quite lovely," Christiano said.

"Yes, he is. Very popular around here. So much so that he's able to be a little particular. He regularly has a full schedule a month or two in advance. But he's usually most agreeable to meeting new members. I'm sure he'd love to accompany you."

"I don't think so. Maybe at a later meeting. For now, I'd prefer someone who is perhaps not so . . . well known. Someone who is not quite as experienced, maybe."

"I understand, sir. Well, Thomas, over there on the dance floor, is fairly new to Club Suque. I believe he is still ignorant. At least I know he was as of last week. This is his third or fourth week here. A couple of our regulars have expressed an interest in Thomas, but so far no one has had him. I think some of our regulars are getting a little lazy and just don't want to deal with initiating a newbie. So, so far he's still unused, and ignorant as far as I know."

Christiano looked at the boy. He appeared to be twenty-four or twenty-five. He was much shorter than Lyle, maybe five feet six or seven. His long blond hair was bathed in sweat and swirled around his head as he jumped up and down on the dance floor and shook his head in beat with the music. He was wearing no shirt, and his tanless and hairless torso shined whenever the fluorescent lights flashed around him.

"Not bad," Christiano said, "but not perfect, either. He seems to be strung out. Probably not the most tasty at this point."

"Of course, you're right, sir. Let me think . . ."

Christiano looked around the crowded bar.

"I'm not sure exactly what your type is, sir," the bartender said a little sheepishly, "but I'd be more than agreeable to accompany you. If you are the least bit interested."

Christiano turned and looked at the young man. He was about the same height as Christiano but several pounds lighter. He looked to be Mediterranean in origin, with olive complexion and light brown eyes. He was well muscled but not to the point of exaggeration. He looked to be in his early thirties, which was just at the cusp of Christiano's preferred age range. Still, he was exceptionally handsome, and Christiano found himself tempted.

"I'm knowledgeable, of course. But if you're sure that doesn't matter . . ."

"No, that doesn't matter. What's your name?"

"Uriel, sir."

"Uriel, you're most attractive, and every bit my type. But I don't normally partake in club staff."

"I understand, sir," Uriel said, with little attempt at hiding his disappointment.

"I'm going to acquaint myself a little more with your charming club. Perhaps I might stop back by here before I leave, however. Though I don't normally partake of club staff, I have been known to make an exception or two. If the offer is still open at that time, of course."

"That would be great," Uriel said, and smiled. "The offer will most definitely still be on the table. I can guarantee that."

"Lovely," Christiano said, and winked at Uriel as he walked past the guard and back onto the dance floor.

Christiano walked around the large dance floor for several minutes. Club Suque was a little larger than many of the other clubs around the world he'd visited, which was a little surprising. He hadn't expected Denver to be such a progressive and inviting city. He knew there were vampires here, but he had no idea the community was large enough to support such a large and extravagant club.

Almost a thousand people filled the club. The vast majority of them were extremely pale, with black hair and fingernails painted black. Most of them wore dark clothes and sunglasses, even in the dark of the club. Still, it was easy enough to pick out the real vampires. They had a special aura around them under the glow of the fluorescent lights that gave them away, at least to other vampires. They followed you as you walked around, and held your gaze for long periods of time. They nodded discreetly as you passed, and smiled, revealing their partially extended canine teeth.

In this group of almost a thousand people, almost a third of them were vampires. Christiano was a little taken aback at how many of them were so careless about how they interacted with the mortals. It was obvious most of the mortals were ignorant. Yet many of the vampires were openly feeding on them in the middle of the dance floor or upstairs in some of the dark corners of the club. Of course, it was possible to feed on humans without killing them. And you could even do it and have them never remember a thing about it afterward. But some of these vampires seemed either not to care enough to take those precautions or, more probably, not to have the skills to execute such a feeding successfully.

But the club was obviously wildly successful, and Christiano imagined it could not be so if it were careless in its killings. He was probably overly sensitive right now, and overly cautious about being in a new city. He didn't know these vampires well enough to make judgments on them yet.

Christiano walked around the club, first the dance floor and then the two upper stories that looked down onto the expansive dance floor. Though it was just about exactly the same physically as almost every other club he'd been to, it was also a little different. Many of the patrons were obviously high on coke and ecstasy, as they were in every other club. They bobbed around the dance floor in a soulless stupor and begged without speech for someone or something to take them away from their meaningless existence.

There were many young men that Christiano found himself attracted to. But after a couple of hours at the club, he still hadn't found anyone he was hungry for. He finished his drink, swirling the thick, warm liquid around his tongue and savoring the warm coppery taste of the blood as it coated his throat when he swallowed it. Uriel had made the third one double-strength, and Christiano found himself feeling slightly buzzed. He wasn't surprised when he found himself ambling back toward the small private bar at the end of the evening.

"I hope you had a nice evening," Uriel said as he smiled at Christiano. He was wiping down the counter and getting ready to close for the evening. Most of the patrons were already gone. The few who lingered were slowly being ushered out by the burly guards.

"I did indeed."

"Good. I'm sorry it has to be over already," Uriel said.

"Maybe it doesn't have to be."

"Really?"

"Really. If you're interested, that is."

"I am, definitely," Uriel said excitedly.

"How soon can you be done here?"

"About ten minutes. I just gotta finish wiping down the bar and then lock up the liquor. Can you meet me outside in ten?"

"Yes."

"Good. Meet me outside the front door. I won't be long."

Chapter Five

Christiano walked toward the entrance confidently, and smiled as the guards nodded at him without smiling and parted to allow him entrance. The rookie of the two grunted as he rolled the heavy wooden door open for Christiano to pass through. Neither of the big guards said a word to him. It had been three weeks since his first visit to Club Suque, and he was well known to the staff by now. Not only did they recognize him, but they also held a reverent fear of him. And that suited Christiano just fine.

As he stepped through the front entrance to the club, he was instantly assaulted with the intoxicating odor of sex and fear and sweat and blood. He inhaled deeply and allowed the odorous vapor to penetrate the membranes in his head and felt his blood vessels expand throughout his body. His cock began to harden instantly, and Christiano knew this would be a good night. He needed a good night. The last couple of evenings he'd ventured out had not been so great. Sure, he'd fed, but he hadn't been satisfied. Something told him tonight would be different.

He ambled up to the back bar. As he passed through the red velvet ropes, he noticed he was being watched even more carefully than on his previous visits. He smiled and adjusted the oversize collar on his black satin shirt as he leaned his elbows against the bar.

"Where's Uriel?" he asked as he smiled at the attractive new bartender.

"Good evening, sir," the bartender answered. He looked at Christiano only long enough to make eye contact and then quickly darted his eyes back down to the bar as he slid the napkin over to Christiano. "He isn't here."

Christiano liked this new kid. He was shorter than most of the other staff. Almost too short, Christiano thought. But not quite. He'd do. What he lacked in stature he made up in looks. His brown, blond-streaked hair was fashionably long and unruly, falling across his forehead and slightly over his eyes. His eyebrows were naturally short, lined with a little makeup to accentuate his almond-shaped eyes. They were light green and sparkled in the dim light of the back bar. Christiano noticed that even in the brief glance he'd gotten from the kid. He had a strong, sharp jawline that was covered with a dusting of dark shadow. He was a little tense and clenched his back teeth, which caused his jaw to tighten and twitch uncontrollably. He struggled to keep his eyes on the bar and not to look at Christiano. But it seemed to Christiano that he was losing the battle, because the kid kept glancing up at him and flirting with his eyes and smiling mischievously.

Christiano reached down and lightly rubbed his rapidly growing cock. The mix of obvious fear and cocky arrogance this kid was projecting was turning him on.

"He isn't working tonight?"

"No, sir, he isn't. Your usual?"

Christiano smiled. "Yes, please." He was honored that this new bartender he'd never seen was already familiar with his cocktail of choice. "When is he returning?"

"I'm sorry, sir. I have no idea. He didn't show up for his last two shifts, and no one has heard anything from him."

"I'm sorry to hear that," Christiano said as he took a sip from his ruby Cuervo nectar. "I hope he hasn't taken ill."

"Yes, sir," the kid said as he held Christiano's glare. He pushed the unruly hair from his eyes and raised his eyebrows at him. "Me, too."

"Well, when you see him, please give him my regards and tell him that I've missed him."

"I'll do that, sir."

Christiano turned and walked away from the bar, and thought he heard the bartender snicker as he left. He almost turned and pounced on the kid, but thought better of it. Perhaps he'd only imagined the snicker. The kid had shown a respectable amount of professionalism throughout their encounter and seemed adequately fearful of Christiano. It simply wouldn't do for him to kill the young man because of a misinterpreted grunt. Maybe the bartender had only been so relieved to have the meeting over with that he'd emitted an uncontrollable moan of relief.

He stopped anyway but did not turn to look at the bartender. He felt an inaudible gasp as everyone around him held their breath for several seconds. When he didn't turn to look at the handsome young man but simply began walking forward again, the air turned warm as the customers in the back bar began to breathe again.

The dance floor was filled to capacity with a young and energetic crowd. Christiano surveyed the throng quickly and spotted at least a dozen or more young men who suited him for tonight's feeding. He felt like more than just a quick feed. He wanted the game tonight. It had been more than a week since he'd last seduced a man for more than just a quick kill. Uriel had been the last, and by their third encounter he'd grown a little too arrogant and confident in his limited grasp on Christiano's affection. It had proven his downfall and, ultimately, his demise. Pity, really. But that was all behind him now, and he was ready once again to seduce and conquer his next victim. It wouldn't be difficult, he knew. It was a game in which he was well skilled.

He leaned against the wooden railing and looked out onto the crowded dance floor again. Then he took a drink of the ruby Cuervo nectar, and rolled the warm blood and tequila around on his tongue for a moment before swallowing.

"Beautiful evening tonight, isn't it?"

Christiano turned to his left to look at the man standing next to him. He was struck by the stranger's beauty immediately. He looked to be in his late twenties or early thirties, with short, spiked platinum hair that was meticulously styled. His black eyebrows were long and tapered. Black eyes sparkled against the ivory skin of his face. A black soul patch was the only hint of facial hair. He was a little over six feet tall, with a solid muscular build that was evident even under the tight black Lycra T-shirt and black jeans he was wearing. Christiano thought he might just be one of the most beautiful men he'd ever seen.

"Yes, it is." Christiano smiled and switched his drink to his left hand so he could shake hands with the handsome stranger. "I'm Christiano."

Yes, I know, the blond young man said without moving his lips as he smiled and shook hands with Christiano.

Christiano felt his throat constrict a little as he tensed up and tried to remove his hand from that of the man next to him. The blond refused to release his grip on Christiano's hand.

I'm Balthazar, he said, again without moving his lips or lowering his gaze from Christiano's eyes. While still shaking Christiano's hand, he brought his drink to his lips and took a large swallow from it. At the same time, he said, *Please don't be shocked. I just find it a little more convenient to have a decent conversation when I don't have to worry about what I'm saying out loud or about someone overhearing something I'd rather not have them overhearing.*

I'm not shocked, Christiano answered without moving his lips as well. He pulled his hand from Balthazar's strong grip and took a long drink from his own glass as he spoke. *Just caught me a little off guard, that's all. I've been here three weeks already, and before now had still not met another vampire. I was beginning to think I was the only one here.*

Don't be ridiculous. We're all around you. Take a look.

Christiano took a long, slow look around him. Everywhere he looked, he saw strangers glaring at him. Standing only a few feet away from him, seemingly, to the untrained eye, to be deep in the flow of the heavy house beat of the music blaring from speakers all around the room. Dancing maniacally on the dance floor in the midst of hundreds of suspecting and unsuspecting mortals. Milling around the various bars, talking with and seducing their own prey for the evening. He'd noticed many of them on his previous visits, and suspected that they were vampires. But he hadn't been sure. They'd been careful in their glances and interactions. And the mortals here in Denver were very dedicated to their craft of impersonating vampires. The truth was, he hadn't really dedicated himself yet to the task of identifying his fellow vampires and integrating himself into their community.

But now they were all around him and not trying in the least to conceal their identities. Their eyes glowed red, and their white skin seemed almost translucent in the fluorescent purple glow of the lights in the club. Some of them even had their fangs exposed as they smiled at Christiano. There were at least 150 vampires staring at him, some with a welcoming smile on their faces, and others with contemptuous glares in their eyes.

Yes, I guess you are, Christiano said as he looked into Balthazar's eyes. *I guess I just wasn't paying close attention. No one identified themselves to me, so I didn't take the initiative.*

I apologize for that, Balthazar said. *They can be such uncivilized brutes sometimes.*

Who can?

"My friends," Balthazar said out loud with a sweep of his arms to the vampires around him. "I've been out of town for a couple of weeks, and it seems my colleagues don't know how to compose themselves in my absence. I apologize for their behavior."

Christiano looked at Balthazar and knew at once that he did not mean it. He was the lead vampire in Denver; it was obvious. And he was proud that his flock had waited for his return to make their presence known. Christiano had met many lead vampires in his travels, and their arrogance and control over their "colleagues" were the one trait they all had in common. They were always the strongest vampires in their communities, and they were at the same time revered and respected and feared and often loathed. They were arrogant and controlling and ruthless. And they always commanded great loyalty. Christiano himself had all the qualities of a lead vampire, but he'd never felt the need or desire to take on that challenge. He didn't like or plan on staying in one place long enough to dedicate himself to the task.

"Don't worry about it," Christiano said. "They were only doing what was expected of them. They are obviously well trained. I'm glad to see there is such a large haven here."

"Yes," Balthazar said as he glanced around the large club. "We are very lucky. We have a great community here. And welcome to it, by the way."

"Thank you," Christiano said, again noticing that Balthazar hadn't meant what he said in the least.

"What brings you to our Mile-High City?" Balthazar said, with more than just a hint of curiosity in his voice, as he turned and stared directly into Christiano's eyes. "If you don't mind my asking."

"I don't know, really," Christiano said as he swallowed the last sip of his drink and waved a waiter over for another one. "I'm just passing through, I guess."

"On your way to where?"

Christiano looked at Balthazar and saw very clearly that he was not just making small talk. Balthazar's eyes held Christiano's own gaze, and Christiano could see that the man was trying desperately not to lose his control. His pupils struggled to stay black and not turn red. Christiano could almost see the little red blood vessels in the whites of Balthazar's eyes pulse with the beat of his heart.

"I'm not sure yet," Christiano said as he smiled and took the new drink from the waiter and looked back into Balthazar's eyes. "And my plans may have changed now. I'm liking Denver more than I expected to."

The veins on Balthazar's forehead throbbed wildly to life, and his eyes narrowed into tiny slits. This was not, apparently, the response he was looking for.

"Maybe I will stay on for a while." Christiano smiled again, this time directly at Balthazar.

"Of course, you are more than welcome here in Denver," Balthazar said. "But I'm not sure this is really the right place for you. We're not really up to your speed."

"What do you mean?"

"I mean that your reputation precedes you, Christiano. I'm sure this is not news to you. You must be quite used to it by now. We all know of your loss of Bernhardt."

Christiano's heart stopped for a short moment, and he struggled to catch his breath in his throat. He looked away to the crowd on the dance floor.

"Some of us even met you and Bernhardt on occasions while visiting Europe several years ago. You two are legendary over here in the States."

"How lovely."

"But we also know that when Bernhardt was killed, you . . . how shall I say this? . . . went a little off the deep end."

"I don't want to talk about this anymore," Christiano said.

"Too fucking bad," Balthazar spit out as he set his drink down and turned to face Christiano. "You're a bad seed, Christiano. You're trouble everywhere you go. And you bring trouble to the rest of us who are around you. You're like the fucking plague. We don't want that kind of trouble here."

"I don't believe you have a say in how and when I come and go. I will do as I please, Balthazar."

"Yes, I suppose you will. But choose your actions carefully, Christiano."

"What do you mean by that?"

"You've already been way too fucking careless. I'd watch my back if I were you."

"Careless? In what way?"

Our members don't take kindly to another vampire killing off their chosen mortals.

I don't know what you're talking about.

Yes, you do. Stop acting stupid with me. Uriel was not just another human being to us. He was very well liked and respected. He knew about us and was discreet and understanding about our needs and our lifestyles.

What does this have to do with me? Christiano asked as he swirled the thick nectar around in his glass and looked around the room.

You fucked up, my friend. Uriel was my lover.

What? Christiano asked, and took a step back from Balthazar. *He never told me anything like that.*

Yes, well, he wouldn't have. He rather enjoyed his little indiscriminate encounters with other vampires when I was away. He had quite a penchant for hot and attractive vampires. And that is all right with me. That's what drew him to me in the first place. And I often partake of the pleasures of other mortals as well. Uriel and I had an understanding about these things, and that was okay.

Christiano looked around the room, avoiding Balthazar's eyes.

So it would have been okay for you to have fucked Uriel. But you do not kill my lover, Christiano.

I didn't . . .

Do not lie to me. I'm not asking for a confession. I don't need one. I know you killed him.

But I didn't . . .

I loved him, Christiano. I have fucked up a lot of things in my life, and I know that I am a ruthless bastard at times. But I loved Uriel. He was the one thing I did right. I know you know what that feeling is like, Christiano. You had it once, too. But just because you lost the love of your life doesn't mean you have the right to kill mine.

Balthazar, look . . .

No, you look, Balthazar spit out as he grabbed Christiano by the collar of his shirt and brought him closer to his face.

Several of the other vampires near them scuttled closer, and Christiano heard their whispered encouragements for Balthazar to take it easy and remember where he was.

Get the fuck out of Dodge, Balthazar said. *I don't want to see your face in here again.*

Christiano took a deep breath and closed his eyes for a moment. Then he opened them slowly and glared into Balthazar's eyes.

You're wrinkling my shirt, he said quietly.

Your shirt is the last fucking thing you should be worrying about right now.

Christiano reached over slowly and took Balthazar's hands in his own. Balthazar's grip on his collar was firm, and his hands were strong. But Christiano's were stronger, and he pried the lead vampire's hands from his shirt and brought them down to his side with little effort.

I am trying to be nice here, because I know you are suffering from the loss of your loved one. But this is my favorite shirt, and I don't appreciate your wrinkling it like this, Christiano said as he swatted at the collar of his shirt. *I will tolerate your discourtesy and your arrogance because you are distressed. And out of respect for your . . . position . . . here in this city, I will not shame you. But let's get one thing clear right now, Balthazar. This is the one and only time I will allow this kind of disrespectful behavior toward me. Are we clear on that?*

Don't fuck with me, Christiano, Balthazar said defiantly.

Oh, I won't; you don't have to worry about that. You're not my type.

Get out of Denver. You won't have many more opportunities to do so.

I think I have just decided to stay indefinitely, actually.

You're a fucking idiot . . .

DO NOT MAKE ME TAKE THIS TO THE NEXT LEVEL, BALTHAZAR, Christiano shouted so loudly that every vampire in the club turned to look at them, even though he hadn't opened his mouth, and none of the mortals in the club seemed to notice a thing. He grabbed Balthazar by the balls and lifted him several inches off the ground as his red eyes glowed in the fluorescent darkness of the club. *You will not like the way this turns out if you do,* he said as he took a deep breath and lowered Balthazar to the floor. *Trust me on this one.*

Balthazar looked around him and noticed that every vampire eye was on Christiano. Some of his colleagues had taken a step or two forward, but many had not.

"This isn't over," Balthazar said, as he smoothed imaginary wrinkles from his shirt and dusted imaginary dust from his sleeves. "Not by a long shot."

"It's over for now," Christiano said. "I believe I want to dance." He picked up his drink and turned his back on Balthazar as he walked toward the dance floor.

On the dance floor, Christiano allowed himself to get lost in the lights and the music and the sting of his third ruby Cuervo nectar. He'd noticed that Balthazar had stormed out of the club half an hour earlier, flanked by ten or twelve of his faithful cronies. And so he'd been able to relax and enjoy himself for the rest of the evening.

He was swaying to the slow, pounding beat of the song when he suddenly felt someone snuggle up behind him and wrap his arms around his waist. Christiano started to turn and snap the newcomer's neck, when he felt the man grind his hips against his ass and felt the hard cock rub against his ass.

"Don't worry," the man behind him whispered, "I'm a friend."

"I don't have any friends," Christiano said, but he stayed where he was and allowed the man to continue dancing with him and rubbing himself up against his backside. It felt good, and Christiano was a little drunk from the nectar.

"Well, you do now," the man said as he licked the back of Christiano's ear. "I like the way you stood up to Balthazar. Not many vampires do that."

Christiano turned to look at the man behind him. He was about Christiano's height and build. His hair was dyed blue, to match the color of his eyes. His skin, like that of most of the others, was milky white. Full, pink lips framed a perfect smile. He looked to be about twenty-five or so, but of course that was misleading. Still, he was a young vampire.

"You're fucking turning me on, man. And I'm hungry. What do you say we share a meal?"

"I'm starving," Christiano said as he leaned in and kissed the vampire on the lips. "Anyone special in mind?"

"Yeah. That dude over there by the larger bar."

Christiano looked over at the bar and shrugged his shoulders.

"The one with no shirt and the gray slacks."

Christiano spotted the guy and took a closer look. He was also looking at Christiano and his new friend and raised his glass to them. He was a couple of inches shorter than Christiano. He looked to be a light-skinned black or Latino man. Maybe a mix of both. His head was shaved, and every inch of his skin, from his head to his chest and arms, seemed to be marble smooth. His chest and arms were muscular and gleamed with sweat. When he smiled, his white teeth glowed in the dark.

"Mesmerizing," Christiano said.

"He's fucking hot, man. Crazy wild in bed, too."

"So you've had him before."

"Hell, yeah. A couple times. He fucking gets off on vampires, man. Can't get enough of us."

"Really?"

"Yeah."

"What's his name?"

"Victor."

"And yours?"

The young vampire smiled and kissed Christiano on the lips. "I'm Lestat."

"Yeah, sure you are," Christiano said, and smiled.

"My name's Shane."

Can you hear me, Victor? Christiano asked the young man at least a hundred feet away.

Victor raised his glass and smiled, then nodded his head.

"I fucking love it when you guys can do that," Shane said, and squeezed his crotch against the back of Christiano's ass.

"Save it for later, kid," Christiano said, and smiled.

"So, what do you say? Wanna fuck him?"

Meet us in the parking lot in five minutes, Christiano told Victor.

The two vampires watched the kid quickly swallow the last of his drink, then kiss and hug a couple of his friends. Then he grabbed his jacket and headed for the door.

"Don't worry about taking it easy on me," Victor said. He was lying in the middle of the bed, with Christiano and Shane sandwiching him on either side. "I can take it as hard as you can give it."

"That's true," Shane said, and started to lift Victor's legs into the air.

"Slow down," Christiano said, and lowered Victor's legs. He was behind Victor and leaned in to kiss his ears and his neck. Victor moaned and wiggled his ass and hips against Christiano's legs and crotch.

"I'm hungry, man," Shane whined. "Let's get to it."

"You won't starve," Christiano said, and winked at him. "Enjoy our friend here. It's the least we can do. Kiss him."

Shane leaned down and kissed the other side of Victor's neck. When Victor moaned louder and shuddered, Shane nibbled his way down Victor's throat and farther down to his nipples.

"Oh, God, dudes," Victor whispered in a hoarse voice, "you're fucking turning me on beyond words." He squirmed and wiggled every part of his body, lifting his hips and back off the bed as Shane and Christiano kissed their way down his entire body.

Shane nibbled his way down Victor's chest and belly. When he reached Victor's crotch he took a deep breath and licked the head of Victor's cock. It was thick and uncut, and took a couple of minutes for Shane to be able to swallow most of it down his throat. Victor moaned and lifted his hips, causing the thick cock to sink deeper into Shane's throat. Shane choked on the big dick and let it slip from his mouth as he took a deep breath.

Victor turned over onto his side and raised his left leg into the air. "I want you to fuck me," he said as he leaned over and kissed Christiano on the lips.

"I will," Christiano said.

"Now."

Christiano laughed and lowered himself down on the bed. When his face reached Victor's smooth ass, he leaned in and spread the marble cheeks apart. He bit lightly on the round mounds on either side and then licked his way between the cheeks until he found the pink hole in the middle. Victor moaned and wiggled his ass. Christiano teased him for a few minutes and then slid his tongue deep into Victor's ass in one move.

"Oh, fuck!" Victor cried out as he slid his ass back farther onto Christiano's tongue.

Christiano slid his tongue in and out of the ass for several minutes, making sure Victor was relaxed and wet. Then he moved back up onto the bed and slowly moved his cock against Victor's ass. He slid his cock up and down the crack between the twin globes, slicking his cock as he moved.

"Stop teasing me, man. I want you to fuck me."

Christiano positioned the head of his cock against the hole of Victor's ass. He pushed forward until just the head slipped inside. His cock head was instantly enveloped in warmth, and he leaned his head back and closed his eyes as he reveled in the pleasure of Victor's ass. Then he slid his entire cock deep inside the warm ass and counted to ten to try to ward off the climax he felt growing already deep in his belly.

"Fuck me," Victor moaned as he rocked his ass deeper onto Christiano's cock.

"I gotta eat, man," Shane whined again as he stroked his cock and watched his new friend fuck his old friend.

"Go ahead," Christiano said hoarsely as he fucked Victor harder and deeper. "I'm afraid this isn't going to last as long as I wanted it to."

Shane leaned down and sucked Victor's fat cock into his mouth for a couple of seconds, and then moved down to just below his balls. He lifted Victor's left leg a little higher into the air, which caused both Victor and Christiano to moan uncontrollably as Victor's ass opened wider to accommodate more of Christiano's big dick. Then he moved Victor's balls out of the way and found the large vein that ran the length of Victor's thigh and down his leg. He opened his mouth wide and gently bit through the skin of Victor's thigh, sinking his fangs into the vein.

Victor moaned lustfully as he felt his skin being pierced, and squeezed his ass muscles around Christiano's cock.

Christiano leaned forward and kissed Victor's neck and then bit down onto the jugular vein. This brought another moan of delight from Victor, and Christiano sucked harder on the neck, savoring the sweet taste of Victor's blood as it hit his tongue and slid down his throat.

Victor rocked back and forth, leaning his neck deep against Christiano's cool lips so that his fangs could have better access to his throbbing jugular, and lifting his leg higher into the air so that Shane could sink his teeth deeper into the vein in his leg. At the same time, he slid his ass back onto Christiano's eager cock.

The two vampires fed on Victor's blood with a thirst that seemed uncontrollable. Victor's hard and eager body drove them to a more heightened sexual desire than they'd anticipated, and they continued to drink even after they'd reached the point when they knew they should stop.

"Hey, guys," Victor said as he continued to slide his ass onto Christiano's cock. "That's enough. We're getting close, and I've still gotta save a little for Balthazar later this morning."

"What?" Christiano said as he lifted his head from Victor's warm neck.

"I'm supposed to meet Balthazar in about an hour. I gotta have some left for him or he's gonna be pissed."

Shane, did you hear that? Christiano asked wordlessly in a voice only Shane could hear, as he continued to fuck Victor.

"Yes," Shane said as he looked up and smiled at Christiano from between Victor's legs.

I don't think we want that to happen, do we?

Nope.

Okay, then, Christiano said, and sank his teeth back down into the supple warmth of Victor's neck.

Shane lowered his head back down to Victor's leg and licked around the still-warm blood that collected around the bite wound, then bit down hard on the exposed thick vein again.

"Hey, guys, I said that's enough," Victor said as he stopped rocking his body between the two vampires. "It's time to stop now."

Christiano shoved his cock deeper into Victor's ass and began fucking him harder and faster as he bit harder and sucked ferociously on his neck. When Victor tried to pull himself off Christiano's cock, Shane held his legs and ass in place with an unnaturally strong grip as he ripped into the vein in Victor's leg and sucked more blood into his mouth.

"Oh, no," Victor whimpered as he realized what was happening. "Come on, guys, you don't have to do this."

Oh, but we do, Christiano said in a voice that Victor could hear, as well, while he continued to drink a steady flow of warm blood from Victor's neck. *Sorry, my friend, but you're going to die tonight.*

Victor's body went limp as he began to lose consciousness. He cried as his head began to get dizzy and he felt himself lose sensation in his legs and neck. "Please don't," he whispered as the tears rolled down his cheek. "I didn't do anything to you. I'm on your side."

Christiano slammed his cock deeper into Victor's ass a couple more times and then moaned loudly as he rested his big dick deep inside Victor and released himself.

He bit deeper into Victor's neck and sucked another couple of mouthfuls of blood into his mouth. It was growing cooler now and more acrid. It wouldn't be too much longer.

Victor took one last deep breath, and his body began to shudder as Christiano stopped sucking on his neck and pulled out of him.

"That's it," he said to Shane.

Shane lifted his head from beneath Victor's legs and wiped the blood that was still dripping from his lips with one hand. He looked dazed and a little confused. "Why did we just do that?" he asked Christiano.

"If Balthazar wants a war, we'll give him a war. Are you with me, Shane?"

"I don't have much of a choice now," he said as he leaned back against the headboard and licked the last drops of blood from his lips.

"Finish him off," Christiano said.

Shane lifted Victor's head from the pillow and felt for a pulse. It was still there, but barely. He leaned down and kissed Victor on the lips and then snapped his neck in one swift and powerful jerk.

"How do we let Balthazar know it was us?" Christiano asked as he leaned over and licked Shane's lips and kissed him.

"He'll know."

Back at the cathedral, Christiano dawdled before going to bed. He was restless and anxious and wound up all at the same time. The blood rushed through his veins at almost twice its normal speed and caused him to pace back and forth and kept him from winding down and being able to sleep.

What had he just done? Why had he killed Victor? The kid hadn't done anything to him. He was a sweet kid and a really good lay. Christiano could have had a lot of good times with him, had he played his cards a little differently. Victor's only sin was that he'd let Christiano know that he had an alliance with Balthazar. He hadn't witnessed the incident between the two vampires earlier that evening, and so he could have had no idea that a war had been established. He couldn't have known that the mere mention of Balthazar's name would be the cause of his death.

And now he'd gotten Shane involved as well. Though Shane had expressed a general dislike for Balthazar, Christiano was fairly certain it was an opinion not so easily shared with others. Shane had confided in Christiano and made an effort to befriend him. And how had he repaid him? By getting him drunk with Victor's blood and then convincing him to help kill Victor. Shane was right: there was no turning back at this point. And on some subconscious level, Christiano had known that from the beginning. He needed someone on his side in this fight, and he'd manipulated Shane into being that someone. Shane, too, seemed like a nice enough kid. Certainly he didn't deserve to be caught up in Christiano's personal feuds.

But Balthazar was abusing his power, and it was he who'd proclaimed war. Christiano didn't want that fight, but he wasn't going to run from it, either. He hadn't known that Uriel was Balthazar's lover, and he surely couldn't be held responsible for killing the lead vampire's lover if he didn't know. It was Uriel's fault, really. He shouldn't have been fucking around behind his lover's back. And if he was, he should have been up-front about it with Christiano so he wouldn't have killed him.

But the battle lines were now drawn, and Christiano was ready. He knew he couldn't do it alone, and so he'd enlisted Shane. Hopefully, others would follow. He'd gotten the feeling that Balthazar didn't hold as much respect and loyalty as he thought he did. All Christiano had to do was show the vampires in Denver that he was stronger than Balthazar and not afraid to face him head-on. Not that he wanted to be lead vampire here, but that he could recognize weakness and step up to confront it. He was strong and a good leader. He could easily identify and train someone to take over the lead vampire position here. But first, Balthazar had to be removed.

Christiano felt his head get light, and he became a little dizzy. The blood slowed down in his veins, and he felt his muscles get achy. A high-pitched ringing sound echoed through his head, and his fingers tingled. That meant only one thing. The sun was just starting to come up, and even though he was deep in the subdepths of the dark basement in the cathedral, he was feeling its effects. He didn't have much time.

He stripped his clothes and ran his hands up and down his body. His muscles were tight and sticky with sweat, and he smiled as he felt how strong and defined his body was. As he caressed himself, his cock began to harden again, and he smiled as he stroked himself while climbing into the coffin.

He was ready for the fight ahead.

Chapter Six

"Come on, Victor," Balthazar yelled as he pounded on the door. "Open up. It's getting late. I don't have time to mess around tonight."

"Maybe he's not home," the skinny kid next to him said as he wiped his nose on his shirtsleeve and looked nervously around the hall.

"Of course he's home," Balthazar said as he gave the kid an annoyed glance. "He knew I was gonna stop by. And for crying out loud, calm down, will you? You're so strung out on that shit, you can't go a second without wiping the snot from your face or looking around like you expect the fuckin' SWAT team to come crashing through the doors at any minute."

"What?" the kid asked, and wiped his nose again, trying very hard not to look around him.

"Open the fucking door."

The boy pulled a ring of keys from his pocket and slid one of them into the lock. He pushed the door open and stepped aside to allow Balthazar to enter.

"What's that smell?" he asked as Balthazar brushed past him and into the hallway of the apartment.

"It's blood," Balthazar said. "Where are the lights?"

"Oh, shit," the skinny teen whined as he stopped walking deeper into the dark room.

"The lights," Balthazar said, with little patience in his voice.

"Over on the other wall," the kid said, and walked quickly to the other side of the room and switched on the light.

The light blinked a couple of times and then filled the room with fluorescent brightness.

"Thank God," the kid said as he looked around the living room. All the furniture was in its place, and the room was immaculately clean. "I thought I was gonna see—"

"Don't get overly excited just yet. You still might see it," Balthazar said. "Where's the bedroom?"

"Over there," the kid said, and pointed to the hallway behind them.

"What was your name again, kid?" Balthazar asked as he turned to walk down the hallway.

"Eric."

"And how long have you been Victor's roommate?"

"Almost a year now. Why?"

"So you know him pretty well."

"Yeah, I suppose."

"Good. Because something tells me we're gonna need to know a little more about Victor and his acquaintances."

"Why?" Eric asked cautiously as he slowed down and let Balthazar get a few steps ahead of him.

Balthazar opened the bedroom door without knocking and fumbled around the wall to find the light switch. When he located it, he flipped it on and stood inside the door frame so that Eric could see inside.

The room filled with light, and Eric thrust his hands against his mouth so that he would not scream. His eyes grew wide, and huge tears began to form in them as he surveyed the room.

Victor was tied to the four-poster bed, spread-eagled, lying on his back. He was naked, and his cock had been cleanly sliced from the groin area and stuffed in his mouth. His eyes were closed, and except for the grotesquely disconnected cock in his mouth, he looked peaceful. The sheets and comforter on the bed were disheveled and soaked with blood. There were also streams of dark red blood splashed across the walls and the floor.

Balthazar looked over at Eric and saw that he was about to scream despite the hands that were turning white as the knuckles pressed against his mouth.

"Don't you fucking dare scream, you little sissy," he hissed at Eric.

Eric looked at him with wide, questioning eyes.

"I don't know," Balthazar yelled. "I don't know what happened. But I swear to God, if you scream I'm gonna make sure you join your friend here. Is that clear?"

Eric nodded and swallowed deeply but kept his hands pressed firmly against his mouth.

"Do you have any idea who might have done this?" Balthazar asked.

Eric shook his head slowly as giant tears fell down his cheeks.

"Move your fucking hands away from your mouth and talk to me, you sissy."

Eric moved his hands slowly from his mouth and took a deep breath as he attempted to speak. Instead, he leaned over and vomited on the floor next to Balthazar.

"Oh, Christ," Balthazar said as he jumped backward to miss the stream of bile that spewed from Eric's mouth. He waited until the kid was finished vomiting, then asked again. "Any ideas?"

"No," Eric said weakly as he looked back over to the bed and what remained of his roommate.

Balthazar walked over to Victor. As he got closer to the body, he noticed something written in blood across the chest of the once handsome young man. He leaned closer to read it.

C M

Balthazar stood up and clenched his teeth until his jaws ground and stood out on his face. His eyes grew red, and his breathing became rapid and labored.

"What is it?" Eric asked.

Balthazar snapped his head to the side quickly so that he glared at the frightened kid.

"Who did this?" he asked as he felt his fangs begin to protrude.

"I told you, I have no idea."

"Don't lie to me."

"I'm not lying," Eric's voice cracked as he whispered.

"You were there with him at the club tonight. Who did he leave with?"

"I don't know, I swear. Tonight was my first night at the club. I don't know anyone there."

"You obviously know someone there, because someone knew enough about you to direct me to you when I inquired about Victor."

"Look, mister, I promise, I don't know who he left with. I saw him talking with two hot guys, and the next thing I know, he was gone. It's not like he hasn't done it a million times before."

"What did they look like?"

"They were both kinda tall. Really good-looking. One of them had black hair and really pretty eyes. Looked to be late twenties or early thirties, maybe. The other dude had blue hair and really white skin. And the most kissable lips I've ever seen."

"Fuck me," Balthazar said quietly.

"What?"

Balthazar stared at Eric for a moment. The more he saw the kid look around himself nervously and wipe at his nose, the more he hated him. He glared at Eric and then smiled.

"Hey," Eric squealed. "What's happening?"

"What's the matter, Eric? What do you feel?"

"My balls! My fucking balls! What are you doing to me?"

"What do you mean, Eric? I'm all the way over here, and you're all the way over there. How can I be doing anything to your balls?"

"I don't know, but you are. Ouch! There it is again," Eric whined as he reached down and cupped his balls in his hands. "Stop it, that hurts."

Balthazar laughed and then watched as Eric was lifted off his feet and slid up the wall behind him. The kid's feet dangled and kicked through the air as he was lifted higher and higher from the floor.

"Stop it, man. Put me down. That's not funny."

Balthazar lifted his arms and waved them around the air, causing Eric to be moved from the wall and spun around the room several feet above the floor.

"I didn't do it, man, I swear. I told you everything I know. You gotta believe me. Let me go. Please."

"Oh, I don't think so," Balthazar said, and slid his lips back to show his canine teeth.

"Oh, fuck," Eric cried as he spun around in circles and caught sight of the fangs every time he was facing Balthazar. "Fuck me."

"No thanks," Balthazar said.

Eric was sobbing openly now, and his head started to dangle as he got dizzy. "Please don't kill me," he whimpered.

"Well, I can't just let you go."

"Yes you can. I won't tell anyone. I swear."

"Of course you won't."

"Really, I . . ."

Balthazar wiggled his fingers in the air, and Eric flew toward him. When he was in grasping range, Balthazar grabbed him and pulled him down to his own level.

"Please . . .," Eric moaned.

Balthazar opened his mouth wide and clamped his lips onto the skinny, cold neck of the kid. He bit deep and hard into the flesh and growled as the first drops of blood met his tongue and lips. He sucked some of it into his mouth and swallowed several mouthfuls.

"Fuck!" he screamed as he flung Eric across the room and against the far wall. "It's sour. How much fucking heroin do you have in your veins?"

Eric moaned and looked up at Balthazar with a dazed look in his eyes.

Balthazar walked over to him and reached down to grab his neck.

"I can't drink this shit."

"I'm sorry," Eric moaned as he struggled to keep his eyes open.

Balthazar twisted the kid's neck with one swift yank of his hand and relished in the sound of the bones popping. Eric went limp immediately and slumped out of his grasp to the floor.

"Fucking waste," Balthazar said as he stepped over the dead young man and to the bed where Victor lay.

"You messed up, old buddy," he whispered into Victor's ear as he lay down next to his dead friend. "You were supposed to go home with me. Why didn't you stick with the plan? None of this would have happened if you'd just stuck with the plan. He's not *that* cute, you know. Certainly not worth getting killed over."

He looked at Victor as if he expected a response.

"Bad news, this Christiano Montez. Fucking bad news. And it looks like he's got a coconspirator. I wouldn't have expected something like this from Shane. Most unfortunate."

Balthazar plucked the flaccid penis from Victor's mouth and rolled it between his fingers.

"A pity, really. Such a beautiful cock. It's no good anymore, now, is it?"

Balthazar kissed the penis and laid it on the bed between Victor's legs.

"What are we going to do with our Mr. Montez, Victor? We can take care of Shane easily enough. But Christiano will be another matter. We'll have to take it a little more carefully with that one. But I'll tell you one thing: if he wants a war, he's got one. He has no idea what he's getting into when he fucks with Balthazar."

He looked over at Victor again and leaned over to kiss him on the cheek.

"Don't you worry, Victor. I'll get him. I'll get him for you."

Balthazar stood up from the bed and walked to the door. He looked back at Victor, lying on the bed, and then over to Eric, who was slumped against the far wall.

"Tsk tsk," he whispered as he walked out of the bedroom and shut the door behind him.

A few steps down the hallway he turned and smiled as he heard a *whoosh* behind the bedroom door and noticed a bright red and orange flicker from the crack between the bottom of the bedroom door and the floor. A second later he saw a thin trail of black smoke seep from the door and drift toward the ceiling.

He smiled as he walked out the front door and out of the building.

It was a couple of evenings later before Balthazar was able to convene his council. They were a group of ten men and two women who had been hand chosen by Balthazar to help rule the vampire community in Denver. He'd chosen the twelve very deliberately, and called them his disciples. Behind his back there were a few snickers about his thinking so highly of himself as to compare himself to Jesus. But no one ever said anything out loud or to his face. Ever. Everyone knew it was Balthazar who was in charge, who had the ultimate word in everything that happened in the community. But one had to get through the council first before anything was even presented to Balthazar for consideration. They relished their position of authority and abused it widely, as did most councils to lead vampires in the United States. They took elaborate bribes, they forced sexual favors from lesser-positioned vampires, and they were excessively violent and merciless.

Balthazar knew of their abuse of power, and it didn't bother him at all. Allowing it to continue helped guarantee their loyalty and their assistance when he needed it. And he needed it now.

"So, what's going on, Balthazar?" Devin asked. He was leaning back in his chair, with his legs spread out in front of him. Some young woman Balthazar had never seen before was on her knees in front of Devin, working diligently at licking and sucking his swollen cock.

"Get her the fuck out of here," Balthazar hissed.

"What? You've never complained before when we brought a . . . guest to these meetings."

"This is different," Balthazar said, and glared at Devin. "This is very important, and it's a closed meeting. I don't know this girl. I've never even seen her before."

"I'm Teresa," the pretty girl said as she let Devin's cock slip from between her lips and smiled at Balthazar.

"Teresa, you have exactly ten seconds to pull your cute little skirt up to cover that pickled twat of yours and get the fuck out of this room. After that I will personally rip your flesh from your body in massive strips and use them to mop up your blood from the floor. Is that clear?"

Teresa stumbled to her feet and clumsily pulled her skirt up around her waist as she tripped over her own feet running out the door.

"What the fuck was that all about?" Devin asked as he pulled up his jeans and buckled them.

"We have a situation," Balthazar said as he sat down at the head of the table and looked around at each of his disciples.

"Well, we figured that much," Devin grumbled. "You don't just call us all together so hastily unless there is a situation. So what is it this time? Somebody make goo-goo eyes at your latest boyfriend again without your permission? You want us to scare them up a little? Have a little come-to-Jesus talk with them?"

There were a few snickers from the table.

Balthazar waited until they died down before responding. "You know, Devin, you are a very short step away from suffering the same fate as I just described to your slutty little friend Teresa."

"You can't kill me like that," Devin said boldly. "I'm not human."

"That's very true," Balthazar said as he locked eyes with the feisty vampire. "But I can make you wish you were, and I can make you beg for a fate as kind as that which I mentioned to your whore. You know that much is true. Now, shall we continue this little debate, or shall we get on with the business at hand?"

Devin was only able to hold Balthazar's gaze for a couple of seconds; then he resituated himself in his chair and moved his eyes to stare down at the table in front of him.

"Good," Balthazar said, and stood up to address the council seated in front of him. "It seems our newcomer friend is up to his old tricks again. Christiano Montez is making quite a nuisance of himself here in our quaint little city. I want him gone."

"What?" asked one of the female members of the council. "We can't just force him to leave town if he doesn't want to go."

"I know that," Balthazar said.

"And besides, what has he done that is so bad? So he's killed a few people, and maybe he's gotten a little careless with one or two of them. But we've all done that. Hell, most of us still get a little careless every now and then. It's nothing to freak out about."

"I think he wants to challenge me for lead vampire."

The group was quiet and looked at Balthazar intently. They each enjoyed being part of the elite council, and all the special privileges that came with the position. But they also knew that Balthazar was a weak leader. He had an ego the size of Los Angeles, and a temper that he couldn't control. But he was young and sometimes foolish and often made irrational decisions based on emotions and personal circumstances rather than on wisdom or for the cause of advancing the vampire movement in Denver. For a long time they'd longed for a stronger leader. But they all knew that none of them—and no one else in the community, either—was any more capable of leading them than was Balthazar. So they'd kept quiet.

But now Christiano was here, and everything was changed.

"That's ridiculous," said Michael, one of the youngest members of the council. "Why would he want to challenge you for leader? From what I know of him, he doesn't even plan on staying in Denver for any period of time."

"I know that, and I don't know why he feels the stupid little need to challenge me. But he does, and I need to know that I can count on you, my friends, for support and for allegiance in this little war Mr. Montez has waged."

"What makes you think Christiano wants to oust you?" Devin asked, leaning forward in his chair now and paying closer attention to the conversation.

"After my little chat with him last week, Mr. Montez seduced our good friend Victor and convinced Victor to invite him to his apartment for a little . . . rendezvous."

"So, all of this really is just a little lovers' quarrel, then. Christiano fucked your cute little boyfriend, and you are not happy with the competition."

Balthazar took a slow, deep breath and glared at Devin for a long moment without saying anything.

"How many of you have slept with Victor?" he asked.

Ten of the twelve council members, including both women, raised their hands.

"And how many of you have fed on Victor?"

All twelve hands were raised.

"Victor was a very special person to our entire community. He understood us and supported our existence here. He loved all of us, and he allowed us to love him as well. And he offered his blood to us freely and willingly and often. We all know how rare that devotion and understanding is among humans. Victor was a very special young man."

"Why are you using the past tense?" Devin asked as he scooted his chair closer to the table and leaned forward on his elbows.

"Because Christiano Montez killed Victor."

There was an audible gasp from the council, and they all began to fidget nervously. Most of them turned their shocked eyes to the ground, unable to look at Balthazar or to fully accept that Victor was dead.

"He ripped him into little pieces, cut his cock off and stuffed it into his mouth, and left him to lie in a blood-soaked bed."

"What? That's ridiculous," Michael said.

"It's true. With total disregard for the sacredness of blood, he ripped through Victor's flesh at all of the most vulnerable spots and then allowed the blood to spill out onto the bed and drain uselessly from Victor's body and stain the bed and the floor. There were gallons of it everywhere."

The council moaned and shifted in their seats again. Wasting valuable blood in this way was forbidden. It was generally considered a sign of betrayal, and often used as a visible declaration of war between individuals or groups of vampires.

"Any more doubts about whether or not our fucking little friend is trying to take my fucking position from me?" Balthazar screamed as spit flew from his mouth. His face was red and his breathing shallow.

No one said a word.

"I won't stand for this," Balthazar said as he took deep breaths and composed himself. "I need to know that you are all with me. Christiano is not stupid, and he is not weak. But he will not come in here and spread his sickly infection and destroy our community. We are a family here, and we need to stick together. I can defeat Christiano Montez, I promise you that. But I can't do it without your help. Can I count on you?"

"We can't just run him out of town. He won't go willingly, and I don't see that he is the kind to get intimidated by us," the more vocal of the two women said.

"No, you're right. We can't intimidate him, and we can't just run him out of town."

"Then what do you suggest?" Devin asked.

Balthazar didn't say a word but just took a moment to gaze into the eyes of every vampire seated at the table.

"You've got to be fucking kidding me," Devin said as he held Balthazar's gaze and leaned back in his chair.

"Have you ever known me to kid about something like this?"

"No, but we've never discussed anything like this before, either. You've got to be out of your fucking mind, Balthazar. We can't do this. It's forbidden, and you know that. The elders in our region are the most conservative in the entire nation. They're almost as fucking conservative as the humans. You've had enough contact with them to know that. They will not support this."

"It is forbidden except in the most extreme and rare cases," Balthazar said quietly as he tugged at invisible wrinkles on his shirt collar.

"This is not the most extreme and rare case," Devin said. "He fucked your cute little boyfriend . . ."

"AND THEN HE KILLLED HIM!" Balthazar screamed as he stood to his feet and pounded his fist onto the table. He took a couple of deep breaths and spoke more quietly and with more control. "And worst of all, he took just enough of Victor's precious blood to write his initials across Victor's chest, and then he carelessly and shamelessly allowed the rest of it to spill out of his body and spoil."

"Balthazar . . ."

"It is also forbidden to intentionally waste human blood. The elders are not so conservative that they will overlook that. Do I have your support?"

"Let's think this out logically, Balthazar. Christiano has a reputation for being a ruthless and merciless killer. He's been in many wars over in Europe. And he always came out the victor."

"Not always. He's been run out of towns, and even countries, before."

"I'm not convinced he didn't leave on his own accord because he was bored or just looking for some fresher, newer meat to exact his revenge on."

"Do I have your support?"

"He is much more experienced at fighting than we are, Balthazar. You know his reputation better than anyone here. Before he showed up here, you couldn't stop gushing about how great he was."

"And now he is not. Now he is nothing more than a stupid vampire who has overstepped his bounds and thinks he can come in here with his European charm and take over our community. The community we've worked so hard to create and preserve. He thinks he is better than us and that he can bend us to his own will and that by sheer brutality he can take over our community. Well, he is not better than us. He is nothing more than a mean and sick vampire who lives to kill and destroy and ridicule."

"Give me a fucking break, man. Yeah, I know he is ruthless, and I know that at times he can be careless. But his hatred is directed at humans, Balthazar, not vampires. And he has a right to hate humans. They killed his lover. And everyone here knows that Christiano and Bernhardt were madly in love. Of course he's going to be a little angry and hateful."

Balthazar squinted his eyes at Devin and glared at him for several seconds before speaking.

"And now Christiano has killed my lover. Are you saying I don't have the same right to be angry and hateful?"

"I'm not saying that at all, Balthazar. What I'm saying is that Christiano's war is with humans, not with vampires. Victor, as wonderful and beautiful as he was, was a human. What makes you believe Christiano killed Victor as a declaration of war against vampires rather than a continuation of his war with humans?"

"It doesn't matter."

"But it *does* matter! That's the whole point of this discussion. It does matter. Because no matter how much you miss Victor, or how angry you are at Christiano for killing him, the elders will not support you killing him because he offed a mortal."

"FUCK VICTOR!" Balthazar screamed. "Do you really think all of this is about Victor? It's not. Victor meant nothing to me. He was a nice piece of ass and his blood was unusually sweet and delicious. Big fucking deal. He was nothing more than a fucking human who happened to be sympathetic to our lifestyle. I am not sad that he is gone. I am not filled with grief over his demise. This is not about Victor. This is about me. It's about us. Christiano thinks he can swoop in here and take over and bend us to his illness."

This tirade had flown from Balthazar's mouth with lightning speed and without a breath. Now Balthazar took a few deep breaths and allowed his heartbeat to return to normal.

"And he's already been somewhat successful. He's already infiltrated our close-knit little circle and contaminated one of our own. You don't really think Christiano killed Victor all by his little lonesome, do you? Of course not. Our stupid little Shane helped him."

This drew a few surprised gasps from the council.

"That's right. Shane helped him kill Victor, and Shane was an accomplice in wasting the sacred blood. This is about so much more than me being jealous because Christiano Montez killed my boyfriend. This is about us saving our very lives. This is about us saving our own community from a tyrant."

Balthazar let this sink in for a moment, making sure he had the attention of everyone at the table.

"I will not allow Christiano Montez to come in here and bully us into his sickness. If I go to the elders with a united front from this council, I know I can persuade them to sponsor our decision. What I need to know now is, do I have your support?"

There were a couple of murmurs among the council, and then they all nodded their heads. All except Devin.

"Balthazar . . ."

"FUCK YOU!" Balthazar screamed. "I'm tired of this little discussion. It's over. DO I HAVE YOUR SUPPORT OR NOT?"

"You're my best friend, Bal," Devin said softly as he looked down at the table and then back up at the lead vampire. "Of course you have my support."

Chapter Seven

Christiano had fully expected a swift retaliation from Balthazar and his cronies. But it didn't happen. For the next two weeks when he showed up at Club Suque, they'd make eye contact and stare each other down. The vampire leader was constantly surrounded by his faithful, who also tried unsuccessfully to intimidate Christiano. But they never made a move, and in fact, after losing the testosterone-laden staring contest, moved swiftly to the opposite end of the club.

Christiano grew bored of the routine and of the club. He hadn't been to Charlie's in months, and decided to go back to the bar he'd had such good luck with before finding the vampire club.

The first thing he noticed when he walked in the door was the thick cloud of cigarette smoke that hung over the room like a storm cloud settling in for days of unrelenting torment. He wrinkled his nose at the odor and swiped it away from his face as he made his way through the dark bar. As always, he became the center of attention as he strode through the entry and made his way to the main dance floor. For the most part, Charlie's drew a local, nonpretentious crowd. They were dressed casually in jeans and T-shirts or nondescript button-downs. There were usually a few cute or handsome young men scattered throughout the various rooms of the bar, but no one whose beauty stuck out or who caused every eye in the bar to turn and watch as they strode through. No one except Christiano.

He ignored or waved off the few attempts at acknowledgment from the middle-aged men at the bar and opened the swinging door that led into the main country-dance-floor section of the bar. It was darker in this area, and the music blared through the speakers with more than a little static. But the dance floor was packed with a wide range of men dressed in a wide range of dress. Thursday evenings drew a mixed crowd because of the half-priced drinks and the mixture of country and alternative music. This night was no exception, and the floor was overflowing with young, half-dressed, spiky-haired men two-stepping with middle-aged, skintight Wrangler-jean-wearing cowboys with thick, bushy mustaches and black felt cowboy hats.

Christiano smiled at the sight before him and sidled over to a relatively uncrowded corner in the back of the bar. He leaned against the wooden railing and waited. It didn't take long.

"Hey," the guy said as he walked up and leaned in close to Christiano's face. Christiano could smell the liquor heavy on his breath. His blood would taste strongly of cheap rum. "Wassup?"

Christiano simply stared at the man without responding. He probably wasn't much older than thirty, but the deep lines that stretched across his face, and the blue veins and little red capillaries that popped up around his nose and eyes made him look at least fifteen years older.

"Hmph," the guy grunted as he staggered away. "Your lost."

"Loss," Christiano corrected, and watched as the guy flipped him the finger just before tripping over his own feet and falling to the floor.

Christiano pushed himself away from the railing and ventured outside onto the patio, where a cool breeze wafted the smoke from around his face and allowed him to take deep breaths of clean air. The ten or so tables with chairs around them were all taken, and so he walked to a back corner and stood where he could have a good view of the entire patio.

His nostrils flared as he caught wind of an old, familiar scent that he hadn't noticed in many years. It had been so long that it took him a couple of minutes to identify it. It was sadness. He looked around to see where it was coming from.

Standing about twenty feet away, at the other corner of his end of the patio, was a young man. His back was to Christiano, and his shoulders heaved and shuddered as he blew his nose into a Kleenex. Christiano admired the broad shoulders that tapered down to a V shape and disappeared at the guy's thin waist. His heart sped up a bit as he took in the sight of the high, perfectly round twin globes of the young man's ass, and his long, muscular legs. With any luck at all, the kid would be at least half sober and would be Christiano's feed for the evening.

He waited for more than five minutes, but when the young man did not turn around, Christiano decided to take a more proactive approach.

"Are you all right?" he asked as he walked up behind the kid and tapped him on the shoulder.

"I'm fine," the guy said as he blew his nose again and then turned around.

Christiano took a deep breath and stumbled backward a couple of steps. Luckily, there was a wall there to catch him; otherwise he'd have fallen on his ass. His knees buckled a little and threatened to give out on him. His breath came in short, struggling gasps.

"Hey, man, are you okay?" the kid asked. "You don't look so well."

"I'm okay," Christiano stuttered through dry, raspy croaks. He was staring at Bernhardt. The hair was blond and cut in a short, modern cut, and his skin was a little paler than it had been so many years ago. But it was Bernhardt. The same exotic, almond-shaped eyes, full, ruby red lips, and strong cheekbones that straddled either side of the long and thin Roman nose. Even the same twin dimples that were chiseled on either side of his extraordinary smile. He looked a few years younger than Bernhardt had, and the blond hair and American accent were certainly new. But there was no mistaking that it was Bernhardt. Christiano's heart beat rapidly and his skin tingled, and his breath caught in his throat exactly the way it had upon their first meeting. "Yes, I'm okay," Christiano said as he took a deep breath and stood up and away from the safety of the wall behind him. "Fine."

The young man smiled and shoved his hands in his front pockets. It was a move Bernhardt had done many times when he felt shy or a little vulnerable, and one that Christiano had always found overwhelmingly charming.

"Good," the kid said as he shuffled his feet. "I'd hate to think that I was the cause of someone not being all right."

Can you hear me, Bernhardt? Christiano asked without moving his lips. *Are you there?*

The kid squinted his eyes a little and cocked his head to the side, as if he were trying to figure something out. But he didn't answer, either with or without moving his lips.

"Wow, that was weird," he said as he shook his head lightly.

"What was?" Christiano asked.

"Nothing. Listen, I really need to get my mind off some really bad news I just received. Come dance with me, okay?" he asked as he grabbed Christiano's hand and led him back inside to the dance floor.

"But, I don't—"

"I won't take no for an answer," the young man said as he pushed his way through the crowd, tightening his grip on Christiano's hand as they maneuvered through the smoke and the mass of men between the patio door and the dance floor.

Normally, Christiano would not allow such behavior and control over his actions. But at this moment he was helpless. His heart was beating at an astoundingly high rate, his breath came in short and labored gasps, and his strong legs threatened to buckle beneath him. Every nerve in his body tingled with excitement. He followed the handsome young man willingly onto the dance floor.

The cute blond wiggled and shook his body unself-consciously and closed his eyes as he swayed to the beat of the music. Christiano was mesmerized and couldn't take his eyes off the boy. Neither could anyone else on the dance floor. The dance moves were foreign to Christiano, but from the looks of those around him, he thought his partner must be quite the dancer.

"So, what's your name," the young man asked as he leaned in so that Christiano could hear him above the heavy bass beat of the music.

"Christiano," he said as he took a deep breath to capture the sweet scent of the boy, and the cool breath that brushed past his lips and down his neck as the boy spoke.

"I'm Chance." He leaned in, wrapped his arms around Christiano's waist, and pulled him closer as he ground his hips against Christiano's to the beat of the song. "Nice to meet you, Christiano."

"Likewise," Christiano said, and tried to arrange his quickly hardening cock so that it didn't press against Chance's leg as they danced.

"Don't worry about it," Chance said as he smiled and leaned in closer so he could whisper in Christiano's ear. "Happens to me all the time when I get into the music. It felt good, actually."

Christiano blushed and took a deep breath as he tried to relax and really start to feel the rhythm of the music. In his day he'd been quite the dancer, and he and Bernhardt had loved to spend an entire evening on the dance floor. But this new stuff was so different from anything he'd known before. It looked silly to him as he watched the young men on the floor around him. But the desire to spend as much time as possible with Chance was much stronger than his worry about looking silly, and after just a couple of songs, he noticed that the men around him were watching him with the same lust and desire that they were watching Chance with. Apparently he was a quick study to the nuances of modern dance.

Chance and Christiano spent the rest of the evening together, dancing, talking, drinking, and laughing. Christiano couldn't remember the last time he'd felt so comfortable with someone . . . the last time he'd laughed. He was surprised when the DJ announced last call and the crowd started thinning out.

"I can't believe it's already time to close. It seems like I just got here."

"I know," Chance said with a note of disappointment as he set his empty glass on a table. "I don't want it to end."

"It doesn't have to," Christiano said, and looked around him at the crowd as they worked their way toward the front door. He couldn't look Chance in the eyes right now.

"What did you have in mind?" Chance asked as he entwined his fingers in Christiano's and spread Christiano's legs apart so that he could snuggle between them.

"I'd love to spend the evening with you," Christiano whispered as he forced himself to look into Chance's eyes. They were light blue and reflected the lights that dangled like Christmas tree ornaments a few feet above them. They sucked Christiano into their beauty immediately, and he'd never experienced a sense of helplessness like this before. He thought perhaps it might be best to end this little rendezvous before it went any further. It made no sense that he thought this man was Bernhardt, and to indulge in that fantasy could bring nothing but trouble. "But it's not very convenient to have someone over to my place."

"Then my place it is," Chance said as he leaned into Christiano's face and nibbled on his ear. "I don't live far from here at all. A couple blocks."

"Do you live alone?" Christiano asked as he closed his eyes and allowed the shudder he felt when Chance's hot, wet tongue licked around the inside of his ear to vibrate across his entire body.

"Yes."

Christiano's cock was so hard it throbbed painfully along his left leg, and he felt a thick drop of precum ooze out of the head of his dick and slide down his shaft.

"Let's go," he said before he had a chance to come up with an excuse not to.

Christiano stared down at the young man lying on the bed beneath him and took a deep breath to help him slow down his rapidly beating heart. Chance's naked body was a vision of perfection unlike anything he'd ever seen. There seemed to be not an ounce of fat on him. His smooth, tanned chest was powerfully muscled, with dime-sized nipples, and a couple of freckles scattered here and there to add character. His abs were hard and defined, with just enough muscle to make them irresistible without looking as if he did nothing else with his spare time but perform endless crunches. They narrowed down into a perfect, thin waist, which gave way to long, muscular legs that had a light dusting of short, blond hairs.

Chance's face was equally beautiful. His features were strong and defined and determined. His blue, exotic, almond-shaped eyes hinted that he was not quite as Wonder-bread white as he might otherwise seem. They were framed by long, curly blond eyelashes. As Christiano stared into them, he knew at once that this young man had seen much pain and yet had not allowed that pain to rob him of his innocence and his ability to love unconditionally. He had high and strong cheekbones, a long, thin Roman nose, and a deeply cleft chin. Chance's lips were what imprisoned Christiano's desire, however. They were rose pink, almost red, and very full—another hint of exotic genealogy that might be missed if one was not astutely looking for it. They shone with a natural sheen that looked as if they'd just been swiped with lip gloss. And they were always parted in a half-smile, just slightly enough to allow a glimpse of the pearly white teeth behind them.

Christiano had resisted Chance for as long as he could stand, and leaned down to accept his defeat. As he leaned in to kiss Chance on those lips that mesmerized him so, he caught a whiff of the young man's scent. It, too, was unlike any Christiano had come across, and the sweet lime-and-ginger scent caused his cock to twitch with anticipation. His lips reached Chance's, and he gently licked them as he counted to ten in his head to keep from shooting his load all over Chance's taut stomach. They were as sweet as he'd expected, and much softer than he could ever have imagined. Christiano licked and sucked on them for several minutes, then slowly slid his tongue inside Chance's mouth. It was warm and soft and wet, and when it wrapped tighter around Christiano's tongue and gently sucked him deeper inside, Christiano moaned softly as his body shuddered and he spilled his load all across Chance's hot, smooth body.

"Christ!" Chance whispered as he kissed Christiano's lips once more before letting them slip from his own. "I've never had that happen before."

"Neither have I," Christiano said as he collapsed on the bed next to Chance. "I'm so sorry."

"Don't be silly. I kinda liked it, actually. As long as this doesn't mean we're finished."

Christiano looked down at his cock, which was still rock-hard and throbbing even as the last few drops of cum dripped from the purple-red head. "Does this look like we're finished?"

Chance laughed softly, then reached down and wrapped his fist around Christiano's hard cock. He slid down on the bed until his face was inches from the throbbing flesh, then reached out with his tongue and licked it. His tongue swirled around the hot head for a few minutes; then Chance opened his mouth and swallowed not only the head but the entire length of Christiano's long, thick, uncut cock.

"Oh, God," Christiano moaned as he lifted his hips to slide his cock even deeper into Chance's hot mouth. "I'm gonna cum again if you keep that up."

"Oh, no, you don't," Chance said as he slid his mouth off the giant cock. "Not so fast this time. I want you inside me."

Christiano leaned up and kissed Chance on the mouth again and at the same time rolled him over onto his stomach. He lay on top of the young man's back and slid his slick cock up and down the length of Chance's ass as he kissed him on the back of the neck and between the shoulders. It was as he was kissing this exact spot on most of his feeds that Christiano's fangs always protruded and he slipped into the zone of no return. So he was surprised when he didn't feel the dull throb in his gums that signaled the ascension of his canines. He even stopped kissing Chance and lifted his head slightly from the shoulders and waited for it to happen.

"What's wrong?" Chance asked breathlessly.

"Nothing," Christiano whispered as he returned his lips to the warm, sweaty flesh of Chance's neck and back. He kissed the young man up and down the entire length of his back, marveling at the fact that he was not hungry and had no intention of feeding on this boy or killing him. This had almost never happened to him, and certainly not in the many years since Bernhardt's death.

"I want you inside me," Chance repeated as he squeezed his ass muscles against Christiano's cock and wiggled his hips teasingly.

Christiano moaned and ground his cock harder against the warm, smooth flesh of Chance's ass. His cock was leaking precum at an astounding rate, and before long there was so much of the slick, sticky fluid that his cock was coated with it from head to base.

Chance's ass was equally lubed from having Christiano's cock sliding against it, and he moved his hips in small circles, reveling in the feel of the fat cock as it slid between his ass crack and every once in a while slid between his legs and massaged his hairless balls.

"Hold still," Chance whispered as he looked over his shoulders and kissed Christiano on the lips.

Christiano stopped moving his cock across Chance's ass and focused on how sweet and warm Chance's tongue was as it slid in and out of his mouth.

Chance moaned as he kissed Christiano, and continued to wriggle his hips and ass against Christiano's cock. When he felt the fat head rub against his twitching hole, he stopped for a moment, relishing the heat and the pulse of the big head against his warm hole. He took a deep breath and relaxed his ass muscles. Christiano's cock slid effortlessly inside.

"Oh, Christ!" Christiano tried to moan as he sucked Chance's tongue deep into his mouth and kissed him.

Chance moaned also as he felt Christiano's thick cock spread his ass open. He held the head inside his ass for a couple of moments and then slid his ass backward onto the fat pole until it was buried deep inside him. He didn't stop until he felt Christiano's heavy balls resting against his own. When Christiano was buried all the way inside him, Chance stopped and welcomed the warm shots of electricity that bolted up and down the entire length of his body. He smiled as he felt Christiano's cock throb heavily even as it just rested inside his ass.

"I'm not going to be able to take much of this, I'm afraid," Christiano said as he felt Chance's ass squeeze his thick cock. "I'm so close already."

Chance stopped squeezing and simply lay still beneath the vampire. "Unh-unh. You're just gonna have to hold it in. There's no way I'm letting this end right here. No way."

"But I can't . . ."

"I swear to God, I'll pull off right now if you can't control yourself."

"No, don't do that. Please." Christiano couldn't believe how desperate he sounded.

"Then let's just sit here and relax for a couple minutes," Chance said as he leaned up and kissed Christiano again. "What do you say?"

"Okay," Christiano agreed, and returned Chance's kiss.

Chance lay completely still for a few moments, not daring to move for fear that it would set Christiano off again. It took every ounce of willpower he had not to squeeze the big dick inside him and lift his ass off the bed to thrust backward onto it.

Christiano continued kissing the back of Chance's neck and shoulders and couldn't help but slide his hips forward and deeper into Chance's ass every few seconds.

"You're not playing by the rules, Christiano," Chance said as he laughed at his new friend's lack of self-control.

"I'm sorry," Christiano whimpered as he stabbed just a little deeper. "I'm trying."

Chance leaned up and backward and kissed Christiano again. "You wanna get started again? Go ahead and finish up?"

"Oh, God, yes," Christiano moaned.

Chance leaned onto his elbows, lifting himself up from the bed, and pushed his ass backward deeper onto Christiano's cock. Though he didn't often admit to being impressed with the size of anyone's dick, or their sexual abilities, he knew at once that he was out of his league with Christiano. He'd never felt this way with anyone he'd ever fucked. It was as if he were really making love for the first time rather than just fucking. Every nerve in his body was on fire and tingled with the excitement of feeling Christiano's huge, thick cock slide deeper inside him and spread his ass muscles beyond where they'd ever been stretched before.

Christiano bit his lower lip as he felt the heat of Chance's ass wrap snugly around his cock and squeeze tightly while he slid up and down the length of it. It had been a very long time since he'd felt anything as sweet or as warm while making love to someone. Making love? When was the last time that term had come to mind while fucking someone? It had been with Bernhardt, nearly a century ago, and it had felt very much like what he was feeling now with Chance.

"I'm sorry," Christiano groaned loudly as he slammed deeper and then pulled out, then slammed back in again. "I can't hold back any longer. I'm getting so close."

"Fuck me, Christiano," Chance said, and squeezed his ass tighter around the fat cock inside him and bucked his ass back and forth along the long shaft.

Christiano grabbed Chance by the waist and slid in and out of his ass with a fury he couldn't control. His cock was on fire, and try as he might to make it last as long as possible, there was no way he was able to ward off the inevitable climax.

"Turn me around on my back when you're getting close," Chance said. "I want you to cum on my stomach."

Christiano moaned loudly and picked Chance up by the waist and turned him over onto his back. Chance's ass gripped Christiano's cock and squeezed it harder as he was manhandled, and that was all it took for Christiano.

"I'm coming!" Christiano yelled, and pulled out of Chance's ass in one swift move.

"Me, too," Chance cried out. A second later he grabbed his own cock and tugged on it lightly. Thick streams of white jism sprayed across his stomach and chest as he writhed below Christiano's towering body, aching to be filled with his giant cock again even before he was finished coming from this round.

Christiano leaned backward onto his legs and pointed his cock at Chance's quivering body. The first few spurts of cum shot out of his cock at lightning speed, flying past Chance's chest and stomach and landing instead across his face.

Chance moaned loudly and reached out with his tongue to lap up the warm cum as it splashed across his cheeks, nose, and lips.

The next several shots landed on Chance's chest and stomach and legs. It took nearly a full minute for Christiano to stop spraying his cum on Chance's body. When the last few drops finally drizzled out of the head of his cock, he fell on top of Chance and wrapped his arms around him.

"That was fucking incredible," Chance whispered as he snuggled beneath his new lover and wrapped his arms around Christiano's waist.

Christiano took several deep breaths and stared at the ceiling as he wondered again why the thought to bite into Chance's neck and feed on him hadn't crossed his mind even once. The only reason he ever fucked a mortal was to feed upon him. It had never once been otherwise. So why didn't he feel that need and that desire now? Why was he not even hungry?

"Yes, it was," Christiano replied as he hugged Chance closer to him and kissed him on the lips. "It was amazing."

Chapter Eight

Chance was leaning against the chrome railing, nursing his drink and watching the action on the dance floor. He'd been coming to Club Suque with Christiano every weekend for the past three weeks. On his first visit it hadn't really been his cup of tea. But it seemed to mean a lot to Chris, and he was getting a little bored of Charlie's anyway, so he'd agreed to give it another try. On his second visit he enjoyed it a little more, and the last time he came, he enjoyed it very much. Chris had been so excited about the fact that he liked it, he'd purchased a yearly membership for Chance that allowed him to move to the front of the always-long line and to be waived the fifty-dollar cover.

For that reason, if for no other, Chance felt obligated to get Chris's money's worth for the membership, and he showed up tonight even though Chris had been called out of town for work over the weekend. It was very different being here without Chris, but he wasn't too uncomfortable. He enjoyed watching the eclectic crowd as they danced, drank, and flirted with one another. About half the people seemed to be straight, and half gay, from what Chance could tell from watching them flirt and make out. The few straight people who came into Charlie's seemed not to be taken aback when they saw men kissing and making out with other men, but he'd assumed that was because they were in a gay bar and had expected as much. But he was surprised the straight people here didn't seem shocked at the open display of same-sex attraction and affection.

He and Chris had been an item now for the past three weeks, since the night they met at Charlie's. No commitment had been spoken out loud by either of them, but it didn't need to be. Chance never once even considered going out with anyone else after the first night he met Chris. And he knew Chris didn't, either, because they were together almost every night. The two or three nights in the past three weeks that they weren't together, he could tell that Chris was in agony over the fact that they couldn't spend the evening together.

The one thing that bothered Chance a little was that they could never spend time together during the day. But Chris had explained that he worked very difficult hours and often was out of the house before dawn, not returning until after dusk. And on the days when he wasn't working during the day, he often found he had to catch up on his sleep during those hours. Chance was not the kind of person to nag about petty things, and so he resigned himself to seeing Chris only in the evenings, and to making as much as he could out of the time together that they had. He had a boyfriend now, and not just any boyfriend, but the one he'd always dreamed of having. Tall, dark, and incredibly handsome. Loving and caring and more passionate than anyone he'd ever known. And so good in bed that Chance often wondered if he'd get through their lovemaking session without going crazy from delirium.

He smiled as he thought about having Christiano inside him, and sipped at his drink as he looked out onto the crowded dance floor.

"Hi," the deep voice next to him said.

Chance looked to his left to see the man who'd spoken to him. He was immediately struck by the young man's beauty. Tall but not too tall, with spiked platinum blond hair and creamy-white skin that looked as smooth as marble. He had a small mole on his cheek, and his eyes bored into Chance with a passion that caused a chill to run up his spine. The guy looked like a taller and blonder version of Enrique Iglesias, and that was all kinds of all right with Chance.

"Hey," Chance said, and smiled.

"I've seen you around here a couple times before, but I just never worked up the courage to come up and say hi."

"Why not?"

"I'm a little shy, I guess. Cute guys make me really nervous."

"*You* think *I'm* cute?" Chance asked, and shuffled his feet. "Are you kidding me?"

"No. I think you're beautiful."

Chance blushed and looked at the floor as he took a large sip of his drink.

"My name is Balthazar," the handsome stranger said as he held out his hand.

"Chance," Chance said as he shook hands.

"What an appropriate name for someone so remarkably gorgeous."

"Stop," Chance said as he realized he'd been holding Balthazar's hand a little longer than he needed to, and pulled it away. "I embarrass easily. Besides, I have a boyfriend."

"Ahhh," Balthazar sighed. "The guy I've seen you with here before?"

"Yes."

"And where is he tonight? I can't imagine he'd let you out of his sight."

"He got called in to work."

"Pity. Do you think he'd mind if I asked you to dance?"

Chance looked into Balthazar's eyes and held his gaze for a moment. He didn't feel completely comfortable dancing with someone he was so attracted to behind Chris's back. But he didn't feel completely uncomfortable, either. Besides, it was only a dance. It wasn't as if he'd be cheating on Chris.

"No, I think it'd be all right."

"Excellent. Let's go."

Balthazar led Chance onto the dance floor, and they mingled their way to the center of the floor, where they were lost in the crowd.

"Christiano, I'm sure you know why we've called you here."

Christiano looked at the panel of five elders before him. They were sitting around a large mahogany table, staring at him intently. They were in full regalia: black velvet pants, blood red shirts with thick heavy collars and ruffles down the front, which were covered with full-length black velvet capes emblazoned with the insignia of the Denver

Order of Vampires. They sat in high-back chairs and held scepters made of white and yellow gold. In front of them on the table were candles and goblets of blood and wine for each of them.

The man who had spoken to him sat at the head of the table and looked to be the eldest. From the way the others watched him and deferred their questions to him, Christiano assumed he was the lead elder. His shoulder-length silver hair and piercing black eyes commanded immediate respect and attention.

"No, sir. I'm afraid I am not certain at all."

"Do you know who I am?"

"No, sir."

"My name is Emiliano."

Christiano's eyes softened at once, and he smiled as he took a deep breath and let it out slowly.

"Am I to assume from your response that you know of me?"

"Yes, sir. My father has spoken of you often and very fondly."

"And I of him. Your father and I were very, very good friends. I begged him and your mother to come with me to America when I decided to settle here over one hundred years ago. But they couldn't leave their beloved Spain. I consider your father my brother. I'm very sorry to hear of his expiration."

"Thank you, sir," Christiano whispered, and looked down at his feet.

"And I am sorry to hear of Bernhardt's passing as well."

Christiano looked up at the old vampire and swallowed hard. He did not reply.

"I'm going to be direct with you, Christiano," Emiliano said as he leaned forward onto the table. "We have been displeased with Balthazar's performance as lead vampire for several years now. He is weak and careless. His arrogance has hurt our community on numerous occasions and has caused us undue stress. We want him out."

"But, sir . . ."

"We want you to replace him."

"I'm honored with your confidence, Emiliano. But I don't want to be lead vampire. I'm not even sure I'm planning on staying in Denver much longer."

"Oh? And where are you thinking of going?"

"My original plan was to settle in Chicago. I got a little sidetracked, but I'm still thinking about moving there. Eventually."

"And do those plans include taking Chance Foster with you?"

Christiano jerked his head up to look at Emiliano.

"Don't be so shocked. Of course we know."

"I'm not sure, sir. I'm trying to be very cautious with Chance at this point. I don't wish to be hurt again."

"You cannot love without experiencing hurt, Christiano. I'm sure I don't have to tell you that, of all people."

"No, sir."

"But caution is a good thing, and very much advised. Do you know where Chance is at this moment?"

"At home, I'd imagine."

"No. He is at Club Suque. And according to one of our faithful, he is engaged in a passionate dance at this very moment with Balthazar."

Christiano felt the blood rise from his heart to his neck and face. "No."

"I'm afraid yes," the old vampire said as he caressed his knuckles and stared directly ahead at Christiano.

Christiano shuffled his feet and looked at Emiliano. "May I?" he asked.

"Go."

Christiano turned and ran out the door without looking back.

The pounding beat of the music and the blinding laser lights that blinked across the dance floor worked their magic on Chance. And the four drinks he'd had didn't hurt, either. When Balthazar pulled him closer to dance, Chance smelled the sweet aroma of his cologne, mixed with his natural musky scent, and allowed himself to melt into Balthazar's embrace. He'd tried looking into the handsome stranger's eyes but found he felt helpless and vulnerable when he did, and quickly looked away. Now he was feeling that way again as he felt Balthazar's hands caress his ass and grind his hard cock against Chance's upper thigh. His own cock was quickly responding to the feel of Balthazar's throbbing dick.

When Balthazar leaned down to kiss his ear, Chance did not turn away or discourage him from continuing. He didn't know why or how he was reacting this way, and he couldn't get Christiano's image out of his mind even as Balthazar nibbled on his ear. He felt horrible about allowing this to happen, but was powerless in stopping it.

"What are you thinking about?" Balthazar whispered into Chance's ear as he sucked on the lobe and licked lightly around the inside.

"My boyfriend," Chance moaned loudly. "I don't think we should be doing this."

"Of course we should."

"Okay," Chance said automatically, and then tried to shake his head to clear it from all the muddle that seemed to congregate there.

"Do you love Christiano?"

"Yes," Chance said, and then realized he hadn't told Balthazar Christiano's name. "How did you know . . ."

"Do you trust him implicitly?"

"Yes."

"Do you believe he is honest with you?" Balthazar asked as he licked his way down Chance's ear and to his neck.

"Yes, of course," Chance said as he moved his neck to the right to give Balthazar's hot, wet tongue easier access. Was it his imagination, or did the fluorescent strobe lights suddenly stop scanning the dance floor, and the few overhead lights suddenly dim almost to nonexistence? Was the music louder and the bass thumping even harder, or was that the alcohol playing tricks on his mind? Were the people around him really moving away from them and forming a circle around them, or . . . ?

"Did he tell you he is a vampire?"

Chance laughed. "Well, he certainly has an unquenchable thirst, but it's not for blood. Believe me."

"Yes, it is," Balthazar whispered as he kissed Chance's neck. "He's a vampire, and so am I."

"What the—" Chance started to question, but was cut short by the sharp pain of Balthazar's fangs as they bit into his neck and pierced the skin. "Hey . . . stop . . ."

Balthazar sank his canines deep into Chance's neck and sucked sharply on the warm, sweaty skin until he was rewarded with the thick, coppery nectar that slid across his tongue and down his throat. It was sweeter than just about any blood he'd tasted, and knowing that it rightfully belonged to Christiano made it even sweeter. He sucked harder on the warm neck.

"Oh . . . my . . . God . . ." Chance tried to scream, but only squeaked out as he felt the strength in his legs fail him and he swayed unsteadily on them. As Balthazar's teeth sank deeper into his neck and his mouth sucked hungrily at the steady flow of blood, Chance marveled at how wonderful the whole thing felt even as the pain coursed down his neck and across his chest and farther down his legs.

Balthazar sucked maniacally on the warm, supple neck of his enemy's lover and held Chance in such a strong grip that he could move little more than an inch in either direction. It didn't take long before Chance slumped to the floor and his eyes rolled back in his head.

The last thing Chance saw before losing consciousness was the crowd moving in around him in a circle, and the movement of their lips as they chanted.

"Chris . . ." he moaned as he felt the last draft of consciousness sway through his veins and away from his body.

The guards outside saw him coming from almost a mile away. The air around him was glowing red and was blistered with a cloud of fog that surrounded his body. He was moving at an astounding speed, and they barely had time to grab the money box and make a hasty retreat. When he was still a couple of blocks away, the ton of wood and steel that was the sliding door into the club exploded from its steel track and blew several feet into the air, above the treetops, and landed a hundred feet from the building.

Inside the club, chaos was rampant. Most of the mortals in the club that night were knowledgeable and could be counted on to keep the truth underground. The few who were not knowledgeable were known to the vampires and were quickly pounced upon. Some of the vampires fed on them, sucking their blood and draining them only to the point of conversion. But others, fueled by the drugs and the energy of the moment, bit into the necks of the mortals and ripped their necks apart viciously, gnawing at the flesh and spitting huge chunks of it onto the floor. Their eyes burned bright red, and they growled like animals.

When the doors blew apart and flew across the air, everyone, mortal and vampire alike, turned their gaze toward the door. Through the now empty frame, moonlight spilled into the club and illuminated a tall and shadowy figure advancing quickly toward them. Everyone moved as close to the back wall as possible, leaving the dead mortals to be trampled on by the man surrounded by red fog.

"Hello, Christiano," Balthazar said as he smiled and wiped the blood from his lips onto his arm.

"Chance," Christiano moaned as he stopped directly in front of his dead lover.

"Oh, he'll be okay," Balthazar said as he kicked Chance's limp leg. "He's in a better place now. He was very tasty, let me assure you. You don't know what you missed by not indulging with this one."

Christiano dropped to his knees on the floor and cradled Chance's head in his arms. "Nooooo," he cried out.

"Yes," Balthazar said, and tried unsuccessfully to hold back a laugh.

Christiano raised his head suddenly and glared at Balthazar. Balthazar flew backward with astonishing speed and slammed, back first, into the far wall. Everyone scattered to get away from him as quickly as possible.

Balthazar stood up and shook himself off as he walked back closer to Christiano. He waved one hand in front of himself and watched as Christiano, with Chance cradled in his arms, rose a couple of feet into the air and spun around weakly in a circle. He concentrated harder, causing the large vein on his forehead to pop out, but still only succeeded in spinning Christiano and Chance around at a pitifully slow revolution.

"Don't fuck with me, Christiano," he said, trying to sound more threatening than he actually felt at the moment. "You can't win."

Christiano floated back to the floor and laid Chance down carefully on the dance floor. He stood up and faced Balthazar, then extended his arm out in front of him quickly. Balthazar went flying backward through the air again, slamming against the railing to the stairs.

"Help me!" Balthazar screamed at the other vampires and members of his council who were standing close to him. "You said you'd help me. Go get him."

No one moved, and as Balthazar got up and shook himself off, he growled at the vampires around him. "Don't just stand there. Get him!"

"You're finished, Balthazar," Christiano said between clenched teeth.

Balthazar tried once again to use his powers to blow Christiano across the room and away from him, but Christiano didn't budge.

"This is the last evening you will live to see," Christiano said as he moved closer to Balthazar.

"You can't kill me, you idiot. The elders would never tolerate it."

"I'm sorry," the voice said from behind Christiano. A second later Emiliano emerged, waving his hands in front of him to clear the red fog that surrounded Christiano still. "But I'm afraid you have been misinformed."

"What . . . ? Balthazar stammered.

"Gentlemen," the elder vampire said as he motioned for members of Balthazar's own council to restrain him.

Several council members stumbled forward and grabbed Balthazar by the arms, twisting them behind his back.

"What are you doing?" he asked his former friends as he looked them in the eyes. "You can't do this."

"Oh, but they can," Emiliano said. "And they will, because I tell them to. You've abused your powers here long enough, Balthazar. We are tired of cleaning up your messes and monitoring your every move."

"You can't be serious," Balthazar cried out as he struggled uselessly against the strength of his council members.

"We are dead serious," Emiliano said as he removed a large wooden stake from a green velvet bag and handed it to Christiano. "Do it."

Christiano took the stake from the elder vampire and walked slowly toward Balthazar.

"No . . . please . . . ," Balthazar begged as giant tears rolled down his face.

"You shouldn't have fucked with me," Christiano said as he leaned to within an inch of Balthazar's face.

"I didn't . . ."

"And you really shouldn't have fucked with my boyfriend," Christiano said through gritted teeth as he pressed the blunt end of the stake against his own chest and leaned forward, stabbing the sharp end of the stake through Balthazar's chest. He heard it pop as it pierced the skin and slid effortlessly through Balthazar's body and out the back side. He kept pushing with the weight of his own body until his lips were touching Balthazar's. He kissed Balthazar on the lips and then spit onto the floor.

Balthazar let out a loud scream and then went limp as his body slumped out of the arms of his council members and to the floor.

Emiliano allowed the slightest curl at the corner of his lips as he watched Balthazar take his last breath. Then he scanned the room, taking note of the looks on the faces of all the humans in the room. Most seemed to be ecstatic at the way the evening turned out, and some were even visibly physically excited at the death and mayhem that had ensued. A few, though, seemed to be catatonic, staring straight ahead with blank expressions in their eyes, their skin as white as that of the vampires around them. They obviously were the unknowledgeable, and had had no idea what they were getting into when they'd entered the club that evening.

"All right, everyone," he said as he made direct eye contact with several of the key members of the vampire community, "we know what needs to be done now. We cannot have news of this evening's events getting out to the press and public. Get busy," he said as he turned and walked over to Christiano. "You can go home, Christiano. We'll talk later."

The club came alive with noise as vampires closed in on the unknowledgeable humans and began feeding on them. The knowledgeable humans and other vampires cheered and whistled as the unknowledgeable humans screamed in horror at the massacre in which they were the main course.

Christiano lifted Chance's lifeless body into his arms and carried him out the doorless front entrance, tears streaming down his face.

Chapter Nine

Christiano laid several blankets on the ground and then laid Chance down on top of them. He filled a copper bowl with cool water and dropped a washcloth into it, and set it beside the makeshift bed. It would come in handy in a couple of hours, he knew, and he wanted to be ready. Then he lay down next to his lover, curled up beside him, and waited. There was no way he could even remotely entertain the possibility of sleep, but he wanted Chance to wake up to find himself wrapped in the arms of his lover.

It didn't take long. A couple of hours after coming home to the cathedral, Chance began to stir and moan. A few minutes after that, he tried to open his eyes but screamed out in pain as he attempted to blink away the sleep.

"Oh, God," he cried out as he threw his arms across his eyes. "Turn off the lights. They're killing my eyes."

"There are no lights in here, babe," Christiano whispered into Chance's ears. He reached into the copper bowl and wrung the water out of the washcloth, then gently blotted it across Chance's warm face. "Only a couple of candles."

"Blow them out. It feels like my eyes are on fire."

Christiano stood up and blew out the candles, then returned to Chance's side. "Okay, honey, they're out. But it won't make any difference to you. Your eyes will burn like that for several hours. They're a little sensitive right now. Keep them closed for now. It'll be less painful tomorrow night."

"What happened? Where am I?"

"There was an . . . accident tonight at the club. You're at my place."

"An accident?" Chance asked as he tried to prop himself up on his elbows.

"Well, not really an accident. More like an incident. With Balthazar."

Chance was quiet for a moment, squinting his eyes in the darkness of the cellar. Then his face went slack, and Christiano knew that his lover had just remembered.

"No, no, no," Chance cried out as he flailed his arms around him, trying to grasp something familiar.

"I'm so sorry, Chance," Christiano said as he pulled Chance to his chest and began to rock him.

"This can't be true. It can't be happening. He said you are a vampire."

"Yes," Christiano whispered.

"Yes?" Chance cried out as he struggled to pull away from Christiano's chest. "What do you mean, yes?"

"I am a vampire."

"No you aren't."

"I am."

"Vampires aren't real. There is no such thing as a vampire. It's all fiction."

"No, it is not. I am a vampire."

"I don't believe you."

"It's true, Chance. I would not lie to you."

"*You wouldn't lie to me?* You son of a bitch. You never told me you are a vampire. What part of that doesn't sound like a lie to you?"

"I'm sorry, Chance."

"Sorry? You stupid motherfucker. You are a vampire and you never told me?"

"I was afraid I'd lose you. People aren't usually very open to accepting us."

"Yeah, well, I wonder why. You freaking flesh-eating monster!" Chance spit out as he shoved himself away from Christiano.

"Chance, I love you. Please try to understand."

Chance reached up with one hand and felt the wound on his neck. "Oh, my God. He bit me. That bastard bit me."

"Yes."

"Does that mean I'm a vampire now?"

"No. Not yet."

"Not yet? What the fuck do you mean, 'not yet'?"

"It'll take three or four days. You're starting to change now; that's why your eyes are so sensitive to even the slightest bit of light. That will get better in a few hours. But I'd still stay away from too much light for a few days. And whatever you do, do not get caught in the sunlight. You can be awake during the day, but you must make sure you are very well protected against the sunlight. It will kill you."

"Dear God, I don't believe this is happening," Chance said as he rubbed his forehead.

"Your fangs will begin to push through your gums in three or four days."

"What?"

"I'm sorry, Chance, there just isn't any easy or painless way to say it. When they push through your gums, it is very painful. Especially the first few times. After that it gets less painful."

"Please tell me this is all a dream."

"It's no dream, baby. It's all real."

"And so when my fangs come out," Chance said and shuddered at the word "fangs," "then I'm a vampire?"

"Yes."

"And then I will have to drink people's blood and kill them."

"You will have to feed on human blood, yes. But you don't have to kill them."

"What?"

"It's optional. Most of the killings are done out of self-preservation. If we kill the person we feed on, they can never tell anyone else that we exist. It just makes it easier."

"I can't believe I'm hearing this."

"But it doesn't have to be that way. There are many humans who know about us and are sympathetic toward us and support our existence. They allow us to feed on them willingly. In fact, they desire it. There were many such people at the club tonight."

"If that's true, then why do you kill anyone at all?"

"I don't know. We get carried away. Sometimes in the passion of the moment . . ."

"Passion?" Chance nearly screamed.

"Yes, it is very intimate. It's not only feeding to fill hunger. But it is also, most of the time, very sexual as well."

"I'm going to be sick."

"I'm so sorry, Chance. I should have protected you better."

"I cannot drink someone's blood. I faint at the sight of it. And I certainly can't kill someone."

"You won't have to kill anyone, Chance. Many vampires don't."

"So, I'm a vampire. I'm *going* to be a vampire."

"Yes."

"And there's nothing I can do about it? Nothing I can do to stop it from happening?"

Christiano leaned up against the wall and pulled his knees up to his chest so that he could wrap his arms around them. He said nothing.

"Chris?"

"Do you love me, Chance?"

"You didn't answer my question."

"And I won't until you answer mine. Do you love me?"

Chance was quiet for a couple of minutes. Then he scooted toward the sound of Christiano's voice until he found him, and sat next to him. "Yes."

"And I love you, too. I already lost one lover, Chance. He was the first true love of my life. And that was a very long time ago. I never thought I'd have another chance at love again. But I love you desperately. I can't imagine losing you, too."

"Christiano, I love you. You won't lose me. But if there's even the slightest chance of me not becoming a vampire, you have to tell me. I don't want to be a vampire."

"You could live forever, Chance. With me."

"I don't want to live forever."

"But . . ."

"I don't want to live forever, Chris. I want to live a long, natural lifespan. I want to grow old. With you. I want to love you and live with you and grow old with you. But I don't want to live forever."

"But I won't grow old. I will live forever. It's too late for me. I'm already almost two hundred years old."

Chance tensed up at this revelation, and he involuntarily scooted a couple of inches away from Christiano.

"By the time you are eighty, I will still only look thirty or thirty-five."

"I don't care. I don't want to live forever, Christiano."

"That means I will have to face losing you again someday."

"Too fucking bad!" Chance yelled. "This is not about you, Chris. This is about me. If I have a choice in this and it is not too late, I want to choose not to become a vampire. If you love me, you will help me."

"I do love you."

"Then help me with this, Chris. I know it will be hard for you when the time comes for me to die. But you'll be okay. You'll have the memories of the decades that we will spend together. You'll be okay. If I become a vampire, I will not be okay," Chance cried, and wiped the tears roughly from his eyes. "Do you understand me?"

"Yes."

"Then help me. Please."

The next seventy-two hours were torturous for Chance. His body was experiencing changes at a rate that was dizzying for him. His muscles tingled, his head hurt constantly, his eyes were sensitive to any little bit of light, and he could feel his heart beating through every muscle and nerve in his body. And he couldn't adjust to sleeping during the day and being awake at night. Not that it was light in the room at any given time, because meticulous measures had been taken to ensure that the cellar was completely dark at all times. But his body clock just didn't like the idea of sleeping during the day and being awake at night.

On the fourth evening, Chance felt a dull ache begin in his gums. In less than two hours the pain was excruciating.

"Chris, I think it's happening," he said excitedly as he opened his mouth so that Christiano could see his teeth. "Do you see anything different?" he mumbled through his stretched-open mouth.

"Yes," Christiano said. "It's time."

Chapter 10

At a quarter to midnight, the moonlight broke through the window and cast a blue-white shadow throughout Chance's bedroom. His queen-size four-poster bed had been moved to the center of the room, and Christiano had placed nineteen red and black candles strategically around the bedroom. Nine candles were situated in a loose circle on the floor around the bed, and the other ten were placed on bookshelves and bureaus throughout the rest of the room.

Chance was lying naked in the middle of the bed, his eyes closed and his hands lightly massaging his jaw. The fangs had now pushed all the way through the gums, and he could still feel them growing and protruding even farther with each passing hour. It felt to him as if his teeth had been pulled on for several hours. He could feel the teeth sliding against the gums and scraping them as they strained to get through the sensitive tissue and be free. He'd prayed the pain and the scraping sensation would stop after a couple of minutes, but it had been over an hour and a half since the pain started, and he could still feel them growing.

At first he'd been fascinated by the sensation and had reached up with his hands to feel the sharp fangs as they broke through the gums. But that fascination passed quickly and gave way to the horrible pain. Chris had given him several Tylenol and even a Vicodin to help with the pain, but it didn't seem to help at all. A few moments ago Chris had also brought him a glass of wine, and the combination of the pain killers and alcohol helped dull the pain to at least a tolerable level.

"You okay, babe?" Christiano asked as he walked over to the bed and looked down at his lover.

"Yeah," Chance said, opening his eyes and looking at Christiano. "It still hurts, but it's now more of a dull, aching pain rather than the excruciating, stabbing flashes of pain like it was earlier."

"I'm glad," Christiano said as he sat next to Chance and stroked his smooth, muscular chest. "It's almost time. Are you ready?"

"Yes."

"Remember what I told you. It's gonna hurt. A lot. Your teeth and your gums are going to hurt like hell. But you've gotta do it."

"I know."

"And you're not going to like the taste, but you can't stop before—"

"Chris?"

"What, baby?"

"Shut up and fuck me."

Christiano smiled and leaned down to kiss his lover on the forehead.

Chance reached up with his hands and cradled Christiano's face in them. He caressed Christiano's smooth skin and leaned in to kiss him on the lips.

"It's gonna hurt, baby."

"I don't care," Chance said, and opened his mouth to kiss the one man he'd ever really loved.

As he opened his mouth to receive Christiano's tongue, he closed his eyes to block out the pain. The farther he opened, the sharper the pain shot through his gums and mouth. His whole head throbbed, but he continued anyway. When Christiano slowly slid his tongue into his mouth, Chance wrapped his lips around it and gently sucked it deeper inside. He loved the taste of Christiano's tongue, and felt his cock grow hard as he sucked the minty tongue further into his mouth and returned Christiano's kiss.

Kissing Christiano and sucking on his tongue made his teeth hurt a little, but the pain also brought a wave of pleasure with it. Chance couldn't deny that the throbbing pain in his mouth was at least partially responsible for the pounding hard-on he now had, which was so hard that it seemed as though the tight skin around his cock might rip open. And the nerves in his ass tingled as if they were ready to burst into flames. Chance had never been this sexually excited, and he struggled not to fall off the bed as he wriggled around trying to contain the sexual energy that coursed through every inch of his body.

"Fuck me," Chance moaned as he broke the kiss and moved Christiano into position between his spread legs.

"Not yet," Christiano said between gasped breaths. "It has to begin precisely at midnight, and last for exactly twenty minutes. I explained all this to you already. There's no room for mistakes."

"I know, I know," Chance said as he lifted his ass and back off the bed and ground his hips closer to Christiano's face. "But I need you inside me. I can't help it."

Christiano smiled and pushed Chance's body back onto the bed. "Maybe this will help," he said as he grabbed Chance's legs and spread them apart.

He leaned down and licked the smooth skin of Chance's upper legs and ass. When Chance moaned louder and spread his legs even further apart, Christiano took that as his signal to continue. He zoomed in on the tiny puckered hole in the middle of the twin silky globes of Chance's ass, and lightly flicked his tongue around it. Chance's low, guttural moans were all the encouragement that Christiano needed, and he slipped his long tongue deep inside Chance's twitching ass in a single, steady move.

"Oh, God," Chance moaned. Though he'd been kissed this way many times before, and even by Chris, it had never felt quite like this. His entire body felt as if he were hooked up to some electrical power source, and the nerves tingled everywhere that Chris touched him. The epicenter of this electrical energy seemed to be centered in his ass, and the feel of Chris's tongue kissing and sliding in and out of him was almost more than he could stand. His cock bounced with excitement, and he felt his balls tighten and the climax already beginning to stir deep in his gut. "I'm already getting so close. Keep doing that, baby."

Christiano pulled his tongue out of Chance's ass quickly, and he scooted himself up so that he was face-to-face with his lover.

"Chance, I told you already. If this is going to work, it has to be precise. You can't cum yet."

"I know. But I need you inside me," Chance whined, and ground his pelvis against Christiano's tight, smooth stomach.

Christiano looked over at the clock on the bureau across the room. Two more minutes.

"I can't make it."

"Yes, you can," Christiano said, and leaned down to kiss Chance again. He held Chance's wiggling body as still as possible and was careful not to let the kisses become too passionate, for fear that Chance would shoot his load prematurely. There was no room for error. Not this time.

Chance, too, was trying to control his desire. He knew how serious this lovemaking session was, and loved Christiano even more for dedicating himself to its success. He knew it couldn't be easy for Chris to do this. Chris wanted him to live forever with him, to share an eternity together. If tonight went right, that would not happen.

He felt Chris's hands massage his ass and lift it gently off the bed.

"It's time," Christiano whispered, and positioned his cock head against the hot, twitching asshole.

Chance took a deep breath and closed his eyes as he felt Chris push his hips forward. The thick head slid effortlessly inside, and Chance gasped with pleasure as he felt his ass muscles wrap around the hot head and squeeze around it lovingly.

"Oh, God!" Christiano moaned. "Don't do that, please. I won't be able to last for twenty minutes if you do that."

Chance stopped squeezing, at least as much as was within his control, and relaxed his ass muscles so that Chris could slide deeper inside with more ease. With every inch that Chris slid into him, Chance thought his body would explode with ecstasy. When all nine inches of Chris's thick cock rested inside him, Chance smiled and tried very hard not to let his ass constrict and milk it. He could tell Chris was struggling as well, and winked at his lover to let him know that he knew what a battle it was for him, and how much he appreciated it.

When Chris started to move in and out of him slowly, Chance thought he might die from the pleasure. With his body this alive, he felt every centimeter of ass muscle that Chris's cock rubbed against tingle and kiss the big dick as it slid in and out of him. With Chris's cock inside him, his ass felt as vital as his teeth and gums did. In both, he felt even the slightest movement as if it were happening in slow motion and lasting forever.

"It's time," Christiano said as he slid deep inside Chance and rested there. He tilted his head to the side, exposing it to Chance's mouth. "You have to bite me now, Chance. I know you're not going to like it, but there's no other way. And you have to keep drinking my blood for the next ten minutes, no matter what. Do you understand me?"

Chance nodded.

"I will start to get a little weak near the end. But it's very important that we both cum at exactly twelve-twenty. Not a minute later or a minute earlier. And you must stop drinking at the exact moment we cum. Otherwise this will not work."

"Okay," Chance said, and leaned forward. As much as he'd thought he'd be repulsed at this moment, he found he could hardly wait to sink his teeth in Chris's neck.

"Remember, I will become unconscious once I cum. Don't be frightened. The most important thing is that my semen and my blood be inside you at twelve-twenty. I will be all right, and I'll wake up again in a couple of hours. At that time you will no longer be a vampire."

"Come here," Chance whispered.

Christiano leaned forward and presented his neck to Chance.

Chance opened his mouth wide and sank his teeth deep into the soft, warm neck. It took a couple of seconds, but when the blood began to trickle onto his tongue, he was shocked to find he wasn't repulsed at all but instead was excited by the feel and the taste of it. He swallowed the first mouthful tentatively, wondering if he'd vomit. He did not, and indeed craved more. He sucked harder on Chris's neck, pulling larger quantities of sweet blood into his mouth, and swallowed each mouthful eagerly.

At the same time, Chris slid his cock in and out of Chance's ass with slow and passionate tenderness. Chance had a hard time concentrating on both pleasures at the same time. Never had he been fucked so wonderfully, or felt as alive or in love as he did at this moment. Chris's cock filled him completely, and with each slide into him, he felt as though his spirit left his body and floated above him. Then, with each withdrawal, he felt his spirit float back inside his body again and rest there for the slightest moment before retreating outside again as Chris slid back into him.

Chris's soft neck had been warm to his lips' touch at first but was now growing colder with each passing minute. The thick blood was sweet and delicious and intoxicating. Chance couldn't get enough of it, and a couple of times Chris had to tell him to slow down and be a little gentler.

It was getting close to 12:20 now, and he felt Chris begin to fuck him harder and faster. He continued to suck on Chris's neck, knowing that he only had a minute left to get his fill of the delicious blood, and reached down to stroke his own cock. It only took a few strokes to get him to the point where repressing his climax was no longer a possibility.

Chris moaned loudly, slid all the way inside Chance until his balls rested against his ass, and whispered hoarsely, "Now."

Chance reluctantly pulled his head back from Chris's neck, feeling the jugular vein grope his fangs as he withdrew. He laid his head on the pillow and shot his own load all over his chest and stomach as he felt Chris's cock expand and throb deep inside his ass. With his nerve endings on fire, he could feel each squirt of Chris's load as it entered his body and swam deeper inside him.

When he finished unloading inside Chance, Chris's body went limp and fell on top of Chance.

Chance fought the urge to cry and panic and instead moved very slowly to disengage himself from his lover. He gently rolled Chris onto his back and moved him over to one side of the bed, where he covered him, and then lay next to him and watched him sleep.

"Let me see your teeth," Christiano said.

He'd been unconscious for almost three hours, and these were the first words he spoke upon waking.

"They're fine," Chance said as he smiled and snuggled up to Chris. "I'm okay."

"Let me see."

Chance opened his mouth wide and rubbed the gums around his canine teeth. "See? Doesn't hurt. And my eyes aren't sensitive anymore, either."

"You're sure?"

"Yes. And most importantly, the thought of drinking blood doesn't give me a hard-on anymore. In fact, it makes me nauseous."

"Good. It worked."

"Yes, I think so."

"It did. I can see it. And feel it, too."

"Yeah, me too."

"Chance . . ." Christiano whispered as he stared at the floor.

"I love you, Chris. Don't ever doubt that."

"What are we gonna do now?"

"We talked about this already," Chance said as he hugged Chris. "We've come this far, baby. Don't back out on me now."

"I won't. I just don't know that I can do this."

"Of course you can. You're the strongest man I know."

"I'm not a man."

"Okay, then, you're the strongest vampire I know," Chance said as he kissed Chris on the lips.

"But it's not what we do, Chance. It's not my nature."

"Then fight your nature. I know you can do it, Chris. You have it inside you to be able to do this."

"I'll come up against resistance. The elders won't like it."

"You don't know that. You said yourself they were tired of leadership like that that Balthazar brought to the table. They want something new and different. And they want you. Accept the challenge and bring some changes with you. It's what they want, and it's what you want."

"But . . . ," Christiano stuttered.

"We've been over this already, Chris. Don't falter now. You can bring about the most positive change for your community in the last two or three hundred years. You're the only one who can do it, and they all know that. It's your responsibility, baby. To your vampire community. To yourself. And to me."

"Yeah, I know."

"I love you, and I want to live with you until I'm old and wrinkled. Until I die."

Christiano pulled back at the last sentence and paced around the large bedroom nervously.

"Get used to it, honey."

"I will."

"But I can't do all of that if you and your friends are out killing people all the time. I just can't."

"I know. I will try. Really I will."

"Thank you," Chance said, and kissed his lover on the lips.

"I'm gonna go now," Christiano said. "It's getting late, and I gotta get to bed. Enjoy the morning and the sunshine. I'll see you later tonight."

"Okay," Chance said, and watched his lover walk away from him. "Chris?"

"Yeah," Christiano said as he stopped at the door and turned to look at Chance.

"I love you."

"I love you, too."

Epilogue

The building sat in the middle of the Sixteenth Street Mall, in downtown Denver. It wasn't inconspicuous at all, with its red brick facade framed in bright silver metal. In large fluorescent red letters above the door was the word *Bloodlines*.

It was an adoption agency like no other in the country. It provided regular adoption services for those who wanted a traditional adoption experience. And in just the two years it had been in operation, it had already garnered a reputation for superior service. Bloodlines paid special attention to providing only the absolute best homes and parents for the children in its care.

But it also provided another service that no other adoption agency in the country offered. For those adopted children who later, as adults, wished to find and meet their biological parents, Bloodlines assisted in making that happen. And for those biological parents who later wished to find and meet their children, the agency also mediated those situations and facilitated making the meeting between parents and the children they'd given up many years before.

Chance had been adopted and had wanted to meet his real parents all his life. His adoptive parents were supportive of that happening, but they couldn't find any place that would help them do it. So, when it came time for Christiano to put in motion his plan of integrating vampires into human society, Chance suggested the founding of Bloodlines.

It hadn't taken long for the vampire elders and community to come around to supporting Chris's suggestions of integration. They'd been tired of their murderous and self-destructive existence for a long time and were hungry for some change. They welcomed Christiano's leadership and his progressive thinking. When he'd suggested starting the adoption agency and having it staffed completely by vampires and knowledgeable humans, they'd eagerly accepted the plan and dedicated their money, time, and resources to its success.

Though he had no real desire to run the company, Chance reluctantly accepted the chairmanship—mostly because much of the business had to be done during the day, and the majority of the leadership in the company were vampires and worked at night. Christiano, of course, was the real leader of the company and was Chance's most trusted and valued adviser and confidant. The frontline employees who worked during the day were all human knowledgeables who were dedicated to the survival of the vampire community and to their mission of integration and advancement of peaceful coexistence and goodwill endeavors.

It was six in the evening, and the shift change was just getting ready to take place. Chance stood outside the building for a moment, smiling at the outward symbol of the success of Bloodlines. Recently there had been talk among other vampire communities about opening branches in their respective cities. Vampires across the nation were openly talking about their own desires to bring about some of the positive changes that they were seeing in Denver. They were realizing they didn't need to kill humans to survive. That most of them had more than enough knowledgeables in their communities who were willing to provide the blood that was needed to keep the vampires alive, without the death and destruction that they'd become accustomed to. And that coexisting with humans and sharing talents between humans and vampires meant more than just mere survival.

Chance walked into the building smiling and whistling.

"Good evening, Mr. Foster," the cute blond receptionist said as Chance walked up to him.

"How many times do I have to tell you? It's Chance."

"Yes, sir," the young man said. "But Mr. Montez is due here any minute, and you know how he insists on all of us calling you by your surname."

Chance smiled. "Of course. But I won't tell if you don't."

"Yes, sir, Mr. Foster."

Chance winked at the blushing receptionist. "Please let Chris know that I'm in my office and am expecting him. But don't let anyone else know I'm here, and whatever you do, don't let anyone else enter my office."

The receptionist blushed deeper and smiled and winked back at Chance. "Yes, sir. I'll make sure you and Mr. Montez are not interrupted."

"Thank you," Chance said, and then started to walk away. He suddenly stopped just before the elevator. "Oh, yeah. I'm expecting Devin for a meeting at eight. Can you please just tell him I'll meet him in his office when I'm done with my . . . meeting . . . with Chris?"

"Sure thing, Mr. Foster."

"And bring me a bottle of champagne before Chris gets here, please."

"Absolutely."

Christiano opened the door and walked into the office without knocking.

"Chance, what's up? Bryce said you needed to see me urg—" He stopped mid-sentence as he saw Chance, leaning against his desk, completely naked. He let his eyes wander the length of Chance's naked body, lingering on the hard cock that jutted out in front of him. "Hmmm, I see what's up."

"I just couldn't wait until later tonight," Chance said as he walked up to Christiano and handed him a glass of champagne. "I need you to know how much I love you."

"I know how much you love me," Christiano said as he took a sip of the champagne.

"Then I need to know how much you love me," Chance whispered.

Christiano smiled and unzipped his pants, freeing his already hardening cock. Then he wrapped his free hand around Chance's hard cock and led him over to the sofa in one corner of the office.

About the Author

Sean Wolfe has had over fifty erotic short stories published in almost every gay skin mag on the market over the past five years. Thirteen of those stories have been reprinted in the erotic anthologies *Friction* (volumes 3, 4, 5, 6, and *Best of Friction*), *Twink, My First Time Vol.* 3, and *Three the Hard Way.*

"Vampires, Inc." is Sean's third novella with Kensington. His first was another vampire novella, titled "Bradon's Bite," included in *Masters of Midnight* and published in June 2003. His second novella was titled "Bad Boy Dreams" and is included in *Man of My Dreams*, published in February 2004.

A single-author anthology of Sean's erotic short stories is scheduled for publication by Kensington in early 2005.

Though much of Sean's writing is erotic, he vehemently denies being a sex fiend and spends much of his free time trying to convince others of that fact. To date, woefully, he has not been very successful.

Sean does hold down a legitimate full-time job as Volunteer Coordinator for Colorado AIDS Project and is very active with his church, the Metropolitan Community Church of the Rockies.